Windsinger

A.F.E. Smith is an editor of academic texts by day and a fantasy writer by night. She lives with her husband and their two young children in a house that was apparently built to be as creaky as possible. She can be found on Twitter @afesmith and online at www.afesmith.com

Also by A.F.E. Smith

The Darkhaven Novels
Darkhaven
Goldenfire

Windsinger

A.F.E. SMITH

Book Three of The Darkhaven Novels

Harper*Voyager*
an imprint of HarperCollins*Publishers* Ltd
1 London Bridge Street
London SE1 9GF

www.harpervoyagerbooks.co.uk

This Paperback Original 2017

First published in Great Britain in ebook format by Harper*Voyager* 2017

A catalogue record for this book
is available from the British Library

ISBN: 978-0-00-818146-8

Set in Sabon by Palimpsest Book Production Limited,
Falkirk, Stirlingshire

Printed and bound in Great Britain

Prologue

It was one of the first sunny days of spring: the kind of day when the relentless chill blade of winter finally lost its edge, and the air tasted of green growing things, and down in the city the workers went bare-armed in hopeful anticipation of summer's return. Miles was able to say his morning devotions to the Sun Lord in the full and certain knowledge of His presence, instead of merely in hope.

Breakfast brought starfruit, the first of the season and his favourite. He sat beside Art, slicing the golden-yellow fruit and enjoying the sweet tang of the juice, while the high voices of the Nightshade children filled the air. Three of them, all under six years old; breakfast was necessarily a noisy affair. Perhaps Miles thought briefly of his own nephew, forever frozen at the age of three in his memory, but if so, he didn't let it linger. He watched the faces around him – Ayla Nightshade, overlord of Darkhaven, his employer and friend; Tomas Caraway, her husband and Captain of the Helm; their adopted son and their two tiny daughters; *Art* – and enjoyed the warm, comfortable sensation of being part of a family once more.

After the meal he went straight down to his laboratory, a

room that had once been a disused wine cellar but that Ayla had converted for his use when she'd invited him and Art to move into Darkhaven. The previous night he had made considerable progress on his latest project – a collar that would afford alchemical protection to ordinary men and women, not just Changers – and he wanted to try it out. So he put it on, and cut his finger, and made notes on the result. Yes, the knife blade still sliced through his skin without any difficulty. Yes, he still bled. But there was no denying that the blood flow was far slower and more sluggish than it would have been without the collar. Give him another year and he'd have the technology perfected.

That was all very satisfactory, and in itself would have been enough to content him. Yet as if the gods were determined to pour blessings on him, Art also had a rare afternoon off. Not that he wasn't allowed time off; he just never took it. But this time he swore to stay out of the fifth ring, and to ignore any summons from Captain Caraway, should it come, and not even to touch the hilt of a sword.

'We'll take a balloon out of the city, Milo,' he said with the twist of a smile. 'Have a picnic. Even grown men need to indulge in romance from time to time.'

Miles scoffed at the idea, of course, but secretly he was delighted. Sometimes he worried that he and Art didn't do enough together, that they were turning into the kind of couple who spent more time fretting about the unwashed dishes than enjoying each other's company. So they had the picnic; and afterwards, eyebrows raised, Art looked around the glade where they were sitting and said, 'Secluded, isn't it? I wouldn't think there's another body about for leagues.'

It was all the invitation Miles needed.

Enjoying the seclusion took longer than they'd planned,

and so the sun was already setting by the time their balloon touched back down in the city. Art went straight up to their room to wash before the evening meal, but Miles lingered in the grounds of Darkhaven, looking at the orange light gilding the temple roofs below him and enjoying being happy. For once, he wasn't listening to the constant whisper of guilt in his ear. He wasn't letting himself feel the simmering dread that one day, everything would come crashing down around him until there was nothing left but rubble. There was sunshine, and the scent of spring blossom, and for once that was enough.

But then, as he turned, he saw a messenger climbing the hill.

There was no reason to believe the message was for him. No reason at all. And yet a shiver crawled between his shoulder-blades. He stood very still, barely daring to breathe, and waited.

The messenger walked right up to him, handed him a folded piece of paper, then – without a word – turned back for the Gate of Death.

It is nothing, Miles told himself. *A note from the university. Something from the fifth ring for Art ...* but his hands were shaking.

He unfolded the paper. He read: *Luka's temple. One week.* And his stomach plunged as if he'd been cast off a precipice.

It had been a long time since he'd received a summons like this. Once a month, he delivered his report to a particular address in Arkannen, along with a letter to his sister Mara; in return, every so often, he received coded instructions and Mara's replies. He'd been doing it for so long, it had become routine – though never without the uneasy edge of guilt. But a face-to-face meeting ... that rarely happened any more. The last time had been almost three years ago, when a Kardise assassin had threatened Ayla Nightshade's life.

Three years. It had almost been long enough to convince himself that his life would stay as it was forever. That, somehow, he could avoid all the consequences of his actions. He should have known that sooner or later, there would always come a reminder of what he was. Sooner or later, the dread always returned.

Still, he would keep going down this path, because what else could he do? On one side of the scales lay Art and Ayla and everyone he loved in Darkhaven. On the other side lay the only family he had left. And he would forever be in the middle, holding them in balance. Because if he let either side fall, even the slightest bit, someone would die.

Just keep going.

He tore the slip of paper into hundreds of tiny pieces, sprinkled them among the new green stems of the sprouting dragonlilies, and went in search of Art.

ONE

The wind had turned cold again, as it often did in the unsettled early days of spring. Ayla felt its icy fingers slip down the back of her neck as she crossed Darkhaven's central square, a reminder that winter still clung to power. Yet for all that, change was coming, and with it something she could almost taste on the air: *peace*.

It had been long enough in the making. Border skirmishes between Mirrorvale and its southern neighbour were almost too common to comment on: a state of affairs that dated from well before Ayla was born. For as long as she could remember, it had gone without saying that Sol Kardis would take Mirrorvale for its own, if it could. Yet last autumn, the Kardise government had sent her a polite and carefully oblique letter that hinted, somewhere between the lines, at the possibility of a treaty. She had replied with delicately worded hints of her own that expressed her willingness to entertain the suggestion of that possibility. And so the correspondence had continued, shaping a shared intent out of allusion and obfuscation until, just before the onset of deepest winter drew a temporary halt to the proceedings, a meeting had been agreed for springtime.

Now springtime was here, and a Kardise ambassador was on his way to Darkhaven.

It would be the most important meeting she had yet held as overlord; Ayla was well aware of that. A peace treaty would put an end to the fighting at the border, fighting that was sporadic but still cost the patrolmen and women limbs and sometimes lives. It would strengthen Mirrorvale's position against its other neighbours. It would increase the flow of trade and information between Mirrorvale and Sol Kardis. And, on a personal level, it would put her in less danger of being murdered. After the first assassination attempt, three years ago, there had been a few others; and although none of them had ever come as close as the first – and indeed, it was some time since any attempt had been made at all – the disquieting possibility remained that one day, an assassin would succeed where the others had failed. Yet once the treaty was signed, she would no longer need to worry about the Kardise trying to kill her.

At least, so she hoped.

Don't promise the fruit before the tree is grown, she told herself. *Just because the ambassador is coming, doesn't mean we'll be able to reach agreement.* All the same, it was a chance. It was far better than anything she'd achieved before, where the question of Sol Kardis was concerned. And for that reason, she couldn't help but let her thoughts leap ahead to what she might be able to do – what *Mirrorvale* might be able to do – when there was no longer the constant need to be on guard. *We can extend our railway. Build new and better airships. Concentrate our alchemical efforts on improved medical remedies, not defence. Tomas won't have to worry about me so much ... and maybe our children can grow up into a world that doesn't threaten war at every turn.*

But first, she had to convince the ambassador that Mirrorvale was strong enough to be worth dealing with as an equal, not a potential conquest.

She found Tomas with two of his men near the door to the transformation room, explaining something that involved sweeping hand gestures and a lot of laughter. Ayla stopped to watch, an unexpected surge of emotion swelling inside her. They had been together for long enough, now, that it was hard for her to view him with any kind of objectivity. It was like looking at one of her children, or her own face in the mirror: too familiar to judge. But every so often, she'd catch him in a moment like this – when he wasn't aware of her presence – and it would be like falling in love with him all over again.

'Captain Caraway,' she said softly. All three of the men turned straight away, drawing themselves upright and saluting. Tomas's expression softened into that particular look she'd never seen him give anyone else – the one that made her feel as though everything and everyone else had faded into the background, leaving the two of them alone – but he greeted her formally, as he always did when they were in company.

'Lady Ayla. Are you ready?'

She walked right up to him, grabbed the lapels of his striped coat and stretched up on tiptoes to kiss him. '*Now* I'm ready.'

The two Helmsmen whooped in approval, and Tomas smiled.

Do you mind? she'd asked him once. *When I break protocol in front of the Helm?*

He'd grinned. *Not at all. I can't do it, because it would demonstrate an alarming lack of respect for my overlord. But please don't let that stop you.*

It was a strange game they played, Ayla thought sometimes. One with many changing roles: overlord and captain for the world at large, equals in private, something in between for the Helm. But after six years they'd found a balance that kept them both happy, and that was what mattered.

'Are you ready?' she asked. 'And the rest of the Helm?'

He nodded. 'Everything is in hand.'

'Then I'd better get going. I don't want to be late.'

She hesitated – it was one thing to play in front of others, quite another to seek genuine reassurance – before winding her arms around his waist and resting her cheek against his chest.

'Safe journey,' he murmured into her hair.

'You too.'

'I'm only going as far as the third ring. It's not quite the same.'

'Even so.'

She would have liked to stay there a while, but instead she stepped back. Their fingers clung together a moment longer. Then Tomas and his men saluted her again, and she entered the transformation room.

The Kardise ambassador was coming in by airship. Perhaps, once, Ayla would have been content to wait in Darkhaven, allowing Tomas and a contingent of the Helm to meet the ambassador at one of the airship stations in the third ring and escort him up through the city to join her. But not today. She and Tomas had decided that where Sol Kardis was concerned, it was vital to display all of Mirrorvale's strength right from the start.

They are bigger than us, more powerful, more advanced, Tomas had said. *But there's one thing they don't have, and that's you.*

And so rather than wait passively for the ambassador to be brought to her, Ayla was going to meet him.

Suppressing a tiny stirring of doubt, she touched the intricate collar at her throat. She wasn't sure how Miles had done it, but this particular piece of jewellery was nothing short of a miracle. It protected her in both human and creature form, allowing her to switch from one to the other without losing the shield that kept her safe from bullets. She could even access her lesser Changer gifts in human form – enhanced strength, heightened senses, the ability to manipulate ice and wood – without having to remove it. And in her creature form, she was genuinely invincible.

As far as anyone can tell, she reminded herself. *We thought Changer creatures were invincible before firearms came along, and look what happened there.*

Still, she was as confident as she could be. Miles had thrown every danger he could think of at her, and none of it had stuck. Now he was busy working on developing similar shields for ordinary people – a far harder task, since they had no alchemy in their blood to build on, but he didn't think it impossible – and she ...

She was going to fly out to meet the Kardise ambassador's airship, alone.

Show him, and show the world, she vowed silently. *Mirrorvale is not afraid of Sol Kardis.*

Letting her hand fall, she summoned the Change.

As the swirling, prickling sensation subsided, she opened her wings to their full extent and arched her neck. She spent long enough in creature form, these days, that it took no more than the space of three heartbeats for her to adjust to the difference. In the past, when her father's shame had kept her out of sight and largely confined to her human skin, it had always taken her some time to settle into her Alicorn form on those occasions she was allowed to enter it. Her creature-self had always been just as much a part of her as her human self, of course; but a somewhat unfamiliar part, alien and awkward like a rarely used limb. Since her father's death, though, she'd exercised that limb more and more – until, now, she considered the strength and single-minded power of her Alicorn form to be *her* no more or less than the more emotion-driven complexity of her human self.

Ducking her head, she pushed open the double doors and left the transformation room.

Outside, the world had come alive. The city was a roar of sound: factories clanking, cartwheels trundling on the cobblestones, hundreds upon hundreds of people talking, a constant hum of voices. Nearer and louder, the clash of steel from the fifth ring, the thud of arrows hitting a target and the grunts of wrestlers; priestesses murmuring devotions, a tune played on the rippling strings of a harp. Darkhaven itself resonated with the soft tread of Helmsmen on patrol, Miles clinking glass in his laboratory, two maids gossiping as they swept the floor; up in the nursery, Marlon chattered about his latest imaginary adventure while Katya sang off-key. A hundred intertwining strands of sound, every one of them distinct. And the smells! In every breath she took, there was something new: hot oil and baking bread and grass and factory smoke and human sweat and a hint of blossom from the distant orchards ...

'Lady Ayla,' her mate said softly. 'Time to go.'

She regarded him steadily. In this form, she found him strange and distant: an incomplete creature, limited to a single way of being. Yet the scent of his skin was familiar, and the rhythm of his heartbeat. He was still the father of her children. So she allowed him to touch her neck with gentle fingers for a moment before stepping back.

Out of the way, she told the Helmsmen. She didn't wait to see if they had obeyed, simply brought her wings down in a powerful stroke and launched herself into the air.

As she rose, Arkannen dwindled below her until she could see the whole of the city: seven rings full of beauty and wonder, industry and ambition and thousands of human lives. Fierce pride and renewed determination gripped her, because this was hers. All of it. And if she had to, she would defend it to the death.

The air changed as she moved away from the city, becoming colder and fresher. Now it tasted of grass and dung, not coal dust and smoke. Southern Mirrorvale wasn't flat and fertile, like the east, which supplied Arkannen with much of its best fruit and grain; it wasn't as rich in timber and coal as the west. It was hill country, inhabited largely by farmers whose small, hardy sheep and cattle were left to graze as they wished, and dotted with market towns where the people spun wool and made the finest cheeses in Mirrorvale. Hard lives, perhaps, but safe ones; yet only a little further south, the hills became less grassy and more unfriendly, rising up into the natural barrier that formed much of the border between Mirrorvale and Sol Kardis. Those hills were the source of all the little streams and tributaries that eventually combined to form the river that passed outside Arkannen's eastern wall; they were also the territory of the patrolmen, whose constant, bitter defence against Kardise incursions was the very thing Ayla was hoping to bring to an end.

As it turned out, she didn't have to fly anything like that far. She'd barely travelled a quarter of the way between Arkannen and the southern border when she spotted the ambassador's airship approaching. Easy enough to identify it – a government ship always displayed the Kardise lion on its envelope, distinguishing it from the striped red and white of a merchant, the gold circle on green background of a passenger ship, or the single plain colour of a wealthy family's personal skyboat. Ayla focused her senses on the airship as the two of them drew nearer to each other, listening through the growl of the engine for the voices of the people who rode in the gondola. All speaking Kardise, of course, but she'd been perfectly taught.

'Sir? Look.'

'Is that –?'

'Gods. She's bigger than I thought.'

'I daresay she can hear you, you know.' That voice was calmer than the others, with a warm hint of amusement. 'They say Changer senses are ten times more acute than our own.'

Make that fifty, Ayla sent into their minds in the same language, then listened to the silence with some satisfaction. Speaking like this, silently, had been another aspect of her gift she'd been late to discover. Her father had been able to do it, but she'd never managed it – something he'd blamed on her hybrid nature, just like her inability to manipulate fire. But once Miles had put her straight on that score, three years ago, she'd begun to wonder if this was another skill that she'd given up on simply because her father had convinced her she was an inferior kind of Changer. And sure enough, as her comfort in her own second skin had grown, she'd found herself able to communicate at greater and greater distances – until now, if she could hear someone talking, she could make them hear her.

Welcome to Mirrorvale, she added, and caught one of the Kardise swearing under his breath.

'Thank you, Lady Ayla,' the calm-voiced man said, ignoring his compatriot. 'I am Carlos Tolino, ambassador for Sol Kardis.'

He'd switched to pleasantly accented Mirrorvalese, which was polite of him. She wished she could see into the gondola – but unlike the smaller ships, this one was fully enclosed, and even Changer eyes couldn't see through solid wood. She'd have to wait to assess the man until they were both back on the ground.

Pleased to meet you, she told Tolino.

'Likewise. I hope you will pardon my aides. They are not used to dealing with people of your ... stature.'

Yet you are?

He laughed. 'No. I have not had the pleasure of visiting Mirrorvale before. But I believe I'm old enough not to be startled very much by anything. Even such a wonder as you.'

By now she had reached the airship. She circled it effortlessly, close enough to pierce the envelope with her spiral horn and send everyone in the gondola to a fiery death on the ground below, if she so chose.

Allow me to accompany you back to the city.

'Thank you,' Tolino said. 'That would be most kind.'

As she headed back in the direction she'd come, she heard one of the Kardise swearing again.

She escorted the airship to Arkannen, as promised; yet once it began to descend towards its allocated docking station in the third ring, she left it behind. Tomas and the Helm would meet the ambassador and his party on the ground – she had seen the carriages waiting. Their journey up to Darkhaven would give her time to Change, get dressed, and be ready to receive her guests.

She was at her station outside the door to the great hall

before two chimes had passed, wearing the kind of long, flowing dress that her father had always insisted she wear and that she'd barely spent any time in during the past six years, because they were so impractical as garments for Changers. The entire thing felt heavy and hampering, tangling around her legs in an irritating fashion. Still, formal occasions called for formal clothing. Warmly amused voice aside, she had no idea what sort of man Carlos Tolino might be, and there was no point jeopardising a possible peace treaty with the chance that he'd object to a woman wearing trousers.

To begin with, automatically, she faced the postern gate; it took her a while to remember that, because of the carriages, Tomas and his men would bring the Kardise in through Darkhaven's vast main gates. The latter had been rarely used in her father's time, and she'd found no reason to change that – the postern was far easier to manage for people on foot, as most of the tower's inhabitants tended to be, and Ayla herself could take off from the central square in creature form. It would have been different if they'd used other methods of transport – carriages, horses, mechanical cycles – but Darkhaven didn't own more than a single carriage and pair. Tomas had hired the other two from somewhere in the city.

Of course, visitors arrived in carriages, but Ayla couldn't remember the last time they'd had a visitor. The Nightshade overlords might make state visits to Mirrorvale's neighbouring countries, and travel the land to fulfil their duties to their own people, but their home remained private. If the stories were true, for centuries that had been by mutual agreement. Back when there were forty or fifty Changers living in Darkhaven, each spending as much time in creature as in human form, it wouldn't have been a place that many ordinary folk dared venture. Yet now ... looking around the square through new eyes, noticing a few cobwebbed windows and the occasional tuft of grass springing up through the cracks in the stone, she wondered what the ambassador would think of Darkhaven. Was it still imposing? Or would he see the worn and shabby seat of a once-great civilisation, a place as much in decline as those who ruled it?

She glanced over her shoulder at the six Helmsmen behind her, three to each side. They must be fed up with waiting by now, yet they didn't fidget or whisper amongst themselves; they remained facing forward, as solid and reliable as the steps beneath her feet. At least she could be proud of the Helm. They knew how important this was, and they wouldn't let her down. Six men, one for each of the first six rings of the city, with herself to represent the seventh; Tomas and another six gone to meet the ambassador. There was tradition in it, as there was in everything here. And although Ayla had broken many Nightshade traditions in her lifetime, she found herself obscurely reassured by this one. She might be the last full-grown scion of a fading line, but she had the weight of history behind her.

Before she turned back around, she noticed that one of her six men was a woman, and couldn't resist giving her a small smile. Ree had saved her life, three years ago; it wasn't the sort of thing one forgot. And besides ... now that Ree was a fully fledged Helmsman, Ayla had the chance to talk to her sometimes, when Ree was on duty at the tower. As much as she loved Tomas, it was nice to spend time with another woman every so often.

Ree smiled back at her – very briefly, as though she thought it was probably the wrong thing to do in such a solemn situation – and Ayla faced the entrance once more. By the time the lookouts at their post above the main entrance called out and ran down to swing the gates open, she was thoroughly cold and fed up with waiting. Still, she summoned another smile as she descended the steps. This was her first chance to assess the ambassador using her human senses. She couldn't let frozen fingers distract her from that.

She scanned the men who were emerging from the carriages, picking out the ambassador straight away. He was of medium height, brown-skinned and dark-haired like so many of his countrymen, with intelligent, jet-black eyes and a kind expression. Ayla hadn't expected the kindness, not in an ambassador. He was dressed without ostentation, much like Ayla herself, although the fabric of his tunic was rich and a Kardise lion worked in gold adorned his belt. As she approached him, he returned her smile with what appeared to be genuine warmth. *Encouraging.*

She flicked a glance at Tomas, standing at the front of the Helm escort in his full captain's uniform – because if anything had occurred to make him uneasy on their way up from the third ring, she'd be able to tell. But his face was untroubled, and he gave her the barest hint of a nod. *Doubly encouraging.*

By now she had reached the carriages, so there was no time left to consider the other men who had made the journey from Sol Kardis – the guards and aides, the ones who had been alarmed by her presence in the sky. They would have to wait.

'Don Tolino,' she greeted the ambassador, with her best attempt at a Kardise bow: dipping her knee, rather than bending from the waist, and ducking her head.

'Lady Ayla.' In return, he touched his fingertips to hers in the Mirrorvalese fashion.

Both countries' honour thus satisfactorily upheld, Ayla

gestured back up the steps. 'Shall we ...?' The two of them climbed towards the formal doors together, with their respective protectors close behind.

'Disheartening, is it not?' Tolino murmured, with the same hint of humour he had shown during their airborne conversation. 'All these people hard on our heels, just waiting for us to try and kill each other.'

She couldn't help but laugh. 'Sadly, yes. Though you, at least, shouldn't take it personally. The Helm are trained to perceive everyone as a potential threat.'

'I assure you, Giorgi does not mean anything personal either.' Tolino threw a surprisingly mischievous look over his shoulder at his burly bodyguard. 'He is merely labouring under the uncomfortable awareness that you outmatch me in every single way. Your power is far beyond anything Sol Kardis has to offer.'

'Which is why we are here,' Ayla agreed with a certain amount of malice – thinking of all those failed assassination attempts – but he only nodded.

'Which is why we are here. And for my part, I am thoroughly grateful for it. Conquest does not suit my ideas of what is best for Sol Kardis at all.' He curled a smile at her like the bow on a birthday gift. 'Trade is far more profitable than war. Don't you agree?'

'Very much so.' They had reached the great hall, where Ayla had planned to install the ambassador and all his aides for their initial conversation. A massive, echoing room – imposing, certainly, but also chilly and inconvenient – where the two of them would face each other amid frozen splendour and beneath the watchful eyes of twenty people ... Impulsively she turned to Tolino. 'Would you ... perhaps we could retire to the library? Just the two of us. An informal talk, a drink to warm us up ... tomorrow is early enough to begin the formal negotiations. And I'm sure your men could do with some refreshment after their journey.'

It wasn't the plan. She and Tomas had agreed that their approach to the Kardise should be polite, but not friendly; that they shouldn't offer anything more than the minimum of courtesy. Sol Kardis might be the larger country, but it was also in the wrong: though none of the councillors with whom she'd corresponded had ever admitted sending assassins her way, it had been an unspoken truth between them that the Kardise were making overtures of peace only because more violent methods had failed. Mirrorvale might desperately want to accept the peace, because it couldn't afford the war, but that was all the more reason to give the impression of cool strength rather than fawning desperation.

Still, plans changed. Don Tolino seemed a pleasant man, and one who was as intent on creating a working treaty as Ayla. If the two of them could agree certain things now, alone and without a score of interruptions, then tomorrow's negotiations could become no more than a rapidly concluded formality.

'I would be very happy –' Tolino began, only to be interrupted by his bodyguard.

'Sir, if I may ... I am not sure it would be a wise idea.'

'Oh, nonsense!' Tolino's eyes met Ayla's in a moment of shared ruefulness. 'No doubt Lady Ayla will guarantee my safety.'

'But sir –'

Ayla looked at Tomas. He didn't like it either, she could tell. Once they would have argued about it, though never in public. But now, he simply scanned her face before moving his fingers in the small, private signal they had developed between them: the one that said *I trust your judgement, and I'm letting you take the lead.*

'If it would make you feel more comfortable,' he told Giorgi, 'you and I can scan the room for concealed weapons together. And while Lady Ayla and Don Tolino are conferring, we can guard the door.'

'Thank you, Captain,' Tolino said firmly, with a quelling glance at his bodyguard. 'That sounds more than adequate.'

Tomas murmured something to one of the Helm, who left his station and disappeared in the direction of the kitchens. By the time Tomas and Giorgi had finished checking the safety of the library, the oil lamps had been lit, a fire had been kindled in the grate and a maid stood patiently beside the two armchairs that faced each other in the centre of the room. Tomas looked at Ayla, eyebrows raised a fraction.

Thank you. She wished she could speak it into his mind, as she would have in Alicorn form, but he nodded as though he'd heard her anyway. Then he saluted, backed out of the room, and left her and Tolino alone.

'Take a seat,' Ayla said. 'Can I offer you a drink?'

'Thank you. That would be most welcome.'

'There's spiced fruit, or ale ...'

'Taransey, surely,' Tolino said with a smile. 'One cannot help but be curious about a liquor that isn't supposed to leave its country of origin.'

'Of course.' Ayla nodded at the maid, who dropped a curtsey before leaving the room. Then she sat down opposite the ambassador, resisting the urge to touch her hair or fold her arms or smooth out the fabric of her unaccustomed skirts. He looked at her expectantly.

'I hope we can reach an agreement, Don Tolino,' she said. 'The unnecessary loss of life at our shared border –'

'Yes.' His levity vanished, Tolino sat forward in his chair. 'Utterly stupid, I agree. You have to understand, Lady Ayla, that my government has been divided on the issue of Mirrorvale for decades. We have debated and wrangled, back and forth, yet nothing was ever decided – and all the while, good men died for nothing.'

It was possible he was genuinely unaware of the assassination attempts, Ayla thought. Hard to be sure, without knowing exactly how the Brotherhood – the shadowy power behind the Kardise government – controlled their councillors. Which also raised the question of whether the Brotherhood were behind this attempt at peace, or whether the government had managed to overcome their inaction of their own accord.

'But you have reached a decision now,' she said, gently probing.

'Reluctantly, yes.' He sighed. 'I won't lie to you: a vociferous faction is still against this treaty. But they are now a minority.'

'They won't interfere?'

'Ah, no. We are a democracy, Lady Ayla. The majority rules.'

A majority can be bought, Ayla thought – but she didn't say it. Whether the Brotherhood had forced a vote for peace or whether it had happened despite their machinations, the outcome was a favourable one.

She opened her mouth to say something more, but at that point the maid returned with a silver tray that bore a bottle of taransey and two glasses. Accepting Ayla's thanks with another bobbed curtsey, she placed her burden gracefully on the small table between the two armchairs and looked up.

'Would you like me to pour, ma'am?'

'No, thank you,' Ayla said. As the maid left the library for the second time, Tolino raised an eyebrow.

'You're going to pour it yourself?' he teased. 'Should I be afraid of poison?'

'I thought, given your curiosity, you might like to study the bottle.' Handing it to him, she added drily, 'You'll notice the seal is intact, so if I'm going to kill you, it won't be with this.'

He took it, examining the thick wax seal with its finely patterned imprint of seven concentric circles, the complicated design of knotted, coloured string. Almost impossible to recreate, though people had tried over the years. 'Taransey has acquired almost legendary status in Sol Kardis, you know. I hear a bottle can sell for thousands on the black market. You could make a fortune if you were to lift the export ban.'

'But then there would no longer be a legend,' Ayla said.

'You prize stories more highly than gold?'

She smiled. 'Given what I am, how could I not? It isn't the Nightshade wealth, such as it is, that's kept Sol Kardis at bay all these years.'

Tolino lowered the bottle to look at her. She returned his gaze without speaking. After a moment, he nodded and passed the taransey back to her. 'Then by all means let us drink, Lady Ayla. I am most curious to see how well the reality lives up to the legend.'

Silently, she broke the seal and poured a small quantity of the amber liquid into each glass, before handing him one. Swallowing some of her own drink, she managed to resist the urge to wince. She'd never admit it to anyone, but she didn't understand the appeal of taransey; it tasted of fire and sharpness, just like every other spirit she'd ever tried. Yet a contented smile had settled on Torrino's face.

'Remarkable,' he murmured. 'Quite remarkable.'

He sipped his drink, gazing at the fire; Ayla matched him. The taransey was growing on her. Though it had a bitter aftertaste she didn't like, she was at least beginning to distinguish some flavours in it beyond mere alcohol.

'Well,' Tolino said finally, replacing his empty glass on the table with a decisive click. 'Thank you. That will give me something to boast about back home. But now I suppose we had better get down to business.'

'I suppose we had.'

They looked at each other a moment in silence. Then, very slowly, Ayla reached up to the collar around her neck. Years of caution were screaming at her not to do it – she could imagine all too clearly what Tomas would say, and Miles too – but her instincts told her that Tolino was to be trusted. And besides, the two of them needed something to break through the polite wall that separated them. Her fingers found the catch, popped it open; before she could change her mind, she dropped the collar beside her own glass.

'I thank you for your trust,' Tolino said. He looked surprised and, Ayla thought, a little pleased. If he brought out a concealed weapon now, it might not go well for her. Indeed, if he were in fact an assassin – if this entire meeting were an elaborate ruse on the part of the Kardise – she had given him the perfect opportunity. But instead he leaned back, hands resting open-fingered on the arms of his chair as though he guessed her doubt and sought to reassure her. 'In return, let me assure you that I have no intention of playing diplomatic games with you – despite what your correspondence with our government may have led you to believe. It is my firm intention to approve a treaty between our countries. Everything else is just a matter of detail.'

'Thank you,' Ayla said, startled in her turn. Taking a moment to hide the sudden rush of relief, she topped up both their glasses. 'That's ... I'm glad to hear you say that. I feel the same way.'

'Good.' Tolino smiled. 'Then shall we begin?'

By the time they had talked through all the most important points of the treaty, the sixth bell had rung, the bottle of taransey was half empty and Ayla was more than ready for a break. They had discussed trade, migration, aid in war, border control and found no desperately contentious areas, only insignificant disagreements that would need hashing out at more leisure. Perhaps she would have continued, pressing for more and more agreement until she was certain that a successful treaty could be signed in the days ahead; but Tolino looked tired, she herself was desperately hungry, and the points that remained to sort out were so minor that she couldn't believe any of them would make a difference. As Tolino had said himself, it was just a matter of detail. So she sat back in her chair, offering him a grateful smile.

'Shall we leave it there? We have days ahead of us. And I think it's clear that we will be able to reach consensus.'

'I admit, I would like something more than taransey to sustain me,' Tolino murmured, and she nodded.

'I'll have someone bring refreshments to your room.'

Yet as she replaced the collar around her neck, the ambassador leaned forward in his chair. 'Before we go, there is, ah ... a rather delicate matter I must raise with you.'

'Yes?'

'You have, here in the city, a young man named Alezzandro Lepont. I believe he is currently working in the warriors' ring ... what number is that? The fifth.' He watched her face as he added, 'Three years ago, he was briefly and falsely suspected of being an assassin.'

Enlightenment dawned. 'Of course. Zander.' She didn't know him, not really. Other than that unfortunate episode, their paths had rarely crossed. Tomas had always spoken highly of him, expressing regret that it would be impolitic to have him in the Helm. And Ree talked about him on a regular basis. But more importantly, in this context ... 'He is the son of one of your councillors, I believe.'

'Yes, Lady Ayla.' Tolino spread his hands. 'And that brings us to the heart of the matter. Marco Lepont is greatly desirous of his son's return.'

'Isn't that up to Zander?'

'Yes and no. He is indeed an adult, and in that sense free to make his own decisions. But Councillor Lepont is an influential man, and Alezzandro his only son.' Tolino paused, then said almost apologetically, 'He has made it a condition of the treaty that the boy leave Mirrorvale and return to Sol Kardis.'

'You want me to deport him?' Ayla asked incredulously.

'If it comes to that. I would hope he will listen to reason, and leave of his own accord.'

She shook her head. 'I'd have to talk to him about this. I couldn't just –'

'That is exactly what we wish,' Tolino said. 'He has disregarded the repeated summons of his father. Perhaps you can persuade him where his own blood cannot.'

Ayla shook her head. 'You don't understand. I wouldn't be seeking to persuade him home. I'd be telling him what you have demanded, and your price if the demand is not met. What he does with that knowledge is up to him.'

Tolino raised his eyebrows. 'Even if the entire treaty stands or falls as a result?'

'Even so,' Ayla said coldly. 'I don't like blackmail.'

He looked at her steadily a moment longer, then smiled.

'Very well, Lady Ayla. I respect your principles, though I cannot agree with your conclusion. We will begin to draw up the treaty in the morning, and as for the problem of Alezzandro ...' He shrugged. 'Let us see what a new day brings.'

Ayla wasn't entirely content with that, but it had to be enough. They had reached agreement on most points, after all. Perhaps in the morning she would be able to convince him to give up the ridiculous idea that it was acceptable to treat a young man like a criminal – and throw a peace treaty into disarray – because his father didn't like the way he was living his life.

'Let me find someone to show you to your room,' she said, and they crossed the floor together. But before she could open the door, Tolino put a hand on her arm.

'Don't look so worried, Lady Ayla. We will find a way to honour both Councillor Lepont's request and your own conscience. I promise.'

Curiously, she found she believed him. She began to say something, but he got there first.

'You know, whatever the legends say, it is my opinion that the reality outmatches them in every respect.'

Then they were outside the library again, with aides and Helmsmen springing into action at this evidence that their employers had not, in fact, torn each other to pieces, and Tomas giving orders for the Kardise to be shown to their rooms and served a late meal. It was only when the ambassador was about to be swept off by his entourage that Ayla managed to get another word in.

'Don Tolino!'

He turned, smiling. 'Yes?'

'Thank you.'

'Not at all. Thank you.'

They clasped hands, briefly. And then he was gone.

Later, once she and Tomas were alone in their bedroom, Ayla stood at the window and gazed out at the stars. It was late, and she was tired, but she didn't yet feel like sleeping. The events of the day kept playing through her mind, challenging her to find a flaw in what she had done. A weakness. Something that would bring all her hopes crashing down. Yet she couldn't find one. Apart from the issue of Zander – and Tolino had as good as assured her that it wouldn't be an issue after all – she couldn't see a single obstacle in her way.

I did it. I actually did it.

'So are you ready yet?' Tomas stepped up behind her, sliding his hands over her hips to encircle her waist. 'To tell me how it went?'

'Well.' She tipped her head back against his shoulder, smiling. 'Don Tolino is a good man, and I really think it went well.'

'I'm proud of you.'

'Oh, Tomas.' Still she smiled. She couldn't stop smiling. It felt like an irrepressible light, bursting out of her despite her exhaustion and the restrictions of her highly annoying dress. 'Thank you.'

'For what?'

'For everything.' She closed her eyes. *Peace. We can have peace. This is really going to happen.*

'You look beautiful,' Tomas said softly in her ear. She chuckled.

'I feel like a trussed-up chicken awaiting the pot. I'd forgotten how uncomfortable these stupid things are.'

His fingertips trailed over her skin, leaving a tingle of anticipation in their wake. His voice held a promise. 'I can help you take it off.'

And he did.

TWO

Outside the library, Ree kept her place in the guard formation – equally spaced, close enough to the Helmsmen either side of her to watch their backs, far enough apart not to get in each other's way. She kept her expression neutral, as she'd been trained to do, but she couldn't help an inner smile. Her childhood dreams of joining the Helm had involved fighting off assailants ten against one, preserving the Nightshade overlord's life at great and heroic personal cost, and single-handedly saving the entire country from deadly peril. *Standing* hadn't featured at all. Whereas the truth was, as she'd once joked to Penn, that all the weapons testing they'd been put through before they joined was far less relevant to their daily lives than whether they could stand without moving for the space of a bell.

Of course, Penn had pointed out that any desperate battles or single-handed feats of heroism would mean there was a very real danger of them failing at their job. Every uneventful shift, he'd said, meant another day of survival for the Nightshade line. And of course, Ree couldn't argue with that. It wasn't as if all the standing had decreased her love of what she did. It was just that, sometimes, it was very hard not to fidget.

Taking a deep breath and releasing it slowly, she did her

best to practise everything she'd been taught. *Stay relaxed but alert*: that was her only physical requirement, a state of loose readiness that could carry her through long periods of waiting and still leave her ready to fight at the end. Tension would exhaust her muscles unnecessarily, but relax too much and she'd be too slow to react if the moment required it. Which led to *focus on the present moment*. Silence and inaction made it too easy for her mind to drift into other times and places, and a distracted Helmsman was a defeated one. Instead, she had to *observe and analyse*. Even if all she had to observe was the stretch of wall ahead of her, the muted sounds of people going about their business elsewhere in the tower, the smell of the oil lamps and the scuff of fabric against her skin – even then, she had to keep thinking about it all. Because failing to notice a change, however slight, could mean the difference between raising the alarm and being taken off guard.

A murmur caught her attention, and she slid her gaze in that direction, but it was only two of the Kardise talking to each other in low voices. The ambassador's bodyguard stood beside Captain Caraway outside the library door, with six Helmsmen stationed three to each side at intervals along the wall, leaving the three other members of Tolino's entourage at something of a loose end. Caraway had offered to send someone to show them to their rooms, but it was clear they felt they should remain within shouting distance of the library, where they could eye the Helmsmen on duty suspiciously and be eyed in return. Decades of fighting between Mirrorvale and Sol Kardis couldn't be forgotten in a single afternoon. And so they stood in a huddle in the vestibule, getting in the way of passing servants and generally making a nuisance of themselves.

Can't really blame them, Ree thought. *I wouldn't want*

to leave either, in their position. She turned her gaze to face forward again, not wanting to make them uncomfortable, and suppressed an inward sigh. That indistinct murmur was the most interesting thing that had happened for the past half-bell. *It's going to be a long afternoon.*

By the time Ayla finally emerged from the library, it was getting late. Anxiously, Ree studied her face; not only was it her job to anticipate her overlord's every need, whim and possible danger, but she was Ayla's friend. As much as anyone could be, anyway. If something had gone wrong, she wanted to know about it. Yet Ayla looked calm and happy, and the parting words she exchanged with the ambassador were warm. It must have gone well.

Once the Kardise party had retreated to their designated quarters, Caraway thanked the Helmsmen on duty for their service and dismissed them to get some rest. Outside, darkness had fallen; the moon hung low in the sky, a misshapen yellow disc. Past the start of sixth bell, but not yet close to seventh. Ree wasn't on duty tomorrow; she had two training sessions to attend, bladework in the morning and firearms in the afternoon, but she'd be able to get up a little later for a change. Maybe she'd call round to Zander's apartment, she thought as she crossed the central square. He'd be interested to hear about the ambassador. And the next morning, they could return to the fifth ring together.

The night shift had already taken over from the day shift, of course, so she had to call down one of the Helmsmen on duty above the postern gate to let her out.

'All right, Ree?' It was Tulia, a tall, broad-shouldered girl with red-gold hair who was the only other female member of the Helm. She'd joined the previous year, having been inspired by Ree's success to attempt the training. Every assessment period since Ree's own had included a few girls, though most of them were unsuccessful, just like most of the boys were. Of course, that didn't stop the snide suggestion in certain quarters that Captain Caraway went easy on the girls. But by now, Ree had learned that some people were far less interested in the truth than in how they could twist that truth to support their own agenda. And there was no point in arguing with people like that, because no evidence – however solid – would ever change their minds.

Sometimes, when a cohort of new recruits turned out to be particularly troublesome on the question of female Helmsmen, Ree and Tulia would go and demonstrate the forms for them. That usually silenced the doubters.

'You just come on duty?' Ree asked.

'Yeah. First night shift of the week. Always the hardest.' Tulia mimed an exaggerated yawn. 'You were in the reception party for the ambassador, right?'

'Mmm.'

'Anything interesting happen?'

'Well …' Ree grinned. 'I got to practise my standing.'

They shared a chuckle, before Tulia unlocked the postern and let Ree out.

''Night, Tu.'

''Night.'

As Ree descended the hill towards the seventh gate, she felt tiredness seeping through her bones – as though leaving Darkhaven, crossing that line between *work* and *home*, had removed her shields and allowed the underlying weakness to reveal itself. Perhaps she'd wait until tomorrow to see Zander. Yet she'd been on day shift and then night shift for the past week, plus the ambassador's visit today … it had been ages since she last saw him.

She shook her head with a sigh. She'd decide when she reached the Gate of Steel – unless she fell asleep on the way. The way she felt now, it was a very real possibility.

Run, Ree. She passed through the Gate of Death with a hand lifted in greeting to the watchmen. *It'll keep you awake.*

As she jogged past the temples of the sixth ring, she noticed that one of the twin swords wasn't sitting quite right on her back. She paused for a moment, rolling her shoulders to redistribute the weight. Those swords had come as a surprise to her. During training, one of the weaponmasters had given a series of lessons on fighting an opponent armed with dual blades, and as part of it they'd all had the chance to try it for themselves. Most of the trainees had grumbled about the awkwardness of having to think about a second sword when they'd just become proficient in the forms with one, but not Ree. For her, somehow, it had fit.

On the last day of the course, Captain Caraway had come to watch them practise. He'd spoken to the weaponmaster. And then, soon afterwards, he'd called Ree to one of the single-combat training floors.

'Captain?' Ree poked her head around the door. 'You wanted to see me?'

'Come in, Ree.' As Caraway turned to gesture her inside, she realised he wasn't alone; a stocky blonde woman stood beside him, arms folded.

'This is Naeve Sorrow,' the captain said. 'She's going to give you extra training. Sorrow, this is Ree Quinn.'

Ree studied the woman in front of her with interest. She'd first met Sorrow, if meeting it could be called, when the other woman had crashed an airship in the grounds of Darkhaven three years ago. Since then, she'd seen the sellsword from time to time, here in the fifth ring or in Caraway's company.

And two sword hilts peeked over her shoulders – which answered one question, at least. Sorrow was renowned for her skill with the twin blades.

'Pleased to meet you,' Ree said, only to be met with a flat-eyed stare. She glanced at Caraway, then immediately regretted betraying her uncertainty when she saw Sorrow's lips curl.

'I'll leave you to it,' Caraway said, either oblivious to Sorrow's antipathy or choosing to ignore it. Ree saluted, and managed not to watch him leave. She was a potential Helmsman, she told herself, not a child.

'I should warn you,' the sellsword said, once they were alone, 'that I'm not very good at teaching people things. If I'd wanted to impart knowledge to snotty brats, I'd have become a weaponmaster.'

Ree blinked. 'Did you just call me a snotty brat?'

'Yes. Got a problem with that?'

Ree flushed. She considered storming out. But after a moment, she said, 'If you're trying to antagonise me into leaving so you don't have to teach me, it's not going to work.'

'Why not?'

'Because I really want to learn the twin blades. *Really*. And since Captain Caraway is going to lock us in a room together every week until I have the necessary skills, you might as well get it over with as quickly as possible.'

The corners of Sorrow's mouth twitched. 'Fair point.'

'Who knows?' Ree added. 'You might end up liking me.'

'Stranger things have happened.' Sorrow studied her face for a moment, then shrugged and stuck out a hand. 'All right. We'll give it a try.'

That was how Ree ended up being trained by a mercenary – a fact, she quickly decided, of which her parents didn't need to be informed. Sorrow didn't talk much, beyond the instructions she gave, but it was good to be around another female warrior. She understood certain things without needing to have them explained. Like when she asked Ree one day, out of nowhere, why she'd been so anxious to join the Helm when everyone knew it wasn't a woman's job, and Ree looked up from unfastening her gloves and said simply, 'Because everyone knew it wasn't a woman's job.' Zander would have pressed her on it. Penn, too. But Sorrow only nodded and went back to her own task. Ree guessed she knew, quite well, what it was like to want something because other people said she couldn't have it.

In addition, she proved to be a far better teacher than she'd made out. Not as good as Zander, of course; no-one was as good a teacher as Zander. But she certainly wasn't horrible. Her way of teaching was to make Ree try to do something, and then tell her what she'd got wrong, and make her do it again, over and over until the lesson was drummed into her head – and then do it again the next week, just to make sure.

'It's how I taught Elisse to shoot,' she said. 'Repeat something enough times that the memory of it settles in your bones, and you'll never forget it.'

'Who's Elisse?' Ree asked curiously, and Sorrow raised an eyebrow.

'None of your business, that's who.'

It wasn't until training finished and Ree was accepted into the Helm that she was able to put the pieces together: as well as being Sorrow's lover, Elisse was the mother of Ayla's half-brother Corus. All the Helm knew about Corus, because he had a special contingent of Helmsmen to live with him and guard him away from Darkhaven, but his existence was largely hidden from the rest of the world. And to all intents and purposes, Naeve Sorrow – infamous mercenary and former scourge of the Helm – was his parent.

Ree wondered how Ayla felt about that.

Sorrow came and went from Arkannen on a frequent basis, visiting Elisse and Corus, but the lessons she gave Ree were enough. By the time Ree joined the Helm, she was proficient with the twin blades; enough so that Caraway gave her special dispensation to carry a pair instead of the usual Helmsman's issue. And she'd also grown to like Sorrow. It was hard not to like someone who had helped her to discover such a fundamental part of herself.

Walking through the fifth ring, now, Ree smiled to remember how nervous she'd once been around Sorrow. They still practised together now that Ree was in the Helm, moving easily from a teacher–pupil relationship to one of ... what? Friends? Comrades? Equals, at least. Sorrow only sparred with people she considered worthy of her notice, which mostly meant Caraway and Art Bryan and a handful of other experienced sellswords and Helmsmen – and Ree. If that wasn't a token of respect, she didn't know what was.

By now she could see the Gate of Steel ahead of her, illuminated by tall gas lamps that made the blades that lined the archway gleam fierce and orange. And there, just inside it – Ree glanced away, thinking she was hallucinating, but when she looked back they were still there, standing stiff and awkward in the company of one of the watchmen from the gate.

Her parents.

As she walked towards them, her father raised his head. He put a hand on her mother's arm, and she, too, looked up. Both of them smiled uneasily, but Ree didn't return the smile. This was too unexpected an occurrence for her to be sanguine about it.

'Hello, Cheri,' her father said when she was close enough. Ree exchanged nods with the watchman, who returned to his post. Only then did she turn to her parents, seeing – with the strange half-surprise that came with looking at something familiar for the first time in a while – the pieces of them that had gone towards making her. Her father's green eyes. Her mother's brown hair: longer than her own, of course, but still the same. Their yellow-brown skin, of a shade that Zander referred to poetically as amber. She was taller than her mother, she realised. That must have been true for a long time; she'd stopped growing years ago. But it was the first time she'd felt it.

'What are you doing here?' she asked.

Her father attempted a hearty chuckle, though it was a shadow of its usual self. 'Can't a father visit his daughter?'

'He can,' Ree said. 'But usually he doesn't.'

'We went to your address, but you weren't there.' Her mother's tone suggested mild rudeness on Ree's part. 'So we came up here to find you, but the guards wouldn't let us in.' Apparently an even greater degree of rudeness. Ree sighed.

'You can't enter the fifth ring without legitimate business. You know that.'

'Visiting our daughter isn't legitimate business?'

Not really, no. Ree shook her head, too tired to pursue the point. 'Does this visit have a purpose? Only I can't believe you'd hang around waiting for me to come off duty if it wasn't urgent.' Belated anxiety gripping her, she peered more closely at them. 'Is someone ill? Dead?'

'Nothing like that,' her father said. Then, with a glance in her mother's direction, 'We just need to talk to you.'

Guess I won't be visiting Zander after all. Ree suppressed another sigh. 'It's late. I've just come off duty. Can we talk tomorrow?'

'Now would be better.'

'Fine.' Ree caught the petulant note in her own voice, and winced. Next she'd be stamping her foot and telling them she hated them. Did everyone revert to childhood when confronted with their own parents?

'I'll take you back to my apartment,' she said, achieving politeness with an effort. 'It would be nice for you to see where I live.'

The Ametrine Quarter was only a short walk from the Gate of Steel, which was a relief with her parents' silence at her heels. Ree led them to the three-storey terraced house that held her apartment, a two-roomed place with shared cooking and bathing facilities that was all she could afford on a junior Helmsman's salary. Middle floor – the worst floor, she always complained to Zander, people above *and* below. Yet as her parents traipsed up the stairs after her, she found herself wanting to point out everything good about it. Her apartment was much like family, in that respect; she could moan about it as much as she liked, but she'd make short work of anyone else's criticism.

Once inside, she divested herself of her weapons and hung up her coat, before – in a sudden panic – glancing around to see what she could offer her parents to sit on. She had one armchair, an old saggy thing with stuffing leaking out of the cushions. And at the tiny table, a rickety wooden chair with a folded news-sheet under one leg. She wasn't convinced that would stand up under her father's weight, so she gestured her mother towards it and said brightly, 'I can fetch you my pillow, if you like.'

'No, dear, that's fine.' Ree's mother sat down on the very edge of the chair. A determined smile was pinned to her face, but the swift glance she cast around the room spoke volumes.

Come on, Ree wanted to say. *It's better than the barracks. Oh, but you wouldn't know about that, would you? Because you never visited me.*

Not that she minded, really. On the whole she'd been grateful for her parents' lack of interference. Her father had called in on her a couple of times over the years, when he had business in the city. And she'd dutifully made the journey home every Harvest Festival, to sit in a corner of the drawing room and pretend not to notice the other merchants' daughters whispering about her hair, her clothes, her *otherness*. After the last visit, when her mother had tried to bundle her upstairs to change as soon as she set foot in the house – *please, Cheri, it's a beautiful dress, and so much more appropriate than that garish monstrosity of a coat* – she'd given herself permission to forego even that small torture. Her parents weren't proud of her. They didn't care that she was the first female Helmsman in history, sworn to protect the very heart of their country, fulfilling a role that most of the young men back home would kill for. No, her mother considered her an embarrassment. Even her father, who'd once indulged her interest in weaponry, was beginning to think better of it. And so Ree had decided that since they were so anxious for her to be someone else, she'd leave them to the company of that imaginary daughter and extract herself from their lives completely.

Yet here they were in her apartment.

Ree installed her father in the armchair, then – after considering and swiftly discarding the idea of perching on the arm in a mockery of happy family relations – settled cross-legged on the floor. She looked from her mother's fixed smile to her father's awkward grin, and her heart lifted a little. Maybe they'd realised how unfair they'd been. Maybe they were here to apologise.

'So what brings you to Arkannen?' she asked.

Her mother glanced at her father. Her father ran a finger around the inside of his collar, and leaned forward to look her in the eye.

'We've found a husband for you, Cheri,' he said.

Ree laughed.

Her parents didn't.

Ree stopped laughing. 'What are you talking about?'

'He's a very nice boy.' Her mother didn't meet Ree's gaze, but directed a tremulous smile somewhere in the direction of her left cheekbone. 'Such a good family. His parents ...'

Ree said nothing.

'You'll like him,' her father said cheerfully. 'He has a wonderful collection of antique swords. Maybe he'll let you try them out sometimes.' He chuckled at his own joke.

Ree said nothing.

'And he doesn't mind at all that you've been working in the city these last few years.' Her mother's smile had slipped at Ree's silence, but she plastered it back in place and pressed on doggedly. 'He said it was refreshing to find a girl who wanted to make her own way in the world. Said it would come in useful when he takes over his father's business, to have a sensible partner by his side and not some empty-headed female ...'

Ree said nothing.

Then, vibrating with fury, she stood up and said in a voice so low and hoarse that it grated in her own ears, 'Get out.'

'Cheri.' An expression of distress replaced the smile on her mother's face. 'That's not very –'

'I said get out. Now. *Now!*'

She grabbed each of her parents by an arm and bundled them towards the door. They didn't resist. Only when they were at the threshold did her mother turn to her again and say, in a weak and pleading voice, 'Cheri ...'

Ree slammed the door in her face.

How *could* they? How could they sit there and say those things to her as if she wouldn't mind, as if she'd just been frittering away her days here while she waited for them to find her a suitable husband? She'd always known that wealthy old families regarded their children as assets to be invested for maximum return, rather than people free to make their own decisions, but she hadn't thought her parents were like that. They weren't *rich* enough to be like that. They might not understand why she'd come to Arkannen, but at least they'd let her do it. They hadn't contracted her off to the highest bidder, her talents and virtues enumerated like a ship's manifest in search of the best possible price. So what had changed?

The Helm was her life. She'd thought they understood that by now. She'd spent a year training. Two more, so far, as a Helmsman. Did they think she'd dedicated all that time and energy to a hobby? To a whim? Did they not know her *at all*?

She wanted to punch something. Or break something. But she didn't have any furniture to spare, and if there was one thing her years in the fifth ring had taught her, it was the importance of restraint. *Violence,* Captain Caraway had said more than once, *is only of value when it's controlled.* So rather than smash up her limited number of possessions, she grabbed her coat from the peg by the door and stormed back out of her apartment in the direction of the training grounds.

It might be close to seventh bell by now, but one of her friends would be awake. There was always *someone* awake.

She found Penn in the boxing ring, practising on one of the punching-bags, which was perfect. Zander would have tried to cheer her up, and failing that, he'd have suggested she work out her aggression in a different way. Sometimes that was exactly what she needed. But not tonight. Tonight she didn't want angry sex, she just wanted *anger*.

And if there was one person on whom she found it easy to take out her raw, unconstrained anger, it was Penn.

She strode forward, grabbing a pair of padded mittens to protect her knuckles. Penn turned at her approach, fists half raised, but he lowered them when he recognised her.

'Ree, are you –'

She threw a punch, which he barely blocked; the impact sent him back a step. His eyes widened, then narrowed.

'What's the matter?'

'My parents,' Ree said through gritted teeth, 'want me to get *married*.'

Another punch accompanied the word. This time it landed, because Penn was too busy laughing to defend himself. The laugh became a wheeze as all the breath was knocked out of him.

'Married?' he gasped, eyes watering, stumbling out of her reach with more haste than technique. 'Have they actually met you?'

'Apparently not.' Ree danced forward and punched him again, but he blocked it and returned a blow of his own. It made her dizzy. Penn was strong. Three years of daily practice had left him far more muscular than he'd been when he started. Which, admittedly, was also true of her – but since Penn was a head taller than her, and considerably broader in the shoulders, he'd had a lot further to fill out. Once she'd been able to knock him down just by punching, but not any more. If she wasn't careful, he'd pick her up and fling her over his shoulder; he had a nasty habit of doing that, these days. Yet the knowledge only made her anger surge hotter.

'Penn?' she panted. *Violence is only of value when it's controlled.* But Captain Caraway had never met her parents. 'Can we go off-book?'

Off-book was what everyone called the no-holds-barred style of fighting that was strongly discouraged amongst professional warriors. Ree and Penn might not be trainees any more, but they were still expected to keep to the Code, just like everyone else in the fifth ring. Not only that, but the Helm were held to it more strictly than most, and with good reason: an incapacitated Helmsman was a temporarily useless Helmsman, and their captain expected them to have more sense than to waste their time on thoroughly avoidable injuries.

All of that went some way towards explaining the wary look in Penn's eyes as he circled her.

'Are you sure?' he said finally. 'After last time? Because you know I won't hold back.'

Ree knew he wouldn't. That's what she liked about fighting him. Last time they'd gone off-book, he'd fractured two of her ribs. Captain Caraway had been furious, thinking someone had jumped her, but she'd told him it had happened breaking up a street brawl down in the first ring. She'd had to listen to a lecture about not getting involved in incidents that were more properly the Watch's business, but at least she hadn't landed Penn in any trouble. She had no desire to do that. It was just that sometimes … sometimes, to really lose herself in anger, she had to release every control she had.

'I'm sure,' she said.

'Even with the Kardise ambassador here?'

That gave her a moment's pause, because he was right: they all needed to be on top form during the ambassador's visit. She certainly couldn't show up for guard duty in Darkhaven with a black eye or a broken nose.

'Nothing that will show,' she conceded. 'But otherwise, no rules.'

As the last word left her mouth, she spun on the ball of her foot and drove her elbow hard into his stomach. He absorbed the blow, twisting aside; she saw the flicker in his eyes as he changed the direction of his own left-handed punch at the last moment – avoiding her face – and so was able to dodge just far enough to let his fist skim past her ribs. Before he could retreat, she caught his forearm in the crook of her elbow and drove the heel of her other hand up towards his chin. He blocked it with his free arm, pushing it back and closing the distance between them until they were chest to chest. Not good. If she wasn't careful, he'd overpower her through height and weight alone.

If they had been truly off-book, she would have headbutted him in the mouth, but that would almost certainly show in the morning. So instead, she turned her head and sank her teeth into his arm.

'Fuck's sake, Ree!' He broke free of her grasp, twisting round behind her, grabbing her arm and pulling it up behind her back until a cry escaped her lips despite her determination. Her knees buckled under the steady pressure. He was trying to force her down, and if he got her on the ground she'd have no chance. She bucked and writhed, trying to wrench herself away, but his grip was inexorable. Anger and frustration boiled up inside her –

We've found a husband for you, Cheri. Maybe he'll let you try out his sword collection sometimes. He doesn't mind at all that you've been working in the city.

With an inarticulate sound of rage, she kicked backwards with all her strength and felt her boot connect with Penn's shin. As his grip on her loosened, she pulled away and spun round to face him, shoving his shoulders and hooking her foot behind his ankles. She went with him as he fell, pummelling indiscriminately at any part of him she could reach until they landed on the floor and she straddled his chest, one arm moving across his throat for a chokehold –

'I yield, I yield!' he gasped beneath her. She swung her leg off him and dropped to the floor on her back beside him. They lay together for a while in silence, breathing hard.

'Wow,' Penn said finally. 'You really don't want to get married, do you?'

Ree shook her head silently. She was trembling all over, now, hit by the cold aftermath of violence. Though her anger was gone, she almost wished it wasn't; the depression it had left behind was harder to shake off.

'Huh,' Penn said, and she frowned up at the ceiling.

'What's that supposed to mean?'

'It's just, I always assumed all girls dreamed of marriage.'

She turned her head to say something blistering, only to find him looking back at her with a smile in his eyes: he was teasing her. It was such a rare event that it eased the chill in her stomach, a little.

Of course, three years ago he'd probably believed it – but why point that out? If Penn had become more open-minded over his years in the fifth ring, Ree thought she herself had probably learned the value of tact.

'What do you think I should do?' she asked instead. His

lips tightened as if he doubted the value of his own advice, but he gave it anyway.

'Tell them you won't do it. If they disown you, that's their choice. Parents who can't accept you for who you are aren't worth having as parents anyway.'

He was thinking of his own parents as much as hers, Ree knew. After he'd failed to take his family's revenge on Captain Caraway three years ago – and worse, stayed to train as a Helmsman under Caraway's captaincy – Penn's father had cut all ties with him. Penn's younger brothers were forbidden even to mention his name. Ree had got that much out of him when they were on night duty together; there was something about the time between midnight and dawn that encouraged that kind of confidence. But he hadn't mentioned it again since, and she hadn't asked. The pair of them upheld a silent agreement that some things were best left unspoken.

Still, Penn was right: her parents didn't deserve her obedience. She was a grown woman, and if she didn't want to get married, they couldn't make her. Admittedly, the families of wealthy investors – and of not-so-wealthy merchants trying to better themselves – had different expectations for their daughters than the ordinary working families here in the city. And also admittedly, it wasn't that long ago that the patriarchs of said wealthy families had thought it acceptable to contract their offspring to each other without consulting anything so trivial as anyone's feelings on the matter. But Ree's parents were thoughtless, not heartless; she couldn't believe they'd do that to her. Besides, one thing she knew for certain was that she had the right to ask the overlord of Darkhaven to intercede in any dispute. Indeed, the overlord of Darkhaven *was* the law. And Ree really couldn't imagine

Ayla forcing any girl to get married against her will, let alone one of her own Helmsmen.

No, there was no chance that Ree might be forced into marriage. It was her parents' obtuseness that had made her angry, not the fear they might prevail.

'Thanks, Penn,' she said softly.

'You're welcome.' He sounded uncertain, as though he wasn't sure she meant it – but before she could say anything else, he sat up and groaned. 'I ache all over.'

'Me too.'

'And we have training tomorrow.'

'Yeah.' She grimaced. 'Sorry.'

'It's all right. I still don't sleep much.' That was another thing he'd told her, in the depths of a long night: he'd first started having trouble sleeping three years ago, when he'd come to the fifth ring with revenge in mind, and somehow that had never gone away. She'd asked him what kept him awake, and he'd said vaguely, *Fear, I suppose. My own thoughts. I don't know.*

'Reckon they've got any spare beds in the barracks?' she suggested.

'Worth a try.'

'C'mon, then.' She forced herself to her feet, before holding out a hand to pull him up after her. 'Let's find out. And Penn ... thank you. Really.'

'It's fine, Ree. You can beat me up any time.'

Resting her head against his shoulder, she smiled. 'I'll hold you to that.'

THREE

Caraway woke with the dawn, despite the fact that for once there was neither an urgent message waiting for him nor a training session to get to, nor – which happened most commonly – a small voice calling his name. Ayla was still asleep, head on his shoulder and one leg tangled with his. Strands of her rosemary-scented hair tickled his cheek. She'd kept it at chin length ever since she was forced to cut it for disguise, six years ago. *It's far more practical,* she'd told him. *With all the Changing, long hair just makes me look like I was dragged through a hedge. And besides* – with the glint of a mischievous smile – *it reminds me that once, you sold my hair to buy me a wig.*

Caraway wasn't sure why she'd want to be reminded of that, given how much she'd despised him at the time. She seemed to view their entire past history through the rosy glass of retrospect, turning every one of their prickly initial interactions into something warm and inevitable. It was much like the stories that were still told down in the lower rings about him, the ones that took a kernel of truth and wrapped it in layers of daydream and wishful thinking until he became a symbol, not a real person. Tomas Caraway, the city's hero.

After six years, he had grown used enough to those stories to accept them with a smile. Easy enough to see heroism, looking back on it. Easy enough to see romance, too. But that was only because, of all the myriad possible paths he and Ayla could have taken – paths along which he drank himself to death, or failed to rescue her from incarceration, or said and did slightly different things that meant the two of them grew into mutual dislike, instead of love – of all those paths, he'd been lucky enough to stumble across the one where everything turned out for the best.

He suspected that was why so many people liked those heroic, romantic tales: it allowed them to believe in fate, the idea that things happened for a reason and the people with the best intentions always won out in the end. The truth was, luck played a far greater part in every single aspect of life than most people cared to admit.

But I know it. He drew Ayla closer in against him, kissing the top of her head. *I've been lucky. And I'm grateful for it, every single day.*

'Are the children up?' she mumbled. Interpreting that through long experience as *Go away and let me get more sleep*, Caraway disentangled himself and slid out of bed. She promptly shifted further over into the warm hollow left by his body. He didn't think her more than half awake, but just as he got his arms into the sleeves of his dressing gown, she said softly, 'I love you.'

Smiling in a way that would have earned some well-deserved backchat from the Helm, if they'd seen it, he pulled the cord of the dressing gown tight and left the room. *Dressing gown*: now there was an odd invention, a piece of clothing designed specifically to put off the necessity of getting dressed. He'd never even thought to own one before he came to live in Darkhaven. You got up, you washed, you put on your clothes, and that was the end of it. Yet Ayla possessed seven of the damn things, as beautifully made and decorated as any of her daytime outfits. And over time, she'd managed to inveigle him into one. It had embroidery on it, and *gold edging*. Why did something that no-one else was ever going to see need to be edged with gold?

Admittedly, it was very comfortable. And it looked nice. He'd probably spend the whole day in it if he thought he could get away with it. But he wasn't going to tell Ayla that.

He poked his head round the door of Marlon's room, but his adopted son was a light sleeper and so Caraway didn't venture too close for fear of waking him. Instead, he stole down the corridor to the nursery, where his daughters were both still curled up under the covers. A strand of night-dark hair was plastered to Katya's cheek; he pushed it gently back from her face, and she mumbled something. Already, at not quite three years old, she looked a lot like Ayla. There was no denying her heritage. Whereas Wyrenne ... Caraway stepped softly away from Katya's bed to gaze down into Wyrenne's cot. His younger daughter's loose brown curls stuck up on her head, and one thumb was planted firmly in her mouth. She didn't look like a Nightshade at all. She looked like him.

That had come as a surprise to Ayla, Caraway knew. This was the first generation without any full-blooded Nightshades, meaning that no-one could have predicted the outcome – and indeed, the outcome was still far from known, until the children turned fourteen and began to manifest their own Changer gifts or lack thereof. But Marlon looked like a Nightshade, despite his birth mother's red hair and freckles, and Katya might as well be a miniature of Ayla herself, all raven-black hair and pale skin, even down to the faint hint of turquoise in her midnight-blue eyes that was the only visible legacy of Ayla's common-born mother. Between the two of them, they'd probably convinced Ayla that Nightshade blood was not so easily diluted. So the arrival of a brown-skinned, tousle-haired baby had startled her, a little. She loved Wyrenne with fierce intensity, but Caraway knew the old doubts still played in her mind: would any of these children turn out to be Changers? What would happen when they grew up and married outside the family, and the amount of Nightshade blood in their own children's veins was halved again? She didn't speak of it often, but the demise of the Nightshade line was an ever-present concern.

It's what I wanted, she'd told Caraway once. *It's not as if much hope lay ahead for the family anyway, with only Myrren and me to continue it. We'd reached the end of the road. I just wish I could find a way to ensure the gift's survival. Because without it, what will Mirrorvale become?*

Caraway didn't know the answer to that question. He wouldn't be where he was if he could envisage a future for Mirrorvale that was independent of Darkhaven and its Changers. But as far as he could see, there wasn't any point worrying about it. Either the Nightshade gift would endure, or it wouldn't – and as long as Ayla and the children were safe, it didn't really matter which. Lord Florentyn and Owen Travers would have had his head for that attitude; but Ayla's father and his Captain of the Helm had always put the survival of the Nightshade line above the welfare of the people in it, whereas to Caraway himself it seemed obvious that it should be the other way round.

That, among other reasons, was why he and Ayla would never have another child. Giving birth to Wyrenne had nearly killed Ayla; once she'd recovered, the physician had warned her against bearing any more children, and given her a medicinal supplement that would prevent it. Perhaps once she would have fought against the advice – insisted that it didn't matter, that it was worth bringing as many Nightshades into the world as possible, even if it put her own life in danger. Her father would certainly have taken that position on her behalf. But Ayla had learned hard lessons from the constant threat of assassination, and one of them was that she had to stay alive, no matter what it cost her in other freedoms. As the only Changer in Mirrorvale, she was too important to do otherwise.

I'm sorry, Tomas, she'd said when she told him the news – tears running silently down her face. *I'm so sorry.*

It's not your fault.

I could ask the physician again if there's any way –

No, Ayla. He'd taken her hands. *I'm glad the physician made the decision he made.*

Why?

He'd hesitated, unsure if his words would help, but he had to be honest. *Because if he hadn't, I would have had to tell you myself that I don't want any more children. I can't live with the possibility that giving birth to my baby might kill you.*

She'd bowed her head. *I don't know what to do, Tomas. I feel so broken.*

Dearest love. You're not broken. It might feel that way now, but you're not. He'd dropped to his knees beside her, willing her to look at him. *We have each other, when I thought for a time I was going to lose you. We have our three wonderful children. And that's enough. More than enough. I can't run the risk of losing you again.*

A tear had fallen on his face, then another. *You won't lose me. I promise.*

Of course, it had taken far more than that one conversation to heal Ayla's grief. He wasn't even sure that it had fully healed now. Wyrenne had only just turned one year old; the wound was still raw. Yet he had told the truth: what they had was enough. Whether it was enough for the survival of the Nightshade line, he didn't know. But it was enough for the people in it.

I love you, Kati. He backed away from the children's beds, noiselessly, so as not to wake them. *I love you, Wren.*

'Are they all right?' someone whispered, and he turned to see Ayla in the doorway. He held out a hand to draw her closer to his side.

'They're fine. Although this never happens.'

'What?'

'Both of us awake before either of them.' He and Ayla had always been early risers, through simple necessity, but an adult's definition of early wasn't anything like the same as a baby's. Wyrenne regularly woke before first bell.

'They were up in the night. I heard Cathrin trying to settle them.' Yawning, Ayla rested her head against his shoulder. 'Do you like this?'

'Like what?'

'Being an old married man with three children.'

'I object to the old,' Caraway said mildly. 'But as for the rest of it, I've never been happier.'

'Is it the lack of time to yourself you like most, or the constant exhaustion?'

He glanced down at her. She tipped her head back to return his gaze, a teasing expression in her eyes.

'Neither,' he said softly. 'Both. Happiness isn't a whole emotion, is it? It's a thousand little moments.'

They looked at each other without speaking. Slowly he

lifted a hand to stroke her cheek, and felt her shiver beneath his touch.

'This is happiness.' He ducked his head to brush her lips with his. 'And this.'

Her body yielded against his, all softness. She didn't feel any more than human. Holding her like this, it was easy to forget that her slight form contained a power that could tear him apart, if she let it.

'It's still early,' he murmured. 'Want to pick up where we left off last night?'

Her teeth grazed his neck – and then she startled back, turning in the direction of the door. A moment later, he caught it: the sound of running footsteps, heading their way.

Automatically he put Ayla behind him, reaching for a weapon. He might be wearing a dressing gown, but there was a knife in the pocket. There was always a knife in the pocket.

'Stay here,' he said, but of course she didn't. The two of them spilled out into the corridor together, in time to intercept a clearly distressed Helmsman. Vane, one of the younger ones, his fair skin flushed red.

'Captain Caraway – Lady Ayla – I –'

'Get a grip, son,' Caraway said. Vane straightened, making a creditable effort to suppress his ragged gasps. He must have run hard, to be that winded. It must be something urgent ...

'Sir, it's the Kardise ambassador. He's dead.'

From within the nursery, Wyrenne began to cry.

Two of the Kardise were waiting in Tolino's bedroom when Caraway and Ayla arrived. One of the Helm had also fetched Darkhaven's current physician, but it was easy to see at a glance that there was nothing he could do. The ambassador lay on the bed, flat on his back, sightless eyes staring up at the ceiling; his face was greyish, his lips tinged blue.

'What happened?' Ayla took a step forward. The two Kardise shifted subtly, moving shoulder to shoulder as if to support each other. One of them was Giorgi, the ambassador's bodyguard; the other, Caraway wasn't sure of.

'I found him this morning,' Giorgi said in his heavily accented Mirrorvalese. 'Resca and I guarded his door in shifts. The whole night passed without a sound. But this morning, he was cold in his bed.'

'Had he been ill?'

'No.'

'And there are no signs of any injury?'

'None. As far as we are able to determine, he died in his sleep.'

'I'm sorry,' Ayla said. She was clearly upset; her gaze kept sliding towards Tolino's body as though she couldn't quite keep it away. She had liked the man on a personal level, that much had been clear. And she'd been so optimistic about the peace treaty, last night ... Still, she was too well trained to let her own shock and dismay overcome her. 'What a horrible thing to have happened. Do you think it was his heart, or ...?'

The two Kardise exchanged glances. 'Perhaps. That is yet to be determined.'

'Of course.' Ayla turned to the physician. 'Gil, I want you to examine the body straight away and determine the cause of death.'

Caraway caught the convulsive movement of Gil's throat. He was a relatively young man, and new to the role, but he had the distinction of having saved Ayla's life after her near-fatal second labour. At the time, he'd been one of several candidates the previous physician was considering as his eventual replacement, but when everything had gone suddenly and horribly wrong it was Gil, and not his predecessor, who had worked out how to reduce the fever and stop the bleeding. After that, it was perhaps inevitable that the old physician would step down. Ayla had begged him to stay longer – he was, after all, the greatest living expert in Nightshade children and their unique ways – but he'd refused. *I failed you, Lady Ayla,* he'd told her. *My hands and brain are slower than they used to be. I can't put your growing children at risk.* And so, since Gil had so ably proved himself, the old physician had selected him as his successor and trained him for a year, before leaving him to take over the role of Darkhaven's medical expert.

Right now, it was clear Gil wished he didn't have that honour.

With a nervous glance at Ayla, he moved towards the bed – but the two Kardise stepped forward to block his path.

'I'm sorry, Lady Ayla,' Giorgi said. 'But we cannot allow that.'

'Not alone,' the other man added.

And with that, the suspicion that had been lingering in the room ever since Caraway entered it became almost strong enough to taste. Ayla didn't seem to notice, though. Her mind was still on dealing with an unfortunate but perfectly natural event, and she frowned at them without comprehension.

'I assure you, Gil is more than competent –'

'No doubt,' Giorgi agreed smoothly, before gesturing at his comrade. 'But we think it best if Resca examines the body. He is one of Don Tolino's aides, but he was also once a doctor and has all the relevant medical training.'

The second man – Resca – nodded. 'I'm sure you'll agree

that in a case of suspicious death, it is better for the cause to be determined by a disinterested party.'

Ayla's face gave nothing away to the casual glance – she'd been practising the art of diplomacy too long for that, by now – but Caraway caught the moment when realisation hit her. It was there in the almost indiscernible creasing at the corners of her eyes, the slight fade of colour from her cheeks.

Suspicious death.

'I understand,' she said. 'But in that case, I'm sure *you'll* agree that we have just as much reason to fear a partisan approach. It would be as easy for a physician to claim foul play where there is none as it would for him to act in the opposite direction.'

'Then what do you suggest, Lady Ayla?' Resca asked.

'You and my physician should examine the body together,' Ayla said. 'That way, we can all be certain of the outcome.'

Once again, the two Kardise men shared a glance; then Giorgi nodded. 'That would be acceptable.'

'Good.' Ayla turned to Gil. 'Please inform us of your findings as soon as possible. I have no doubt that you and Resca will discover nothing untoward, but it's better to be certain.'

'Y-yes, Lady Ayla.'

She looked back at the Kardise. Caraway thought she might say something dangerously heartfelt – protest Mirrorvalese innocence, even, though that would have been unwise at this stage – but in the end, she simply inclined her head. 'Do let me know if you need anything else.'

The Kardise were silent. Ayla hesitated a moment longer, then turned and left the room. With an encouraging smile for the nervous-looking physician, Caraway followed.

Once they were alone again, Ayla pressed the heels of her hands to her eyes. 'How can this be happening?'

'I don't know.' He put his arms around her, searching for words of comfort and reassurance – but none came. His mind was busy jumping from one disastrous scenario to another. One of Darkhaven's people had killed the ambassador. One of the *Kardise* had killed the ambassador, and this entire visit had merely been to provide an excuse for war ...

'It's terrible bad luck,' Ayla muttered. 'I just hope one of Tolino's aides will be competent enough to take over the negotiations.'

Caraway shook his head. While his thoughts had been running to murder, Ayla was still assuming an unfortunate coincidence. But in his experience, when it came to dead men there was no such thing as coincidence.

'Let's wait and see what happens,' he said noncommittally. She drew back, narrowing her eyes at him.

'You believed their insinuations, didn't you? You suspect foul play.'

He shrugged. 'I think it would be wise to prepare for the worst.'

'Perhaps,' Ayla agreed. 'But we can still hope for the best, can't we? I know you're usually right about these things, but Tomas ... this is one time when I really, really hope you're not.'

'You know I'm usually right about these things,' Caraway echoed. 'Can I have that in writing?'

She managed a smile, but he could tell her heart wasn't in it. Briefly he thought back to the morning, how content he'd been. He'd believed himself lucky, and now his luck was going to be tested again. Because of all the paths that led away from this point, only a very few didn't end in full-scale war.

Still, there was another side to luck, wasn't there? As Ayla always told him, his luck would have come to nothing if he didn't have the skill and determination to back it up. So he might not be able to control the outcome of all this, but he could at least make the favourable paths more likely. And to do it, he was going to have to assume this was a murder. Better to be prepared for something that never happened than to wait for the worst and then discover it was too late to do anything about it.

'Don't worry, love,' he murmured. 'Whatever the truth, we'll find a way through it.'

Art and Miles came down to breakfast to find all three Nightshade children and one rather harried nursemaid, but no sign of Caraway or Ayla. That was unusual enough that Art stopped to exchange a few low-voiced words with the Helmsman stationed at the door to the breakfast room, before taking his seat beside Miles at the table.

'It's the ambassador,' he muttered. 'Died in his sleep.'

'Died?' Miles swung round to face him – though he remembered to keep his voice down. 'Of what?'

'No-one knows.' Art sent a brief, frowning glance in the children's direction. 'But it's bloody bad news, regardless.'

Ayla will be devastated. She has been planning this treaty for months. Years, even. Miles saw the deep crease between Art's brows and wanted to smooth it with his thumb, but he settled for covering Art's hand with his own. Art gave him an absent smile, but it was obvious he was deeply troubled. *Does he suspect foul play? But surely –*

'Uncle Art, you said bloody.' Marlon broke the silence. 'Papa will be cross with you.'

Miles felt some of the tension leave Art's body. 'Oh, I

doubt it, lad. I've heard your father use some interesting words in his time.'

'I know *that*,' Marlon said indignantly. 'But *never* at the breakfast table.'

'Oh dear. I have got myself into trouble, haven't I?'

'Well ...' Marlon directed a sly look across the table at him. 'P'raps I'd forget, if you were telling me a story from when you were Papa's teacher.'

Art chuckled. 'Come on, then. Sit round here and I'll tell you the one about the runaway horse. I'm not sure –' sharing a sideways smile with Miles – 'but I think that's your favourite.'

While he was telling a story they'd all heard several times before, and encouraging Marlon to eat his breakfast at the same time, Miles entertained Katya by drawing pictures on a scrap of paper. Zoelle, one of the children's two nursemaids, had enough to do cajoling porridge into Wyrenne – and besides, Miles often thought Katya needed a little extra attention. It wasn't easy, being the middle child.

That reminded him, obliquely, that he was due at Luka's temple in two days' time, and all his guilt came flooding back. He looked up at Art, slicing fruit while he recounted his tale to a rapt Marlon – *but then, guess what? Your papa leapt onto its back, just when I thought I was a goner* – and prayed that whatever lay behind the summons wouldn't have any significant impact on his life.

How many times had he wanted to tell Art the truth? Confess it all to him, and pray he would find a way to rescue Mara and her family, as well as free Miles from his double life? Yet he couldn't. Not without losing Art himself in the process, as well as Ayla and Tomas and everything that mattered to him in Mirrorvale. Either he lived a double life, or he lived no life at all. Because it had been too long. Five years since he first met Art, and he had never breathed a word of the truth. First because they had only just met. Then because he was too busy falling in love to think about anything else. And finally … finally, because once he'd fallen in love, he'd become terrified of losing it. Telling Art the truth now would entail having to admit he'd been lying all this time about his identity, his family, his purpose in Arkannen. Lying, and passing information – however harmless – to a foreign power. Art wouldn't forgive him for that. He could barely forgive himself.

Besides, he had it all under control. He worked as hard as he could on behalf of Ayla and her family. He gave the Enforcers just enough to keep them happy, whilst preserving Darkhaven's most important secrets. No-one was being harmed. And it kept Mara safe.

It kept Mara safe, and it kept Art by his side.

'Uncle Milo?' Katya asked, shaking him out of his thoughts. All the children had picked up on his nickname and used it with abandon. 'Can I have a firedrake now?'

'I am not sure if I can draw a …' He looked at her small, pleading face. 'All right, Kati. I will give it a try.'

He and Katya were busy creating elaborate curls of flame and smoke from the firedrake's mouth when Caraway and Ayla finally arrived. They both looked worried, but they greeted the children easily enough. Ayla crouched down beside Katya to look at the pictures, while Marlon tugged on his father's sleeve and said urgently, 'Papa! Uncle Art telled – *told* me the story of when you saved him from the runaway horse. Was it scary?'

'Terrifying,' Caraway said cheerfully. 'I nearly fell off at least three times. But I had to impress your Uncle Art, didn't

I?' He ruffled Marlon's hair and added in a low voice, to Art, 'You've heard the news?'

'Yes.'

'I need to let the rest of the Helm know. They're training this morning. Will you –'

''Course I will, lad.' Art pushed his chair back from the table. 'Another story tomorrow, Marlon, all right?'

The boy nodded. Art gave Miles a look: slight smile, eyebrows raised. *I'll tell you all about it this evening.* He never kept anything back. The knowledge didn't make Miles feel any better.

Caraway kissed his children goodbye – *I always kiss them,* he'd told Miles once, *just in case it's the last time* – before he and Art left the room.

'Tomas!' Ayla called after them. 'Aren't you going to eat any – oh, never mind.' She turned to Wyrenne just as the baby threw her bowl on the floor and started to scream. 'Yes, I know what you want.'

'Do you mind, Lady Ayla?' Zoelle asked anxiously. 'Only she's been grumpy ever since she missed her morning feed –'

The worry was still in Ayla's face, but she managed a smile. 'Of course not.'

She settled down with Wyrenne in her lap, while Zoelle occupied Marlon and Katya with a game on the floor. Miles barely blinked. After Ayla had recovered from delivering the baby, she'd come to him with a very particular problem that she'd hoped could be solved by alchemy. And once you'd helped a woman restore her lost milk supply, it was hard to be embarrassed by seeing it put to good use.

'Do you have any idea what killed him?' he asked, going straight to the subject that was clearly on her mind.

'No. I'm hoping his heart gave out, or …' She looked

down at Wyrenne, stroking the tousled curls of hair back from her face, and added softly, 'But Tomas thinks it was murder.'

'Murder?' The idea was alarming. If the ambassador had been murdered, it must have been by someone in Darkhaven, and Miles found it hard to believe that anyone he knew would have –

Concealing treachery is easy, his conscience reminded him. *You know that.*

As with Art, he was seized by the urge to tell her everything. Yet once again, he was prevented by the knowledge that it had already been three years since she welcomed him into her home. How could he confess, without making her doubt his friendship? And if there was going to be trouble with Sol Kardis, she would need him more than ever.

'He thinks we should prepare for the worst,' Ayla said. 'You know what Tomas is like.'

Wyrenne pulled away from the breast long enough to say firmly, 'Papa,' which made both of them smile. Then Miles got to his feet, knowing that probably the most useful thing he could do was to keep trying to perfect his collars – but before he left, he put a hand on Ayla's shoulder.

'If you need anything,' he said. 'Anything at all ...'

She nodded. 'Thank you, Miles. I know I can rely on you.'

FOUR

'Well,' Ree said, looking down at the half-eaten dish of stew in front of her. 'This brings back a few memories.'

Tell me about it. Zander scooped some of the beige stuff off his own plate and let it rain down through the tines of his fork. He shook his head, caught between amusement and disgust. 'It seems they haven't changed the recipe since we were trainees.'

'No.' She glanced at Penn, who was sitting next to her reading, and grinned suddenly. 'In fact, I'm pretty sure we ate the exact same meal the night you two had your famously epic fistfight.'

'An epic that will never be re-enacted,' Zander said. 'These days Penn would destroy me without even breaking a sweat. And I'd hate *this* to be the very last thing I ate.'

He looked down at his plate again. The three of them didn't often spend time in the fifth ring's mess hall – now they were no longer trainees, they had to pay for their own food, which meant they preferred being able to identify what it was. But they'd all been hungry after the morning's training session, and even their quarters in the fourth ring had seemed too far away, so here they were: shovelling down plates of mysterious gloop and chatting with the laconic ease of people who had known each other for years. At least, Zander and Ree were chatting. Penn's head was buried in a news-sheet, from which he surfaced only if they said his name repeatedly.

'Did you see the new recruits for Helm assessment?' Zander asked, gesturing over his shoulder towards the huddle of young people on the far side of the room. 'There's a couple of girls in there again.'

Ree's gaze moved briefly past him to scan the group, before returning to settle on his face. 'Yeah. Captain Caraway asked me to speak to them, same as always.'

'You realise you're their idol, don't you?'

She nodded. 'I think that's why they're always so disappointed when I give them a huge lecture about how difficult it's going to be to get into the Helm. But some of the girls who come ... they're not ready. They come because they know I got in, and Tulia after me, and they think that must mean it's easy, or that the weaponmasters will give them special treatment.' One corner of her mouth lifted in a lopsided smile. 'Flattering, I know. But the ones who are ready ...' The smile faded. 'I remember how lonely I was, when I first came here. I think it's nice for them to have someone to talk to who's been through the same thing.'

'You're welcome to use me as an example,' Zander said solemnly. '*See that man over there? The really handsome one? He's a fabulously accomplished warrior. One of the best the world has ever seen. An astonishing lover, too. And even* he *didn't get into the Helm*. I wouldn't mind.'

By now Ree was shaking with silent laughter, which was exactly what he wanted; he loved it when her eyes crinkled at the corners and her smile lit up her whole face. Sometimes it felt as though making Ree laugh was the main purpose of his life. He watched her in delight until she got hold of herself, wiped her eyes, and said breathlessly, 'But you'd make a terrible example. It's only politics that stopped you getting in.'

Politics. Yes. But maybe once this peace treaty is signed, things might be different ... He didn't say it, not out loud. It was a hope too close to his heart to share with anyone, even Ree. But he felt his mood changing, so he gave her a smile and a wink before leaning across the table and saying loudly, 'Whatcha reading, Penn?'

No answer.

'Penn!' Ree elbowed him in the ribs. He lifted his head, scowling.

'What? Can't you leave me in peace for even the space of a meal?'

'If you'd really wanted peace, you would have gone home,' Ree retorted. 'The truth is, you love us and you love our company.'

The corners of Penn's mouth twitched. 'What do you want, Ree?'

'Zander asked you what you were reading.'

Penn turned his head to look blankly at Zander. 'A news-sheet.'

His tone was that of a man trying very hard to be patient. Zander gave him an affectionate grin. 'Surprisingly enough, we can see that for ourselves. What's the story?'

'It's about an airship,' Penn said vaguely. His gaze drifted back towards the sheet of paper, as though he had decided the conversation was over, but Ree elbowed him again and he sighed. 'I don't know why you two don't just buy your own news-sheets. The Parovians have built the world's largest passenger airship, big enough to carry nearly a hundred people. And for its inaugural flight, sometime soon – it doesn't say exactly when – they'll be bringing it to Mirrorvale.'

'To Arkannen?'

'Apparently it's too large for the city docking stations. They're going to land at that new town over to the east. The one that Lady Ayla wants to become a base for trade between us and Parovia. Remember, Ree? She said we have to increase our ability to export Mirrorvalese goods and technology if we want to remain strong enough to hold our own against our neighbours, and new trade centres like Redmire will be one of the ways we do it. There's an airfield there, of course, so ...'

Zander raised his eyebrows, doing his best to ignore the renewal of Ree's silent laughter. Penn shrugged.

'What? I pay attention when it's something important. And international relationships are important.'

'Speaking of which,' Ree said, suddenly serious, 'the Kardise ambassador's death ...'

Penn nodded. 'Even if he died of natural causes, it's going to mean trouble.'

Zander stared at them both. It was at times like this he really wanted to give his friends a good shaking: first, for forgetting that he wasn't part of the Helm, and second – which was the more important in this case – for forgetting that he was Kardise.

'The ambassador is dead?' he said faintly.

Ree bit her lip. 'Zander ... I'm sorry ...' She reached across the table to clasp his hand. 'He died last night. They're trying to find out how. You didn't ... know him, did you?'

'The most I knew was that an ambassador was coming to Darkhaven. They don't hand out the details to everyone in the fifth ring, you know. What was his name?'

'Carlos Tolino.'

The name was familiar, of course; one couldn't grow up as a councillor's son without learning the names that made up the government. But Zander was relieved to find that this one had been an acquaintance, at most. He nodded.

'My father knows him. Knew him. I don't think I ever met him.' A smile touched his lips. 'To be honest, my father tended not to introduce me to his colleagues if he could possibly avoid it.'

'Zander!' Ree said in mock outrage. 'You're not telling us you were a troublemaker, are you?'

The funny thing was, he hadn't been. Not to start with. Until he was about twelve or thirteen, he'd done everything he could to be the model of a councillor's son. He'd worked hard at school. He'd studied every night. He'd been polite and respectful to his father. But then ... he wasn't sure how to explain it. Though he'd been trying just as hard as ever, his grades had begun to slip. Nothing came to him with the ease it had. His father had hired tutors for him, and made him study even longer in the evenings and on free days, but it made no difference. It was as if his brain had stopped working properly.

Of course, his father hadn't accepted that. He'd accused Zander of being lazy. Of simply not trying hard enough. And after a year or two, Zander had accepted that judgement – because at least if he was lazy, his failure was through choice and not through lack of ability. Being lazy meant he didn't even have to try. So he'd abandoned the books that made no sense to him and gone looking for other things to be good at. Unfortunately for his father, what he'd discovered was a boundless talent for mischief.

'My father started leaving me out of formal dinners after

I substituted a live piglet for the grand centrepiece,' he told Ree. 'But I don't think it was until I destroyed his second-best carriage that he decided to keep me out of sight for good.'

'Destroyed?'

'Well ... exploded, really.'

She laughed, but her eyes searched his face. Maybe she saw some of the truth that lay beneath his flippant answer. He did as he always did, and turned the moment aside.

'But tell me more about the ambassador's death. What happened?'

'We don't know yet,' Ree said. 'Not exactly. He arrived in Darkhaven about halfway through fourth bell, and he and Lady Ayla were alone in the library until ... I'm not sure, but the sixth bell had already sounded. Then the Kardise all trooped off to supper and bed, and I went off duty and found my parents waiting for me.' She grimaced. 'We all know how that went. Anyway, next thing I knew, Captain Caraway was calling us together before the training session this morning and telling us the ambassador had died in the night.'

'That's all he said? That the ambassador had died?'

'Mmm. And that Darkhaven's physician and the Kardise are looking into it. So naturally, Penn and I have been speculating about what happened and what it will mean ...'

'Ree speculated,' Penn put in. 'I mostly listened.'

'... and I'm so used to you training with us that I forgot you weren't there to hear the news. I'm sorry.'

'It doesn't matter,' Zander said absently. *Died in the night.* He remembered enough of the strange and unspecific language of government to know that it could mean anything from *cruelly murdered* to *faked his own death for political reasons.* But the one thing it couldn't possibly mean was *we are certain this death was unsuspicious in any way*, because if that were the case, Darkhaven would have every reason to make it known as swiftly and as widely as possible.

'Zander?' Ree asked. 'Are you all right?'

He nodded – for once in his life, unable to produce a smile. 'I just hope it doesn't mean war.'

She frowned. 'Do you really think Sol Kardis would go that far?'

'I don't know.' It would depend entirely on how the ambassador had died, and how Darkhaven could *prove* the ambassador had died, and thus far it was impossible to tell. 'I just ... I don't know.' With an effort, he summoned the smile that had eluded him. 'Let's talk about something else. What are you two doing this afternoon?'

Soon after that, Ree and Penn went off to firearms training, bantering about the lack of improvement in Ree's aim – *it's been years, Ree, you'd think you'd at least be able to hit the target by now* – but Zander stayed in his seat, staring at the cold remains of his rapidly congealing food.

War. His friends might not want to believe it, but if there was any suspicion around Tolino's death, it would come to that. Zander knew it would have been difficult enough to get the Kardise government to consider a treaty in the first place; Sol Kardis had had its eye on Mirrorvale as a potential acquisition ever since he could remember, so it was a significant concession for the larger country to give up any possible future conquest. No doubt their failed attempts to assassinate Ayla Nightshade had contributed to the decision, but it would have been a contentious issue in parliament. So if the ambassador's death turned out to be murder, those Kardise councillors who were against the treaty would use it as evidence that Mirrorvale was not to be trusted. And, if everything Zander had heard was true, they would have the backing of the Brotherhood.

In fact, it wouldn't be entirely surprising if the Brotherhood themselves had ordered the ambassador's death to create precisely this situation.

Zander wondered if he should mention that to Ree, but came to the conclusion that she already knew – or, if not her, at least Captain Caraway. Because she'd said the cause of death was being investigated by both the Kardise party and Darkhaven's own physician. Both sides must be keenly aware of the possibility of treachery. Only a unanimous verdict of some natural cause would be enough to prevent a war.

And if war did break out, Zander would have to decide what to do: whether to obey his father's wishes at last, and return home, or to stay in Arkannen despite the fact that a declaration of war would officially make him an enemy of its people.

He'd originally come to the city for several reasons. Though he might have lost his academic abilities, he hadn't lost his skill with a sword – so he'd thought he might be able to make something of that, once he didn't have his father looking over his shoulder. Being away from Sol Kardis, and all the expectations that came with being a councillor's son, had held undeniable appeal. And, of course, he'd known it would infuriate his father not to know where he was. Yet being framed as Ayla's intended assassin, not two months into training, had meant he hadn't been able to conceal his location any longer. His father's aide had arrived from Sol Kardis to escort him home – but by then Zander's name had been cleared, and he'd flat-out refused to go.

Tell my respected father, he'd said in the polite, formal

style used among Kardise councillors, *that I have been accepted onto a prestigious training programme here. Tell him I intend to return once I am qualified.* Then, because he knew the aide by name, and because he found it impossible to maintain formality for long, he'd added, *Come on, Leo! All I ever do under my father's roof is get myself into trouble.*

Don Alezzandro, the man had replied austerely, *that is exactly why your father wants you where he can see you.* Yet then he, too, had unbent. *The truth is, Zander, he knows all about this training programme of yours, and he doesn't understand it. I'm not sure I do, either. What do you want with learning to be a Helmsman? You're Kardise. You have as much chance of joining the Helm as you do of becoming a Changer.*

Tell my father I'll come home when I'm ready, Zander had answered stubbornly, and Leo had said no more.

Yet, of course, the aide had been right: Zander couldn't join the Helm. At the end of training, just before the successful candidates were officially announced, Captain Caraway had taken him aside and very apologetically told him so.

If it were down to merit alone, I'd have you in a heartbeat, he said. *I admitted you to training because you deserved it, and because I had the vague idea that something might change ... But with the relationship between Mirrorvale and Sol Kardis as precarious as it is, we simply can't have a Kardise councillor's son in the Helm. I'm sorry.*

It was at that point Zander realised he'd been hoping for a miracle. He'd been hoping the gods would smile on him, that somehow Caraway would be able to make an exception in his case – but of course he couldn't. While the recruits Zander had trained alongside might accept him, the older

Helmsmen certainly wouldn't. There would always be that degree of suspicion, of uncertainty, in case he turned out to be a traitor. And on the Kardise side, the government might very well take it as an insult. His father, Zander thought with the slow creep of resignation, certainly would.

What will you do now? Caraway asked him. *Will you go back to Sol Kardis?*

I'm not sure ... Zander thought about it, then added slowly, *Or maybe I am.*

Caraway nodded. *If you need anything, just ask.* He clasped Zander's forearm, then walked away.

Captain! Zander called after him. *Did Ree –?*

Caraway stopped and glanced back over his shoulder, smiling. *Of course she did.*

Later, Zander considered that smile and decided that the captain hadn't pressed him on the question of his return to Sol Kardis because he'd already known exactly what would happen. Zander stayed in Arkannen. He got a job as a junior assistant weaponmaster and an apartment in the Ametrine Quarter. More often than not, he joined Ree and Penn when they were training. Except for the little matter of not actually doing the job, he might as well have been a Helmsman.

Of course, his father wasn't at all happy with the situation. Soon after that conversation with Caraway, Leo had arrived once more to escort Zander back to Sol Kardis, and again Zander had refused to go. The following week he'd received a long letter from his father, demanding his return, and an even longer one the week after. After that, the letters had become increasingly angry and increasingly terse until the last one read, simply, *WHY ARE YOU STILL THERE?*

Zander hadn't even tried to answer that question. He suspected the truth was both too simple and too complicated for his father to understand. The complicated answer was all bound up with Ree, and friendship, and a sense of belonging; with carving a place for himself in the world that was separate from his identity as his father's son, and finding something he was good at without his father's name to smooth his way. The simple answer was that he didn't want to leave.

He hadn't had any more letters since that one, months ago now. He rather thought his father had given up on him. That ought to hurt, but it was mostly a relief.

Or at least, it had been.

Because while Mirrorvale and Sol Kardis were heading for peace, Zander had been able to convince himself that he belonged in Arkannen. But now they were heading for war, he wasn't sure he belonged anywhere. If he no longer had a place in his homeland, but he would soon become anathema in his adopted country, where did that leave him?

Abruptly, the noisy chatter of the mess hall became unbearable. According to the clock on the wall, he had a little time before fourth bell, which was when he was due to continue the thankless task of showing a bunch of incompetent young idiots how to hold a sword without cutting themselves. As the fifth ring's most junior assistant weaponmaster, he was given this task every time a training period came round: take the sons of wealthy Mirrorvalese who believed they could buy talent, attempt to drum some basic techniques into them, and help the weaponmasters to decide whether any of them had enough potential to stay for further training. Based on what he'd seen of the current lot so far, his answer was a resounding no. Still, they deserved his full attention; maybe if he walked up to the Gate of Ice and back before starting work, he could clear his head.

He got halfway there before someone called his name, and

he turned to see Captain Caraway emerging from the armoury. After the night's events, Zander would have been surprised if Caraway *hadn't* wanted to speak to him sooner or later, so he stopped and waited for the other man to join him.

'Can I talk to you for a moment?' Caraway asked, with a gesture that indicated they should continue walking.

'Of course.' Zander smiled at him. He liked the captain; always had. Even when Caraway had arrested him for planning regicide, he hadn't been cruel about it.

'I expect you've heard about Don Tolino's death,' Caraway said. 'I know this puts you in a difficult position, Zander, and I'm sorry for it. But I have to ask ...'

He indicated a quiet spot at the edge of the stable yard, and they sat down together. Zander expected a question about what the Kardise government might do next, perhaps a request for advice – but when Caraway spoke again, it was something very different.

'Last night, before Tolino died, he and Ayla spent some time discussing the treaty. And one of the clauses in it ...' The captain frowned at his hands, before glancing up at Zander. 'Your father explicitly requested that the final treaty be contingent upon your immediate return to Sol Kardis.'

So he hasn't given up on me after all. Zander wasn't sure whether to be angry or relieved.

'There you go, Captain Caraway,' he muttered. 'If you want to meet a man who'll do anything to get his own way, up to and including the subversion of a peace treaty, look no further than my dad.'

Caraway smiled, but it was perfunctory.

'I have to ask,' he said again. 'Zander, did you know your father was going to make that request?'

'Know? I had no idea. Why do you –' But even as he started to ask the question, he knew the answer.

You think I arranged a murder.

In an instant, it was as if he were back in the fifth ring as a new recruit, subject to an accusation he had no way to disprove. The same helplessness, the same frustrated sense of injustice.

Haven't you already made this mistake once, Captain Caraway?

Zander didn't look up straight away, for fear that his unexpected bitterness would show in his eyes. Yet when he did meet Caraway's gaze, he could see that the exact same thought was in the captain's mind. That made him feel a little better.

All the same, he thought, *this is what it will be like, if Sol Kardis and Mirrorvale go to war. I'll always be suspect number one.*

'Zander.' Caraway spoke gently, as if he knew how Zander was feeling. 'I'm not accusing you of anything. I just need all the information I can get. Every piece of the puzzle will fit somewhere.'

'I had no idea,' Zander said again. 'I haven't heard from my father in months. Though it's not unlike him to escalate a situation far beyond the reasonable.' With his earlier musings in mind, he added, 'But surely, sir ... I mean, from what Ree and Penn said, you don't even know that there's a puzzle to solve. Don Tolino could have died of natural causes.'

'He could,' Caraway agreed. 'But I'm not optimistic about it. The timing is too much of a coincidence.' One side of his mouth turned up in a not-quite smile. 'Ayla always says I'm paranoid. Let's hope she's right.'

'I'm afraid she might not be in this case,' Zander admitted. 'The Brotherhood –'

'I know.'

He did, of course. The assassination attempts had seen to that. But Caraway couldn't know, because he'd never been there, what it was like to be the son of a Kardise councillor and hear and see certain things, growing up, that convinced him beyond doubt that all the rumours were true: the much-vaunted Kardise democracy was not a democracy at all.

To be the son of a Kardise councillor and have every reason to believe that his father didn't always act on behalf of the people who had elected him.

'They're quite capable of doing something like this,' he said, not meeting Caraway's gaze. 'The individual lives of their own people matter far less to them than what they see as the greater good, so they'd be quite happy to have killed Don Tolino if they thought it would get them what they want. I expect you know that already.'

'I was afraid of it,' Caraway agreed. 'Thank you, Zander.'

He got up to go. But before he'd gone too far, Zander gave in to the promptings of his need to know the worst and called after him, 'Captain Caraway! Do *you* think there will be a war?'

Caraway turned. He looked grave, and incongruously young; as though he were more vulnerable than he cared to reveal, and just for a moment, he had let it show.

'If Tolino was murdered,' he said, 'and if we can't prove very quickly that we didn't do it – then yes, Zander. I'm almost certain of it.'

FIVE

When Naeve Sorrow travelled between the Mallory family farm and Darkhaven, she usually took the train.

The original plan for the track hadn't brought it anything like so close to her door; it had been a straight line between the city of Arkannen and its nearest mine. But once Ayla Nightshade had found out where her half-brother Corus and his mother Elisse were living, she'd ordered a minor detour. Far more convenient to be able to send Helmsmen and messages back and forth by train than by horse or carriage, and less expensive than chartering an airship. Not that the train had been intended to carry people – its purpose was coal – but a few words from Ayla, and suddenly the goods trucks were joined by a coach.

And so, Sorrow thought with the mental equivalent of an eye-roll, *the course of the world is altered by a single woman's whims.*

Not that she minded. Lana Mallory, Elisse's mother, grumbled about the train on a regular basis. Too loud. Too dirty. It shed a blanket of coal dust across the far meadow and made the air taste like a factory. But to Sorrow, who found country air far too bland and country landscapes far too green, the train tasted like home. The rattling, grumbling assertiveness of it suited her temperament: a little piece of Arkannen on the move. And strangely, riding in Ayla Nightshade's coach helped her forget that more often than not, she was on Ayla Nightshade's business. Hers or Captain Caraway's; it was all the same.

Sorrow hadn't intended to get herself mixed back up with Darkhaven. But once it had been agreed that Ayla had a right to know where Corus lived, and that it would be sensible to set a guard on him and his mother, Sorrow had found herself acting as a go-between for Elisse and Ayla. It was the sort of shitty position she'd never wanted to be in, but since she often travelled to Arkannen for work, it made sense for her to carry news to and from the farm where Elisse and Corus were staying. Elisse and Corus, and Elisse's mother Lana – because that was where Elisse had chosen to go, back to the place she'd grown up in.

Lord Florentyn told her he'd give me a better life, Elisse had explained. *He gave her money and everything. But I never got ta visit her, and then when I ran away from Mirrorvale I couldn' see her any more. She'd like ta meet her grandson.* She'd hesitated a moment, before adding with rare shyness, *And I think she'd like ta meet you, too.*

Sorrow had never thought she'd end up meeting someone's parents – well, not in *that* context, at least – but Lana Mallory had turned out to be all right. It must have been strange for her, seeing her daughter leave with the most powerful man in Mirrorvale, only to return with a child of Nightshade blood and a woman of dubious morality. Yet she hadn't said anything about it at all. Upon meeting Sorrow, she'd given her one long, appraising look before setting her to work on the farm. That was fine by Sorrow. She'd far rather get her hands dirty than make any kind of attempt at heartfelt conversation.

She'd stayed with the Mallorys for several months, long enough for her wounds to heal, but soon after that she'd begun feeling restless again. It had been Elisse who suggested she go back to Arkannen.

You're not happy stuck here, she'd said. *I'd rather see ya occasionally and willingly than all the time under duress. It wouldn' be any less than I had in Sol Kardis.*

So Sorrow had returned to the city. To start with, she'd assumed she would go back to her old life: find the kind of work she always found, and visit Elisse and Corus as often as she could. It wasn't as if carrying messages for Ayla was enough to earn her a living. Yet she'd discovered that, somehow, certain jobs no longer appealed to her. She was still perfectly happy to steal, to threaten, even to kill if the occasion demanded it; but not on behalf of the wrong people.

The wrong people, she'd mocked herself when she'd first caught her thoughts tending in that direction. *You know perfectly well there's no such thing as the wrong people. Everyone's as guilty as each other.* It was the fundamental principle by which she'd always operated. But now, she found there were some lines she was no longer willing to cross. Some actions that were unacceptable, even to her conveniently flexible morality.

That was why, when a trafficker had approached her in search of someone to guard his contingent of stolen slum children on their way to slavery in the Ingal States, she'd taken the job and then alerted the Watch. It had required a considerable amount of ingenuity on her part not to be identified as the snitch, but she'd managed it. The children had been reunited with their families, and she'd even given them some of the money ... though not all of it. She wasn't that much of a mug.

It was also why she'd accepted an extortionate fee from one of Arkannen's idle young men to kidnap an heiress and carry her off to a deserted place, where he could convince her to marry him by fair means or foul. That all seemed a bit old-fashioned to Sorrow, but apparently the wealthy families of Mirrorvale still believed that women who'd lost their so-called virtue should be married off as quickly as possible, even if the prospective husband had forced them into it. So Sorrow had delivered the girl to the arranged location with the small addition of a loaded pistol. She'd heard the boy still walked with a limp.

And it was why, a few months later, Captain Caraway had offered her a permanent job.

I'm sure you'd be good at it, he'd said. *And I need someone who knows how to bend the law without breaking it.*

What exactly do you want me to do?

Keep me informed of what happens in the city. Obtain information for me, when I need it. Darkhaven's spies perform many roles, and I need intelligence from within Arkannen as much as from without it.

She'd given him an incredulous look. *You want me to be a spy for Darkhaven?*

Why not? You'd be perfect for the job.

But the last thing I want is to be tangled up with bloody Changers!

He'd smiled. *That's exactly why you'd be perfect.*

She'd had to stop and think about it properly, then, because he had a point. No-one who knew her would ever suspect her of working for Darkhaven. The Helm had hated her for years, and she'd made no secret of her own antipathy towards them. She was the least likely person in the entire city to be carrying tales back to the tower.

And if she took this job, she wouldn't have to worry about crossing the wrong lines any more. She might have little respect for Caraway, but he was unlikely to ask anything of her that she couldn't countenance. As much as she was willing to make such a judgement of anyone, he was *the right people.*

Besides, she was already working for Darkhaven in a way, wasn't she?

All right, she'd said. *I'll give it a try. Temporarily.*

That had been almost a year ago, and so far it seemed to be going as well as could be expected. Caraway didn't ask anything particularly taxing of her. He paid her an acceptable fee – not, admittedly, at anything like the level she was used to commanding for her most dangerous commissions, but it came at reliable intervals and didn't involve nearly dying on a regular basis. Perhaps that last point would have been a negative, rather than a positive, but the information he wanted was often tricky enough to obtain that the mental exertion involved went some way towards making up for the lack of excitement. The only downside – if such it could be called – was that as a spymaster, Tomas Caraway seemed to take all his tips from the lurid espionage novels Sorrow had read when she was a child, before she was old enough to know any better.

She looked again at the slip of paper in her hand, the message that been carried to the Mallory farm the previous afternoon on the very same train she was riding now. It requested her immediate return to Arkannen, and gave a time and address for her meeting with Caraway. Nothing wrong with that. Only the message was written in some stupid code she'd been forced to learn, and she'd be willing to bet the location was a ruined warehouse or a seedy back alley or something equally daft. It obviously hadn't occurred to him that only an amateur would arrange a clandestine meeting in an obviously clandestine place.

The train made its penultimate stop on the south bank of the canal, where Sorrow had to wait for an age while the coal trucks were unloaded by the vast waterside crane, ready for use in the industrial quarter on the north bank. It would have been easier if she could have got out there, too, but there was no way across the canal for people. The north bank was part of Arkannen, but the south bank wasn't; while authorised merchant barges unloading their wares at the docks were allowable, building a walkway across the canal that allowed entry on foot would have been too much of a security risk. And so she waited, until the last thunderous rattle of coal subsided and the train started again with a jerk, sweeping her across the new river bridge and round to the terminal station near the Gate of Birth.

Emerging from the station, Sorrow regarded the scene before her with a considerable amount of pleasure. For years, she'd come and gone from Arkannen by airship, which was an enjoyable enough experience; she always liked seeing the seven rings laid out beneath her as regular as the pattern on a game-board, their order belying the messy lives of the people who inhabited them. Yet arriving by train always hit her in a way that arriving by airship never had. Perhaps it was because that was how she had first set eyes on the city, as a young girl trudging up to the gate on foot with barely an ennol to her name. Perhaps she just preferred chaos to order. Whatever the reason, she never failed to appreciate it: the vast archway made of undressed stone that was the Gate of Birth, the sole entrance to Arkannen; the bridge that led to it, its balustrades lined with carved stone creatures; the wide wall that stretched out to either side, windowless and smooth, barely even starting to curve before it vanished from sight; the roofs peeking out above it, rising up and back until they faded into the smoke from the factory chimneys. From the air the city might be orderly, but from the ground it was bloody *huge*.

She crossed the bridge in a tangle of other people, some on foot and some on horseback, taking a small secret pride in the fact that she was the only one who had arrived by train. At the gate, she waited in line to show her border pass before walking through the archway into the open square beyond. It was one of the largest open spaces in Arkannen, designed primarily – or so Sorrow surmised – to allow people to stop and gawk without getting in each other's way. Around the square were a hundred shops selling everything from food to fabric, as well as lodging-houses for the weary traveller – though any traveller who had visited the city before knew that the better, and certainly quieter, lodging-houses were to be found by turning right, to the fashionable shopping district and the leisure quarter beyond. Left led deeper into the heart of the mercantile quarter, and also to the first stop on the tramline, which was Sorrow's own destination.

She checked the address she'd been given once more, then hopped on the tram and rode it all the way through the industrial quarter to the edge of the Night Quarter. Then she walked briskly through the narrow streets, dodging the usual crowds of hawkers and pushers and the occasional nervous-looking tourist – or rather, since she never entered Arkannen less than thoroughly armed, allowing them to dodge her. Fourth bell chimed while she was still picking her way past some kind of erotic street theatre, which meant she was late, but she maintained an even pace. Caraway would just have to wait.

Her destination, when she reached it, was just as bad as she'd feared: a boarded-up smoke den at the end of an alley. No way anyone would come here for less than nefarious purposes. Still, she'd only draw more attention to herself if she hesitated, so she ducked through a gap in the half-rotten door and found herself in a cool, shadowed room through which bright beams of sunlight leapt from holes in the broken shutters. Sure enough, the man himself was sitting on an old crate, writing something down in his notebook; he glanced up sharply at her approach, but then his expression softened and he stood up to greet her.

'This was a ridiculous place to choose, Captain Caraway,' she muttered, glancing around at the mould-streaked walls. 'I suppose I should be glad you aren't wearing a terrible wig and a false moustache.'

He smiled. 'Where would you have chosen?'

'Anywhere! Nowhere! Since you at least had enough sense not to wear your rainbow-coloured coat, no-one would look twice at you. The two of us could have stood and talked on any street in the city. And that way we soon would have noticed if anyone was listening, too.'

'They might not look twice at me, Naeve, but I rather think they would look twice at you. Your reputation has only grown in the years since you came back from Sol Kardis.'

'Yes, Captain Caraway.' He'd made her free of his first name, once. But since he insisted on calling her by hers, even though he knew she didn't like it, she'd decided to be equally stubborn and stick to his full title. 'Which is why anyone who saw me coming in here would assume I was up to something secretive. Whereas anyone who saw me having a chat on the street with some scruffy-haired man would assume I couldn't possibly be up to no good, because if I was, I'd be in a place like this!'

'Were you followed?' he asked calmly.

'Not that I know of.'

'Well, nor was I. And I didn't see anyone when I came in, and I assume you didn't either, so I think we can relax.'

Sorrow forbore from pointing out that she'd once followed him and Ayla without them being any the wiser; given that she'd subsequently sold their whereabouts to the old Captain of the Helm, leading directly to Ayla's capture and near imprisonment, she didn't think it would be a helpful recollection.

'So what's up?' she said instead. 'Let me guess ... someone's murdered the Kardise ambassador.'

Caraway said nothing, but the expression on his face spoke volumes. She shook her head in disbelief.

'You've got to be kidding me.'

His lips tightened. 'Does it seem like the kind of thing I'd joke about?'

'Shit. And you're sure it was murder?'

'We'll find out soon enough,' Caraway said. 'Ayla wants to believe it's just bad luck, but ...'

'But this is Darkhaven we're talking about,' Sorrow finished for him. 'Nothing is ever coincidence with you people.'

One corner of his mouth twisted upwards in acknowledgement of that statement. 'Which is why I'm speaking to you now. If this does turn out to be murder, which I'm expecting it will, we're going to have to move fast to uncover the culprit. Because it's not just our chance at a peace treaty that's at stake. It's any kind of peace at all.'

'You think the Kardise will declare war over this?'

'Unless we can offer a damn good explanation for their ambassador's death, I'm almost sure of it.'

Sorrow nodded. 'So what do you want me to do?'

'If it's murder, the only possible conclusion is that someone wants to send us to war with Sol Kardis. Maybe it's the Kardise themselves, manufacturing an excuse to reject peace. But if not ... war is a vast thing, Naeve. Bigger than individual people. This doesn't strike me as a personal crime. There's power behind it, organisation ... someone in the city has something to gain from war. And I want to know who.'

'I'll do my best,' she said doubtfully. 'But it's a lot to ask without anything more to go on.'

'I know. Like searching for a rat in a barn full of hay.'

'It's not finding a rat that will be the problem,' Sorrow said. 'It's finding the right one. Your barn is teeming with rats, Captain Caraway. Throw a stone on any city street and you'd probably hit *someone* who had something to gain from war.' She shook her head at him in mocking disapproval. 'How'd you live in the first ring for five years and stay this naïve?'

He ignored the barb. 'You're telling me people *want* war?'

'Not everyone. Most people are probably too consumed by their own petty concerns to think about it either way. But off the top of my head, I could list about ten different groups who might be in its favour.'

'Please do,' Caraway said. She gave him a long look, suspecting him of laughing at her, but he appeared perfectly serious.

'Fine. Sellswords, for the pay. Merchants, for the profit – sure, black-market Kardise firearms are going to be harder to source, but the price of Parovian steel will shoot way up.

Factory owners who can sell their products to the cause. Factory workers who could use the extra shifts. Rich men who can invest in all this, then sit back and watch the spoils roll in without ever having to see, hear or smell a battlefield.' She quirked an eyebrow at him. 'How am I doing?'

'Five,' he said. 'But so far, they're all about money.'

'That's because war is expensive, Captain Caraway.' She shrugged. 'Still, here you go: anyone who's ever had a friend or relative killed in all the unrest at the southern border. Anyone who thinks we Mirrorvalese are naturally superior, our country is unfairly oppressed, and we need to show the world what we're capable of. Anyone who thinks Arkannen is too crowded and could do without all these immigrants coming into the city, thank you very much. Anyone who fantasises about killing and would welcome a socially acceptable reason to do it ...' She smirked. 'And people like me, who throw themselves behind the most suicidal cause there is going, because they'd far rather life was dangerous than dull.'

'And here was me thinking you wouldn't do anything without getting paid for it,' Caraway said. 'You win, Naeve. The city is crawling with people who'd love nothing more than for Mirrorvale to go to war with Sol Kardis.' No doubt about it, this time: he was laughing at her. 'But presumably most of them don't have the skill or resources to arrange a murder within the walls of Darkhaven, so that must narrow it down somewhat.'

She narrowed her eyes at him. 'You can laugh. But not all of us are heroes of your stature, Captain Caraway. Most people are just out for what they can get.'

'On the contrary, I think most people are exactly like me,' he replied. 'Decent enough, doing the right thing most of the time – though more by luck than design – and fucking it up monumentally every now and then. But the important thing is that our intentions are good.'

'You're including me in this pretty little worldview, are you?' She couldn't stop the scorn dripping from her voice, but he only smiled.

'I wouldn't employ you if I didn't.' To her mingled surprise and dismay, he gave her a friendly clap on the shoulder. 'Good luck, Naeve. Let me know what you find out.'

After he'd gone, Sorrow relieved her feelings by kicking the wall. Then, because she'd unthinkingly used the foot that had been shattered three years ago – which ached in cold weather, let alone being driven at high speed into something large and solid – she spent a good deal of time swearing. Once she'd finished doing that, she stayed where she was, digging at the crumbling mortar between two bricks with the point of a knife and thinking about what Caraway had said. *Decent enough, doing the right thing most of the time, and fucking it up monumentally every now and then.* She found it almost alarming that he was willing to apply those words to her. Not the fuck-ups – she'd freely admit to more than a few of those. But never, not since she was a little girl, had she been motivated by trying to do the right thing. She'd learned while she was still young that morality was simply a way for other people to take advantage of you.

'The right thing,' she muttered. 'The wrong people. I'm losing it.'

The point of the knife caught in the brickwork; she dropped it and sighed. She ought to quit working for Darkhaven and go back to what she did best: getting paid as much as possible. No matter how dirty the job. No matter how corrupt the client. And yet, she didn't want to.

Why?

Because Elisse believed in her.

Because she had a responsibility towards Corus.

Because she kind of, sort of, a little bit enjoyed being trusted by the Captain of the Helm. Being given steady work that she knew wouldn't involve torture, or murder, or kidnap. Being part of something bigger than herself.

Because she cared about her country ...

She swore again, long and low. Then she retrieved her knife, and went to carry out Caraway's orders.

SIX

Unless she had business that took her outside the tower, Ayla always spent the last three chimes of the second bell with her children. She had started the practice when it was just her and Marlon, trying to make up for the distance she'd allowed her brother's death to put between them. Being the overlord of Darkhaven could consume her if she wasn't careful, until it was all that mattered to her in the world – she only had to recall her own father to know that. She didn't want her children to grow up feeling the lack of warmth she'd experienced herself as a young woman. She'd come close enough to that with Marlon as it was.

Of course, it was often difficult to carve the time out of her day; there was always a crisis somewhere that needed fixing. But over the years, one of the most important lessons she'd learned was which tasks *had* to be done by the overlord of Darkhaven and which could be left to someone else. She had more than enough competent people working for her, starting with Tomas and the rest of Darkhaven's staff, and spreading out to all the magistrates and overseers who applied her law across the whole of Mirrorvale. Between them, they could handle all but the most pressing of emergencies. For a precious segment of time each day, they could spare her to her children.

In all honesty, Ayla hadn't expected to be a very good mother. It wasn't as if she'd excelled during the first two years of Marlon's life. Her own drive to have children had come purely from the knowledge that the more Nightshade babies she brought into the world, the more likely her family gift was to survive. And yet, once she actually started spending time with Marlon, she found herself enjoying it. Not only that, but he responded to her tentative parenting overtures with such delight that she could never have withheld her attention from him again, even if she'd wanted to. By the time Katya was approaching two and Wyrenne was about to be born, Ayla had become so enamoured with motherhood that she was determined to have a huge family solely on her own account, not because it was her duty.

But then everything had changed again.

Giving birth to Wyrenne had nearly killed her. She had bled far too much, for far too long; it had been touch and go whether she'd survive at all. Tomas had sat beside her for days on end, never letting go of her hand, whilst tiny Wyrenne was cared for by a wet nurse and Marlon and Katya played in whispers, and Ayla herself swam through fever dreams and clung to life by a thread. Though she didn't remember any of that, she remembered very clearly the moment when she'd first come round afterwards.

She was awake. That was the first thing. Awake, when before she had been ... something else, walking on the cusp between dreams and darkness. Whatever it was had left her weak, as if her limbs had lost their purpose. And there was an empty ache inside her ...

One hand went instinctively to her belly, but found nothing except her own shrinking skin. *Where –*

'The baby?' she whispered hoarsely.

Tomas was at her side in an instant, bearded and dishevelled. 'She's fine. You're fine. We're all fine.'

Tears shone in his eyes, sending the panic inside her spiralling higher.

'Tomas,' she said. 'The baby.'

It was only once she had Wyrenne in her arms that she allowed herself to believe there hadn't been a terrible disaster. And it was later still they told her that it had been her life in danger, not Wyrenne's. That she could never bear another child.

'Was it really that bad?' she asked the old physician, once she'd recovered enough to contemplate the idea of going through it again. He took her hands in his and looked her straight in the eyes.

'You are lucky to have survived at all. Lysael wasn't so lucky.'

Lysael was Myrren's mother, who had died giving birth to him.

'It runs in the family,' the physician added. 'Increasingly so in recent generations. I'm sorry, Lady Ayla. There's no arguing with Nightshade history.'

No, there was no arguing with Nightshade history. The family had nearly killed itself off in its drive for purity. Her ancestors had thought their strength lay in rigidity, exclusivity, lack of change. They'd built a fortress around themselves and defended its walls with vigour, all the while ignoring the cracks at their foundations. It was as if they'd taken a beautiful sculpture with a worm at its heart and hidden it away so no-one else could touch it, guarding it jealously while the worms multiplied through the wood and turned it all to dust.

Really, they deserved everything they got.

Yet the knowledge was a bitter seed, because she was the one who had to bear the weight of it – she and her daughters. That gave her sorrow a keen edge. She'd lost her dream of a large family, only to gain a premature fear in exchange. The Nightshade line might still fail, and it might kill her girls in the process.

She let it all consume her, for a while, before confiding in Tomas. As always, he knew just what to say.

'You're only half a Nightshade, Ayla. Your father never tired of reminding you of that. And as far as I can see, that just makes you stronger.'

'I nearly died,' she objected.

'But you didn't. That's what matters. You survived, and our daughters will too. They're only quarter Nightshades. If there's a weakness in your blood, they don't have much of it.'

'Yes,' she said. 'But surely that means they have less chance of inheriting the Changer gift, as well.'

'You're assuming the two go hand in hand. But Nightshades have been Changers far longer than their women have been dying in childbirth.' He tucked a stray lock of hair behind her ear. 'Besides, our daughters might not even want to have children of their own. So it's a very far-off problem you're worrying yourself over, love.'

Ayla began to protest that it would be their duty to have children, to continue the line, but caught herself before she got too far. For all her rebellion against tradition, maybe she'd absorbed more of it into her bones than she'd realised.

'Do you ever wonder?' she asked softly, instead. 'If they've inherited the gift? Two chances for it to survive … it's a slender thread to hang my hopes on.'

'No slenderer than when you and Myrren were children,'

Tomas reminded her. 'But it's not two chances, is it? It's four.'

He was right, of course. She had not only Katya and the new baby, but Marlon and – out in the wilds of Mirrorvale – their cousin Corus. Four chances for the Changer gift to survive. She'd worried that her own children wouldn't inherit the gift. But perhaps it didn't matter if it was one of her daughters or one of the boys, as long as *someone* turned out to be a Changer.

'Now,' Tomas said, squeezing her hand. 'How about we give this one a name?'

She nodded. She'd originally wondered whether Tomas would want to give his children names from his own family – Marlon and Corus had both been named for their maternal grandfathers, neither of whom were Nightshades. Yet as it turned out, he'd been surprisingly insistent on continuing the pattern of naming that had been followed in the Nightshade line for generations.

It's not a tradition that needs breaking, he'd said with a smile. *And Nightshade names are pretty.*

With that decided, it hadn't taken them long to settle on Katya for their first daughter: a name that was as close as they could get within the Nightshade tradition to Ayla's mother Kati. That had been easy. But now, gazing at the new baby cradled in her arms, Ayla found herself at a loss. Not because she couldn't think of anything, but because she was very aware of the fact that this was the last child she'd ever give a name to.

'Do you want to name her for your mother, this time?' she asked hesitantly.

'My mother's name was Pearl,' Tomas said. 'I don't think you'll find that anywhere in your family history.'

'Then ...'

'Don't worry. We'll think of something.'

To that end, with the baby sleeping peacefully against Tomas's shoulder, they spent an evening poring over the leather-bound tome that held the family records, starting at the back where the ink was fresh and bright. The last completed page held only four records for the past sixty years, each one written – like most of the entries – by several different people. Ayla lingered over each entry in turn, starting with her own.

Day 7 of the Frozen Moon, 1756: Ayla Nightshade. Daughter of Florentyn Nightshade and Kati Farrier. Change: unknown. That was in her father's hand, the last word darker and more vehement than the rest. She'd crossed it out later, replacing it with *Alicorn*. And then in her own hand, from the day of their wedding, *Married: Tomas Caraway, Longest Night, 1777.*

Day 22 of the Fallen Moon, 1753: Myrren Nightshade. Son of Florentyn and Lysael Nightshade. Change – and here Florentyn had left an eloquent gap, which she'd defiantly filled with *Wyvern* before concluding the entry. *Died Day 8 of the Flame Moon, 1774.*

Day 13 of the Leafless Moon, 1736: Lysael Nightshade. Daughter of Tylon and Dynelle Nightshade. Change: Griffin. Married: Florentyn Nightshade, Longest Day, 1752. Died Day 22 of the Fallen Moon, 1753.

Day 19 of the Flame Moon, 1721: Florentyn Nightshade. Son of Samlyn and Jeryssa Nightshade. Change: Firedrake. Married: Lysael Nightshade, Longest Day, 1752. Married (2): Kati Farrier, Longest Night, 1754. Died Day 2 of the Flame Moon, 1774.

A great deal of tragedy lay between the dry lines of that single page: Ayla's brother and her father, both gone within a week of each other, and Myrren's mother, who had married her far older cousin out of duty and died at the age of seventeen without ever seeing her first and only child. Not to mention Ayla's own mother, whose death – belonging as it did to a mere commoner – had gone unrecorded in the Nightshade annals. *Perhaps I should change that … yet what does it matter? I loved her, and she loved me. Everything else is irrelevant.*

Before that were Lysael's parents and Florentyn's, and back and back beyond that: turning the pages of the vast old book was like peering through a tiny window into the past. A long list of Nightshade ancestors, broken only rarely by other names – an occasional second marriage, a younger daughter allied with a Parovian prince or Ingalese lordling who was willing to give up his own home to live in Darkhaven. Barren alliances, for strategy or perhaps for love. With such a large extended family, there had been no need to procreate outside the bloodline – or at least, if any such children had existed, they hadn't been recorded. The ink grew more and more faded, the handwriting increasingly archaic, and the family … the further back she went, the more complex and densely populated the family tree became, until within a dozen generations it was impossible to tell who was related to whom.

They had been sowing the seeds of their own downfall, Ayla thought. And even her father, nearly at the end of the line, had been too blind to see it.

She only realised she was staring blankly at the open book when Tomas murmured, 'If you're considering one of those, love, you should know I can't even pronounce half of them.'

She glanced down the page, picking out the female names one by one from the cramped lines of writing. *Corythys. Myanisse. Fenylla.* He had a point, but she raised her eyebrows at him anyway.

'I thought you said Nightshade names were pretty.'

'They are. But whichever we choose, I'd like to have at least a fighting chance of being able to spell it ...' He paused, finger tapping on a name near the bottom. 'How about this one? Wyrenne.'

'It's a big name for a little girl,' Ayla said doubtfully, and he smiled.

'But it can be shortened to Wren. I like that. It suits her.'

Nicknames were not at all a Nightshade tradition; Ayla couldn't imagine she'd ever call her second daughter Wren. She'd heard Art Bryan refer to Tomas as *Tom*, once, and it had taken her far longer than it should have to understand who he was talking about. On the other hand, Tomas was right – it did suit her.

'This Wyrenne was a Phoenix,' she said, glancing up at him. 'Maybe ours will be, too.'

'Maybe.'

They were quiet a while. Surreptitiously, Ayla watched her husband – one hand cupping the baby's downy head against his shoulder, his expression content – and the ache of loss gripped her all over again.

'You should write them in,' he said, turning to her as if he could read her thoughts from her silence. 'All of them. It's about time we did it.'

And so she flipped back to the end of the book and wrote, in a bold hand that left plenty of space for all the Changes and weddings she hoped were to come:

Day 8 of the Flame Moon, 1774: Corus Nightshade. Son of Florentyn Nightshade and Elisse Mallory.

Day 1 of the Butterfly Moon, 1775: Marlon Nightshade. Son of Myrren Nightshade and Serenna Raine.

Day 25 of the Petal Moon, 1778: Katya Nightshade.

Daughter of Ayla Nightshade and Tomas Caraway.

Day 12 of the Awakened Moon, 1780: Wyrenne Nightshade. Daughter of Ayla Nightshade and Tomas Caraway.

'There,' Tomas said gently. 'That's not so bad, is it?'

'You do know I'll love them whatever happens, don't you?' she said – suddenly anxious for him to know that she'd never turn out like her father. 'Whether they can Change or not, I mean.'

He smiled. 'I know.'

Now, Ayla picked up the sturdy, squirming bundle that was one-year-old Wyrenne and planted a kiss on each of her cheeks. The difficult circumstances of her birth hadn't affected Wyrenne in the slightest; she was the most robust child of the three of them. Marlon was a serious, inquisitive boy, and Katya a bright little ray of sunshine, but Wyrenne appeared to be made of pure determination. Already she rebelled against everything that didn't match what she wanted – and since it was difficult to tell what that was, given her current lack of intelligible speech, almost daily battles were waged between her and her nursemaids.

Ayla had always thought that Marlon took after Myrren, in many ways, and she imagined Katya's sunny temperament to be much like Tomas's had been when he was a child, but Wyrenne ...

'You remind me of myself,' she murmured, kissing the baby again. 'Which means you're going to be trouble.'

'She already is,' Marlon said solemnly. 'Cathrin and Zoelle say she's the terror of the nursery.'

'Good for her.'

'Were you naughty when you were a baby, Mama?'

'Almost certainly.'

'Was I?'

Ayla released Wyrenne to run across the floor, and scooped Marlon onto her lap instead. 'Oh, not at all. You were very, very good.'

'And Kati?'

'Yes, Katya too. Wyrenne is the only one who inherited my rebellious streak.'

She expected him to ask what *rebellious* meant; yet instead, he thought for a while before saying softly, 'Tell me again 'bout how I was made.'

'My brother Myrren made you,' Ayla said. 'Not for himself, but for me and your papa. Because he knew we'd have two beautiful daughters, but we'd also want a little boy of our very own.'

It was a story she'd told many times before. She and Tomas had agreed that although they were Marlon's parents in every way that mattered, it was important to bring him up knowing in some way who Myrren had been to him. Time enough for the full complexity of the truth when he was old enough to understand it.

'That was good of him, wasn't it, Mama?'

'Yes, it was.'

'Where is he now?' Marlon asked, and Ayla replied as she always did.

'Part of the wind and the rain and the sun.'

Of course, it wasn't true; the Nightshade overlords weren't returned to the elements as other people were. Myrren lay in the vault alongside his father. Nevertheless, she liked to believe that some small part of him had escaped the tower and found freedom.

'Mama!' Katya came running up, a book clutched in one hand. Two dimples showed as she held it out and said, 'Read this. Pleeease?'

Ayla was in the middle of a tale about a clumsy duck, hampered only by Wyrenne's tendency to wander off halfway through the narrative and start climbing the furniture, when a knock came at the nursery door. At the sight of a Helmsman's striped coat, Ayla jumped to her feet. If Tomas had sent someone to disturb her here, it must be urgent.

'Excuse me, Lady Ayla. Captain wanted me to let you know, the physician and the Kardise doctor have reached a conclusion.'

They know how Tolino died. Ayla's pulse began to race. She took a step towards the Helmsman, before glancing back at the three expectant faces grouped around the book. *But the third bell hasn't rung yet ...*

'Don't worry, Lady Ayla.' Cathrin, one of the nursemaids, came forward from the corner where she'd been mending a hole in a pair of Marlon's trousers. 'I'll finish the story.'

Ayla hesitated a moment longer – but she had to go. However much she didn't want being overlord of Darkhaven to distance her from her children, in the end, it always had to come first.

'I'll be back later if I can, my loves,' she murmured, and followed the Helmsman out of the room.

Rather than Tolino's bedroom, this time, the Kardise had gathered in one of the reception rooms. Tomas was waiting for her at the door; they entered together, to find three of the Kardise grouped awkwardly on the chaise longue, while Darkhaven's physician, Gil, and the Kardise doctor, Resca, stood in front of the fireplace. Gil looked troubled, but Resca's expression was impassive. Already fearing the worst, Ayla sank into an armchair opposite the Kardise, while Tomas took up his usual position to one side. In the past he had tried standing at her shoulder, as tradition dictated, but neither of them had liked it. They couldn't read each other, or exchange the little wordless signals that helped them to present a united front, unless they could see each other, however obliquely.

'Thank you for joining us, Lady Ayla,' Resca said. She couldn't quite work out from his tone whether he meant it as a veiled insult. 'Your physician and I have examined Don Tolino's body, and we are in full agreement.' He paused a moment, glancing at his compatriots, before completing his statement. 'Don Tolino was poisoned.'

A hiss sounded from the opposite side of the room, a collective intake of breath from the Kardise party. Unseen by anyone, Ayla dug her nails into her palms. *Stay grounded. Concentrate.*

'Poisoned?' she echoed, directing the question at Gil rather than Resca. 'How? When?'

The physician didn't look at her. Gaze fixed on the rug in front of his feet, he mumbled, 'Zephyr. It's a slow-acting poison. The evidence suggests he ingested it sometime during fifth bell, the evening before he died.'

Zephyr. It was one of the rare poisons strong enough to sicken even a Changer, if the dose were big enough. It certainly would have killed Tolino. Yet there was a reason no-one ever tried to incapacitate a Nightshade overlord with zephyr: it had a strong, bitter flavour that was instantly detectable to enhanced Changer senses. In fact, only someone with a very dull sense of taste would fail to notice it. And as an ambassador, Tolino would have been trained to recognise a wide range of poisons, just as she had been as a young woman. Surely there was no way that someone could have got him to take zephyr without ...

Belatedly she registered the other half of what Gil had just said. *Sometime during fifth bell.*

'But that was when he was with me in the library,' she said blankly. 'No-one else was there. So how could –'

Now everyone was looking at her. Tomas with concern, the young physician with discomfort. And the Kardise ... now the rest of the Kardise, just like Resca, were utterly expressionless.

She shook her head.

'No. Of course I didn't – no. There must be some other explanation.'

'Did anyone else enter the room whilst you and Don Tolino were together?' Resca asked her.

'No, I – no. We were alone. You know that! Giorgi and Captain Caraway were guarding the door. No-one could have got in, and we would have seen them if they had.' She paused, then added more slowly, 'Of course, there was someone else right at the beginning of our meeting. The maid with the taransey. But she just brought the tray in and left! She didn't even pour the drinks. I –' She stopped, looking around at their faces, and finished quietly, 'I did that myself.'

Taransey. It explained part of the problem, at least. For an ordinary person, one without the benefit of enhanced Changer senses, taransey was strong enough to mask even the flavour of zephyr. And Tolino couldn't have been familiar enough with the liquor to know what it *should* taste like. But how –

'The glasses,' Tomas said quietly. 'Could the poison have been in the ambassador's glass when the maid brought in the tray?'

Ayla threw him a grateful look. 'Yes, it's possible.'

'Not really,' Giorgi said. 'It would have been impossible for anyone outside the room to have known which glass would be yours, and which would be the ambassador's. If the maid had poured the drinks, then perhaps she might be our culprit …' He shook his head, sadly, as if Ayla had committed a basic tactical error. 'But you said yourself she didn't.'

'Then both glasses,' Tomas persisted. 'Or the bottle itself.'

'I …' Ayla pressed her lips together. She had been about to say that she would have detected zephyr, hidden in liquor or not. Yet it wasn't as if she drank much herself; Tomas didn't drink at all, and out of respect for him she tended to avoid it too. She'd tasted taransey, what, four or five times before? Would that have given her enough familiarity to notice the difference?

There had been that faint bitterness, she remembered now. She'd thought it part of the drink.

'The bottle was sealed,' she said. 'Perhaps the glasses …'

'But you drank with him, didn't you?' Resca said. 'And yet you are alive.'

Yes. From what she knew, it was almost certain that a dose that killed an ordinary man wouldn't kill a Changer. But she would have been ill, at least. She wouldn't have walked away completely unaffected.

'Did you have any symptoms that night, Lady Ayla?' Gil asked, as if reading her thoughts. 'Perhaps a fever, an upset stomach …'

His expression was hopeful. Tomas's too. They wanted that to be the explanation. They desperately wanted her to say yes. And if she had any sense, she would. She'd lie, for the sake of the treaty. It wouldn't remove suspicion from her entirely, but it would at least cast a shadow of doubt. If she and Tolino had both been given poison then it would become a completely different sort of crime, one that was aimed at Sol Kardis and Mirrorvale together.

She should lie. And yet she couldn't.

'I was fine,' she said. 'I don't think I can have swallowed any poison at all. There must be another explanation.'

Silence. Everyone was looking at her again. And though she knew it to be unwise, she couldn't help but respond.

'I didn't kill him!' she said, addressing the Kardise directly this time. 'Why should I have done? It doesn't make any sense. Don Tolino and I had come to an agreement. We were going to start working out the terms of the treaty in the morning. Why on earth would I kill him? And in such a way that the doubt was sure to fall on me?'

'I can't answer the second question, Lady Ayla,' Giorgi said. 'But as for the first ... I'm afraid we have only your word that you had reached a compromise.'

'Are you calling me a liar?' The question came out fiercely enough that he sat back as though she'd slapped him. Tomas's hand tightened briefly on her shoulder, and she realised he'd moved into the traditional guard position behind her. *I have to keep my temper.*

'I've told you the truth,' she said more calmly. 'Every detail. I could have claimed that the bottle was open, that the maid poured the drinks, that I was sick all night after drinking. But I didn't. I've been completely honest. Why would I do that, and lie about the details of my conversation with Don Tolino?'

'Only you can tell us that,' Giorgi replied. 'But in the meantime, a man has been murdered.'

That was unanswerable. She was still searching for an answer when, to her relief, Tomas stepped into the breach.

'A vicious crime, and one we need to solve as swiftly as possible. I assure you, we will do everything we can to uncover the culprit.'

Giorgi's eyebrows lifted. 'There seems little left to solve, Captain.'

'I tell you, I didn't –' Ayla began, but again the pressure of Tomas's hand silenced her.

'I don't know how you'd run a murder investigation in Sol Kardis, but here in Mirrorvale, we don't accept the first explanation to present itself. There must be a thorough investigation.'

'In the course of which, no doubt, your highly dedicated men will uncover evidence that completely exonerates your overlord of the crime,' Giorgi said with a contemptuous curl of his lips. The implication was so clear that a small, detached corner of Ayla's mind found itself thoroughly impressed with Tomas's unimpaired calm.

'You are welcome to be part of the investigation yourself. Assure yourself that everything is above board.'

Giorgi exchanged glances with Resca. The doctor shrugged.

'We will give you a week.'

'A week? That isn't long enough to –'

'We cannot in good conscience allow his body to remain unburied any longer than that. Besides, if there really is another explanation for Don Tolino's death, it should be easy enough to find.'

'All right.' Ayla felt the tension in Tomas's hand, but still he kept his composure. 'Then we'd better get started. Gil, Resca – thank you for your work on this. I have no doubt we'll need to call on your expertise again.' Then, to the other Kardise, 'Gentlemen.'

That was her cue to leave, she realised dimly. She stood up, but she couldn't look at anyone for fear she'd start begging them to believe her. Tolino's unexpected death had been bad enough, but *this* ... How many times in her life must she be falsely accused of murder?

And this time, the consequences ranged far wider than herself.

Keeping her chin up so her tears wouldn't fall, she swept out of the room.

Rage and fear boiled off Ayla like steam as she stormed through the corridors. It was all Caraway could do to keep up with her until, finally, she reached their bedroom. By the time he'd stepped in after her and closed the door behind him, she'd already begun pacing the floor. Back and forth. Back and forth. He stood where he was and watched her, aching with love and anxiety. That, and the frustrated desire to grab the Kardise by the shoulders and shake them until they saw the truth.

'Poison!' Ayla flung a wild-eyed glance in his direction. 'Tomas, I didn't poison him!'

'Of course you didn't.'

'But all the evidence says I did! The ambassador's team have no doubt about it. They listened to me politely enough, but I could see it in their faces. They'll carry the news back to Sol Kardis, and you know what that will mean!'

War. Caraway didn't need to say it. He stepped into her path, catching her gently by the shoulders to halt her pacing. 'You know, love, I could almost wish you had lied.'

'We need to find the truth. Not conceal it with lies.' She lifted her chin, eyes flashing defiance at him. 'And we *will* find the truth.'

'Of course.' Resting his forehead against hers, he admitted, 'But I don't know how to protect you against this.'

'You did it before,' she whispered. 'You believed in me when everyone else had already found me guilty.'

'And I believe in you now. But that's not what I mean. There's no visible enemy here, Ayla, only shadows. Someone is trying to kill you or to set you up, and I'm not even sure which. But either way, it happened right under my nose. And I don't know how.'

'Then you protect me by helping me find out,' she said fiercely. 'It's not your fault, Tomas. Whoever did this is clever. We just have to be cleverer.'

I might not be clever enough. Or quick enough. Or strong enough. There's only so far my luck can stretch. But he didn't say that. Instead, he said, 'We have a week. It's not long, but enough. And I've already set a few wheels in motion.' With half a smile, he added, 'Maybe there are some benefits to extreme paranoia.'

She buried her face in his shoulder. After a long time, her muffled voice said, 'Have you considered the possibility that I did it after all?'

'What?' He drew her away from him, searching her face, but her gaze was averted. 'Ayla, what are you talking about?'

'Maybe death in childbirth isn't the only cruel flaw that runs in my family.' Still she didn't look at him. 'Maybe there's madness, too. Myrren killed our father without even knowing he was doing it. What if I ...'

'No.'

'But surely, if that darkness was in him –'

'It's not the same.'

'Why not?' Finally she met his gaze, her green-blue eyes spilling out distress and fear as clearly as her words. 'I don't remember poisoning the man, but that doesn't mean it didn't happen.'

'You had no reason to kill Tolino. You wanted him alive.'

'But madness doesn't need a reason, does it? Look at Myrren. He was a good person. A better person than me. He would never have chosen to murder anyone, let alone his own father, yet that's what he did. So who's to say ...'

Her voice wavered. Her arms were wrapped tightly around herself, fingers clinging bloodlessly to her own elbows. Caraway reached out for her, only to let his hand fall when she shied away from his touch.

'Ayla, listen to me. Myrren's situation was completely different. He attacked people without forethought, out of fear and love, and he did it when he wasn't himself. It's simply not possible to poison someone that way. You would have had to conceal the poison on your person, find a moment when Tolino wasn't paying attention to slip it into his glass ... poisoning is a crime of planning, not passion. Temporary madness doesn't cover it.'

She looked at him doubtfully, but at least she was listening. Hoping to convince her, Caraway hurried on.

'Besides, love, don't you think I'd have noticed that darkness in you, if it existed? I sleep beside you every night. I wake up with you every morning. We know each other more intimately than either of us has ever known anyone else. Don't you think I'd see it?'

Tears welled in her eyes. 'You can't see inside me, Tomas.'

'Yes,' he said firmly. 'I can. I see you here –' he touched his head – 'and here.' He grabbed one of her hands and laid it flat against his chest, above his heart. 'I *know* you didn't do this. And I'll prove it. I promise.'

She drooped back against him. Her shoulders shook. Caraway held her close, and began to make a mental list of everything he needed to do to fulfil that promise.

SEVEN

Miles knelt at the Sun Lord's altar, head bowed. Silence lay heavy around him; the sixth ring might offer shrines to foreign gods alongside the older powers, these days, but no-one except the foreign-born ever ventured into them. Outside, Luka's chariot was setting; the vast stained-glass window above the altar spilled the mellow light of evening over Miles's face and his clasped hands. To either side, thick, black shadows gathered in the alcoves – and one of them held a man.

'You summoned me,' Miles said without turning.

'Yes,' the voice said, cold and precise in the darkness. A new man, Miles thought. Not the contact he'd last spoken to, three years ago. But without ever seeing their faces, it was hard to tell. 'I wanted to talk to you about the Kardise ambassador's death.'

'But when you sent the message, it had not yet –' He stopped as the implication caught up with him. *Flaming Luka.*

'*You* killed the ambassador?' he said, barely believing it.

'I arranged his death,' the faceless man corrected him. 'We thought it best not to risk implicating you and thus losing your unique access to the Nightshade bloodline. So we took alternative measures.'

'But why?'

'*Why?*' The voice held an edge of impatience now. 'Because this peace cannot be allowed to go ahead. Why else?'

'But surely – I have spent these past three years keeping Ayla alive –'

'Yes, Miles. We do not want Sol Kardis to use her death to gain Mirrorvale as an asset. But nor do we want an alliance between them! Either way, the effect is the same: the two of them together are stronger than we are. And if the Kardise discover the secret of the Change ... No. Constant unsettlement was our preferred option, but failing that, let them go to war. Mirrorvale is better able to face Sol Kardis now than it was three years ago – you have seen to that.'

'But people will die,' Miles said stupidly.

'Some. Does it matter?'

'Of course it matters! Passing on information was one thing, but *this* –'

'Is an extension of the same process,' the faceless man finished for him. 'Particularly since it was information you gave us that allowed us to kill the ambassador in the first place.'

What? Miles opened his mouth to deny it – foolishly, because the denial might well have involved admitting that he never passed on anything that could be a danger to Darkhaven – but the part of his brain that thrived on solving problems was already putting the pieces together.

The poison was in the taransey. Both Ayla and Tolino drank it, yet only Tolino was affected. The only possible conclusion is ...

'My antidote,' he whispered.

'Indeed. I have the formula here, written in your very own hand.'

Yes. It was one part of his work that had seemed safe to give to Parovia, rather than Darkhaven. He had to send the Enforcers regular information, to prove he was doing *something* – and what harm could there be in an antidote? It was designed to save lives, not take them. And since zephyr wasn't fatal to Changers, and thus a thoroughly useless tool as far as assassination went, it wasn't as if he'd thought Ayla would ever be in a situation where she needed to counteract its effects.

I made the wrong choice. I did not think it through. And now a man is dead. Miles closed his eyes as hard on the heels of that thought came another, far more selfish one: *If anyone ever finds out about this, they will never believe it was unintentional.*

All the same, he couldn't stand by and let this happen. He wouldn't be bullied into letting a preventable war happen, the same way he'd been bullied into spying for Parovia in the first place. If ever there was a time to tell the truth, this was it. He'd lose Art – that hurt, even to think, but he steeled himself against it. He'd lose everything that mattered to him. But at least, perhaps, if he told Art the truth in secret, he could keep the faceless man from finding out he'd done it. And that way Mara would be safe.

'If you are thinking of revealing that a Parovian agent within Darkhaven murdered the ambassador,' the cold voice said, 'then I should point out that according to all the evidence, Miles, that agent is you. I only have to ensure that the Helm discover your handwritten formula and they will assume you are the traitor. A spy of several years' standing, and one who had plenty of opportunity to administer an antidote that only he knows about.'

Yes, Miles thought. *But perhaps they will still listen, if I tell them everything. If I tell them how my family has been threatened. How I have done my best to keep Darkhaven's secrets, despite that.*

'You are considering a confession,' the faceless man said contemptuously. 'You think you can throw yourself on their mercy. Let me make this easier for you, Miles. If Mirrorvale and Sol Kardis fail to go to war over this, for any reason at all, your sister will die. Her children will die. And your weaponmaster will meet a nasty end.'

'No –' The word fell out before Miles could claw it back. He had half risen from the altar, turning towards the alcoves, before he got a grip on himself. Slowly, he forced himself to kneel once more, facing straight ahead. His heart pounded loud enough to hear, but still he caught the faceless man's low laughter.

'It is your choice. But let me assure you, war will come to Mirrorvale. The only question is whether you are willing to sacrifice the people you love in a futile attempt to stop it.'

Miles said nothing. He could feel himself quivering like a frightened animal. Finally, he whispered, 'Why did you tell me the truth?'

'To see where your loyalties lie,' the faceless man said. 'And it seems they have drifted far from where they should be.' He sighed. 'You will report to me on a regular basis. I want to know what you are doing. And remember, Miles – there will be war. Either that, or your weaponmaster will gain first-hand experience of the nastiest, most lingering poison that Parovia has to offer.'

Miles couldn't speak. He nodded, then bowed his head and listened as the soft footfalls of the faceless man receded into the distance.

He should get up. Art would be wondering where he was. Yet he didn't move. Instead, he closed his eyes and wished, desperately, that he'd never been noticed by the Enforcers in the first place.

It had been his fault, all of it. He hadn't set out to become an agent of the crown; as a young man, even the idea would have been laughable to him. Speaking whatever was on your mind had never been the first prerequisite for a spy. No, he had arrived in Rovinelle – the capital city, where his older sister Mara lived – with the sole aim of studying alchemy at the Royal College, the most prestigious university in the country. He would live with Mara and her family for the five years it took him to complete his studies, graduate with high honours, and then take up a research post at one of the lesser universities. That was his entire career plan: a life of peaceful academia. That was all he wanted.

Yet within days of his arrival, he began to hear rumours that the Royal College of Parovia had a second purpose: that the brightest and best of the students would be approached silently, in the darkness, by a king's agent offering them a secret task. *Where do you think the king gets his spies from?* the whispers ran. *He has to recruit them from somewhere.* And gradually, those rumours became Miles's greatest spur. Because how better to prove himself, a young unknown provincial amongst all these moneyed sophisticates, than to be selected as one of his majesty's eyes-and-ears? He was already gaining a reputation for being far too gauche to engage in the scintillatingly witty repartee favoured by the school's elite. Yet if the Enforcers approached him ... well, that would show his detractors he was worth something. That would show them he was more than their equal: he was their superior.

He didn't stop to think what it would mean, to be a spy. He didn't stop to wonder what, exactly, would be used to ensure his loyalty.

The years passed. The rumours continued, but no-one ever seemed to know anyone who had been selected to carry out the Enforcers' will. Perhaps, after all, it had been no more than idle gossip. Miles put the idea to the back of his mind and got on with his studies, but he never quite forgot it. Not when the other students still looked down on him. Not when all his academic achievements and the praise he received from his tutors apparently counted for nothing beside his lack of urbanity.

Then, shortly before the end of his final term, he returned to his sister's modest house to find her gone. His nephew, too. To start with he thought nothing of it, though they would usually be there when he came home from his lectures, but as the day shaded into dusk he began to worry. Finally he left the house, walked down to the law office where his brother-by-marriage worked. He hadn't been in that day, the other clerks told him. No message, no reason given. He just hadn't shown up.

Miles ran back to the house, but it was still empty. He walked from room to room, opening cupboards, searching for a sign that this absence was normal: a family trip, perhaps, one he'd forgotten about. But everything was still there. Their winter coats. Mara's cosmetics. The big travel case she kept under her bed. Nothing was missing … except the people.

He made a list of all the places they might be. Favourite haunts in the city. Friends' homes. The hall of healing – perhaps one of them had been taken ill, perhaps it had been an emergency. All through the night he walked from door to door, knocking and asking questions. But no-one had seen

Mara and her family. They had vanished without a trace.

Finally, as the sky began to lighten, he returned to the abandoned house. He sat down in a chair, staring at the list in his hand, every item crossed off to no avail. He meant to think, to regroup, to come up with the obvious place he'd missed – the one place, no doubt, he'd find them. But instead, he fell asleep.

When he jolted awake again, a short time later, two men were sitting across from him.

'We have a job for you,' one of them said.

'What?' He rubbed his eyes, his face, trying to shake off the foggy strands of sleep. 'Who are you?'

They just looked at him. And as he blinked in the dim morning light, he saw the small silver token that each man wore openly on his lapel. The King's Enforcers.

'What have you done with my sister?' he whispered.

'She is safe. Her child and husband too.' The man leaned forward and, suddenly and shockingly, smiled. 'Call them an incentive.'

'But where –'

'They are safe.' The other man spoke for the first time, his voice even and without expression. 'They have been given a new life. A good life, if different from the one they had. And if you want them to keep it, you will do your job.'

Miles swallowed, his throat suddenly parched. When he could speak, he said, 'What do you want me to do?'

They told him. When they'd finished, he protested faintly, 'But my exams – if I fail –'

'You will not fail.'

'How do you know?'

The first man smiled again. 'Because you love your sister.'

A week later, Miles sat his final exams, graduating top of

his class. Shortly after that, he packed up the few belongings he had and took an airship to a new country. To Arkannen, in Mirrorvale, where a post had been found for him at the university.

To start with, alone in a strange city, he tried to comfort himself with the idea that he was a patriot doing what was best for his country. That he and he alone had been selected from a classful of intelligent, ambitious boys, just as the rumours had suggested: the best of the best. Yet he didn't think it could be patriotism if he was doing it through fear, rather than love, and eventually it dawned on him that he hadn't been chosen because he was the best. He had been chosen because, unlike the young noblemen being educated alongside him, he had a family who could be threatened without outcry or reprisal. He had been chosen because he was *nobody*.

For months he passed through his new life in a blur, living only for the instructions he received from time to time in secret: communications that always included a letter from his sister, though sometimes the details were blacked out. They were doing well. The boy was growing taller. The husband had started a better job. A new baby was on the way. Miles clung to those snippets of information as if they could lead him out of the nightmare. For Mara, he kept telling himself. He was doing it for her.

Then, after a while, the fog cleared. He found that almost despite himself, he was making friends. Connections. Doing the job he had been given, burying himself deep in the heart of city life. He decided it wasn't so bad, what he'd been asked to do. It was no more than reporting gossip, really. What the university academics were saying about Mirrorvale's trade relations with other countries. What was whispered on the streets about the Nightshade line. He might have written the very same things in his letters to Mara.

Yet he had been sent to Arkannen for more than that. After the deaths of Florentyn Nightshade and his heir, Parovia had thought it wise to keep an eye on Darkhaven; with a single Changer left alive, a young woman, Mirrorvale was on the brink of collapse. Street rumours and university gossip were all very well, but the Enforcers needed more. They needed information from closer to the source.

Before they could instruct him on how to go about getting that information, he'd met Art. A chance encounter on a city street, leading to several intense, heightened evenings of conversation that culminated in one equally intense, heightened night. Miles hadn't even thought about how Art could be of use to him. Art's job had barely registered with him at all. But when he stumbled home through the pre-dawn chill after a night that had been everything he'd hoped for, he found his masked contact waiting for him – ready to congratulate him for something he'd never intended.

'You have done well there,' the voice whispered from behind the mask. 'Very well. Forming a relationship with a weaponmaster would have been useful enough, but forming a relationship with Art Bryan ...'

His stomach twisted in a mixture of guilt and giddy delight. 'You want me to continue the relationship?'

'Of course. He is former mentor and close friend to the Captain of the Helm. And everyone knows what the Nightshade girl likes doing with her captain.'

Miles nodded. The relationship between Ayla Nightshade, overlord of Darkhaven, and Tomas Caraway, her Captain of the Helm, was the subject of fully half the rumours and gossip that swirled around Arkannen like complex ocean currents. He had heard more than enough over-romanticised versions of their story for one lifetime. And indeed, Art had mentioned Tomas several times during the course of the previous few days. Miles simply hadn't registered who he was talking about, because he'd been too busy focusing on the way Art's eyes crinkled at the corners when he smiled.

He truly was a terrible spy.

All the same, he went along with the plan – still telling himself it was for Mara, when the truth was that he'd have seized any excuse to see Art again. He fell in love, hard and fast, until one day he found himself moving out of his tiny apartment into Art's equally tiny apartment, knowing he had the full blessing of his Parovian employers. He began to think himself ever so clever, letting the faceless man believe he was doing it for his country when really he was doing it for himself. It wasn't as if anything Art told him was more confidential than what a keen ear could pick up on any street corner. So although Miles might not be revealing the whole truth about himself, he could still convince himself that he wasn't betraying Art's trust.

And then an assassination threat arose, the Kardise plotting to kill Ayla Nightshade. The Parovian spy network heard of it almost as soon as Darkhaven did.

'We need to ensure the attempt is unsuccessful,' the faceless man told Miles. 'Parovia is not yet in a position to take advantage of Mirrorvalese weakness. If Ayla Nightshade dies, Sol Kardis will take Mirrorvale – and we cannot have that. Soon enough the Kardise would be pushing at our borders.'

'What do you want me to do?' Miles asked.

'You are an alchemist. She is a creature of alchemy. Find a way to keep her alive.'

A lot to ask, perhaps – yet once again, it seemed luck was

on Miles's side. He was still trying to come up with a way of suggesting to Art that he should be introduced to Ayla when she sent for him herself. Let him into Darkhaven. Allowed him to test her capabilities. He learned a great deal more about the secrets of the Nightshade line than he'd ever learned before, which pleased his Parovian contact no end. And, of course, his mission was ultimately successful. He figured out how to enhance Changer strength using alchemy. His work saved Ayla's life. Not only that, but he and Art were invited to live in Darkhaven for good.

'Perfect,' the faceless man whispered. 'We will have the secret of the Change in no time.'

And, for a while, it had been perfect. Miles had got on with his work, enjoyed his relationship with Art, forged friendships with the inhabitants of the tower, and fed the Enforcers just enough information to keep them happy. He'd known it couldn't last forever, yet that hadn't stopped him hoping – because everything had seemed to be going so well. Even when the possibility of a peace treaty between Sol Kardis and Mirrorvale had arisen, he'd assumed that Parovia would be pleased, because it meant there was no longer a risk that Ayla would fall to a Kardise bullet.

Apparently he'd been wrong.

I should still tell the truth, he thought. Testing the idea. Trying to find a way back to that one precarious point where he could stand and hold everything in balance and not let anyone fall. Yet his mind only ran in circles, like a rat in a trap.

But if I prevent the war, Art will die. Mara and her children. I will lose them all. And for what? The Enforcers will only find another way to make it happen.

At least Ayla would be warned. She could tell the Kardise.

With both countries on guard, surely Parovia would be unable to manipulate them into conflict ...

But Art would be dead. Mara would be dead. I have fought too long for her life to let that happen.

He dug his nails into his palms, trying to ground himself with pain, and sank down lower before the Sun God's altar.

Great Lord Luka, please! Surely there is a way for me to keep them safe? To keep everyone safe?

And like a reply, the thought came to him: *If I could just perfect these collars ...*

He had already been told that if he found a way to create genuine alchemical protection for ordinary people, he wasn't to share it with Darkhaven. Such a technology would give whichever country controlled it an insuperable advantage, rendering its troops almost invincible. Thus, obviously, it must go to Parovia – and thus, just as obviously, he could never let them have it. He had always been a patriot through coercion, not belief; the thought of Parovia getting hold of a power that would allow it to wipe every other country off the map chilled him to the core. But maybe, if he could get it right soon enough, he could create enough collars to protect the people he loved in the inevitable war with Sol Kardis, and Parovia would never have to know.

Love. Therein lay the problem. He had done his utmost to hate the Mirrorvalese – for their godlessness, their arrogance, their misuse of alchemical powers. Maybe then he'd be able to convince himself he was a patriot and not a traitor. Yet he couldn't. He'd fallen in love, not just with Art but with Ayla, her family, even her country. Though his own beliefs remained unshaken, there was nothing irreligious in Mirrorvalese worship. In truth, there was no difference, but that one revered the alchemy and the other, the alchemist.

Sometimes, in the darkness of deepest night, Miles wondered whether the Enforcers had sent him here knowing he would fall in love. Perhaps the only convincing traitor was one whose treachery struck at his own heart as much as that of the one he betrayed. And strike it did, because it went against every bit of morality he possessed. Mirrorvale wasn't a threat to Parovia; it was simply struggling to keep its place in the world. Parovia wasn't neutralising a risk, but seeking to make an acquisition. So he couldn't tell himself that he acted to protect his country. Nor could he believe that the preservation of Art's life, or of Mara's, was worth the death of thousands. Any objective morality would tell him that it was right to let a handful of people die, if by doing so he would prevent a war that claimed many more lives.

Except he couldn't prevent it, not really. He was quite sure of that. If this attempt failed, the Enforcers would only try again. And next time, they'd use an agent who was far more ruthless than Miles himself – one who was willing to destroy as many lives as it took. No, war would come, whether he confessed or not; and that being so, surely it was better for him to remain in place, doing what he could to mitigate the effects of Parovian treachery and keeping his loved ones alive in the process. Without his work, after all, Ayla wouldn't possess the collar that kept her safe. That alone put Mirrorvale in a good position to win the war. And his current research might give them even more of an advantage.

If Mirrorvale and Sol Kardis remained enemies, as Parovia wished, but Mirrorvale sustained minimal losses in any conflict ... why, then, everyone would be happy. Mara and her family would be alive. Ayla and her family would be alive. *Art* would be alive. Miles's troubled conscience would be soothed. And everything could go back to the way it had been before.

He could only hope.

EIGHT

Perched on an arm of the single chair in the small living room that belonged to Diann Rawleigh, Darkhaven's housekeeper, Penn exchanged a glance with Ree. *I'll find her for you,* the housekeeper had said, when they'd asked her if they could interview the maid who had attended Lady Ayla in the library on the night of the Kardise ambassador's arrival. *Just wait here, please.* But time had passed, and she still hadn't returned.

'Want the seat?' Ree asked.

'I'm fine.' He glanced around the room, noticing vaguely how tidy it was, and said half to himself, 'I really hoped it wouldn't be murder.'

'Me too.' Ree tilted her head to rest against the back of the chair, looking up at him. Her greenish eyes were solemn. 'I keep thinking … what we're doing now, trying to prove Lady Ayla didn't kill the ambassador, is the most important job we've ever done. It's not just protecting her. It's preventing a war.'

Penn nodded. Ree fidgeted a moment in the armchair, then added softly, 'So don't let me mess it up. All right?'

'Only if you do the same for me,' Penn said. 'I'm not –'

He fell silent as Rawleigh swept back into the room. A girl followed in her wake, dressed in the plain black uniform of Darkhaven's servants. She had a freckled brown face and neatly plaited dark hair, and her eyes were downcast.

'Here she is,' Rawleigh announced. When she'd first heard their request, she'd taken it for granted that she would stay in the room whilst the interview was conducted; it had taken all Ree's tact to convince her that if the maid did know anything, she might be more willing to open up if she were alone. Now, Rawleigh gave Ree and Penn a searching glance before saying reluctantly, 'I'll be down in the laundry if you need me again.'

'Thank you,' Ree said as the housekeeper left the room, then gave the maid an encouraging smile. 'Please, sit down.'

The girl did so, sinking onto a low footstool opposite the armchair as if her knees would no longer support her. She looked scared. It was the coats, Penn thought. He and Ree and the maid were all much of an age, young people who in another time and place might have sat down and talked to each other without any constraint – or rather, Ree and the maid would have talked, while he drifted away into the places his mind still went when faced with the need to produce inconsequential chatter. Still, it would have been pleasant enough. He probably would have enjoyed it, even, as long as he knew himself to be among friends. But as soon as he put his arms into a Helmsman's striped coat, he became something else. A symbol. People didn't look at him and see a socially awkward young man. They saw power, skill, authority. The fact that he still *felt* like a socially awkward young man had no bearing on the matter.

'What's your name?' Ree asked the maid.

'Sia.'

'I'm Ree. This is Penn. Don't mind him, he always looks like that.'

Penn realised he was frowning, and hastily smoothed it away.

'Do you know why we're here?' Ree asked.

'N-no …' Sia shifted a little on the stool. 'Because the ambassador died?'

'Yes. He was murdered. And we need to find out who did it.'

The maid wrapped her arms around herself. 'I didn't do anything.'

'Of course not,' Ree said. 'We just need to ask you some questions …'

It was one of those situations in which Penn felt thoroughly uncomfortable. He wasn't good at coaxing information out of people; he couldn't see beneath their skin as others apparently could, to the hopes and fears and feelings that were written there as clear as newsprint for those who knew how to look. Ree had turned out to be one of those people – she was talking in a friendly way to the maid at this very moment, calming her anxiety as easily as turning off a tap. He could understand why Ree was here. What he couldn't work out was why Caraway had sent *him*.

Probably to learn how it's done, he thought mordantly.

'So all we need you to do is tell us what happened that afternoon,' Ree was saying. 'Is that all right?'

Sia nodded. Her arms no longer formed a barrier between herself and the rest of the world; her hands sat loose and relaxed in her lap. That was probably a good sign.

'A Helmsman asked me to attend Lady Ayla in the library,' she said. 'She was there with the ambassador. She asked him what he'd like to drink, and he said taransey.'

'Tolino was the one to suggest taransey?' Penn asked, and Sia shot him a quick glance.

'Y-yes.'

That's probably important. Particularly if the poison turns out to have been in the bottle all along. He wrote it down in his notebook.

'And then?' Ree prompted the maid.

'And then I went back to the kitchens to get it. First me and Hana fetched a bottle of taransey from the cellar –'

'Hana?'

'She works here too.' Sia shuddered. 'None of us like the cellar. All them shadows. And rats. So Hana said she'd come with me.'

'How is the taransey stored?'

'There's a rack for it. Square thing, lot of holes. The bottles lie on their sides. You can't store taransey upright or it'll spoil.'

'How many bottles are down there?'

'Maybe twenty? Not sure, but the rack is nearly full. Dusty, too.' Sia added with a touch of mild reproach, 'The bottles don't need replacing so often, now that Lady Ayla is in charge.'

'So then what?'

'We grabbed a bottle from the rack and took it back upstairs.'

'Did you notice anything unusual about it?'

Sia shrugged. 'It looked like a bottle of taransey. Though I suppose ...' She paused a moment, eyes unfocusing briefly in thought, before concluding, 'I suppose it wasn't as dusty as the rest of 'em.'

Interesting. Penn wrote that down, too.

'What then?' Ree asked.

'When we got back upstairs, I put the bottle on a tray and took two glasses from the sideboard. The good glasses, the crystal ones. And I carried the whole lot through to the library.'

'You didn't look away from the tray at any point after that? Or put it down, say to open a door …'

'It didn't leave my sight,' Sia said with blunt certainty. 'And if I had to put down a single tray to open a door, I wouldn't be very good at my job.'

'So then what happened?'

'I asked Lady Ayla if she'd like me to pour the drinks. She said no, so I left.' Sia shrugged. 'And that's it.'

'Do you know what happened to the bottle of taransey afterwards?' Penn asked. It was one of the things Captain Caraway had asked the Helm to find out. Sia nodded.

'I went back into the library to tidy up after Lady Ayla and the ambassador left. The half-empty bottle was on the table. It should've gone in the drinks cabinet, but that hasn't been used since the old Firedrake's day. The key's been missing for years. So …' Her gaze dropped, a blush tinting her cheeks. 'I locked it in the drawer of the old desk in the corner. I figured if I was the only one who knew it was there, it would be safe enough.'

Probably meant to retrieve it for herself when she was sure no-one else had missed it. Still, Penn noted it down without question, because at least it was one thing they could tell the captain. Then Gil and Resca would be able to test the remaining contents of the bottle, which would answer the question of whether it had held the poison.

'Thank you, Sia,' Ree said. 'I think that's –'

'Hold on.' Penn frowned down at his notes. He'd written *S/H to cellar, took bottle, S put on tray, S took glasses from sideboard, S carried to library,* but there was one thing missing. 'Did you take the bottle of taransey from the rack yourself? Or did Hana pass it to you?'

'I … lemme think. Hana took it down. She was nearest.'

Does that matter? I suppose it might. Penn lifted his head, and he and Ree exchanged glances.

'Can we speak to her, too?' Ree asked.

'It's her day off. She'll be in tomorrow, though.' Sia grinned. 'She always does the breakfast service for Lady Ayla and her family. She likes seeing the children.'

'All right,' Ree said. 'Thank you, Sia. We'll talk to Hana tomorrow.'

They all stood up. Sia bobbed them a curtsey, which made Penn shuffle in awkward discomfort. She opened her mouth as if she might be about to say something else – but in the end, she simply nodded, before leaving the room.

'That's why the captain sent you,' Ree said as they walked back towards the library, which the Helm were currently using as a base for the investigation. Penn frowned.

'Why?'

She smiled. 'For your relentless logic.'

'You're cleverer than I am.'

'I don't think so,' she said, after giving it due consideration. 'Differently clever, maybe. I leap about. Sometimes I make connections that way. But you …' She elbowed him in the ribs, though not hard. 'You see the holes in things.'

'So you think it's important? That Hana took the bottle from the rack, not Sia?'

'Definitely,' Ree said. 'I mean, there are only two possibilities, aren't there? One is that both glasses were poisoned, because there's no way anyone could have poisoned just one and known for certain it would be given to the ambassador.

If that's what happened, Sia must have done it herself, because no-one else had any control over which two glasses she took. And it's not as if anyone else could have slipped poison into them later, either. She said they were in her sight the whole time.'

'She could have lied about that.'

'Yes, but why? If she's innocent, there'd be no reason to. And if she's guilty, it would be far more to her advantage to lie the other way, and invent a moment at which someone else could have done it when she wasn't looking.'

Penn nodded. 'All right. So the second possibility is that the poison was in the bottle, in which case the person who made sure the poisoned bottle was selected was Hana, not Sia. Though without speaking to her, it's hard to know how damning that really is.'

'What do you mean?'

'She might simply have taken it because it looked cleaner than the others.'

'I suppose so,' Ree said doubtfully. 'But putting a poisoned bottle in a rack with lots of others and assuming that someone would take it first because it wasn't as dusty would be a very chancy way to commit murder.'

'That's assuming it was meant to happen the way it did,' Penn replied. 'And I don't think we can assume anything yet.'

'No.'

Silence fell between them. Ree was looking solemn again, even a little unhappy, as if she hadn't gained nearly as much from their interview with Sia as she'd hoped. For once in his life, Penn found himself actively wanting to make conversation, in order to distract her from her worries, but unfortunately there was only one change of subject he could think of. Still, even if it made her angry, that was probably better than sad. Probably. To tell the truth, he wasn't at all sure which she'd prefer. But he took the plunge anyway.

'So ... have you seen your parents again?'

She rolled her eyes. 'I found them waiting for me yesterday when I came off duty. My father had the cheek to ask if I'd calmed down.'

'And?'

'I swore at him. Obviously.'

'Obviously,' Penn echoed. Ree shot him an irritated look.

'Well! We'd just found out about Tolino's death being murder, so I was in no mood for their nonsense. My father said they'd call on me in a couple of days and he expected me to have a civil tongue in my head by then.' She grimaced. 'Something to look forward to.'

Penn didn't reply. He knew what it was like to be pushed into doing something by a parent. He also knew what it was like to make a stand against it. *Tell them you won't do it,* he'd advised Ree. *If they disown you, that's their choice.* Yet it was a lonely path to take, with plenty to lose along the way. Penn might have defied his father, but he'd lost an entire family. His mother, who sent him a secret letter from time to time but didn't dare visit him because *your father is still very angry, dear, I don't want to upset the applecart.* His two younger brothers, who no doubt were growing up hearing all about the iniquities of Tomas Caraway the murderer, just as Penn himself had done – only now, Penn was part of the story. Part of the debt to lay at Caraway's door. A traitor who no longer deserved a name, who'd turned against his own kin to serve under the captain he'd sworn to kill.

Sometimes, in the middle of the night, Penn worried about his brothers. The older, Conor, must be a young man by now. A new receptacle for their father's bitter hatred. One day, he might arrive in the city with revenge in his heart – against Caraway, against Penn himself. And what if Penn couldn't stop him?

What if he *could*?

If he had to choose between his captain's life and his misguided brother's, he wasn't at all sure where the blade would fall.

'You have siblings, don't you?' he asked Ree.

'A brother and two sisters.'

'And you won't lose them if ...' He didn't know quite how to finish the sentence, but Ree shook her head as though she'd understood anyway.

'There's nothing to lose. I barely see them. They're too busy with their houses and their children.' With a sidelong glance, she added, 'But I'm the youngest. It's different for you.'

'What is?'

'Feeling responsible.' She shrugged. 'But there's nothing you can do about it, Penn, honestly there isn't. You just have to hope your brothers grow beyond your father. Like you did.'

'But I nearly didn't,' Penn said. 'You know that. I came this close –' his finger and thumb hovered next to each other – 'to making a terrible mistake. Anyone can become a murderer, if enough hate is poured into them.'

'If you'd wanted to kill Captain Caraway, you would have. You didn't do it because you're better than that.'

'I don't know,' Penn said miserably. 'I think maybe it was just because I hadn't been indoctrinated long enough. I was fifteen when my cousin died and my father began plotting revenge. Nearly a man already. But Finlay, the younger of my two brothers ... he was only seven. By the time *he's* old enough to come to the city, he'll have been soaking up bitterness for more than half his life. What chance does a child stand, against that?'

Ree slipped her arm through his, giving it a squeeze.

'I want to give you some wonderful advice,' she said. 'Something that can solve this for you. But I don't think there is anything, is there?'

Penn shook his head. This was one reason why he didn't like making conversation: it could take you too deep, too quickly, into places you were trying to keep hidden from yourself.

Admittedly, he'd succeeded in distracting Ree. Though she still wore a frown, he suspected it was now on his behalf rather than on Ayla's. Yet that wasn't any better, was it? He should have been more like Zander, and said something to make her laugh. Instead he'd given her something else to worry about, as well as bringing things into the daylight that he usually kept for the darkness of the seventh bell. As friends went, he was utterly useless.

'Here we are,' he mumbled, jerking his head at the library door ahead of them. Yet as he reached out to open it, Ree touched his arm.

'Penn. It's all right, you know.'

'What?'

'Telling me things. That's what friends are for.' She smiled at him. 'And thank you for trying to take my mind off it all, for a little while.'

She could read him as easily as she read everyone else. Shaking his head, Penn followed her into the library.

NINE

Alone in his laboratory, Miles did his best to focus on research. Yet where, before, his ideas had flowed freely and he had seen the shape of what he had to do, now – when it was urgent, when it really mattered – his fingers were slow and his brain slower.

Come on, he told himself. *You have to do this. You have to! Otherwise you will be letting them go to war unprotected.* But the more he thought about that, the more the panic swirled inside him and the harder it was to think about anything at all.

Finally, giving up, he walked away from his experiment bench and stared wildly around the room as though it might reveal undeniable evidence of his perfidy. Bottles and glassware stared back at him, glinting greyly in the light from the high, barred window. Ayla was due at the laboratory any moment, to consult him on the matter of the Kardise ambassador's death. And he had nothing to offer her except lies.

I could give her a hint, he thought. *Lead the investigation to the right place, and the Enforcers would never know I had done it ...*

But the tiny flare of hope died as quickly as it had arrived.

If Mirrorvale and Sol Kardis fail to go to war for any reason at all, the faceless man had said. Which meant that Miles couldn't give anything away. He had to choose his words carefully, or Art would die.

Though he was expecting it, the knock at the door startled him. He forced himself to straighten, to ignore the pounding of his heart. 'Come in!'

'Good afternoon, Miles.' Sure enough, it was Ayla. She pushed the door closed behind her and leaned on it, as though trying to shut the world out.

'Lady Ayla,' he said. 'You are well?'

'Not really.'

'No. Of course not. Why would you be? I mean –' *Stop talking, Miles.* He spread his hands and smiled helplessly at her.

'You know why I wanted to speak to you?' Ayla asked. He nodded.

'You are investigating the Kardise ambassador's death.'

'To be honest, I'm not even sure you can help me. But you've helped me so much in the past ...'

She sat down abruptly on the floor, reminding him with bittersweet clarity of the times they had spent together working on the collar that now kept her safe. Not daring to speak, lest his voice betray him, he followed suit.

Traitor, his relentless conscience threw at him. *She trusts you. She is your friend. She took you into her home, gave you a job, and this is how you repay her?*

He expected Ayla to keep talking, to ask all her questions, but she was equally silent. She looked tired, Miles thought; tired and afraid. Regret burned inside him until he wanted to stand up and confess everything – but he couldn't. So instead, he prompted her gently, 'Lady Ayla?'

'Sorry.' She looked up, forcing a smile. 'Miles, how much do you know about poisons?'

'Enough to be of some use, I should think,' he said. 'That is how the ambassador died?'

'Yes. Someone gave him zephyr.' Ayla sighed. 'I wouldn't trouble you with it, but I couldn't get the answers I needed from Gil.'

'Really? But surely, as a physician –'

'He told me all about its effects,' Ayla agreed. 'And that there's no known antidote. But I already knew those things. I grew up learning about poisons.' Her mouth curved downward. 'There's no denying it, Miles: I was very well placed to kill the ambassador, should I have wished to do so.'

I am afraid so, Lady Ayla. That is the point. He waited a moment before asking, 'What do you need to know?'

'Gil told me that the only way of administering zephyr is in food or drink. But I remember learning about plenty of poisons that work by touch, or by inhalation ... is it possible that Gil is mistaken?'

Miles shook his head. 'Zephyr must be ingested. It has no effect on the body otherwise.'

'All right,' Ayla said. 'Then assuming Gil and Resca are correct about the time of death – and they both assure me they are – the only thing Don Tolino consumed was taransey. So the poison must have been in there.' She massaged her temples. 'And this is where I really hope you can help me, Miles, because I can't see my way through it. The poisoner couldn't have known which glass would go to whom, so the zephyr must have been either in both glasses or in the bottle. A sealed bottle, but that's almost beside the point. Because the point is, I must have swallowed just as much poison as he did, and yet I didn't so much as feel nauseous!' Her laugh had a wild edge to it. 'It's not hard to see why the Kardise don't believe a word I'm saying.'

Guilt gnawing at him, Miles waited. She took a deep breath, drawing the appearance of calm around her like an embroidered robe, and began to ask him questions.

'Is it possible for a person to be naturally immune to zephyr?'

'Not that I am aware of.'

'Is there an antidote that Gil might not know about? Something I could have eaten, or –'

Yes. Yes, I discovered it and I gave it to your enemies. Miles swallowed over a dry throat and managed, 'Gil was correct, in that respect. There is no known antidote.'

'My collar, then. Is it possible that the collar protected me from the effects?'

'In creature form, perhaps,' Miles said. 'But in human form, I doubt it. We have tested you with poisons from time to time before, Lady Ayla, but I am still working on protecting you from them. The collar has to be calibrated individually for each one, and that work is not yet done. And since zephyr is so easy to detect, it was not high on the list. Still, it is possible ...' But he stopped, because Ayla was shaking her head.

'No,' she said softly. 'I'd forgotten, but I took off my collar when Tolino and I sat down in the library.' Her lips twisted in acknowledgement of the irony. 'It was an attempt at friendship.'

They sat in silence for a time. Then Ayla said, in a tone of voice that suggested all too clearly that she was clutching at straws, 'I don't suppose that during your testing, you gave me enough small doses of zephyr that I built up an immunity to it?'

'If I had asked you to consume zephyr, you would have

noticed it straight away,' Miles reminded her. 'As I said, it was not high on the list, mainly because I assumed you would detect its presence well before you needed to be protected from it.'

'Usually I would. But apparently not when it's in a bottle of taransey.' Ayla sighed. 'So where does that leave us? It's impossible for someone to have poisoned the ambassador without poisoning me. And yet someone did.'

If you would just stop trusting me, you would see the answer. The words almost slipped out; it was only by calling his loved ones' faces to mind that he kept them back.

'I am sorry I cannot be of more help, Lady Ayla,' he said instead, and meant it. She gave him a tired smile.

'It's all right. I just need some new ideas.' She tipped her head back to rest against the door, closing her eyes. 'If you were going to poison the ambassador and frame me for the crime, how would you do it?'

Miles stared at her, unable to find a single word of reply. *Think. Make a joke. Make something up. Think!* But even as he opened his mouth to say something, the gods knew what, Ayla shook her head.

'I'm sorry,' she said. 'That wasn't a fair question. Ignore me.'

'No need to apologise, Lady Ayla.' Then, knowing the answer but unable to stop himself asking the question, 'So what will happen now?'

'If I can't satisfy the Kardise that I had nothing to do with their ambassador's death, I fear it will be war.'

'Would that be so bad?' Miles asked, trying to assuage his own burning guilt. 'You are strong, now. The Kardise have no way to defeat you.'

She looked at him blankly, as if he had just said something

very stupid. 'But people will die, Miles. What does being invincible matter if I can't protect my people?'

'I thought –'

'A single Changer creature can defend Darkhaven. A single Changer creature can't win an entire war. The blood of every person whose life is lost will be on my hands.' She ground the heels of her palms into her eyes and muttered, 'I should have lied after all.'

'What?'

'Tomas said I should have lied to the Kardise, and he's right. I should have.'

Miles had never seen her so overset. For the first time, the sheer magnitude of his crime dawned on him. He'd thought about the people he cared about, Art and the Nightshades and the young Helmsmen he'd first given training in firearms, and dismissed the rest as *minimal losses*. By focusing all his guilt on the abstract act of betrayal, he had been able to ignore the real and terrible consequences of his silence. *Let Mirrorvale and Sol Kardis go to war with each other,* he'd been told, not *Send people to die*. And yet, on some level, they were one and the same.

He couldn't create collars for everyone. He wasn't even sure he'd be able to create them for those he loved most. The blood of every single person whose life was taken by a Kardise gun would be on his hands, not Ayla's.

'But don't worry,' Ayla added. 'I won't send Art to the battlefield, much as we could use his experience. I'm selfish enough to want to protect the people I love most, so he can stay here with you and Tomas.' She smiled sadly. 'They won't like it, but I think they'll obey me all the same. Because if the worst happens, and I don't come back, someone has to protect the children until they come of age.'

Miles nodded, feeling sick to his stomach. It was what he'd hoped for, and indeed relied upon – that Art would be needed in Darkhaven and thus be kept away from the battlefield. Yet now, truly appreciating for the first time that *someone* would have to die, he realised that such a hope had been unbearably self-centred.

'I am sorry, Lady Ayla,' he said. 'More sorry than I can express. I wish … I wish it did not have to be this way.'

'So do I.'

They sat in silence for a while. Miles could only guess what Ayla was thinking. His own head spun with guilt and regret. He wished he could stop time, freeze it somehow, so that he would never have to face the consequences of his decision. Yet finally, Ayla sighed and got to her feet.

'I'd better go.' She frowned at him, as though seeing him properly for the first time that day. 'You look tired. I hope you're not working yourself too hard.'

'I am so close to a breakthrough, Lady Ayla. And if I could just get these collars right –' He didn't need to finish the sentence. They both knew what that would mean for the coming war. Desperate hope sparked in Ayla's eyes, but somehow she managed to shake her head and smile at him.

'It would be wonderful, of course. But I can't have you killing yourself over it. You're too important to me for that.'

Miles didn't trust himself to speak. He nodded mutely, and Ayla put a hand on his shoulder before turning for the door.

'Thank you, Miles. As always, you've been a great help.'

Once she'd gone, Miles lowered his head onto his knees and let out a long, silent cry of despair. *I am sorry, Ayla. I am sorry.*

He had only told one lie. But that was bad enough.

Even after leaving Miles, Ayla couldn't stop thinking about him. There was no denying that if he could produce a reliable collar for the protection of ordinary people, the threat of war would be far less severe. She wanted that as much as she'd ever wanted anything. Yet she had been polite when she'd told him he looked tired: he looked terrible. Red-rimmed eyes, a newly lined face, with a hint of grey beneath the ochre-brown of his skin that implied long nights of wakefulness. She'd never been sure how old he was – perhaps around thirty? A fair bit younger than Bryan, anyway. Older than her. But he looked like he'd aged a decade in the past few days. Clearly the possibility of war had hit him hard.

It's hit us all hard, she reminded herself. *Let him work. If he can find the solution, it will be worth the sacrifice.* Such cold-heartedness didn't sit well with her at all, but she had no choice. War had a way of rendering individual lives meaningless.

By far the best thing she could do would be to stop it happening at all.

To that end, she went straight to the library. Tomas and Giorgi were both in there; she could hear their raised voices from the other end of the corridor. She wanted to find out if they'd located the leftover taransey yet, but she had to draw on every bit of willpower she possessed before she could make herself open the door. At the start of the investigation yesterday, when they'd come to ask her about it, Giorgi had as good as accused her of disposing of the half-empty bottle in an attempt to cover her tracks. Who knew what he'd accuse her of today?

The men were over by Florentyn's old desk, facing each other across it much as she'd once faced her father. Her physician and the Kardise doctor were also in the room, off to one side as though trying to avoid being drawn into the argument, and a couple of Helmsmen lingered near the door. All of them looked uncomfortable.

Tomas straightened up and saluted at her entrance. Giorgi gave her a bare nod. Between them, on the desk, stood a half-empty bottle of taransey and a glass containing a finger's width of the amber liquid.

'Is that –' she began, and Tomas nodded.

'The maid had locked it in a drawer for safekeeping.'

'Have you tested it?'

'Gil and Resca have, just now. There's no doubt it contains zephyr.'

'Well, then,' she said. 'That proves this was a crime aimed just as much at me as it was at Don Tolino, since we shared the bottle. I don't know how I managed to escape unscathed, but surely the important question now is who put the poison there, and how they did it without breaking the seals.'

'I made a similar suggestion to Giorgi,' Tomas agreed. 'But he insists we should have different priorities.'

He was furious. Perhaps as angry as Ayla had ever seen him, though he was just about holding it in check. She wondered exactly what Giorgi had been saying about her before she entered the room.

'If a person is untouched by a deadly poison,' the Kardise aide remarked, 'the obvious conclusion is that they failed to consume any of it.' For the first time that afternoon, he looked directly at her, eyes dark and cold. 'It is easy enough to pretend to share a drink of friendship, Lady Ayla. Particularly in a room with no witnesses.'

Right. All right. But maybe there's a way to prove it ...

She walked over to the desk. Miles had said it was impossible to be immune to zephyr – but Miles didn't know everything, surely? It had to be worth a try, if only to rule out a line of investigation.

Tomas frowned when she picked up the bottle. 'What are you doing, Lady Ayla?'

'We need to know if zephyr doesn't affect me for some reason.' She didn't look in Giorgi's direction, wishing he wasn't there. If it had been the Helm alone, she could have asked Tomas about this instead of telling him. But in front of the Kardise, they had to be overlord and captain, not partners. So without waiting for a reply, she topped up the glass.

'Ayla ...' The dropped honorific would have told her the level of Tomas's unease, even if she hadn't been able to hear it in his voice. 'This could kill you.'

'I'm sure Lady Ayla knows exactly what she's doing.' The double meaning in Giorgi's words was clear. He thought it was all a ploy. No doubt neither of the possible outcomes would satisfy him: if the poison affected her, it would *prove* she didn't drink it last time, whereas if it didn't, it would *prove* she'd already known there was no risk. But Tomas needed as much information as possible – and she desperately wanted the truth.

Ignoring Giorgi's sneer, she sniffed the taransey, then let it touch her lips. Just like last time, she detected nothing unusual. A hint of spice, a touch of sweetness, a subtle bitter aftertaste – was that the zephyr? – and, most of all, strong alcohol.

She lifted the glass a second time, but stopped before it reached her mouth. *What if this does kill me? What if everyone is wrong about the limited effects of zephyr on a Changer?*

It's less than I drank last time, she reminded herself. *There can't possibly be enough poison in there to cause me serious harm.*

With a flick of the wrist, she gulped the contents down.

'I will let you know the results of this experiment,' she announced directly to Giorgi, summoning all the chilly formality she employed when people tried to use her age, her size or her gender as excuses to treat her with less respect than she deserved. She couldn't look at Tomas; the concern on his face was too raw. *It won't kill me. It won't.*

Without another word, she headed for the door. According to Gil and his Kardise counterpart, it had been the best part of two full bells before the poison had taken hold of the ambassador. She would just have to wait and see what it would do to her.

TEN

Ree and Penn were meant to be on shift together, but – like the day before – they'd been pulled off their usual duties to help with the murder investigation. They were about to go to the library for their orders when a young Helmsman caught up with them and directed them to one of Darkhaven's small receiving rooms instead. When they got there, they found both Caraway and Ayla waiting for them.

'You won't report to the library any more,' Caraway said. 'You'll report to me here, every morning and every evening. The Kardise are being ...' He paused, obviously choosing his words carefully, before concluding, 'Intractable.'

'They're convinced I'm guilty and they won't hear of anything that says different,' Ayla added. She looked even paler than usual, and dark shadows lurked beneath her eyes. 'I'd almost say they're determined to slow this investigation down until it reaches a standstill. And we can't let that happen.' She shivered, pulling her robe tighter around herself. 'We only have a week.'

Ree frowned. 'Are you well, Lady Ayla?'

'Zephyr poisoning,' Ayla said. 'I wanted to prove a point, so I drank from the poisoned bottle. I've been up all night.'

Her lips curled in a wry smile. 'Captain Caraway isn't very pleased with me for endangering myself, but I think it was worth finding out what would happen.'

'It was,' Caraway said. 'But it wouldn't have been if you'd died.'

'According to the accepted wisdom, zephyr doesn't kill Changers. I was almost certain it was safe.'

'*Almost.*'

They looked at each other with identical expressions of affectionate exasperation. Ree ducked her head to hide a smile.

'So you're not immune to zephyr,' Penn said – and Ree had to hide another smile at his total obliviousness to any kind of emotional interaction. 'But the zephyr was definitely in the taransey, and you drank the taransey before without any effect ...'

'Which means something must have stopped it working on you before,' Ree concluded. 'An antidote.'

Ayla nodded. 'But there isn't one. I was taught that myself, and both Miles and Gil agree.' She sighed. 'The only logical explanation is that I'm a murderer.'

'There's another explanation,' Caraway said firmly. 'And we'll work it out. But for now ... Ree, Penn, you'll be setting aside the question of Ayla's temporary immunity, and focusing on how the poison got into the taransey in the first place. We already know the bottle must have been tampered with, but the seals on those things are bloody complicated. Not just anyone could open a bottle of taransey, add poison and reseal it without leaving any sign of the intrusion.'

'So if we find out *how*, we might find out *who*?' Ree asked.

'That's right.' Caraway handed Penn a half-empty bottle of liquor. 'It's been opened again since, of course, but I'm hoping that if you take this back to the distillery, they'll be able to tell you how it was done.' He held out a letter. 'You'll also need this. Ayla's signed it and added her own seal. That place is guarded better than Darkhaven, and they don't usually open their doors for anyone less than the overlord herself. I'd go in person, but I don't suppose I'd be at my best in a place like that – and besides, it should be a simple enough job.'

Ree wondered briefly if it troubled him, working on a case that centred around poisoned liquor. He'd handled the bottle without any sign of discomfort, and that oblique reference to his own past relationship with alcohol had been made with the same self-deprecating honesty he brought to all his dealings with the Helm. All the same, the metaphor must cut too close for him to approach it with total equanimity: a precious drink, with poison at its heart.

'Yes, sir,' she said, tucking the letter away in an inside pocket. 'We'll do everything we can.'

Ree would have expected the distillery to be located in the first ring, somewhere in the industrial quarter with all the other factories, but in fact it was in the second. Not on the busy eastern side, either, with its noisy smiths and smelters and the constant rumble of the tram line. It was tucked down at the end of a secluded street, surrounded by hundreds of little workshops where the finest artisans plied their trade.

'Says a lot about how they see themselves,' Penn muttered.

Ree tore her gaze away from the most beautiful, intricate piece of jewellery she had ever seen: a golden bracelet in the shape of a firedrake with the tip of its tail in its mouth, every scale individually shaped and carved, with tiny rubies for eyes. Earlier she'd been caught by a series of exquisitely detailed paintings of Mirrorvalese flowers, each no bigger than her little fingernail; and before that, a bubble of the thinnest, most delicate glass supported by a stem so slender it must surely be about to snap. It was hard not to get distracted in this part of the second ring.

'Sorry?'

'The distillery.' He gestured at the tall, barred gates that were the only way in. 'They're not manufacturing a product. They're making *art*.'

'Yeah.' Her gaze fell on the guard standing stern-faced on the other side of a small gate set into the larger. '*Expensive* art.'

As they approached, she could sense Penn trying to make himself look as imposing as possible, and realised she was doing the same. It was the way the guard stared at them: as though they were feral dogs coming too close to a feast table, and in a moment he would chase them off with a stick.

Captain Caraway should have sent older Helmsmen, she thought in dismay. *No-one here is going to take us seriously. Why did he pick us?*

Though she hadn't thought she knew the answer, some part of her brain supplied it anyway. *Because he trusts us the most. Because the older men were already part of the Helm before he became captain, but he trained us himself.* It made her proud enough that she was able to step forward to the gate and hold up Caraway's letter without so much as a quiver.

'We're here to see the foreman,' she said. 'Ayla Nightshade's orders.'

The guard reached through the bars to pluck the letter from her hand. His eyebrows lifted as he examined the seal, and he cast a brief, curious glance at the wrapped bottle nestled in the crook of Penn's arm. 'Wait here, please.'

When he returned, he was accompanied: a woman walked

beside him with neat, rapid steps. Her hair was greying, her face lined, but she had a wiry kind of strength about her. The guard unlocked the small gate before stepping back to allow her through.

'Aires,' she said, touching her fingertips to Ree's and then to Penn's. 'I'm the foreman here. I understand you have a taransey problem you wish to consult me about.'

Ree nodded mutely. For some reason, she hadn't expected the distillery's foreman to be a woman. She thought of taransey as something that belonged almost exclusively to men, like ... well, she couldn't think of another example. But then she noticed Aires studying her with an equal amount of interest, and had to suppress a grin. *Like the Helm, Ree. That's the comparison you're searching for.*

'We're here on Ayla Nightshade's business,' Penn said, recalling Aires's attention. 'Can we come in?'

'I suppose so. But you'll have to agree to be blindfolded.'

Ree and Penn exchanged swift, startled glances, and the foreman gave a rusty chuckle. 'Honestly, your faces! You won't learn the secrets of taransey just by looking. Come on in, both of you.'

Feeling more than a little foolish, Ree followed her. Once everyone was inside, Aires led the way towards the distillery while the guard relocked the gate and resumed his position. Ree studied the building with interest as they got closer, but there wasn't much to see – just a little complex of chimneys releasing different shades of smoke into the air, no different from any other factory in Arkannen.

'Some from the stills, some from the kilns, and one from the engine that runs the mill,' Aires said, following her gaze.

'Are you allowed to tell us that?' Ree asked doubtfully, and Aires laughed again.

'There's no secret in it. Making liquor's much the same the world over. It's the precise ingredients that make the difference.'

She pushed open a door, releasing a grumble of steam-powered machinery – that must be the mill – and a waft of spice. As they climbed a flight of steps, the air became warmer and warmer until it was almost uncomfortable. Then Aires opened another door, releasing a wall of scented heat. Ree took a deep breath, trying to separate out the different components: sweet woodsmoke, yeast, coal, some kind of roasted grain, and above it all that spicy flavour that made the back of her throat tingle with the ghost of the drink it would become. Aires raised her eyebrows.

'Any the wiser?'

'No,' Ree admitted.

'Good. Come on, then.'

She led the two of them along a walkway that seemed to be a kind of overseer's platform. Ree glimpsed three brick-walled structures that must be the kilns, a large vat of liquid being stirred by two men pushing a rotating paddle – Aires stopped briefly to look at that, then called something down to one of the workers, who slowed his pace a fraction – and what looked like a big wooden tank. Finally the gleam of copper caught her eye and she saw the stills themselves, shaped like bells with long pipes leading out of the top, connected in pairs: one larger, one smaller. She would have stayed there longer to examine it all, but by then they'd reached the other end of the walkway and Aires was ushering her and Penn into what looked like an incredibly compact office.

'Standing room only, I'm afraid,' she said. 'I don't usually have visitors. So, how can I help you?'

Unwrapping the bottle he'd been carrying, Penn held it

up. 'We need you to tell us everything you can about the history of this bottle.'

Aires raised her eyebrows. 'What about it?'

'Well, for a start,' Ree said, 'is it possible to find out who bought it?'

'Perhaps. Sometimes we sell an entire batch to a wealthy customer. I'd have to check the log ... here, hand it over.'

Penn did so. Aires took it, running her fingers over the seals as though she could read the information they conveyed through her fingertips.

'Let me see, now ... this one was bottled only recently. At a guess, within the last three months. We mature taransey in casks, you see, and bottle it once it's ready to drink. Each batch of bottles gets a different serial number, to allow us to trace them and detect forgeries.' She pointed at a complex set of wedge-shaped marks in the wax around the neck of the bottle. 'So if I look this one up ...' She turned to grab one of the books from her desk, flicking through the pages until she found what she was looking for. 'Here you are, see? Bottled this year, the month of the Awakened Moon.'

'Just last month, then.'

'Yes. Not long in the world.' Aires moved her finger across the page, frowning. 'But this particular batch was down for individual distribution within Arkannen, so it's impossible to identify with any certainty exactly who bought your bottle.'

'But it was someone in the city?'

'Oh, yes. We often have orders for a single bottle at a time. Many of those are inns – your average inn patron doesn't tend to drink taransey all that often, so they get through it quite slowly – but they could be individual households, boutiques, brothels ... anyone, really.' She gave them a sly, sidelong glance. 'Even the Helm. We used to sell entire batches to Darkhaven, but I understand Lady Ayla doesn't have the taste for it.'

'Do you have a list of the individual customers who were sent the bottles from this batch?' Ree asked.

'Here.' Aires passed her a different book. 'This is the customer log. The list you want is on that page – see? Same serial number.'

A batch turned out to consist of two dozen bottles. Ree copied down the twenty-four names and addresses, while Penn picked up their taransey bottle from the desk and handed it back to Aires.

'Is there anything else that strikes you as unusual about this bottle, ma'am?'

'No, it looks fine ...' She removed the cap, took a sniff and winced. 'But someone's put something in it that isn't meant to be there.'

'That's why we're here,' Penn said. 'I don't know if you heard, but the Kardise ambassador died recently, and –'

'This is what killed him?' Aires suggested with flippant swiftness, still pulling a disgusted face at the bottle.

'Yes.'

The foreman lifted her head sharply. 'What?'

'There's poison in it,' Ree explained, tucking her completed list of names away and passing the log book back. 'And of course the ambassador didn't know what taransey was meant to taste like, so ...'

'But how did the poison get in there?'

'That's the difficult part,' Penn said. 'The bottle was brought to the ambassador untouched.' By unspoken agreement, Ree noticed, neither of them was mentioning Ayla's involvement. 'He broke the seal, drank from the contents, and it killed him.'

'Murder,' Ree added.

Aires frowned. 'I hope you're not suggesting *we* –'

'No, of course not. How could you be sure it would go to the intended target? But that being the case, we need to know how it's possible for someone to have opened a sealed bottle of taransey, added poison, and resealed it in such a way that no-one could detect the difference.'

The foreman picked up the bottle, rotating it slowly. After a few moments, she pulled an eyeglass from an inner pocket and used it to examine the seals.

'I wouldn't have said it was possible,' she said finally. 'Not with this bottle, anyway. The seals are wax, as you know, and patterned according to our own design. For someone to open the bottle, they would have had to snap the seals and then melt the edges back together afterwards – but I see no sign of any damage in the wax, no hint of melting and rejoining. Maybe it would be possible to lift the entire design using a very thin, very sharp blade, but again you'd have to fix it back onto the bottle afterwards. And that would be incredibly tricky, because to get the wax to stick to the bottle, we usually have to melt an entire lump and imprint the seals and patterns while it's drying. So again, either you'd end up with a faulty set of seals – which they're not – or the wax wouldn't adhere properly to the glass and so wouldn't be convincing as an unopened bottle.' Lowering the eyeglass, she shook her head. 'I really can't see how –'

'May I look at that bottle, Aires?' At the sound of the new voice, the foreman straightened much as Ree or any other Helmsman would have if Captain Caraway had entered the room. She turned to see a man standing in the doorway, his height and presence crowding the already crowded office.

Perhaps her parents' age, Ree thought; neat brown hair, fair skin, wearing a coat and breeches that spoke of understated wealth. Despite the polite phrasing of his request, his outstretched hand left no doubt that it was really an order.

'Yes, sir.' Aires handed over bottle and eyeglass, and the man subjected the seals to his own intense scrutiny.

'Ah, no,' he said finally. 'It has been done very well, but this bottle has most certainly been resealed.' He glanced up, and Ree was struck by the bright, mesmerising blue of his eyes. 'It is not so much the rejoining; Aires is correct that there is no sign of that. Yet the texture of the wax tells its own story. One does not get such a dull surface without melting and resetting several times. And ... yes, *here* and *here* are imperfections in the pattern. Not visible to the naked eye, but there all the same.' He lowered the bottle, nodding thoughtfully. 'Interesting. Very interesting.'

'How do you know this, sir?' Penn asked. The man turned to him with a pleasant smile.

'My apologies. Clearly I failed to introduce myself.' His gaze moved from Penn's face to Ree's, where it lingered for a moment in amused curiosity. 'Derrick Tarran.'

He gave his name as if he fully expected them to recognise it – and Ree did, though perhaps not entirely for the reasons he was assuming. Tarran was one of the oldest names in Mirrorvale. Hundreds of years ago, a Tarran ancestor had founded this distillery and given his name to the liquor it produced, and the distillery had stayed in the family ever since. Derrick Tarran was the current owner – a rich and powerful man, and certainly a knowledgeable one when it came to questions over taransey and its production.

That much was probably known to most people in Arkannen, but Ree had an additional reason for recognising the name. The village she'd grown up in and where her parents still lived, Torrance Mill, was named for the Tarran family. They had an estate just outside the village. Of course, that didn't mean Derrick Tarran would recognise her, or have any idea who she was. The Tarrans spent most of their time in the city; she didn't think she'd ever seen any of them before, and they certainly wouldn't have seen her. Still, it was a link to home that she hadn't expected.

'Then you're certain this bottle was tampered with?' she asked.

'As certain as I can be, ah …' He paused delicately, and Ree realised she'd failed to observe the basic courtesies. Her mother would have been mortified.

'Ree Quinn,' she said, extending her hand for the traditional greeting. Once again, she saw both laughter and curiosity in his eyes as he touched his fingertips to hers.

'Delighted to meet you.' He studied her face a moment longer, before turning to Penn. *I guess no-one told him there are women in the Helm now.* Ree wasn't sure whether to be disgruntled or amused.

'Penn Avens,' Penn said.

It was the name he'd used when he first came to the city, hiding the secret of his family connection to the previous Captain of the Helm, who had kidnapped Ayla and who Caraway had killed. After learning the reasons behind that death, and losing his desire for revenge in the process, Penn had stuck with the alias. Yet Derrick Tarran smiled at him and said, 'Ah, yes. Young cousin to the late Owen Travers.'

Penn nodded mutely.

'I find it pays to keep abreast of the goings-on in the city,' Tarran explained, almost apologetically. He handed the bottle back to Penn. 'I do hope I have been of some assistance.

Please, if you find you have more questions at any time, don't hesitate to come back and ask them.'

It was a dismissal, albeit a polite one – but Ree stood her ground.

'I do have one more question, sir, if you don't mind. You said the tampering was very well done. Can you tell us what kind of skills it would have taken to do it? Or what tools?'

'A good question,' Tarran said approvingly. 'It would not have been easy. I suggest you look for a very clever forger. Someone who is used to copying intricate patterns. But other than that ...' He shrugged. 'I am afraid my extensive knowledge of Arkannen does not extend to criminals.'

'No. Of course.' Ree offered him a short bow. 'Thank you, sir. Thank you, Aires.'

Once she and Penn were out on the street, making their way back to Darkhaven, they compared notes. An expert had testified that the bottle really had been tampered with, which proved that it was possible for someone other than Ayla to have added the poison. They also had a list of twenty-four names, one of whom must have bought that particular bottle. Surely it wouldn't take long to visit them all, and then ...

'One step closer,' Penn said, and Ree smiled.

'Yes. You know, Penn, I really think we can do this.'

That evening, Ree had just got back to her apartment with a hot snack she'd bought from a street vendor when someone knocked at her door.

'You said a couple of days,' she said when she opened it to find her parents standing there. 'I make that one.'

Her father chuckled uneasily. 'Can we come in?'

'I suppose so. But only if you keep well away from the subject of finding me a husband.'

'Please, Ree ...' Neither of her parents moved from the doorway, but her father took her hand. 'Will you at least hear us out? I really think you'd like Lewis Tarran, if you just got to know him.'

Tarran. Ree frowned at him. 'This boy ... is he related to Derrick Tarran? The distillery owner?'

'Only child,' her mother said enthusiastically. 'Just think, Cheri, your children would inherit an entire –'

Her husband gave her a look, and she subsided. Ree paid very little attention to them. She was remembering the interest with which Derrick Tarran had studied her – hardly surprising, if he was planning to accept her as his daughter-in-law. Yet she wasn't at all the sort of girl whom young, wealthy heirs married. They wanted beauty, compliance and a good family, not an ex-Helmsman from lesser merchant stock who would challenge her husband every time he failed to treat her as an equal. It was curiosity over why the distillery owner should even have considered the match, as much as a vague thought that she might glean useful information to help with the murder investigation, that led her to step back from the doorway and gesture her parents inside.

'Come on, then. I'll listen. But make it quick.'

They settled into the same places as before. Her mother cast a disapproving glance at the cooling butty in Ree's hand, but made no comment. *Probably doesn't want to get thrown out again,* Ree thought. She unwrapped the butty and took a defiant bite.

'Listen, Cheri.' Her father spoke firmly. 'I know you think you want to stay in the Helm, but sooner or later your time there has to end. It's a young person's job. And if you wait until you're too old to keep doing it before you move on, it'll be too late. You'll have no family, no home of your own, no man to share your life.'

'I don't want a family,' Ree said, though she'd had the same conversation with her parents often enough to know it was fruitless. 'And retired Helmsmen get good –'

'Every girl wants a family,' her mother interrupted. 'You just don't know it yet.'

'I'm nineteen years old. I'm old enough to know what I want.'

Her mother gave her an indulgent smile. 'When I was nineteen, Cheri, I thought I wanted to elope with the chandler's son. My parents had to guide me onto a better path –' she darted a glance at Ree's father – 'and that's what we're trying to do for you.'

It's not up to you to say what's better for me. With an effort – she almost felt it scrape down her throat – Ree swallowed her anger. This argument would circle around and around until all three of them were tired and frustrated. Better to try a different line of attack.

'I know you mean well.' She had to force the words out. 'But you don't seem to understand how important my work is to me. Not only that, but I'm good at it! I saved Lady Ayla's life when I was still a trainee!' She didn't want to bring that up again, after the lukewarm response she'd received from them originally to the fact that she'd *saved the overlord of Mirrorvale's life*, but any weapon would do in an emergency. 'I know for a fact she won't want to see me go, and Captain Caraway won't either.'

We're talking about the two most important people in the country, she added silently. *Surely that has to mean something to you?*

'I know you've done well,' her father said. 'And we're

proud of you.' He could at least have tried to sound as though he meant it. 'But your first duty is to your parents. Lady Ayla and Captain Caraway know that.'

'We're on the verge of war,' Ree contradicted him. 'My first duty is to my country.'

He shook his head. 'All the more reason to get out now.'

'Oh, Cheri ...' Her mother extended a hand, then let it fall. 'War isn't a game. Why go and get yourself killed? You'd be much better off settling down with a nice boy and letting the real warriors deal with the Kardise.'

Ree couldn't reply to that immediately. She discarded the congealed remains of her butty on the floor next to her, taking a deep breath. Her hands were shaking. She wanted to throw her parents out again, for good this time. Or better still, drag them up to the fifth ring and show them how much of a real warrior she was. But instead, once more, she made her best attempt to reason with them.

'I don't understand why this means so much to you. You have two other daughters. A son. Six grandchildren already.'

'Seven,' her mother corrected.

'There you go, then! So many I've lost count! You can't possibly need me to churn out more of them. And it's not as if you need me to make a strategic marriage –'

Her parents exchanged glances. Neither of them spoke. And Ree felt something cold and heavy settle in her stomach alongside the food.

'What is it?' she demanded, anxiety sharpening her voice. 'What aren't you telling me?'

'Cheri ...' Her father tried to put an arm around her shoulders, but Ree shrugged him off and he made no further attempt to touch her. 'I made a bad investment,' he admitted. 'I owe Derrick Tarran a lot of money, with no way to pay.

But since his son has his heart set on you, we agreed that as part of the betrothal bargain, the Tarrans would write off the debt –'

'Lewis has his heart set on me?' Ree repeated slowly. 'Why?'

Her father looked uncomfortable. 'I talked about you, Cheri. Before all this blew up, I spent some time with the Tarrans both here and at home, and Derrick kept wanting to hear more about my sword-wielding daughter. He found the stories ... entertaining, I suppose. And Lewis was there a lot of the time, listening ...' He crossed his arms defensively beneath Ree's stare. 'I wasn't to know he'd think of you as a marriage prospect! As far as his father and I were concerned, you were an amusing anecdote!'

'Then surely Derrick Tarran can't want me as a daughter,' Ree said, pushing aside the insult in favour of the one piece of information that might help her. But her father sighed.

'Lewis is an only child. His father's pride and joy. What the boy wants, he gets. And since his father more or less owns me, Ree ... that means he gets you.'

Ree shuddered. If she'd known, that morning at the distillery, that she was face to face with her prospective father-in-law, she would have ... what? The thought derailed as she realised there wasn't anything she could have done. Not without damaging the investigation.

'He might own you, but you don't own me.' The words had been burning in her throat all this time – *I'm a grown woman, you don't own me* – but now they were finally free, she felt hollow. Because in the end, it didn't matter whether she was legally obliged to obey her father or not. If she didn't marry Lewis, his father would find other ways to call in her family's debt. She'd effectively have reduced them to penury.

Their house and possessions would be sold, her father would lose his merchant's licence, and they'd be left with nothing.

Given that, what choice did she have?

'No, I don't own you,' her father said, as if he could read her mind. 'But I'm begging you, Cheri ... please do this thing. For all of us.'

'We wouldn't ask it of you unless we thought you'd end up happier, too,' her mother added with a tremulous smile. 'Honestly, chicken, it's the best thing for everyone.'

Chicken. Ree's mother hadn't called her that since Ree was a little girl. That, as much as anything, convinced Ree that her mother was telling the truth. She really did believe that Ree would be happier married; that this awful, necessary bargain was a blessing in disguise. And though she couldn't have been more wrong, Ree found it impossible to hate her for it.

'Does he know I'm not a virgin?' she flung at them, in a last-ditch attempt to free herself. So-called virtue was one of those things prized in the kind of girls who were expected to make good marriages. One had to know one's heirs were one's own, after all. So surely, a family like the Tarrans would never accept a girl who wasn't ... intact.

Yet once he'd got over his very obvious embarrassment, her father spread his hands – ignoring her mother's scandalised spluttering – and said, 'To be honest, Ree, I don't think he cares. It wasn't even mentioned when we were drawing up the contract.'

'There's a contract?'

'Well, yes. Since this marriage will also be the settlement of a debt. And, you know, these grand old families ... they are used to things being more ... transactional.'

'Grand old families are also used to brides who haven't

slept repeatedly with one of the fifth ring's junior assistant weaponmasters,' Ree said. 'So why are the Tarrans willing to waive that requirement? Especially when there's so much money involved?'

'I ...' her father began, but this time he was drowned out by her mother.

'Cheri! You slept with a *weaponmaster*?'

'Junior assistant weaponmaster,' Ree corrected with a certain amount of malice, before adding innocently, 'I can introduce you if you like. He's from a very good family.'

'I don't care if he's a Nightshade! You can't marry a weaponmaster!'

'Who says I want to marry him?'

'*Cheri!*' Her mother looked as dismayed as if Ree had just told her the world was coming to an end. 'As far as I can see, young lady, it's lucky we've managed to arrange this marriage before –'

Ree's father shot her a warning glance.

'Well, sweetheart?' he asked gently. 'Can you do this for us?'

I think I have to. For a moment, Ree couldn't speak. She felt tears sting her eyes, but she'd had plenty of practice at keeping them back over the years.

'Let me at least meet Lewis first,' she said, a little desperately. 'Give him the chance to know me, not some fantasy he's dreamed up. If, after that, he still wants to go ahead with the marriage ... I suppose I'll do it.' Raising her hand to block out her mother's glad cry and her father's stammered thanks, she added, 'Now please go away and leave me alone.'

After they'd left, she hugged her knees and stared at nothing. This was it, then. The end of the life she'd chosen for herself – because she couldn't believe the Tarrans would accept her desire to stay in the Helm once she was part of the family. That sort of thing was for *less important people*, those without a name and reputation to maintain. No, her job would be making witty conversation at dinner parties and ensuring everything went smoothly when her husband entertained business guests. Running a household. Looking pretty. Having babies. All perfectly valuable work, for the right person – which she was most definitely not. Yet in a few short months, she would have to be.

If, that was, Lewis went through with it.

She sat upright, a new tendril of hope creeping through her. The marriage wasn't a foregone conclusion, even now. If Lewis backed out of the deal, that would be a renegement on his family's side; Derrick Tarran would thereby be put in the wrong, giving Ree's father a good basis for negotiating manageable terms of repayment. So maybe it was possible for Ree to avoid the trap ahead of her without throwing her family into poverty.

She just had to convince Lewis Tarran that marrying her was a terrible, terrible idea.

ELEVEN

Two days after the ambassador's death was announced as murder rather than misfortune, Zander emerged into the early morning chill to find his father's aide, Leo, waiting on his doorstep.

'Gods,' he muttered. 'What did you do? Fly through the night to get here?'

Imperturbable as ever, Leo held out a letter. 'Your father asked me to give you this, Don Alezzandro.'

Zander broke the seal, then scanned the content of the single sheet with increasing unease. He hadn't been exaggerating: news of the murder must have been sent straight to Sol Kardis by airship as soon as it came out, and a reply returned with Leo the very next day. Apparently his father had strong feelings on the matter.

Alezzandro –

The Nightshade woman murdered one of your countrymen, a man who went to that godforsaken country looking for peace. They cannot be trusted.

If you do not return home with Leo, I will have no choice but to name you traitor and disown you for good.

At that point, his father's formal script degenerated

abruptly into an agitated scrawl. *Have some sense, Zander, for pity's sake. I can understand a young man rebelling against his father for a few months to indulge in foreign wine and exotic whores, but this is frankly ridiculous.*

Marco Lepont

Zander looked up. 'Do you know what this says?'

'Your father conveyed the gist of it to me, yes.'

'So that's what he thinks I do here,' Zander murmured. 'Wine and whores.' A smile curled his lips as he remembered saying something similar to Ree, back when they'd only just met. 'Good to know he holds my work in such high esteem.'

'He means it, Zander,' Leo said gravely. 'If you don't come home this time, you'll no longer bear your father's name. Surely you realise that an insult of this magnitude sets every right-thinking Kardise man at odds with Mirrorvale?'

For the first time, Zander wondered if his father would have gone so far as to order the ambassador's death for the sole purpose of forcing his errant son back to Sol Kardis. He had, after all, been willing to put an entire peace treaty in jeopardy for that very same purpose. But the thought didn't last long, because although Marco Lepont might be a bossy old man with a stick up his arse who'd far rather go to war with strangers than understand them, he would never countenance anything as fundamentally chaotic as murder. The Mirrorvalese aphorism *killing is wrong except in law or at war* could have been written specifically for him. While hacking a man's limbs off was sometimes a necessary evil, it had to be done according to the rules.

'I suppose,' he said slowly, 'I must not be a right-thinking Kardise man, then. Because it hasn't yet been confirmed that Lady Ayla killed Don Tolino – and that being the case, cutting all ties with Mirrorvale would be an over-hasty step to take.'

'It's all but confirmed,' Leo replied. 'She was the only person with Tolino when he drank the poisoned liquor that killed him – and by her own admission, she was the one who gave it to him. I understand the Helm are going through the motions of an investigation, but it can only be a delaying tactic. The answer is clear enough.'

He gave Zander a sympathetic smile, as though he knew how much the truth must sting. And sting it did. Ree and Penn hadn't given the same picture at all, last time Zander had seen them. They'd talked about trying to find a traitor within Darkhaven's walls, someone who had killed Don Tolino and nearly killed Ayla in the process. They hadn't even mentioned the possibility that Ayla herself could have committed the crime, let alone that she was the only plausible suspect.

'So why do you think she admitted giving him the poisoned drink?' he asked, clutching at twigs because all the branches were broken. 'With so many possible opportunities to murder a man who was her guest, why would she choose to do it in such a way that suspicion fell squarely on her?'

Leo shrugged. 'Madness. That's what they say.' Then, perhaps reading the doubt on Zander's face, he added, 'Her brother ripped their father's throat out, Zander. Hardly a stable family background.'

A chill danced over Zander's skin. He didn't know Ayla. He'd seen her once or twice, that was all. But he knew Caraway, who loved her. And he knew Ree, who had become her friend. Surely both of them couldn't be mistaken in their regard?

'Changers have always been dangerous,' Leo said. 'By their very nature, they are just as much animal as man. And while you might make use of a wild animal, should the occasion arise, you can never trust it. How can you? Its motivations would be as alien to you as yours to it.'

'She's not –' Zander began, before realising he didn't know how to finish the sentence. Not dangerous? That wasn't true. Not wild? Hard to say. Unless you were a Helmsman, or another member of Darkhaven, there was little to go on beyond rumour. Most citizens of Arkannen had only ever seen their overlord as a swift golden flash of wings overhead, nearer than the sun but just as distantly involved in their lives – and he was no exception.

Instead, he said, 'I have friends here, you know that. Good people, whatever you may think of Ayla. It would be a hard choice to leave them.'

'Take a little time to consider it,' Leo said. 'But only a little. Your father expects me to depart from Mirrorvale again tomorrow, and he expects you to accompany me.'

A day? I can't decide in a day! I can't say goodbye to Ree and Penn, leave my job – Swallowing his protests, Zander gave a stiff, formal bow.

'All right, Leo. I will inform you of my decision in the morning.'

By the time he arrived at Ree's apartment that night, his head ached with conflicting worries. The Helm didn't have long to prove Ayla's innocence – and from what Leo had said, they were unlikely to succeed. That would lead inexorably to the war he'd feared since he first heard of Tolino's death. It seemed stupid to become utterly estranged from his father for the sake of staying in a country that would soon no longer want him.

And yet, if he left, he'd be leaving forever. Submit to his father's will this once, and he knew quite well he'd never find a way to defy it again. Was it really worth losing everything he loved in Arkannen out of fear of a conflict that might never come?

If Ayla was guilty, he'd be foolish to stay. But if Ayla was innocent, leaving Mirrorvale would mean abandoning his friends for a lie.

He thought he was concealing his turmoil as well as he ever did, using a smile as disguise. In fact, for a while, he was able to put it right to the back of his mind. As he and Ree cooked a late meal over a single gas burner in the shared kitchen, and he listened carefully to her account of her parents' unreasonable behaviour and her own predicament, he was conscious of no more than the desire to help her in whatever way he could. As they ate, huddled together on her saggy old armchair, he produced several suggestions of things she could do to put Lewis Tarran off marrying her – each more outlandish than the last – until he had her laughing once more. And as they tumbled into bed together, he forgot everything else in the world except the feel and the scent of her. Yet afterwards, she rested her head on his shoulder and murmured, 'Now maybe you'll tell me what's wrong with you.'

'What do you mean?'

'You keep looking at me like you're saying goodbye.'

He couldn't hide from her. She had always seen through him, right from the start. He sighed, staring up at the shadowed ceiling.

'Ree … you know Ayla quite well, don't you?'

'I suppose so.'

'How likely is it that she's telling the truth, do you think?'

He half expected her to rise up in fury. *You've been listening to your father. You think she's a murderer. You hate Mirrorvale.* But instead, she wriggled round until her legs were tangled with his and her upper body was far enough away that she could focus on his face. He turned his head; she wore a small frown.

'Do you want me to answer that question as a Helmsman, or as a woman?'

'Both.'

'All right. Well, as a Helmsman, I say of course Ayla is innocent. I've sworn my life to her service. I believe she is worth fighting for. But in the back of my mind, there's a little squirm of doubt. Because so far, we haven't found much evidence that points to anyone else. Because if there is another explanation, it's far more convoluted than the very simple one that's staring us in the face. And because she's not human. Not really. We tend to forget that, but it's true.'

'And as a woman?'

'As a woman ... I just can't believe she did it. I've seen her kill someone before, remember. She took her other form to do it. And I think ... I think, if she was going to kill someone again, it would be like that. Fierce and bloody. Not with poison.'

Zander opened his mouth to say something, but she put a finger to his lips.

'I've heard what some people are whispering,' she said earnestly. 'That there's darkness in the Nightshade line. That her brother was mad and so is she. But poison isn't the weapon of a madwoman, Zander! Poison is premeditated.'

'You didn't tell me she was alone with Tolino when he consumed the poison.'

'No,' Ree admitted. 'I didn't think it mattered.'

'Of course it matters! If she had a clear opportunity to administer it, then –'

'But that's just it. Everything points to her. *Everything*.

Which would have to mean she's either too stupid to have covered her tracks or too crazy to care, and I don't think she's either. Given that, it doesn't matter what evidence there is against her. The more damning it becomes, the less I believe it. What matters is finding out the truth. And after what we learned today at the distillery, I think it's at least possible that Penn and I are starting to do that.'

Doubtful, Zander said nothing. Ree grabbed his hand, gazing intently into his face.

'Think of it this way. I know Ayla a little, but I know Captain Caraway a lot better. *You* know him a lot better. So you must have seen how much he loves her, and how much he believes in her. If you trust his judgement, that should be enough.'

'I'm not sure,' Zander said miserably. 'People can be blinded by love.'

Ree nodded. 'But it can also help them see more clearly.'

I don't think I'd stay, if it weren't for my love for you. So does that mean I'm seeing more clearly, or that I'm blinded by you? Unable to look her in the eyes any longer, Zander turned away again. They lay side by side, gazing into the unimaginable future.

'I don't want to go,' he said softly.

'Then don't.'

'But I think I have to.'

'Then do.'

'Ree ...'

She propped herself up on her elbows to look down into his face. Unshed tears gleamed in her eyes.

'It has to be your decision, Zander,' she said. 'It's what you believe that's important, not me or your father or anyone else. I could try and convince you to stay, but if your heart tells you Ayla is guilty, you'd only resent me for it. And besides ... I'd be afraid for you, if you stay. I remember what was said about you, back when we first started here and the other trainees found out about the Kardise assassination threat. How much worse do you think it'll get if our countries go to war?'

Zander had thought of that already. He had, he realised, been hoping that Ree would talk him so decisively into staying that he wouldn't have to worry about it any more. It was the knowledge of his own unfairness, as much as anything, that drove him to say with a certain amount of petulance, 'Then you don't want me to stay?'

'I didn't say that, and you know it,' she retorted. 'I'm saying you don't get to use me as an excuse either way.'

'If I stay, my father will disown me.'

'You'd be in good company. Penn's family have already cast him off, and once I talk Lewis Tarran out of wanting to marry me, I daresay I'll be heading the same way.'

'I'd find it difficult,' Zander said softly. 'I don't want him to control my life, but ... I still want him to be my father. You know?'

'I know.'

They were silent. Then Ree added, 'Even if you do stay, it might be more difficult than you think. Many of the warriors in the fifth ring will be called to battle. Training might continue, but it will be training for war against your country. Will you be comfortable teaching your pupils the skills they require to kill the people you grew up with? And even if you are, will the weaponmasters believe it?'

'You're saying I might lose my job.'

She nodded. 'And if you do, you won't be able to stay in the fourth ring any more. They're strict on the requirements, you know that. If you're not related to someone here and you don't have a decent job, you get kicked out. That's what happened to Caraway before he became captain.' She gave him a sympathetic smile. 'Your life in Arkannen would change completely.'

'I could get another job.' But even as he said it, he knew it wasn't true. If the people who knew him best, the warriors of the fifth ring, were willing to mistrust him because of where he came from, why should the citizens of the lower rings have any problem doing the same? They'd look at him and see the enemy. Soon enough, he'd be reduced to nothing: no job, no money, nowhere to live. Faced with that, how long would it take before he ran back to Sol Kardis after all?

Of course, all this was no more than hypothetical – and just like that, he had a hypothetical answer.

'I could change my nationality,' he said, half joking. 'Secure my place in the fourth ring for good.'

Ree frowned at him. 'How?'

'It would solve your problem as well. Quite ingenious, really.'

'Zander –'

'I mean, think about it. Your parents wouldn't be able to marry you off to someone else, and I –'

'*Zander*. We are *not* getting married.'

'Why not?'

'Because that's not who we are.'

'I love you.'

'And I love you. What does that have to do with it?'

He was silent, and she added, 'It wouldn't help, anyway. Sure, you could live here with me –' her gesture took in her tiny bedroom – 'but having a Mirrorvalese wife wouldn't get you a job. How long do you think you'd be able to stick it out, with nothing to do, knowing your birth country and your adopted country were tearing each other apart?'

'But I'd be able to stay in Arkannen,' he said softly.

'Why does that matter so much to you?'

'Because it's my home, now. Because you're here, and Penn. Because I'm more myself here than I ever was in my father's house ...' He paused, then added slowly, 'And because, whatever the evidence says, I don't believe Ayla is a murderer.'

He looked at Ree. She was smiling.

'Well, then,' she said. 'I guess you're staying.'

TWELVE

Caraway had called a halt to the current Helm assessment period as soon as he'd found out the cause of Don Tolino's death; with the Kardise allowing him only a week to investigate, he couldn't spare much time for anything else. Yet nor could he stay out of the fifth ring entirely. As well as uncovering a murderer, he had to prepare for a war he hoped would never come. Ayla had already arranged for reinforcements to be sent to the border – not enough to be an obvious threat, but certainly enough to be a first line of defence – and Caraway was busy building an army. He'd spoken to the weaponmasters, asked them to send out word across Mirrorvale for anyone who had trained in the fifth ring to be ready to return to the city. That way, if she needed to, Ayla could call up a host of fully prepared warriors within the space of a day. Many of the weaponmasters themselves would take command positions, while the rest stayed behind to train the reserves.

He and Ayla had briefly considered requesting help from elsewhere, if it came to it. The long civil war in the Ingal States had left the lords of the demesnes with no capacity to involve themselves in the affairs of other countries, but

Parovia was another matter. It had been the bitter enemy of Sol Kardis for centuries, so there was no chance it would take the Kardise side in any war – thankfully, given that if the two large countries ever combined forces, they would crush Mirrorvale between them like a nut. The obvious question, therefore, was whether Parovia would be willing to stand alongside Mirrorvale if it meant standing against Sol Kardis.

Unfortunately, Ayla and Caraway had soon reached the conclusion that the price would be too high. Mirrorvale and Parovia might currently be at peace, but that didn't make them allies. Too great a weight of history lay behind them: centuries in which Parovia and Sol Kardis had eyed each other across Mirrorvale like two dogs coveting the same bone. Any aid that came from Parovia would be accompanied by demands: concessions here, information there, a hundred little things that moved Mirrorvale closer to being a vassal state rather than a country in its own right. Not only that, but asking for help would give the impression of weakness – and Mirrorvale had always to appear strong if it were to survive. Which meant, if war did come, it would have to stand alone.

Caraway hoped desperately that matters would never reach that stage. Even if he couldn't unmask Tolino's murderer in the time allowed, he'd keep working to find the culprit before the war progressed too far. But if he failed, and the casualties started mounting, it would be his job to call up the reserves. Anyone between the ages of sixteen and twenty-five. Anyone between the ages of fourteen and forty. Anyone old enough to carry a sword and young enough to run with it. Anyone at all. He knew how it went, the relentless culling of the population in wartime, an expanding net that dragged everyone in. He'd have to watch them arrive at the fifth ring, go through a hasty few weeks' training and be sent out to die. Until, finally, the Kardise army reached the walls of Arkannen, and he and the Helmsmen who hadn't gone with Ayla to the border made their last, desperate stand to protect Darkhaven. To protect Ayla's children, and the future of Mirrorvale itself.

That was the worst-case scenario. Sometimes he found himself losing sight of the best.

And through it all, a little voice whispered to him that he was doing a terrible job. That it had been a mistake for him ever to take up the role of Captain of the Helm, and that if he'd thought about what was best for Ayla then he never would have done it. Because the truth was, he had very little idea of how to plan for a war. He'd been trained primarily in defence; the Helm weren't meant to be an attacking force. If Ayla had appointed an experienced soldier, the man might have stood a chance. But what did Caraway have? A year or so as a young Helmsman. Five as an outcast. And six years as captain, during which time he'd almost convinced himself he was doing well. Easy enough to believe he was good at the job when in reality, he simply hadn't been challenged hard enough to show otherwise.

Of course, he wouldn't have to lead the army. Ayla would. He wouldn't even see the battlefield. But that made it even more important that he get everything right.

He was in the middle of another long discussion with the weaponmasters when a message arrived that the Captain of the Watch needed to speak to him with some urgency. No doubt there had been a firearms-related incident. The problem of illegal weapons in the city seemed far less significant to him now than it had even a week ago, but nevertheless, it was part of his job. He couldn't have Arkannen breaking out in self-inflicted violence as well as everything else. So half a bell later, when his conversation with the weaponmasters concluded, he went in search of Larson – finally running her to ground in one of the older watch houses, down in the first ring's leisure quarter.

'You wanted to see me,' he said, ducking under the lintel to enter the small holding cell that was currently acting as a makeshift office. The Captain of the Watch looked up from the report she was frowning over.

'Ah, Caraway. Thank you for coming.'

'Is it another shooting?' He'd been relieved to find that his dire predictions regarding the number of firearm-related deaths in the city had not entirely come to pass. Though the collection of confiscated firearms in Darkhaven's safe had grown steadily, it hadn't been as rapid as he'd expected. And though in his more doubtful moments he wondered if that was because people had simply become better at hiding their illegal weaponry, rather than because the Helm and the Watch between them had succeeded in greatly reducing the flow from Sol Kardis, there was no denying that the number of shootings in Arkannen had plateaued. There were still more of them every year than he'd have liked, but not as many as he'd feared. Maybe a few gory deaths had taught people caution. Or maybe arming the Helm with pistols had helped. He and Larson had discussed that last point a few times over the past year, when she'd tried to convince him that the Watch should carry firearms too.

How are we supposed to defend ourselves, otherwise? she'd asked him, quite heatedly. *We're the ones who have to deal with every damn fool who thinks waving a gun around makes him invincible.*

I understand, he'd replied. *I really do. But overall, I think it would only escalate the situation. If you demand firearms to protect yourselves from our citizens, next thing we know, the citizens will be demanding firearms to protect themselves from* you. *Giving pistols to the Watch would legitimise them as a weapon.*

She'd skewered him with a sceptical glance. *And giving them to the Helm doesn't?*

Not in the same way, no. We've always been separate. We're meant to be separate. Our job is to protect our overlords, and we do whatever it takes to achieve that. The Watch, on the other hand ... you belong to the people. And that means there can't be one law for you, and another for them.

That's Lady Ayla's opinion, is it?

Only mine.

She'd snorted. *Comes to the same thing.*

That's what you think, Caraway had said. *I assure you, Captain Larson, our overlord disagrees with me at least half the time. So don't let me dissuade you from taking your case to her.*

Despite that, Larson hadn't yet approached Ayla. Perhaps she still hoped to convince Caraway first; perhaps she was more frightened of Changers than she let on; perhaps she'd even been swayed by his argument. Stranger things had happened. Whatever the truth of it, he'd come here fully expecting a firearm-related death and all the debates that went with it – but to his surprise, Larson shook her head.

'Nothing to do with pistols, for once. I need you to identify a body.'

'I'm sorry?'

Setting the report aside, she got to her feet. 'We've a dead girl in the chiller, and I need you to identify her for me. Got a few moments?'

'Of course. But who –'

'I'll explain as we go.'

They left the watch house and walked in the direction of the mortuary. Caraway waited patiently for the promised explanation, but Larson wore a preoccupied frown and seemed lost in her own thoughts. They were already more than halfway to their destination when she shook her head briskly, shot a sideways glance at Caraway as though she'd forgotten he was there, and said, 'Right, then.'

'You were going to tell me about your victim?' he prompted.

'Yes. She was found in an alley, the night before last. Stabbed. Missing coin-purse. No sign of any sexual motive for the crime. Looked like a simple mugging.'

'I see,' Caraway said, although he didn't. 'So ...'

'There was nothing on her to show who she was. Her dress was pretty but inexpensive, the kind of thing half the girls in the city wear on a night out. We drew up a sketch yesterday morning, took it around, asked questions – nothing. No-one in the lower rings recognised her as an employee. No-one in the fourth ring identified her as lover, relative, friend. But then ...'

By now they had reached the mortuary, an underground room built with thick stone walls and no windows. Larson descended the steps and swung open the door, releasing a wintry draught. Responding to the impatient glance she cast over her shoulder, Caraway followed.

'Then, we came across a woman who thought the sketch looked like a friend of her sister's. She said both girls worked in Darkhaven.' While she talked, Larson was leading him past benches and rows of tools to a table at the far end of the dimly lit room, where the unmistakable shape of a body lay beneath a sheet. 'And of course, your maids live in the tower, don't they? So that would explain why we couldn't trace her down in the city.'

She twitched back the sheet, and Caraway found himself looking into the face of a girl. Her skin held the greyish tinge of the dead, but her blonde hair and small, regular features were undeniably familiar. After a few desperate, blank moments, he was able to put a name to her.

'Hana,' he said softly.

'You do recognise her, then? She's one of yours?'

'Yes. She is – was – a maid in Darkhaven, just as you said.' To himself, he added, 'Most mornings, she brought us breakfast.'

'Good.' Larson lifted the sheet to draw it back into place. Caraway rounded on her almost savagely.

'I wouldn't put it that way!'

The Captain of the Watch looked steadily at him, but said nothing. Because he'd been unfair. He'd been aware of it even as he made his response. Both of them had known perfectly well what Larson meant. He took a deep breath, running a hand over his face as if he could wipe away the fruitless anger.

'I'm sorry. Really. I just – she was very young.'

Larson nodded. Her job was far more difficult than his, Caraway thought dully. It was rare that he had to deal with the aftermath of murder. But he kept seeing Hana's face in his mind's eye – both the way it was now, and the way it had been last time he saw her – and so he said nothing as Larson finished covering the dead girl and led him away down the room.

'I'm sorry,' he said again, when they were back in the smoky air of the street. She waved a dismissive hand at him.

'Forget it.'

'Do you have any idea who did it?'

'Not yet.' Larson sighed. 'To be honest, Caraway, it's not likely we'll find out. Whoever it was disposed of her very neatly: the maximum amount of damage with the minimum amount of mess. Probably didn't even get blood on his clothes.' She shook her head. 'And all for the sake of a few coins.'

The preoccupied frown had already settled back on her face, Caraway noticed.

'Is something worrying you, Captain Larson?' he asked. 'More than this, I mean.'

She shrugged. 'Trouble brewing in the city. Nothing I can't handle. But Caraway …' She gave him a level look. 'Sort out this Kardise business, will you?'

He nodded, feeling suddenly tired. 'I'm trying.'

'I didn't know what to make of you, in the beginning,' Larson said. 'Too young for it. There for all the wrong reasons. You've done well enough, as it happens. But war …' She shook her head. 'That's another beast entirely.'

'I know.' He had nothing better to offer than to say again, 'I'm trying.'

She clapped him on the shoulder – as stoic as ever, but her eyes held a hint of sympathy. 'I know.'

After they'd parted, Caraway walked slowly back up through the rings towards Darkhaven. He couldn't stop thinking about the murdered girl, and he knew it was partly because he felt responsible. Not that the Helm had any official duty to protect anyone who wasn't a Nightshade, of course. But as their captain, his protective instinct extended to his men, too; and naturally, over time, that instinct had widened to encompass everyone who lived and worked in the tower, whether warrior or servant, physician or alchemist. A girl who fell under his care had been killed, and he hadn't prevented it. He hadn't even known about it.

Worse than that, he had the terrible, guilty feeling that he could have done something, if he'd only put a little thought into it.

Because this wasn't a random crime, or at least, he didn't think it was. *Talk to Hana* had been on his long list of tasks that needed doing ever since Ree and Penn had returned from interviewing the other maid, Sia. Hana had gone with Sia to fetch the taransey; she might have been the one to ensure the correct bottle was picked. But they'd been unable to ask her about it, because it was her day off.

If Caraway had taken it seriously – if he'd tried to find her that afternoon – then maybe he'd have prevented one murder as well as solving another. Instead, he'd decided it could wait until she was back ... and that very same night, she'd been killed.

Of course, it could be a tragic coincidence. Yet when he'd first heard of the ambassador's death, he'd thought to himself that when it came to dead men, there was no such thing as coincidence – and that went for dead women, too. He couldn't recall another time that a servant from Darkhaven had been killed, either during his time in the Helm under Captain Travers or in the past six years since he'd taken on the captaincy. In fact, setting aside the rash of fatal shootings, murder wasn't all that common in Arkannen generally. Injuries of all kinds, certainly – people didn't seem happy unless they were racing or brawling or blowing themselves up with unstable machinery. But not death.

Surely it wasn't paranoia to surmise that these two murders, a Kardise ambassador and a Darkhaven maid, were connected.

And in that case, he needed to find out what Hana had known that was so significant, so incriminating, that it had required her death. Uncover that, and maybe it would lead him to the longed-for proof that Ayla wasn't guilty.

He also needed to find out why no-one had told him Hana was missing.

When he got back to the tower, he went straight in search of Diann Rawleigh. He found her in her living room, making entries in the ledger that held the household accounts, but she rose to her feet as soon as she saw him and gave the very tiny curtsey that she reserved for him and Ayla alone. Caraway suspected she considered herself to be the third most important person in Darkhaven – and she was probably right, at that. As a Helmsman, he had known very little of the day-to-day running of the tower, and cared even less; but as Ayla's husband, he was fully aware of how much work it took to put food on multiple tables multiple times a day, launder clothing and bedsheets, and keep every room in the rambling maze that was Darkhaven clean, warm and illuminated. It was a logistical problem no less complex than waging a war, only it never came to an end. And the men of Darkhaven – the Helm, the physician, the handful of clerks and officials – very rarely noticed it. To them, the people who served their meals, washed their linen and cleaned their floors were barely more than invisible.

It wasn't just the men. Ayla didn't see them either.

Before I admitted Ree to the Helm, you told me it was lonely not having any other women in Darkhaven, he'd said to her once. *But there have always been women here. The maids. The kitchen staff. The housekeeper.*

She'd given him a blank look. *They're servants, Tomas.*

It was the first time she'd ever said something that made him genuinely angry. He had to swallow several heated responses before managing to say, quite mildly, *If it comes to that, so am I.*

You're my husband.

I was your employee first.

Perhaps hearing some of his imperfectly suppressed emotion in his voice, she studied his face for a long, silent moment before replying.

After my mother died, there was a girl ... Lily, her name was, like the flower. She was my maid. She spoke to me kindly a few times, when I'd been crying and couldn't hide it. We became ... not exactly friends, I suppose, but close enough to hold a proper conversation. Sometimes she'd come to my room when she'd finished her daily duties and I'd finished my lessons, and we'd talk ... A half-smile touched Ayla's face, then faded again. *When my father found out, he sent her away. Just like that. She had nowhere to go, no other job to take, and he had her thrown out of Darkhaven with no more than the clothes she was wearing.*

Ayla –

I argued with him, of course. I told him it wasn't her fault, she was just doing as I asked her. I told him I'd needed a friend. He said, 'We don't have friends, Ayla. We have subjects. And the sooner you accept that, the happier you'll be.'

Caraway nodded. *I understand.*

I'm not sure you do, Tomas. She took his hand in tacit apology for the contradiction. *I'm doing the best I can to be a good person and a good overlord, but those two things aren't always the same. I can't be friendly with the servants.*

A little more so with the Helm, but even there I have to keep my distance.

But –

I was brought up to set myself apart. To believe I was better than everyone else. Her laugh had a jagged edge to it. *Not as good as my father or Myrren, of course – not as good as a pure-blood – but still a Nightshade. And whether I believe it or not, I have to behave that way. Because that's what everyone expects of me! I have to be separate, and I have to be feared. Otherwise people will stop believing in my right to rule them, and that's as sure a way to end the Nightshade line as any.*

Caraway had turned the subject, then, and let that particular conversation die. The truth was, he understood better than she thought. He was, after all, married to her. Their relationship might be one of equality in private, but in public he deferred to her as her Captain of the Helm should. He was well aware of both the difficulty and the importance of maintaining appearances. Yet he couldn't help but feel that there was a difference between keeping a proper distance and treating people as if they were no more than furniture. No ... that wasn't quite fair. Ayla was polite to her staff. If they had problems or grievances, she listened to them and treated them fairly. But she didn't *care* about them, not in the way she cared about Bryan and Miles and some of the younger Helmsmen.

He couldn't fault her for it, really, on a practical level. She had a whole country to protect. But his responsibility was limited to Darkhaven, and as such, he couldn't help but care.

For that reason, he got Rawleigh to sit down before breaking the news, as gently as he could, of Hana's death.

He had seen her react to various disasters before with a remarkable degree of calmness, so he wasn't surprised when she didn't cry or even make a sound. What he hadn't expected, though, was the averted gaze and the flush of colour staining her cheeks. She was upset, yes, but she also felt guilty.

He didn't press her on it, merely talked through the details and whether anyone might need to be notified. It was only as the conversation drew to a close that Rawleigh's lips pressed together briefly, as if she had made up her mind to an unpleasant task, and she said, 'Captain Caraway? There is something I need to tell you.'

He gave her an encouraging smile, and waited.

'Two days ago, it was Hana's day off. She should have returned to the tower that evening, ready for work the next day, but as I understand it she … ah, she didn't. Another of the maids, Sia, came to me yesterday morning and told me that Hana hadn't returned. I told her to wait a little longer – it happens from time to time, that a servant disappears on us, and usually it's because they've fallen ill or enjoyed their time off rather more than they should have. Nothing more serious than that.

'Anyway, Sia came back at the end of the day. Hana still hadn't showed up. Sia was worried, so I told her I'd take it up with you or with Lady Ayla …' The housekeeper hesitated for only a fraction of a moment before concluding, 'But I didn't. My apologies, Captain Caraway.'

'Why didn't you?' he asked, and the hint of discomfort in her face became more prominent.

'I … Captain Travers never wanted to be bothered with that kind of thing. It wasn't Nightshade business, so it wasn't his concern. And I didn't judge it appropriate to approach Lady Ayla with such a trivial matter.'

'Not trivial,' Caraway said, with more steel than he'd intended. 'A girl is dead.'

Her spine stiffened. 'I wasn't to know that.'

He let her stew in it a moment before conceding the point. 'No. And though it was for the wrong reasons, I think you were right not to take it to Ayla. But for my part ...' Seeing how offended she still looked, he softened his tone. 'Please keep me informed of anything like that in the future, Rawleigh. Please. If someone is missing from Darkhaven, I need to know about it.'

'Why?'

Was it really such an odd request that she needed to ask? Caraway frowned at her. 'Because that way, if someone is in trouble, I have the best chance of doing something about it. Why else?'

She gave him a level stare, but said nothing.

'I couldn't have done anything for Hana, as it happens,' he added. 'She was killed before Sia even knew she was missing. But on another occasion, things might be different.'

The housekeeper looked at him a moment longer. Then she said calmly, 'Would you like a cup of tea, Captain Caraway?'

By the time he left her, she had unbent towards him more than she ever had before, and it was clear that his request had borne completely unexpected fruit: Diann Rawleigh had given him her approval. It was something he hadn't even realised he was missing, until it was bestowed upon him. Perhaps that should have pleased him, but instead it left him itching with unease. Six years he'd been in Darkhaven, now, and yet the housekeeper had misjudged him enough to believe a missing maid would be beneath his notice. Had his predecessor left him other legacies that were yet to be discovered?

Struggles and concealments that had been the way of life under Owen Travers, never coming to Caraway's notice because he simply didn't know they existed?

In the months after he'd married Ayla, he had met some resistance from Darkhaven's staff. The Helm took it in their stride; they had come together as a fully coherent unit under his captaincy by then, and it made little difference to them whether he was their overlord's lover or her husband. But the rest of the community, particularly those who had been there since Florentyn was overlord and Travers was captain ... to them, apparently, there was a big difference. It was by no means unknown for a Nightshade overlord to take a common lover, but exceedingly rare for the affair to end in marriage. Of course, there was the recent precedent of Ayla's mother Kati, but she had one very important factor in her favour: she hadn't worked in Darkhaven before she married Florentyn. Whereas Caraway, who had started out as a mere Helmsman ... they saw him as an upstart. His marriage to Ayla crossed that invisible line between the Nightshades and their subjects, in a way they couldn't approve or comprehend. There had been whispers about his sudden rise: *came from less than nothing to be Captain of the Helm,* the gossip ran, *and now this?*

They had expected him to be untrustworthy. To bully them. To push Ayla aside and take control – as if, he thought with a smile, anyone could push Ayla aside unless she wanted to be pushed. But that was what Owen Travers would have tried to do. *For the good of the Nightshade line*; no doubt that's what he would have told himself, while he pursued his own desire for power. And Darkhaven's staff had no reason to believe any better of Caraway. He might have helped Ayla against Travers, but who was to say it was for acceptable reasons? One ambitious, ruthless man was much like another.

Caraway would have protested he was neither ambitious nor ruthless ... except he'd killed Travers, hadn't he? That was ruthless enough. And if loving Ayla Nightshade could be classed as ambitious simply by virtue of who she was, he was that as well. Besides, denying a rumour only ever gave it more credence. So he'd dealt with it by ignoring the mutters and the sidelong looks, and offering every single member of Darkhaven his trust. Sometimes, to convince people to trust you, you had to trust them first. He'd thought it was working, too ... but maybe it hadn't worked as well as he'd hoped.

If he had done more, would Hana still be alive?

It was a stupid thought. Her death had occurred while everyone had still believed her to be enjoying her day off. And though he might wonder if it was linked to the ambassador's murder, he didn't know that for sure, or have any reason to believe she would have confided in him even if she'd known him better. But he let himself feel the guilt anyway, because if there was one thing he'd found about guilt, it was that it drove him to improve things.

All the same, it burned in him as he found Hana's friend, Sia, in the kitchens and took her aside to give her the news. He'd never seen such instant devastation on anyone's face before. She wrapped her arms around herself, shoulders shaking, tears rolling down her cheeks, while he stood there in silence – wishing he could help her, but knowing it was the kind of pain that had no cure.

'I'm sorry,' she said finally. Caraway shook his head.

'No need to be. It's a horrible thing to have happened.'

She looked up, scrubbing the tears from her eyes with the back of one wrist in a gesture that made her seem very young. 'Did they catch him?'

'Not yet.' He saw no point in repeating Larson's pessimism to her, so he simply added, 'They're doing everything they can.'

'Bastard,' she said fiercely. 'I hope he rots.' Colour flooding her cheeks, she turned her gaze down to the floor. 'Sorry, sir.'

'No need,' Caraway said again. 'I feel the same way.'

He let her cry a little longer, before asking, 'Sia ... you say *he* and *him*. Was there someone Hana was close to? Someone you think might have ...'

Leaving the suggestion open-ended had the desired effect; the maid frowned at her shoes before saying slowly, 'I'm not sure.' She shot a quick, nervous glance up at him. 'I didn't tell them before. The lady Helmsman, and the man you sent. I didn't want to get Hana in trouble.'

She still seemed to be hesitating over it, so Caraway said gently, 'Whatever it is, it can't hurt her now. And it might help us find her killer.'

'It's just ... the day the ambassador came, she was dead excited. More than usual, I mean, and she always acted a glass over sober anyway ...' Sia sniffed back tears. 'She was giggly all through us fetching the taransey, and even more when I came back to the kitchen after delivering it. She brushed it off when I asked her about it, but I figured she'd fallen in love with someone. She falls in love a lot.' A pause, before the inevitable sad amendment. 'Fell.'

'So then ...'

'Well, next day we heard the ambassador had died. Hana was subdued, but so were we all – I mean, it was an awful thing, wasn't it? Her reaction didn't strike me as odd. But two days later, when we found out he'd been murdered ... that was different. She was sad, withdrawn. Maybe even a bit scared. She couldn't concentrate on her work at all. I asked her what was wrong, and she said she was trying to decide whether she should confess to something.'

'Did you find out what?'

Sia shook her head. 'I tried to get it out of her, but all she said was, *He told me it would help.*'

'He told me it would help,' Caraway echoed. 'Who do you think she meant?'

Sia wiped her eyes again. 'I don't know. I'm sorry.'

'No, that's fine,' he reassured her. 'You've been very helpful.'

Shortly after that he left her, feeling more than a little perturbed. His instinct had been correct: Hana had been connected to the ambassador's death in some way. It was proof, if he'd needed any, of Ayla's innocence – though he knew the Kardise wouldn't take it as such. Hana had known something, and now Hana too was dead.

The trouble was, he had absolutely no way of finding out what.

THIRTEEN

Crouched in the alley between two warehouses, Sorrow dropped a pair of dice onto the cracked stone in front of her and glanced casually over her opponent's shoulder as she did so. The warehouses on the other side of the street were identical to those that currently provided her cover, but she was only interested in one of them. Four men had walked through its front door not long ago, and they were yet to re-emerge.

'Oi,' her opponent said, wiping his nose on the back of one hand. She wasn't sure of his age – probably twelve or thirteen – but the flick of his wrist as he spun the dice across the pavement suggested a long familiarity with games of chance. 'You playin' or what?'

'Yes.' Paying scant attention to the uppermost faces of the dice, she pushed a coin towards him. She'd followed the four men from the docks, where they'd been part of a barge crew. The part most trusted by its owner, presumably. They'd waited until the shipment of fine fabrics was unloaded and the rest of the crew had gone before starting a second unloading process, this time from the hidden compartments in the base of the boat. Illegal firearms. They'd brought them to this warehouse, and taken them inside, and now she was trying to decide what to do next.

'You're bettin' silver on a *five*?' the boy said. 'Must be pretty sure of yer luck.'

'Hasn't let me down so far.' Sorrow turned her gaze back to the game in time to see him cast; each of the seven-sided dice showed a single pip. *Two*. She raised her eyebrows at him. 'Well?'

He scowled. 'Best of three?'

'I've already won twice.'

'Best of five, then?'

'If you say so.' She scooped up the dice, then raised her head sharply as a door opened on the other side of the street. Three men left the warehouse, one by one, the last of them locking it behind him. Sorrow studied the dice as each of them passed, apparently intent on her game to the exclusion of all else, but her mind was racing. *Three men*. What had happened to the last one?

She was going to have to find out.

Without another word, she pushed herself to her feet and jogged across the street towards the warehouse.

'Hey!' the boy called after her. 'We got a game goin' here, lady! What about yer stake?'

She glanced back over her shoulder. 'You can keep it. Now get lost.'

He didn't need telling twice. He scrabbled the assorted coins up from the ground and took to his heels as if a rabid dog were chasing him. Once he'd disappeared round the corner, Sorrow examined the warehouse. The door was locked, of course, and the windows tightly shuttered. There'd be another, larger door on the other side of the building – something big enough to admit a cart, for cargoes that were safe to show in public – but no doubt that was equally secure. However, like many of the larger warehouses, it probably had a loading hatch set into its flat roof, allowing small airships to unload their cargoes straight through it. And into the wall to one side of the door were set some crumbling rungs, presumably to provide a way out in case of fire. They looked narrow and treacherous, designed for emergency exit rather than entrance, but a determined enough person should be able to climb them.

She went at it in a rush, getting halfway up the building through momentum alone. After that it was a slow, painful matter of jamming fingers and toes into whatever insufficient crevices presented themselves, and hoping for the best. She nearly fell off twice, but finally she crawled over the side of the warehouse and onto the roof. In comparison, getting the hatch open was easy; though it was locked and bolted from the inside, the hinges were exposed, allowing her to unscrew them.

Once she'd eased the door downward as noiselessly as she could, she stuck her head through the hole. As her eyes became accustomed to the dimness inside, she saw that the hatch lined up with a square opening in the floorboarded rafters of the loft, creating a channel for goods to be lowered all the way down to the warehouse floor below. It was a long drop. If she screwed it up she'd break a leg, or worse. And so she went for it before she could change her mind, hanging by her hands from the hatch frame and swinging herself past the gaping hole to land on the loft floor beyond.

Her landing sent a thud reverberating around the loft, and also produced a large cloud of dust. She crouched where she was for a while in silence, holding her breath so that she wouldn't sneeze and straining to listen above the rush of her heartbeat for any sounds from the warehouse below. There was nothing. Slowly she rose to her feet and set off across the floor, stepping from rafter to rafter to avoid the holes in the worm-eaten floorboards.

As she moved further away from the hatch and its square of daylight, the shadows descended and it became harder to see where she was putting her feet. She began to wonder if this was a fool's errand. Yet then, as she approached the front of the loft, she finally heard something: a metal clunk, the creak of a door, a low murmur of voices. Crouching again, she peered down through the nearest gap and caught a glimpse of lamplight. Several people were passing beneath her. Hard to tell how many, since only one of them carried a lamp – and that was telling in itself. If they'd been here on legitimate business, they'd have unshuttered the windows and thrown open the vast doors at the front of the building to let in the daylight.

She tracked the orange glow through the cracks beneath her feet, following it further away from the hatch she'd entered by and into the deeper darkness. Finally it stopped, and again she heard the murmur of voices. The light flared brighter through a gap ahead of her, as though the single lamp had been joined by several others. Acutely conscious, now, of even the slightest creaking sound caused by her movements across the floor of the loft, she lowered herself to her stomach and eased forward along the nearest rafter until she could see through the gap. Yet it didn't help much. Although she now had a clear view of the half-dozen people standing in a tight circle below her, ringed by lamps, all of them were hooded and masked. She couldn't make out any identifying features, only the glitter of eyes and the muffled murmur of voices.

Bloody stupid theatrics. Like children playing at revolution. It was almost funny, until she remembered that it could very well lead to war. If these people really had murdered the ambassador then they were too dangerous to laugh at, silly masks or not.

She lay still, breathing as quietly as she could, trying to pick out their voices; yet the damn masks distorted everything. She might as well have been listening from outside the warehouse – would have been a damn sight safer, too. Then one voice lifted forcefully above the rest, and finally she was able to distinguish individual words.

'She's done her job. Now we need to keep her quiet.'

'Yes, but surely ...' The second speaker sank back into a mumble. Sorrow gritted her teeth in silent frustration and waited for something more audible.

'... useful ... someone in Darkhaven ...'

'I don't think ... outweighs the risk ...'

She couldn't make out the whole of the rest, but from their gestures and the rise and fall of their voices, the thing she wasn't hearing was an argument. According to the snatches of conversation she could piece together, the group had an agent in Darkhaven who had performed a task on their behalf – though whether that was poisoning the ambassador or something else, it was impossible to tell. Three of the six seemed to be arguing that this mysterious girl could be useful again in the future; the others thought she was a liability. One of the latter was a softly spoken man who had been the one to connect them with the girl in the first place. His chief opponent was a tall man who spoke with the accent of the Mirrorvalese elite and gave the impression of being in charge. He was of the opinion that being able to pass on orders to someone on the inside was worth any degree of risk.

'Well, then,' he said at last, raising his voice just enough that the individual words became distinct. 'At least we can all agree that it's important to make sure she doesn't talk.'

'I am glad to hear you say so,' the softly spoken man replied. 'Because, as it happens, I have already taken care of it.'

'What does that mean?'

He shrugged. 'I silenced her for good.'

'*What?*' That was nearly a shout. One or two of the masked men glanced over their shoulders; they moved in closer still, and the indistinct murmurs began again. Sorrow made out just a single word: *murder*.

She pressed her cheek against the splintered wood, her heart thudding against her ribcage. So, the softly spoken man had taken matters into his own hands. He had brought the girl on board, and disposed of her just as easily. Which meant she'd been right: these people were dangerous, despite their melodramatics. If they could kill one of their own with such little care, then they'd have no hesitation in dispatching Sorrow herself, if they caught her.

Admittedly, the rest of the group hadn't known about the murder. But listening to them, she heard no remonstrations with the softly spoken man for his actions, only a certain amount of anxiety that the crime shouldn't be traced back to them.

'What's done is done,' the rich man said finally. 'As long as her death can't be connected to …'

And then it was all mumbling again, broken by the occasional phrase that suggested more than it revealed.

'The Helm already know … asking questions about the taransey …'

'… believe the seal was tampered with. So there is nothing to connect …'

'... unaware of the antidote. That part remains our secret.'

Finally, the rich man held up his hands for silence, projecting his voice even through the mask.

'Thank you, brothers. We have done well. We have brought an end to the false peace that would have been a betrayal of everything our country stands for. Soon the Kardise scourge will come to an end. We will drive them from our towns and cities, crush them at the border, and Mirrorvale will belong to the Mirrorvalese once more!'

Each of the six figures extended a hand into the centre of the circle; six voices spoke as one. *Free Arkannen.*

'Good night,' the rich man said. 'I will send word of our next meeting time and place through the usual channels.'

They began to disperse, each taking a lamp and carrying it off through the darkness towards the door; yet the ringleaders, rich man and softly spoken man, remained where they were, conversing in whispers. Sorrow scrambled to her feet as quietly as she could, using the noise of the others' departure to cover her own. If she was quick, she could get back out to the street before the final two conspirators emerged. That way, maybe she'd have the chance to find out who they were.

She picked her way back to the square of daylight on the other side of the loft, leapt out across the plummeting drop below with scant regard for anything so limiting as safety, and caught the frame of the open hatch with both hands. Once she'd hauled herself back up to the roof, she darted across – keeping low – and peered down over the side of the building. If anyone caught her climbing down the fire ladder, she'd be a goner for sure.

Two of the men were already disappearing in different directions down the street; as she watched, two more left the warehouse and did the same. Once she could no longer see the second pair, she swung her legs off the roof of the warehouse and descended the ladder in a rush, hoping the final two had been in deep enough conversation to delay them a while longer. She landed just as the door swung open again, and whisked herself round the corner of the building, where she flattened herself against the wall and tried not to breathe loudly. Had they seen her? She thought not. A few more low-voiced words were exchanged, before one of the men in his hooded cloak passed by the mouth of her alley. The softly spoken man.

She hesitated only a moment. He was the one who'd murdered a girl; he was the one who had been able to offer a connection inside Darkhaven. Uncovering his identity must surely be the most beneficial action she could take.

She stole to the end of the alley and peeped out. The rich man was striding away in the opposite direction. The softly spoken man hadn't stopped or turned; he must not have seen her. So she followed him. Along the street, round the corner, back towards the canal –

He glanced over his shoulder. She glimpsed the mask beneath his hood, still in place despite the fact that he was walking in broad daylight. For an instant she froze, reaching for a weapon, thinking him about to return for her.

Then he broke into a jog, slipped down a side alley, and was gone.

She stood and swore for a moment, but only a moment. Because she might not have succeeded at identifying any of the group, but she'd still gained some valuable information. She'd take it to Caraway and see what he made of it.

Later that day, once she'd sent a message up through the city and received a meeting-place and time in response, she and Caraway sat in an inn – which was, admittedly, a far more sensible location than last time – while she related what she'd overheard. He listened in silence, occasionally scribbling a note.

'Interesting,' he said when she'd finished. 'So how, exactly, did you identify this group in the first place?'

'By the content of their barges.' Sorrow smirked at his obvious confusion. 'Trade is a wonderful weather-vane, Captain Caraway. I assume you've noticed that in summer, the merchants' investors request ice, and in the winter they demand firewood? When a new factory opens on Canalside, the price of coal goes up. When we have a good harvest, the price of wheat goes down. And in times of peace, people stop smuggling black-market weaponry into the city, because demand for it lessens and so the profit they can make isn't worth the risk.'

'All right,' Caraway said doubtfully. 'What's your point?'

'My point is that when it comes to wealthy investors, there is nothing more predictable than money. They chase it like hounds on the scent. And so when I heard that one particular set of barges was due to bring a vast shipment of illegal firearms into the city, despite the impending peace treaty between us and Sol Kardis, it got me asking questions.'

'You mean ...'

'When the news broke of the ambassador's murder, the price of a pistol doubled almost instantly,' Sorrow said. 'So I had to wonder whether the investor behind my barges had known about it in advance.'

'Which he had, if the conversation you just described is anything to go by,' Caraway agreed. 'I'm impressed, Naeve.'

She shrugged. 'I know this city far better than you and your men. Well, maybe not you. The years you spent drowning your guilt in the lower rings must have been good for something. But a lot of your young Helmsmen come to the fifth ring, do their training and disappear into the tower. They never feel the city in their veins like I do.'

'So who is the investor?' Caraway asked, dismissing the insult to the Helm with a wave of his hand. 'I'll bring him in for questioning as soon as –'

'I don't know,' Sorrow interrupted before he could get too enthusiastic. 'I looked into it, of course. But the merchants who run those barges were all commissioned by Jack Malone.'

'Jack Malone,' he repeated. 'Why does that sound familiar?'

She rolled her eyes at his blank expression. 'It's the name investors use when they don't want to be identified. Stops them being tied to any illegal activity.'

'All right. That's useful to know.' He flicked back through the pages of his notebook. 'But there's also something I've heard recently ... ah. Damn it.'

'What?'

'Jack Malone is also the name of the person who bought the taransey that was used to poison the ambassador. Ree and Penn got a list of possible purchasers from the distillery and spent all day yesterday following them up, but everyone could account for their own bottle except one. Jack Malone. His address turned out to be a lodging-house, but there was no longer anyone of that name staying there.'

'Right,' Sorrow said slowly. 'So it's likely the same person bought the taransey and invested in the barges, but we're no closer to discovering his identity. I can give you a few names of merchants involved in gun-smuggling, but that won't help you with your murder problem.'

'No,' Caraway agreed. 'But if you never found out who the investor was, how did you come to overhear the group?'

'Well, the barge workers unloaded their legitimate shipments at the docks, and then a handful of them took the black-market stuff across to a warehouse. So obviously I followed them. Most of them didn't hang around, which makes sense under the circumstances, but one man stayed. That seemed odd enough to investigate, so I broke in –' she raised an eyebrow at him – 'off the record, of course. And that's when I heard them talking.'

'Right. Then for a start, we can find out who owns that warehouse –'

'One step ahead of you, Captain Caraway.'

'Well?'

'He died several years ago. The deed has remained in his name, but I think we have to assume he's not stocking up on illegal firearms.'

Caraway absorbed this new blow with barely a flinch. 'Give me the name anyway. Just in case.'

'Maurais. Giovano Maurais.'

He wrote it down. 'Sounds like a Kardise name.'

'Yes,' Sorrow agreed. 'But given that he's dead, that could be a piece of misdirection on the group's part.'

'And what about the barge worker? Would you recognise him if you met him again? Presumably he's the only one whose face you saw.'

'I don't know,' Sorrow admitted. 'It was only a glimpse. I suppose you could get the names of everyone who was working on those barges, haul 'em all in and let me try to identify which one was playing dress-up in a warehouse down on Canalside. But I can't guarantee to get it right. And if I were him, I'd go to ground for a while anyway.'

'It's something for us to be working on, at least,' Caraway said. 'And what about the man you followed?'

'Nothing, I'm afraid.' She scowled. 'I picked him because he was talking about having murdered someone. The rest of the group were taken aback by it. They came round to his way of thinking easily enough, but it still indicates he's the most ruthless member of the group. So it seemed important to know who he was.' She looked Caraway in the eyes, daring him to respond in a way she didn't like. 'But I lost him almost straight away. Whoever he is, he's bloody good at keeping out of trouble.'

'They seem to have covered their tracks very well,' Caraway agreed. 'Hana was their only possible weak point, but Hana is dead.'

'Hana?'

'The girl your man killed. She was a maid in Darkhaven.'

'You think she was part of the group?'

'It would seem that way, from what you've said. She was involved somehow. Her friend gave the impression that a man had talked her into it. I asked the staff, but none of them had any idea who it might be – not surprising, if it was your softly spoken man. She must have seen him on her days off.' He looked sad. 'It's hard to believe of her. She always seemed such a sweet girl.'

Sorrow rolled her eyes. 'Your problem, Tomas, is that your natural paranoia is in constant tension with an almost pathological desire to believe the best of people. *Sweet* tells you nothing. Fuck it, I could be sweet if the occasion demanded.'

They looked at each other. Caraway's lips twitched. Sorrow glared at him for a moment before conceding.

'Maybe not. But you take my point.'

'I do. I also didn't fail to notice that you called me by my name. Which, since I have an almost pathological desire to believe the best of people, I'm going to take to mean you're finally beginning to like me.'

'Think what you want,' Sorrow said. 'What difference does it make?'

He shrugged. 'I prefer to like the people I work with.'

'So you like me, do you?' She said it mockingly, but he nodded.

'Of course.'

'Why?'

'Because I trust you.' He gave her a warm smile, ignoring her incredulous look, and proceeded to confound her further by clasping her hand. 'Thank you, Naeve. I really appreciate it.'

'It's not much to go on,' she muttered.

'It's a lot more than we had before.' He stood, ready to leave, then turned back to her and said, 'And they definitely mentioned something about an antidote?'

'Yes.'

'Thank you.'

Once he'd left the inn, Sorrow propped her head on her hand and sighed. *First he accuses me of trying to do the right thing, and now he tells me he trusts me. What am I, a fucking priestess?*

Still, she was working against the kind of people who thought peace with an old enemy was a betrayal, rather than a genuine chance for change. The kind of people who would happily engineer a war, because they'd never have to fight in it. The kind of people who could use the phrase *Kardise scourge* to refer to ordinary citizens of Mirrorvale, getting on with their lives, who happened to have one or more foreign-born ancestors somewhere in their family tree.

Yes: if there was ever a right side, she was on it. That had to count for something.

FOURTEEN

With all the work on the murder investigation, it came as a surprise to Penn when he was assigned to a new task. The vast Parovian airship he'd read about in his news-sheet only the previous week was coming in to land at the airfield in Redmire, and Ayla would be there to meet it – which meant a contingent of the Helm to guard her. Yet Penn's role would be a little different.

'Marlon wants to see the airship,' Captain Caraway told him. 'I need you to make sure he's safe.'

'Yes, sir.'

'I don't need to remind you how important this is.'

'No, sir.'

And so he found himself heading off towards the eastern border in one of the larger Mirrorvalese airships, with six other Helmsmen and young Marlon riding in the gondola with him, and Ayla flying alongside in her Alicorn form.

'Penn?' Marlon fidgeted in his seat, testing the limits of the safety harness. 'How big is the airship?'

'I'm not sure, exactly. But I read that it can carry nearly a hundred people, passengers and crew combined.'

'How many can this one carry?'

'Ten.'

'That's not nearly so much, is it? Is it, Penn?'

'No,' Penn said. 'Hush, now. We're about to land.'

On the ground, while Ayla shifted back to human in a swirl of black dust and the other Helmsmen made an outward-facing ring to protect her while she dressed, he grabbed Marlon's hand despite the boy's protests that he was too old to hold hands like a baby. A crowd had already gathered around the edges of the airfield; it would be easy enough for Marlon to wander off or be snatched. And Penn wasn't going to let that happen.

He knew why Captain Caraway had given him this job. It was because three years ago, he had stolen Marlon with the intention of using him as a weapon against Caraway himself. Putting Penn in charge of the boy today achieved several things: it reminded him what it was he'd been working to atone for ever since, it proved the extent of Caraway's faith in him, and it showed Ayla that he was to be trusted – though the lingering glance she gave him when she emerged from the centre of the circle made him think that trust was still some way off.

'Penn!' Marlon yanked on his hand. 'I can see it! Look!'

Penn followed the direction of the boy's pointing finger. Sure enough, there was something in the sky. It could almost have been a normal airship approaching the airfield – but as time passed, he realised that what had seemed like a small airship quite close was actually a large airship far away. The thing was shaped like a bullet, like an elongated version of a Mirrorvalese ship's envelope, yet there was no gondola underneath; only fins at the back and engines to the sides. As it got closer and closer, and bigger and bigger, he could make out the trimmings of Parovian royal purple against the brown of the outer skin.

'There's a name on the side!' Marlon hopped from foot to foot as though controlled by wires. 'I can see a W, but the rest's a bit hazy. Can you read it?'

Penn shook his head. At this distance, the name on the side of the airship was nothing more to him than a blur. He wasn't sure if Marlon was already beginning to develop heightened Changer senses or if his own eyes simply weren't up to the job. 'I'm sorry, I don't know –'

'*Windsinger*,' Ayla said softly. 'It's called the *Windsinger*.'

As the ship made its long descent towards the airfield, Penn was able to confirm the truth of that for himself. He also began to feel a little of Marlon's dizzy excitement. Because the ship was *huge*. Bigger than any transportation he'd ever seen, be it airship or carriage or boat. Mirrorvale tended to favour small, fast vehicles. But this ... it reminded him of something he'd read a long time ago, about the great expanse of water called the Bluegreen Ocean that lay at the western edge of the Ingal States, and how, once – before they'd lost their drive to do anything more than war with each other – the Ingalese had sent a vast boat out across the water in search of land on the other side, one that had never returned. He could imagine the entire sky as an 'ocean', and the *Windsinger* as a boat strong enough to search for adventure: sailing on and on, into the blue.

'Penn?' Marlon interrupted his thoughts. 'Why doesn't it have a gondola?'

'It doesn't need one. The people travel inside.'

'How?'

'Um ... the thing that looks like a giant version of one of our envelopes is divided into two compartments, using a wooden frame to keep its shape. A big one at the top for the gas cells, and a little one at the bottom for passengers and crew.'

That was about the limit of Penn's understanding of airship technology, but it didn't stop Marlon asking questions. He kept asking them while the *Windsinger* landed and was tethered, while a gangplank was lowered, while Ayla and the Helm greeted the airship captain. Penn answered as best he could, but he was relieved when the captain invited them all aboard for a tour. That thrilled Marlon sufficiently that he ran out of questions for a little while, looking around him with wide eyes as they walked up the gangplank and into the belly of the ship.

Determined not to be distracted from his task of guarding the boy, Penn didn't take in a great deal of the tour. They visited cabins and a dining room and an observation deck, but after a while all the rooms blurred into one. Marlon seemed to feel the same way; when they returned to the entrance area, ready to leave, he piped up, 'But Mama! We haven't seen any of the good bits yet!'

The airship captain smiled at him and suggested, in his accented Mirrorvalese, 'Would you like to visit the pilot's room?'

So they all traipsed off to the crew's quarters, where Marlon got to look at the controls and peep through a hatch at the gas cells above, and even walk out to one of the engine cars. He was directing his questions at the captain instead of Penn, now, which came as a relief.

'Time to go, Marlon,' Ayla said at last. 'But you can come back another time.'

The captain nodded. 'I am sure we will have you on board again before we return to Parovia.'

Penn already knew the *Windsinger* would be staying for a while, though the captain had been vague about how long. *We will keep giving tours for as long as your people are interested,* he'd told Ayla. *We want them all to get used to the sight of our airship in Redmire. No doubt it will make many more journeys here once our trade agreements are completed.*

No doubt it would, Penn thought. People would want to ride in a big passenger airship like this just to say they'd done it. If Ayla wanted to encourage the flow of goods and ideas back and forth across the border, he couldn't think of a better way.

On the flight back to Arkannen, Ayla rode in the Mirrorvalese ship with Marlon and the Helmsmen, and joined in all Marlon's excited chatter with a creditable amount of enthusiasm. To Penn's dismay, the boy appeared to have memorised his hopelessly insufficient answers on the subject of the *Windsinger*, and offered them up to his mother with all the reverence of an acolyte quoting a sacred text. *Penn says there's enough gas in the* Windsinger *to fill twenty of our airships. Penn says you can go on an actual journey on the* Windsinger *and eat food on it, can we go one time? Penn says if there was a race between the* Windsinger *and an eagle, the* Windsinger *would win, but you're the fastest of them all, Mama.* It got so embarrassing that when Marlon stopped to say something to one of the other Helmsmen, Penn had to lean over to Ayla and say, apologetically, 'I really don't know that much about airship technology, I'm afraid.'

She smiled. 'It's still more than I do.' Her gaze rested on Marlon for a moment, and she added, 'He likes you.'

'I have two younger brothers,' Penn offered uncertainly. Ayla gave him a thoughtful look, but said no more. Still, he hoped he was a little closer to earning her trust than he had been before.

When they landed in Arkannen's third ring, they found

Captain Caraway waiting for them with a couple of carriages. By that time Marlon was almost asleep; he mumbled something about the *Windsinger* when Caraway gathered him onto his lap, then rested his head on his father's chest and closed his eyes.

'If he sleeps now, he'll be up all night,' Ayla said. Caraway looked ruefully down at the boy's dark head.

'I don't think I can keep him awake.'

'Probably not.' She shot a sly glance at Penn. 'New job for you, Penn. Spend the rest of the afternoon tiring Marlon out with more facts about the *Windsinger* so he stands some chance of being in bed before sixth bell.'

Caraway smiled at Penn. 'Sounds like I've been missing out.'

After that, they talked about the Parovian airship all the way back to the seventh ring, and it was only when Penn saw Darkhaven's big gates swing open ahead of the carriage that he realised he'd been talking just as much as his captain and his overlord. Not only that, but he'd actually been enjoying himself. It had been, he thought dazedly, a rather startling day.

Then he saw the Kardise waiting in the central square.

All of them were there: Giorgi, Resca, the two other aides whose names Penn had never been given. With them, wrapped and bound, was a long, oddly shaped package that could only be the ambassador's corpse. They wouldn't leave it here in Mirrorvale. They would take it back to Sol Kardis, to his family.

Caraway handed Marlon to Penn, and he and Ayla descended from the carriage in haste.

'Lady Ayla,' Giorgi said, stepping forward to meet them. 'We have stayed long enough and must take our leave.'

'But the investigation –'

'Has gone as far as it can, I think.'

'You gave us a week,' Caraway said.

'Today is a week since Don Tolino's death.'

'That's not what you said.'

'Do you really think a couple of days will make any difference, Captain?'

'It might. We know there is a dissident group here in the city who plotted the murder. We suspect they got a maid to supply the poisoned taransey and killed her afterwards. We also suspect the same maid may have administered an antidote to Ayla to stop her being affected. I've shared all this with you!'

'And you provided no evidence to support it, beyond the second-hand account of a mercenary. Hardly the most incorruptible source.' Giorgi raised his eyebrows. 'Unless you now have something more solid to offer?'

Caraway was silent. Giorgi nodded as if that were answer enough.

'Very well, then. We will carry all this to the councillors and see what they say.' He paused, then added politely, 'If anything further comes to light, do please let us know.'

Ayla hesitated, but she seemed to read in their faces that arguing would be futile, because after a moment she said, 'Please, take one of our carriages.'

'No need. Our own is on the way.'

'Your airship –'

'Ready to go.'

'Then there remains nothing for me to do but wish you a safe journey,' Ayla said. 'May the winds carry you swiftly home.'

They bowed to her, one after another: short bows that

conveyed a certain amount of insolence. Lips pressed tightly together, Ayla stepped back.

'Carriage approaching!' called the lookout above the main gates. At a nod from Caraway, two of the Helm ran to swing them open for a second time. The luggage – and the ambassador's body – was secured to the rack, before the Kardise filed into the carriage one at a time. The Helm saluted them, but received no acknowledgement. And then the carriage was gone, the driver flicking the reins, the wheels churning up dust in their wake.

'Mama?' Marlon asked in a small voice. He was still in Penn's arms, blinking sleepily. 'Why do those men hate us?'

For a moment, Ayla appeared not to have heard him. She was gazing after the carriage, and though Penn wasn't all that good at identifying the nuances of people's expressions, he saw both sadness and fear in hers. But then she touched the little boy's cheek and said quite calmly, 'They don't hate us, Marlon. They're just angry their friend died.'

'Ayla,' Caraway said softly. 'Do you want me to –'

She looked up at him. 'Just get them what they're asking for, Tomas. I beg you.'

Taking Marlon from Penn, she hurried away across the square. Penn glanced back at his captain, but Caraway was watching Ayla's retreat – and sadness and fear filled his face, too. As if he were aware of Penn's gaze, though, he turned and managed a smile.

'Right, then. We've got evidence to find.'

FIFTEEN

After another long, fruitless day of research, Miles got back to his room in Darkhaven to find Art waiting for him. They didn't see each other very much at the moment. Since the Kardise had left the tower, Art had spent most of his days – and some nights – down in the fifth ring, preparing for war. Meanwhile, Miles kept working on his collars and trying to convince himself he could atone for the secrets he was keeping. But now, here was Art, sitting back in one of their two chairs, sleeves rolled up to the elbow and a cup of ale in front of him – and Miles was seized by a rush of love almost frightening in its strength. *I will not let you die.*

'You're late tonight,' Art said, pouring a glass of the Parovian wine Miles still preferred and sliding it across the table towards him. 'How's it going?'

'Not well.' Miles slumped into the other chair, taking a long gulp of the wine. 'And the fifth ring?'

Art sighed. 'Turns out, even war is a load of bloody paperwork. We've written hundreds of letters to former students of the fifth ring. We've drawn up training plans and battle plans. We've prepared everything we need to requisition goods and weapons. And all the damn talking! I swear, if I have to listen to another argument about the most effective way to structure the bloody army ...' He shook his head. 'I'd rather be at the border than endure any more of this.'

'Would you?' Miles asked softly. Art met his gaze, and a rueful smile touched his lips.

'No. Of course not.'

They sat in silence for a while. Miles poured himself more wine, hand shaking so violently that the bottle chinked against the rim of the glass. *Maybe I should go back to the laboratory after Art is asleep. If I try again to make the third flame reaction work –*

'Miles.' Art's hand covered his, lowering the bottle gently back to the table. 'You look exhausted. You can't keep pushing yourself like this.'

'I am fine.'

'You're not fine,' Art said. 'I should know, I have to live with you. You're working too hard on those damn collars.'

'No,' Miles snapped. 'Not hard enough. If I can get them right, hundreds of lives will be saved.'

'But –'

'Leave it, Art!'

Silence. Art looked taken aback, as well he might. Miles had never raised his voice to him before. He never raised his voice to anyone.

'Sorry,' he mumbled, hunching his shoulders and looking down at the table.

'Oh, Milo ...' With rare tenderness, Art hooked a finger under Miles's chin and lifted it until they were gazing straight at each other. His grey eyes searched Miles's face. 'You're not single-handedly responsible for keeping everyone alive, *rishka*.'

Rishka. It was the Parovian word for *sweetheart*. Art must be concerned about him, if he was using that term of endearment outside the cover of darkness.

I am going to lose you, one way or the other. Tears stung Miles's eyes; he closed them so Art wouldn't see. He should push Art away. End their relationship. Destroy what lay between them so that Art could no longer be used as a weapon against him. Maybe then he could stop the war *and* keep Art alive.

But the faceless man wouldn't believe it. Of course he wouldn't. He'd kill Art out of spite, if the Enforcers didn't get what they wanted.

'War may not come,' Art said, though he didn't sound as if he believed it. Miles opened his eyes and met Art's gaze once more.

'It will,' he said dully. 'We both know that. The Kardise party would not have left as they did, otherwise. The declaration will come, and –' *And it will all be my fault. Because I could have stopped it. Because I should have stopped it, and let you and Mara die ...*

A tear escaped, despite his best efforts. He could still stop it. If he told Art everything, he could stop the war. He just had to be willing to sacrifice the people he loved most.

Why could it not be my own life at stake? That would be easy. I would give it up in an instant, as the price of peace. But his ...

'Milo.' Art brushed the tear away with his thumb. His voice was gruff; no doubt, Miles thought with an affectionate ache in his chest so powerful it left him breathless, that meant he was about to say something heartfelt. 'Listen. We're strong, you and me, all right? Us and Ayla and the children, Tomas and the Helm, all the people of this beautiful bloody country – we're strong. We'll take whatever the Kardise throw at us and we'll come through it. Because we have each other, and we won't let each other down. All right?'

I have already let you down. The words were on the tip of Miles's tongue, ready to break free at last. *And I do not know if we are strong enough for this. Because I have something to tell you, Art, something terrible –*

Someone knocked on the door. Art took Miles's face between his hands and kissed him, fast and fierce, before going to answer. A Helmsman stood on the other side, but Miles didn't hear any of the subsequent conversation. He stared at his shaking hands and waited until, finally, Art turned.

'I'm sorry. I have to go. Will you be all right?'

Miles nodded. The words he'd been about to speak had gone, if they had ever really been there. He knew he wouldn't try again. It was too late. Much too late.

'You know you mean the world to me,' he said as Art walked through the door, torn between love and utter despair. The tears gone from his eyes, only to lodge as a hard ball in his throat. Art stopped and looked back at him.

'I know, Milo. That's what we're fighting for, isn't it?'

Days passed. Miles spent all the time he had in his laboratory, despite Art's obvious worry, but he couldn't get any further forward. He had nothing more than an imperfect prototype, and he couldn't even duplicate that. He was failing. He was failing everyone.

He tried to get some sleep, but even that eluded him. Every time he lay down, the same doubts began circling like hungry vultures. He was doing the wrong thing. He was doing the right thing. Whatever he did, people were going to die. Eventually, those thoughts always drove him out of bed and back to the laboratory, mind slow with exhaustion and hands unsteady. And, once again, he would fail to achieve anything worthwhile.

Finally, he went to see the physician.

'I need something to help me sleep,' he told Gil. 'Perhaps I should brew it myself, but I do not trust myself to get it right ...'

'Certainly.' The young physician gave him a searching look. 'Is there something on your mind?'

Cold fear hit Miles, for a moment, before it receded into equally chilly relief. Gil didn't know anything. The question had been far more general than Miles's guilty conscience had made it out to be.

'I am concerned, that is all,' he said. 'If it comes to war ...'

'We must all hope that doesn't happen.' Gil turned to grab a bottle from a nearby shelf. 'In the meantime, let's try this. I'll make it up for you at what I guess to be the correct dosage, but it's bound to need adjusting. Sleeping draughts are tricky to get right.'

'Thank you.' Miles watched in a daze as the physician mixed his ingredients. Medicine was far more impressive than murder, he thought stupidly. It proved nothing, to kill a man. A man was no more than flesh and bone, and flesh and bone were easily severed. By far the harder task was keeping a man alive.

'It shouldn't be that difficult, in your case,' Gil said with a quizzical glance. 'But by the sound of it, you're in urgent need of this draught.'

Miles realised he had spoken at least some of his thoughts aloud. For all he knew, he could have incriminated himself through sheer exhaustion ... yet the physician's expression remained calm. He must still be safe. By now, he could barely remember why that mattered.

Mumbling his thanks, he took the sleeping draught from Gil's hand. Then he returned to his bedroom, swallowed twice the recommended dose, and sank into the first deep sleep he'd had in days.

The formal declaration of war arrived by airship and was carried up to Darkhaven by four messengers. Ayla met them at the gate herself; it seemed the right thing to do. The foremost messenger read the declaration aloud in two different languages, in a voice that trembled ever so slightly, whilst the other three ranged themselves behind him, shoulder to shoulder as if they expected her to attack them. No doubt that was what they said of her in Sol Kardis, now: that she was mad and murderous, just like her brother had been. The end of a line that had descended into uncontrollable bloodlust and must be destroyed. She confounded their expectations by listening silently and receiving the rolled-up parchment with grave courtesy. Then she stood and watched them as they descended the hill, until they blurred into smears and she realised her eyes were brimming with tears.

She had expected this moment ever since the Kardise party had left the tower, their ambassador's body wrapped in linens for its journey back to their homeland. She'd known the flimsy evidence she had to offer for her innocence – an overheard conversation, a resealed bottle, a murdered servant – was not enough to convince them. Yet somehow, having seen it coming didn't make it any easier to bear now it had arrived.

'Are you all right, Lady Ayla?' Tomas was behind her, with a handful of the Helm. She blinked the tears back before turning. She had to be seen to be strong, now more than ever.

'Fine.'

He scanned her face. She could see in his eyes how much he wanted to comfort her, but he wouldn't touch her. Not in public. In this situation he was her Captain of the Helm, not her husband.

She wanted her husband.

'I do need to consult with you, Captain Caraway,' she added. 'On the matter of the forthcoming war.'

Tomas nodded. He dismissed the Helmsmen with a few quiet words, and the two of them climbed the steps to the lookout post above the main gate. Tomas directed the sentry to go off duty, before taking Ayla's hands in his.

'Are you all right?' he asked again, softly. She managed a smile.

'I could be worse.'

'You don't have to pretend with me, love.'

She shook her head. 'I have to. I have to keep pretending all the time. Because if I let the fear in, I won't be able to push it back out.' She gripped his fingers, and added in a voice that she couldn't quite keep from shaking, 'Though I would like you to hold me, for a while.'

He drew her closer without a word. She rested her cheek against his shoulder, closed her eyes, and breathed deeply. *Be strong. Be strong.*

'It's not inevitable, even now,' Tomas said. 'War is a slow process. There's still time to find the evidence we need to convince the Kardise of your innocence before anyone has to die.'

'Perhaps,' Ayla said, though she doubted it. The investigation had made very little headway in all this time; whoever was behind the ambassador's murder had planned it too cleverly to be discovered. Still, she saw no reason to deprive Tomas of his hope. 'But we need to fly our troops to the border, all the same. The reinforcements we've already sent won't be enough against the full Kardise army. And I ...' She swallowed, hard, against the sudden lump in her throat before concluding, 'I have to go there myself. Tomorrow.'

As close to him as she was, she felt him tense; yet like her, he seemed determined to speak calmly and quietly of the things that could destroy them. 'Yes. I'll talk to the weaponmasters, call up the warriors. Everyone is already prepared. Most of the Helm will stay here to defend Darkhaven, of course, but I've spoken to the ten of them who will be your personal guard ...' He paused, before adding softly, 'I wish I could go with you.'

'I know,' she whispered. 'But I need you to stay here. For the children, and for Darkhaven.' *Someone has to protect them if I die,* she didn't need to add. They'd talked about it often enough before.

'They'll be safe here,' Tomas said. 'And you'll be safe, too. You have Miles's collar.' He hesitated. 'I know you want to protect the whole of Mirrorvale, but if it comes to it, fall back to Arkannen. This city was built to break invaders.'

Ayla doubted he even heard the shade of eagerness in his own voice. He didn't want the Kardise army in Mirrorvale, of course he didn't – yet at least, if it happened, it would give him an active role to play in the defence of his country. She knew it fretted him that he'd be sitting here in Darkhaven while she went to war.

'I'm sorry,' she said.

'For what?'

'I should have lied. If I'd thought more strategically when the Kardise made their accusation, instead of focusing on my own innocence –'

If anything, he held her tighter. 'I can't blame you for that, love. Perhaps for the overlord of Mirrorvale it was foolish, but for yourself it was the right thing to do.'

'That's just it,' Ayla muttered. 'What I want for myself doesn't matter. I have to be overlord of Mirrorvale all the time. The truth isn't worth a war, is it?'

Tomas said nothing to that. Maybe there was nothing he could say. Instead, he simply repeated, 'It's not inevitable.'

'Even so.' Reluctantly she pulled away from him, gathering herself together, taking on a new form from the many she'd had to inhabit during her life. Not daughter or mother or lover or friend. Not even overlord. *Warlord.* 'I think, now, the time has come for us to behave as though it is.'

That afternoon, amongst all the final preparations for a war she didn't want to fight, Ayla spent as much time as she could with her children. That night, she and Tomas barely slept, turning to each other both for solace and in the knowledge that there might not be another night to come. And in the morning, she Changed into her other form, and set a course for the Kardise border.

SIXTEEN

The day after Sol Kardis declared war on Mirrorvale, a woman walked right up to Zander in the streets of the fourth ring.

'Kardise scum,' she hissed at him. And spat in his face.

A couple of days after that, Zander began to notice a change in his cohort of rich young pupils. There were whispers, sidelong glances, insolent comments spoken just softly enough that he couldn't be sure he'd heard them – until, finally, one boy responded to a mild rebuke by calling him *filthy Kardise vermin* and storming out. The rest of them simmered down a bit after that, but his lost trainee never returned, and the tension never fully dissipated.

A few more days after that, Zander and Penn were down in the first ring when they noticed a street vendor being hassled by a group of young thugs. While the two of them hesitated, unsure whether to get involved, snatches of the conversation drifted over to them through the noise of the crowd. Or not so much a conversation, really; the vendor himself said nothing, just bowed his head and gripped his tray as if protecting his wares were all that mattered.

Traitor.

Warmonger.

Go back where you came from.

At that, Zander started forward without further conscious thought, only to find Penn keeping pace with him. The sight of a Helmsman's striped coat was enough to subdue the little mob; no doubt Penn's height and broad shoulders helped, as did the hilt of his sword at one hip and the butt of his pistol at the other. While he was busy sending the miscreants on their way, Zander approached the street vendor. Easy to see, now, why the youths had picked on him. By the colour of his skin and the cast of his features, he could have been Zander's older brother.

'Are you all right?' Zander asked. The vendor's gaze flicked up, then quickly back down again.

'Sod off.'

'I just wanted to ... I mean, I'm Kardise too, so ...'

The man's head lifted again, a scowl touching his features. 'I'm not Kardise. I'm Mirrorvalese.'

'I'm sorry, I –'

'Just stop talkin' to me, will yer? Anyone sees us havin' a chat, they'll think we're plottin' a murder.' He turned his back on Zander and began to walk away, flinging a glare over his shoulder. 'A pox on you and your bloody country.'

Zander hadn't planned on telling Ree any of it – and knowing Penn's disinclination for gossip, he hadn't expected any word of it to reach her from that quarter, either. Yet this was obviously one of those things that Penn considered important enough to talk about. Zander had barely taken two steps past his own front door, that evening, when Ree arrived in a flurry of indignation and demanded to know who had been making trouble for him.

To start with, he tried to make light of it. He'd known it

would happen, and so had she. No point making her feel as though she had to protect him as well as perform her duties for the Helm. Yet as a joke, it was a poor one – and soon enough, the litany of incidents emerged in a great tumbling rush of pent-up words. The way people looked at him, now, as if they suspected him of being about to kill them, or were trying to work out how best to kill *him*. The way conversations died away when he entered the mess hall, and rose up again when he left. The way people avoided touching his hand or meeting his gaze.

'It's like I'm contagious,' he said finally. 'No-one sees me any more, only the disease I'm carrying. The disease of being Kardise.'

'It'll stop,' Ree said. 'I'm sure it will. Just as soon as the war is over.'

He shook his head. 'For the Mirrorvalese to turn on us that quickly, that violently ... it makes me think, maybe they hated us all along. Why else would they be so unable to separate a country from its individual descendants? Maybe they never looked at me and saw a person. Maybe they always just saw a Kardise boy.'

'I see you,' Ree said softly. 'I know that's not much to set against the rest of it, but it's all I have.' She took his hand, gripping it tightly. 'I wish I could do something to stop it, Zander. I wish –'

'Don't,' he said. 'It's all right.'

'It's not all right.'

'No.' He glanced down at their interlocked fingers, and felt tears sting his eyes. 'Don't let go, Ree.'

It was all he could manage, but she squeezed his hand as though she understood. 'I promise.'

* * *

As she did each day at dawn, Ayla-as-Alicorn walked through the camp and let herself be seen. She was their greatest weapon and their best protection; everyone knew that. Her presence each morning gave the soldiers of her army – the Helmsmen, the weaponmasters, the warriors trained in the fifth ring – both reassurance and courage. Unlike the councillors of the Kardise government, who thus far had kept themselves shut away from the battle and let their army do the work, she had to be there all the time. Fighting alongside her people. Fighting *for* her people. That was what being overlord of Mirrorvale meant. That was what she gave her subjects in exchange for their obedience.

'Lady Ayla.' They always stopped as she passed. Ducking their heads, awe glimmering in their eyes. Helmsmen who'd been openly scornful of her in her father's day – warriors who wouldn't have lifted a finger to prevent her from being unlawfully incarcerated for murder, six years ago – they all loved her. It would have been satisfying, were it not for the fact that it had taken a war to bring them to it.

Good morning, she always told them, and watched them shiver as if she'd sent a thin sliver of ice straight into their hearts. They feared her as much as they loved her. And that was how it should be.

She'd spent most of her time in Alicorn form since arriving at the border, returning to human form only to eat and sleep. It wasn't that she couldn't eat as an Alicorn, but it was easier to feed a woman – even one with a Changer appetite – than a giant winged horse. Perhaps it would have been safer for her to remain in her stronger creature form to sleep, but that would have required even more energy, and her collar kept her safe no matter which form she was in. Besides, she'd found she didn't sleep well as an Alicorn. On the one night she'd spent out on the plains in creature form – because neither the campaign headquarters nor the camp's tents were large enough to hold her – she'd found herself overly alert, waking at the slightest sound. Maybe she'd spent too long in her human skin when she was younger. Maybe her senses in Alicorn form were just too sharp. Whatever the reason, the only way she could get any sleep was to Change back into human form and curl up in her bedroll in the darkest corner of her quarters, imagining herself home.

Her quarters were located in one of two small forts that faced each other across this section of the border between Mirrorvale and Sol Kardis. Much of the rest of the border consisted of steep, rocky hills – not completely impassable, but more suited to stealth raids than to the open march of an army. Those hills had been the site of many clashes between the Kardise and Mirrorvalese patrols, yet any large force that tried to approach the same way would soon become strung out in single file along the steep slopes and narrow, winding tracks – easily spotted and picked off by the Mirrorvalese who manned the watchtowers. Thus for an invading Kardise army, the only viable route into Mirrorvale was the Whispering Plain, the one place along the border where the hills tapered down into flat grasslands. That was where both the road and the canal from Sol Kardis entered Mirrorvale, and where the checkpoints were located for travellers by foot, horse or boat. Each checkpoint included a compact but sturdy oak fort, usually housing border guards and any travellers who needed somewhere to stay the night. Now, though, the forts had become the headquarters of two opposing armies, with the soldiers' tents spreading out beyond and behind each fort like mushrooms rising after rain – and between them, the plain of dry, yellow-green grass. The battlefield.

Not that it had seen much use as yet. The war, so far, had been blessedly slow. There had been skirmishes, mainly involving the scouting parties from each side who had been sent out to assess the size and position of the opposing army; yet for the most part, the two sides had reached a standoff. Sol Kardis and Mirrorvale had been sniping at each other in small, undercover raids for so long, they'd forgotten how to do anything else. The Kardise were too wary of Ayla's creature-self to mount a full-scale assault, fearing the loss of too many men. She had encouraged that wariness early on, moving close enough to their front line to let them shoot her and allowing their bullets to bounce harmlessly off her skin. It had stung, but she'd remained there long enough to show them she was uninjured, before lunging towards the riflemen and scattering them like a flock of startled birds. For her part, Ayla kept her army on the defensive, hoping for as little bloodshed as possible. She was still holding out for a miracle. She was still holding out for the war to end.

Because the truth was, once the Kardise overcame their reticence, she wouldn't be able to keep them back for long. The smaller Mirrorvalese force would be overwhelmed by superior numbers, even with all the skill of the fifth ring on their side. Even with Tomas's plan to train and send more warriors as rapidly as possible. Even with an Alicorn. She didn't have twenty other Changer creatures to call on, as her ancestors might have done when the Nightshade line was thriving. She only had herself. And although she was the hope and pride of her army, she knew she wasn't enough.

That was why she had gathered some of the patrolmen and women to the battlefront, leaving the rest to protect the borders as they usually did – since it would be no surprise if the Kardise tried to sneak a raiding party through the hills while everyone's attention was focused on the main army. The patrolmen were the best resource she had: years of hostility with the Kardise meant they were well placed to predict the enemy's movements and give her valuable intelligence about the terrain. Not only that, but they carried firearms, and had done for years. Guns might be illegal in most of Mirrorvale, but it would have been unwise to extend that to the people who had to face them as a real threat on a daily basis.

Though they'd been cagey about it to start with, Ayla had discovered that the patrolmen had even begun to develop their own technology. The Kardise were making improvements to their firearms all the time: increased range, increased accuracy, even a double-shot gun that could fire two bullets at once. If the Mirrorvalese patrolmen didn't keep up, they would soon find themselves at a disadvantage. And so, using captured firearms and a few ideas of their own, they had entered the race. They had two alchemists. They had a small foundry. They had even started to make their own powder. It was, after all, unwise to rely on your enemy for the very thing you needed to fight him.

Ayla had taken it all in with a mixture of amazement and guilt. She'd always made sure the patrol units at the southern border were well funded, of course. When the occasional request came in for additional supplies, she never hesitated to grant it. The fifth ring kept up a steady supply of warriors to replace those who were injured or killed. Ayla even visited the border every so often, to speak to the patrolmen and hear first-hand of relations between Mirrorvale and Sol Kardis. Yet the news had always been the same: sniping, skirmishes, never outright battle. And so she'd let the situation continue as it was, and never thought to ask what her people were doing to make sure they weren't outmatched. She hadn't seen the innovation. She hadn't seen the brilliance. And because her views on firearms were well known, they'd never dared to show her.

It made her realise how short-sighted she'd been, to cling to her ban on firearms out of fear for her own life. They were in the world, and that could never be reversed. Instead of burying her head in the sand, she needed to accept the future. Mirrorvale needed to start manufacturing its own pistols and those other things, the long-barrelled things that allowed a bullet to travel with accuracy across a much greater distance ... rifles. It needed to be more advanced in all aspects of industry than its neighbours. And she knew that already, didn't she? That was why she'd built the railway. That was why she'd been opening Mirrorvale ever more widely to trade and ideas. Yet when it came to firearms, she'd let fear outweigh reason. That had to stop.

If she got out of this war alive, it would stop.

Of course, she had at least agreed with Tomas that the Helm should be armed with pistols. Which was all to the good, because the ten Helmsmen she'd brought with her were the only people apart from the patrolmen who knew how to use them. The rest of her army, the weaponmasters of the fifth ring and the assorted warriors who had trained under them, might be wonderfully skilled with bladed weaponry, unmatched in unarmed combat, and yet all that would come to nothing when faced with an ordinary Kardise soldier with a pistol in his hand. The archers helped, striking from a distance just as the Kardise riflemen did, but their arrows were less destructive than bullets and slower to fire. No, there was no denying that at war, the Mirrorvalese ways of fighting were far less effective.

To be fair, I didn't expect a war, she thought.

You should always expect a war, came the imagined reply. She rather thought it was her father's voice. And he was right – she had been stupid. Six years ago, firearms had been rare even in Sol Kardis; three years ago, they had been on the increase; today, they were numerous enough to equip entire army divisions. And she hadn't had the foresight to match that.

That was why it was so important that she protect her people from the consequences of her folly.

SEVENTEEN

A person could only worry about so many things at any given time. What with her ever-present fear for her colleagues and countrymen at the border, her rising alarm at the unrest within Arkannen, and her sharp, impotent fury at what was happening to Zander, Ree had almost forgotten the prospect of her own forced marriage. It simmered away at the back of her mind, but only rarely did it present itself as important enough to take her attention away from one of her more pressing concerns.

Unfortunately, though, it seemed her father didn't feel the same way. A little over a week after the declaration of war, he sent her a message to say that he'd arranged a meeting for her with Lewis Tarran – *just as you wanted, Cheri,* he wrote as though he were granting her a long-held wish. And so that was how, despite the fact that her country was at war and there were a million more important things she could be doing with her time, Ree found herself walking into the private lounge of an expensive guest house, ready to drink tea and make polite conversation with her theoretical future husband. Or rather, she reminded herself, do everything she could short of setting the place on fire to convince said future husband that he'd be making a terrible mistake by marrying her.

Lewis was already waiting for her, reading in an armchair on the far side of the room. At least, she assumed it was Lewis; he didn't look much like his father. Ree's main memory of Derrick Tarran was one of *presence* – a man who was imposing in both person and personality – but she remembered his light skin, like Penn's, and his bright blue eyes. In contrast, Lewis Tarran was brown-skinned and dark-eyed and slender. Far from dominating the room, he gave the impression he'd rather take up as little space as possible. Yet when he put his book down and stood up to greet her, she saw that he was tall, even though he tried to hide it; that the shape of his nose and cheeks and hairline was almost identical to Derrick's; that the set of his jaw revealed a force of will with the potential to match his father's. He was a Tarran, all right. He just wasn't completely one.

'Lewis?' she said, just to make sure.

'Ree.' He gave her a nervous smile. She'd expected arrogance, but saw no sign of it. Nevertheless, she stuck to her guns.

'I had a bit of a job getting in here. I don't think I'm at all the sort of person this kind of establishment is used to entertaining.'

She gestured to her striped coat. She'd worn her uniform, despite the fact that she was off duty. She'd wanted to show him that she was a Helmsman, not a suitable wife – and besides, it wasn't as if she had much else to wear.

Her mother would have told her off and forced her to change. She imagined Derrick Tarran would have looked at her in amused disdain. But Lewis only smiled.

'Terribly dull, these places. I like your uniform.'

Of course, Ree chided herself, he had enjoyed her father's stories about her. He probably thought of her as an exotic novelty. She'd have been better off wearing a dress.

'What are you reading?' she asked, wanting to change the subject to something that would allow her to demonstrate how hopelessly incompatible they were, but not quite finding herself able to be rude to him without provocation.

'Oh … a novel. An adventure story, actually. Do you like to read?'

This was better. 'I never read,' she said firmly. 'Don't have the time.'

He looked a little daunted, but recovered swiftly. 'That's understandable. You're out doing all the things I like reading about. But I really think you'd enjoy this one. It's –'

As he spoke, he turned the book towards her, and the cover was so familiar that she finished his sentence without thinking. '*Tales of the Darkhaven Defenders*!'

'You know it, then?'

'It's been my favourite book since I was about seven years old. Um.' She caught herself, hastily reining in her enthusiasm. 'Not that I like reading or anything.'

He looked at her. She looked back at him. And they both burst out laughing.

After that, she found it impossible to maintain her resolution to prove they had nothing in common. They curled up in the armchairs and talked: about books, about combat, about Arkannen and Torrance Mill, about the war. Lewis told her how disappointed his father had been when all his theoretical knowledge of weaponry had failed to translate into the slightest bit of practical aptitude; how much he was dreading being called up to the fifth ring to train in the reserve army, as he knew would happen sooner or later. He told her how much he wanted to teach reading and writing in Arkannen's free school, which took any children whose parents couldn't afford to pay for tutors – *only my father won't hear of it. He says it's unbefitting any man, let alone a Tarran.* Incensed by that, Ree told him in turn about her initial struggle to join the Helm, which led on to all the details of her current life. *I love hearing about it,* Lewis said. *I just wouldn't want to do it myself.* Finally, after she'd shown him her pistol – which he handled with a greater degree of familiarity than perhaps he had meant to betray; no doubt the Tarrans, like many wealthy families, had access to firearms despite their illegal status – he sat back in his chair and looked at her, a hint of his original shyness creeping back into his face.

'Ree,' he said. 'Do you think ... I mean, maybe we ought to talk about why you're here.'

She nodded. She felt equally shy. Yet they had talked easily enough, before, that she felt he would understand – and so she forced herself to tell him the truth, straight away.

'I like you, Lewis. A lot more than I expected, in fact. I think we could be friends. But I really don't want to marry you. I'm sorry.'

'It's all right.' He slumped down deeper in his chair, despondent gaze settling on the table and his discarded book. 'The truth is, I don't want to marry you either.'

Ree studied him for a silent moment. Then she said, in a voice that couldn't entirely hide her exasperation, 'So why are we even having this conversation?'

'I ... you wouldn't understand.'

'Try me.'

'I'm my father's only child. His heir. He's been talking about me getting married since I was fifteen.'

'But you're only, what ... twenty-five, now? Still plenty of time. Particularly,' Ree said with a slight residual bitterness at the constraints of her previous life, 'for a man.'

'He keeps talking about passing on his legacy. He wants

to know his line is going to continue. But I …' Lewis swallowed. 'I've never been interested in girls that way. And he knows it. That's why he keeps *pushing* and *pushing* –'

'So you like other men?' Ree's mind was already jumping to people her parents had known, back before she left home. Same-sex couples posed something of a problem in the highly formalised world of father–son inheritance, but there was usually a way round it. A younger sibling, a nephew: potential heirs abounded in most families. A couple could adopt a child, just as Lady Ayla and Captain Caraway had done with Marlon. Or a contract could be made with a parent-by-blood, someone who agreed to bear or father the child but relinquish all claim to it afterwards … Yet Lewis was shaking his head.

'I'm not interested in anyone,' he said vehemently. 'I'm just … not interested. No-one seems to understand that. My father keeps telling me I simply haven't met the right girl yet – as if I'll come face to face with someone and a switch will flick inside my brain. But I know different.'

'That seems perfectly reasonable,' Ree said. 'Surely he has no choice but to take your word for it.'

Lewis snorted. 'When I was sixteen, he took me to a brothel. Make a man out of me, he said – you know, since I hadn't shown any signs of wanting to corner a maid on the back stairs as he did when he was my age.'

'That didn't make him a man,' Ree said. The more she heard of Derrick Tarran, the less she liked him. 'That just made him a bully.'

Lewis lifted a shoulder; she couldn't tell if he disagreed or was simply uncomfortable with hearing overt criticism of his father, however justified.

'He paid for a whole night. The girl and I spent it talking about politics and playing strategy games with an old pack of cards she found in her bedside drawer.' He rubbed the line of his jaw reflectively, as if recalling an old bruise. 'My father was furious.'

His father's pride and joy. The words flashed into Ree's mind, her own father's explanation of the situation. *What the boy wants, he gets.* That might have been the story Derrick Tarran had sold, but it clearly bore only a distorted resemblance to the truth.

'So why did you tell him you wanted to marry me?' she asked.

Lewis looked down at his hands. 'I thought ... I thought if I had to marry, at least it would be to someone I found interesting. And you are.' He glanced up at her face, then away. 'Interesting, I mean.'

'But that's not a good enough reason for me,' Ree said softly.

'No. I'm sorry. I shouldn't have – I'm sorry.' He ran a hand over his face. 'I'm just so tired of it all. And your father told these stories about you, like a joke –' he winced – 'sorry, but they were. Only I didn't think it was funny. You sounded like someone who might ... understand. And your father kept saying you'd be leaving the Helm soon anyway and needed to settle down in a good marriage ...'

'He did, did he?'

Lewis raised his head at her sharp tone. 'I'm sorry,' he said again, helplessly.

'I'm not angry with you,' Ree said. 'My father, on the other hand ...' She pushed that aside as being unhelpful in the current situation, and added, 'You do know I can't marry you, though, don't you?'

'Are you sure? We could live in the city. You could stay in the Helm. Your life would be exactly as it is now, only you'd have more money. Is that not even worth considering?'

Maybe it was. Not so much for the wealth – however much her parents might look down on her tiny apartment, it was all she needed. But the marriage would rescue her family from debt and make her mother happy ... She sighed.

'It would be dishonest, Lewis. You know that as well as I do. And it wouldn't solve your problem, either. As soon as you were married, your father would be pushing you towards having children – that's the whole point of this, for him – but I don't want any. Never have. So what would we do then?'

His eyebrows lifted. 'You don't want children?'

'No.'

'And your parents accept that?'

'Not really,' Ree said drily. 'That's why I've ended up here with you. But at least they have other offspring to supply them with grandchildren.' She gave him a sympathetic smile. 'I do understand, Lewis. I honestly do. But that doesn't mean I can marry you.'

He nodded. He looked so unhappy that she reached out impulsively to touch his hand.

'There's no rush, you know. Even if your father thinks there is. It's worth waiting until you find someone you want to share your life with and who feels the same way about everything as you do. And then, if you don't want to take the necessary steps to have a child of your own blood, there's always adoption –'

'My father wouldn't like it,' Lewis muttered. 'He's always going on about how the Tarran line has been unbroken father to son for the past five hundred years.'

Ree shook her head. 'With the greatest respect to your father, it's not up to him.'

'What's that?' The question came from the far side of the

room; both Ree and Lewis jumped and turned. Derrick Tarran stood in the doorway. After Lewis's gentleness he seemed hard and imposing, the clear-cut original of whom Lewis was a blurred copy. Ree lifted her chin defiantly.

'I was just telling Lewis that I never want to have children.'

Smiling, Derrick walked towards them. An aide followed at his shoulder, a blank-faced man who took up a position by the wall while Derrick stopped in the middle of the room. Instinctively both Ree and Lewis scrambled to their feet at his approach.

'My dear,' the elder Tarran said. 'As your father's daughter, you must surely know what is expected of girls who make good marriages.'

'But I'm not going to make a good marriage.' Ree shot Lewis a pleading glance, and he moved forward to stand beside her. He looked nervous, but his voice was steady.

'We've decided we don't suit.'

Derrick's frown deepened. It held enough anger that Ree tensed, her hand drifting towards the hilt of a sword that wasn't there – but it wasn't directed at her.

'You little freak,' he snarled at Lewis. 'Are you telling me that even with *her* –'

'Ree has a life here, Father. I don't have any right to drag her away from it.'

'I own her entire family,' Derrick snapped. 'That's the only right that matters. You'll keep the agreement and that's final.'

Lewis swallowed hard. 'No.'

Derrick's arm drew back, and Lewis flinched. Ree moved without conscious thought, catching the blow before it could fall. The impact jarred her arm, but she forced herself to stand still and look Derrick in the eyes.

'Leave him alone.'

He grabbed for her wrist, but she twisted it out of his grasp. His narrow-eyed glare should have been enough to wither her where she stood.

'I suggest you stay out of this, *Cheri*, unless you want me to call in your father's debt and leave your family homeless.'

'I'm not afraid of you.'

His fists clenched again. She expected him to try and hit her, and she braced herself in readiness. Yet instead, and perhaps more frighteningly, he wound himself back. The threat of violence was still there, coiled beneath the surface, but he had it under full control. And Ree knew quite well that a calm opponent was a good deal more dangerous than an angry one.

'You silly little girl,' he said. 'You have no idea what you're dealing with.'

Ree's nails dug into her palms. 'I know exactly what I'm dealing with: a man who thinks his wealth entitles him to order everyone else's lives for them. You're a bully, Derrick Tarran, and nothing more.'

He smiled. His head tilted towards her, just a fraction. And in response, someone grabbed her wrists and wrenched them behind her back. Struggling to no avail, she turned her head to remonstrate with Lewis – *I stood up for you, and this is how you repay me?* – but it wasn't him. It was the aide, the one who'd entered with Tarran senior. Not an aide: a bodyguard. She should have realised it as soon as they came in. Instead, she'd forgotten his existence. *Stupid.*

'Father,' Lewis said uneasily, 'I really don't think you should –'

But Derrick Tarran grasped her chin in one gloved hand, still smiling, and struck her across the face. Even through the pain that bloomed across her cheek and into the socket of one eye, she recognised the precision of it. He might be rich, but that didn't make him soft. He knew exactly how to hurt someone efficiently.

Wrenching her head out of Tarran's grasp, Ree glanced at Lewis again, but he was staring at the floor. She didn't blame him, not really. He'd grown up with this; he'd probably learned through long and bitter experience what defiance would cost him. But she saw no reason why she should put up with it.

'For a businessman, your negotiation skills aren't up to much,' she said, trying not to wince at the renewed heat in her face. 'If you think you can intimidate a Helmsman with physical violence, you can think again.'

Tarran nodded at his bodyguard, who released her wrists.

'That was for the insult,' he said. 'I have no need to intimidate you. You'll marry my son or see your family ruined. The choice is entirely yours.'

'But Lewis doesn't want to –'

'Lewis will do his duty by his bloodline.' Tarran remained calm, even slightly amused, but the steely glance he shot at his son left Ree in no doubt as to his true feelings. She concentrated on breathing through the pain in her skull, while her thoughts tumbled over each other in search of a solution. No help would come from Lewis. And she didn't believe her parents would accept destitution to save her from this marriage, even if her father-in-law was happy to hurt her to prove a point. Indeed, she couldn't expect it. Derrick Tarran was a powerful man, and few merchants of her father's stature would be willing to oppose him.

Which meant Ree could see only one way forward, even if she didn't like it: invoke a powerful name or two of her own.

'You can't bully me,' she said. 'Like I said, I'm a Helmsman. All I have to do is speak to Captain Caraway –'

'You breathe a word of this to him and I'll destroy you.

Do you think I can't? Defy me, and you'll find yourself accused of a terrible crime and thrown out of the Helm. Your friends will turn against you, your family will be gone and you'll end up whoring for coppers, because no decent employer would dream of taking you in after what I make it appear you've done.' He snorted. 'Your captain might think himself incorruptible, but incorruptible men are by far the easiest to goad into righteous action.'

'He won't believe it of me. Especially if I tell him what you've said today.'

'You do that,' Tarran said. 'It'll give me an excuse to bring him down with you.'

Ree shook her head. 'A threat to Captain Caraway is a threat to Lady Ayla. You may be powerful, but you're not that powerful.'

Still he smiled. 'Ayla Nightshade isn't here, Cheri. She's gone to war. And in wartime, many things can happen.'

You're delusional. Ree opened her mouth to say it, but stopped herself before the words came out. She didn't really believe the man could affect the course of the war, but she had no doubt he could make life very difficult for Caraway while Ayla was gone – and Caraway already had more than enough to deal with. They all did. So although she had no intention of marrying Lewis, perhaps grudging agreement was her best course for now.

'All right,' she muttered. 'I suppose I'll consider it.'

In a fatherly gesture that she found utterly horrifying, he patted her bruised cheek. 'Welcome to the family, Ree.'

EIGHTEEN

Caraway stood at the lookout post above the main gate, gazing south through the darkening air towards Sol Kardis. That was his habit, now. Every evening during the first two chimes of the sixth bell, while the Helm were eating together in the mess hall, he maintained a solitary vigil. Darkhaven was always secured for the night by that time, with only a handful of trusted people carrying keys to the postern, so there was little security risk. There would be plenty of warning of any invading force.

Once, the men coming off day shift would have been allowed to leave the tower before it was locked, but war had put a stop to that. Caraway kept two-thirds of his remaining Helmsmen in Darkhaven at any one time, one shift on and one shift resting, while the third shift took time for training and family outside the tower. It was important to be ready for anything. If the war at the border went badly, he'd have to put them all on permanent duty, but not yet. He wanted everyone to spend as much time with their loved ones as possible.

Ayla. He wished he could send his thoughts to her mind as she did in creature form, closing all that distance between them. Yet even she couldn't speak that far. *Be safe. Please be safe.*

Two notes rang out in pleasant harmony, the two smallest bells from the Temple of Time in the sixth ring. On cue, the door from the mess hall opened and the Helmsmen who were on night duty emerged to take up their posts. Tulia was to be stationed at the lookout; she exchanged salutes with Caraway, before he descended to the courtyard. A messenger had just been admitted through the postern and now waited at the foot of the steps.

'Evening report, sir.'

'Thank you.' Caraway took it. This, too, had become routine. Ayla had commandeered two small, fast airships to act as couriers between Arkannen and the border, and closed off an entire docking station to all except military traffic. One courier ship left the city every morning at dawn, and returned as dusk fell; the other was stationed with the Mirrorvalese troops and did the same in reverse. That way, the army was never more than half a day away from getting anything they needed.

Of course, a lot could happen in half a day. Especially when it came to war.

He took the report to the transformation room, as he always did; with Ayla gone, it made a convenient temporary war room. He had maps in there, of Arkannen and its surrounding lands and the terrain between here and the border. He had plans for what he'd do if Ayla fell, or was overwhelmed enough to retreat, and the Kardise advanced on the city. With any luck, he'd never have to use any of it, but it never hurt to be prepared. And if nothing else, the room kept him awake long enough to do everything that needed to be done. One glance at the uncomfortable makeshift bed in the corner and he miraculously found enough energy to keep him going another half-bell.

If he concentrated very hard, he could almost convince himself that the bed was there because he found it more convenient to be close at hand in case of any trouble, and not because his own bed felt unbearably lonely without Ayla to share it.

At the desk, he scanned through the report. He always had to read them twice. The first pass, with heart racing and palms sweating, took in nothing but the answer to a single question: whether Ayla was alive and unhurt. He had every confidence in her abilities, but that didn't stop him fearing for her. How could it? Anything could happen, in a war. The Kardise might reveal a surprise weapon that could destroy her. She might be hurt trying to protect her people. Someone could assassinate her while she slept ...

Once he'd convinced himself that no such disaster had occurred and that the report was, as usual, a dry summary of the day's action plus a request for resources, he read it a second time with the buoyancy of relief and made a list of everything he needed to send back to the border with the dawn courier. As yet, there had been few requests for more warriors, which was good – not only because it meant limited casualties, but because it gave the reservists currently being trained in the fifth ring a little longer to prepare themselves. Mostly, the demands were from the quartermaster. Feeding an army was a costly business.

There was also a short report that had arrived earlier that day from the Mallory farm. The train ran at night, now, as well as in the daytime – the need for coal was urgent, what with the increased output from the factories – and so Caraway was able to exchange frequent messages with the Helmsmen guarding Corus. He and Ayla had decided that it was safe enough to leave the boy and his mother where they were, for now; if the war went badly and the Kardise crossed the border, Elisse and Corus could take the train and be in Arkannen long before the Kardise army got there. Still, a daily report reassured him that all was well – and reassured Sorrow, too. Her natural instinct had been to return to the farm when war broke out, and he'd had to convince her that she'd better serve her loved ones by staying put. With the Helm so stretched, he needed Sorrow more than ever if he were to stand any chance of finding out who was behind this war and putting a stop to it.

Seventh bell had already rung by the time Caraway had finished sending Helmsmen out with messages to various importers and manufacturers around the city, then writing his own reports to be sent back to the border and to the Mallory farm. He'd have to be up before first bell to get down to the third ring in time to see the laden courier ship take off with the dawn. He really ought to lie down on the uncomfortable bed and get some sleep. Yet instead, he found his feet carrying him back out of the transformation room and towards the postern gate, where he exchanged a few words with the sentry before leaving Darkhaven and descending the hill to the sixth ring. A familiar itch had started at the back of his mind: the one that said *you're failing her* and *you'll never be good enough* and *you know as well as I do what would make all this easier to bear*. And except when he was with Ayla herself, or with their children, there was only one place in the city that could suppress it for a little while.

The Changer temple was situated exactly halfway round the sixth ring from the Gate of Death, a small building made of blackstone. It had seven sides, just like Darkhaven; one held the door, another a high window, while each of the other five was carved with one of the pure Changer forms. The door itself was kept locked – yet now he was part of the family, Caraway had the key. And although maybe it was stupid, he often came here to make a private dedication of his own.

Inside, moonlight polished the dark stone to a silver gleam. The temple was almost empty: a little bare room, holding nothing but the wide black slab of the altar beneath the window. Unlike the outside of the temple, that altar acknowledged the possibility of far more Changer creatures than just the five single-element forms so beloved by Ayla's ancestors; it was carved with a multitude of little creatures all jumbled together, hydras with wings and firedrakes with feathers and griffins with unicorn horns. Caraway had studied it many times, finding an alicorn like Ayla and a wyvern like her brother Myrren had been, and fifty other creatures he couldn't name besides, but now it was too dark to make out the details. He tiptoed to the altar, kneeling on the cold stone where he and Ayla had once knelt together. A dedication. *My life to yours, Ayla. My life to yours, and to our children's.* Turning to the Changer temple for solace was far better than turning to a pitcher of ale. He almost thought Ayla's ancestors might approve.

He hadn't known, until he married a Nightshade, that there even was a temple dedicated to Changers – but of course they were a power in the world, just as much as the sun or air or time. Yet he doubted that many people knew of its existence, for the simple reason that it was closed to the citizens of Arkannen – and unlike the other temples, it didn't have a priestess to tend it. Not even Ayla's mother had been admitted; Florentyn's second wedding had taken place in Darkhaven itself, just like the few other weddings in the family history that had involved people who weren't family. That was the single law by which the Changer temple had operated for centuries: only members of the Nightshade line were allowed to enter.

The Nightshade line, and now him.

Are you sure? he'd asked Ayla, when she told him of her plan to take him there. *I mean, it's not my place to –*

She'd shaken her head. *Your place is with me.*

But I'm not –

I am, she'd said. *I'm the overlord of Darkhaven and the only living Changer, and I say we do this right.* She'd lifted her chin defiantly. *It's only a building.*

Only a building. Maybe so. Yet all the same, he had been properly awed by it on the day of their wedding.

Fourth bell had only just rung, but already the sun was beginning to set. Caraway had spent most of the day trying to work out what a man should wear to his own wedding, but in the end he'd settled on his captain's uniform, which had the twin virtues of being presentable and readily available. He'd bathed and shaved and spent some time staring at himself in the mirror in bewilderment, trying to convince himself this was really happening. He'd kissed Marlon goodnight. The Helm had showered him with a mixture of good-luck herbs, good-natured insults, and good advice of a kind that would have made him blush if he hadn't already been used to it. And now the time had come for him to get married.

The shadows were lengthening fast as he walked through the sixth ring, turning the familiar shapes of the temples into something far more mysterious. A sensation very much like fear unfurled in Caraway's stomach. He was about to set foot in a place that no-one but Darkhaven's overlords had entered for hundreds of years. He was about to marry a woman whose gift was considered one of the great powers, and have his name inscribed in the book that held a record of every Nightshade birth and marriage and death since the line began. Suddenly, against all that weight of history, his love for Ayla seemed a very little thing: a candle-flame in the darkness. Her father would have laughed at it, right before he ripped Caraway apart for his presumption. Yet her mother, whose life Caraway had failed to preserve ... oddly, he rather thought she would have given her blessing. She had married for love herself, after all. She would have wanted her daughter to be happy. And so it was with Kati Nightshade's memory in mind that he walked the last few steps to the temple door.

By tradition, Nightshade weddings were held at either midsummer or midwinter. Longest Day or Longest Night. It was said that a Changer child conceived at midwinter would have the power of ice or steel, whereas a midsummer child would be made of wind or flame. Not that it made any difference to him or Ayla; their child was already growing in the womb. But Ayla had proposed to him in the autumn, and so they'd set their wedding for Longest Night.

The ceremony will be at sunset, Ayla had said. *And we stay until dawn. Are you sure you don't want to wait for midsummer? We could marry in the daytime, then. I hear a summer wedding is very beautiful, all flowers and sunlight –*

It sounds lovely. But I'd rather not wait.

She'd smiled up at him. *That's what I hoped you'd say.*

Now, as he pushed open the temple door, he was met by a flickering glow. He locked the door behind him, then walked the few paces through the entryway to the single chamber beyond. And stopped. Candles lined the walls, hundreds of them, from tall white pillars in gleaming black metal stands to tiny flames in silver saucers. And among them, wound around the stems of the candle holders and spilling across the floor in perfumed curls – winter roses, their delicate creamy petals and green leaves standing out bright against the dark stone.

Flowers and sunlight. Oh, Ayla. Caraway swallowed, hard, because he didn't want to go to her with tears in his eyes, even if they were of happiness. He lifted his head, looking past the candles to the altar at the far end of the room. And there she was, wearing a dress that shimmered scarlet and amber and gold. The colours of candlelight. The colours of Alicorn wings. Her expression was grave, almost remote, and for a moment he couldn't move. History pressed down on him again, the shades of a hundred Nightshade ancestors whispering his unworthiness. What made him think he could stand in this place, a place consecrated to the power that ran in her blood, and pretend himself her equal?

But then she smiled, a tentative, tremulous smile, and Caraway forgot everything except the need to be at her side. He strode forward to meet her, catching her outstretched hands in his. Up close, the dress was even more stunning, changing and shifting as if made of the firelight that surrounded them. Yet he barely saw it. He only saw her.

'Ayla. You're beautiful. The most beautiful thing I've ever seen.'

'You looked almost frightened,' she said softly. 'I was afraid you had changed your mind.'

'I was thinking I should be here to worship you. Not marry you.'

Her smile turned playful. 'It's perfectly acceptable for you to do both.'

They gazed at each other in silence. The candlelight danced across Ayla's face and glinted in her hair. Caraway wondered what she saw in his eyes. Whether, like him, she saw forever.

'I brought you something,' he said at last. The idea of giving it to her made him nervous, now, but he had to go through with it. He felt in his pocket until his fingertips brushed the velvet of the little bag. 'I know it's not a Nightshade tradition, but they've always been worn in my family, so I thought maybe you might ...' Words failing him, he upended the bag and tipped the ring out onto his palm. 'Only if you want to.'

Wordlessly, she extended her hand, and he slipped the ring onto her middle finger. The interwoven strands of metal shone against the paleness of her skin. *Gold for joy, silver for passion and copper for fidelity.* That was what his grandmother had always said.

'Is it all right?' he asked anxiously.

'It's perfect.' Ayla looked down at her hand. Her smile had changed again; this one was happy and wistful at the same time. 'I'm sorry I don't have anything to give you.'

'You gave me flowers and sunlight in the depths of winter. Isn't that enough?'

She glanced up. 'You like it?'

'It's wonderful.' Unable to resist touching her any longer, he slid a hand to the small of her back and drew her closer. The dress might look like flame, but it slipped over his skin like cool water. His other palm cupped her cheek, thumb brushing her lower lip – and then it was the natural next step to lower his head and kiss her. When they finally parted, she clutched the front of his shirt and looked up at him with mischievous eyes.

'Captain Caraway. Are you really telling me you desire me here?'

'I desire you everywhere,' Caraway said. He rested a hand on the gentle swell of her belly, a barely visible indication of the child growing within. 'Is that wrong?'

'No.' She interlocked her fingers with his. 'But it will have to wait, just a little while. We have a ceremony to perform first.'

And so it began. They knelt together, facing each other, hands still clasped. *Traditionally we face the altar,* Ayla had said, *but hang tradition. We're marrying each other, not my ancestors.* Caraway didn't know the words, but it didn't matter; Ayla said them, looking very solemnly into his eyes, and all he had to do was say them back to her. Yet that didn't steal their meaning. They lay weighty on his tongue, the truth of every one of them burning into him like a brand.

All that I am, I dedicate to you.

My heart to yours.

My body to yours.

My life to yours.

Now and forever.

Blood and bone.

Breath and life.

'Blood and bone,' Caraway echoed now, alone at the altar. 'Breath and life.'

He thought of them often, those words they had spoken to each other. When he and Ayla argued, when they were both short on sleep, when she said or did something that made her seem, for a moment, like a stranger again. Or it would hit him in little moments of contentment: when she caught his eye across the breakfast table and smiled. When Katya learned a new word or Wyrenne took her first steps. The memory was always there, a reminder of how much they had promised and how much they had meant it. He found it kept the little seed of *wanting* at bay: the urge to throw everything away so he couldn't lose it later, to prevent his own future failure by failing now. He had dedicated himself to Ayla, and that meant he no longer had the right to choose self-destruction.

She still wore his ring, though not on her finger. It had fallen to the ground the first time she Changed. But Miles had found a way to attach it to the front of her collar, so now it sat in the hollow of her throat, fluttering with every heartbeat. *It's only right,* Ayla had said. *It shows you're part of what keeps me safe.*

Yet he hadn't kept her safe this time, had he? He'd failed to prove her innocent of murder, and now she'd gone to war. He'd let her down in the worst possible way, and he really ought to resign his post before he could do any more damage, find an alehouse somewhere –

Caraway let the black despair smother him for a moment, before deliberately pushing it away with another memory: the rest of his wedding night. He didn't think about that very often, because it approached the status of something sacred in his mind – and he knew very well that turning a memory over and over caused it to tarnish and fade, like a pebble worn smooth by the sea. He didn't want those particular moments in his life to take on the blandness of familiarity. Yet tonight, more than ever, he needed to hold on to everything that was bright and true and use it as a defence against the fear that threatened to consume him. And so he let himself remember.

The spoken ceremony was over, the wedding was done. Caraway wasn't sure what time it was, but he didn't think the sixth bell had rung yet. On midwinter's night, that meant plenty of time until dawn. He looked at his new wife, and there must have been a question in his eyes, because she smiled.

'You're wondering why we have to stay in here the whole night.'

'It did cross my mind, yes.'

In response, she lifted a hand to the back of her neck, and her flame-coloured dress fell shimmering in a pool around her feet. His mouth suddenly dry, Caraway swallowed.

'Ayla –'

'Usually it would be to conceive a Nightshade child,' she said. 'But since we've already taken care of that –' her fingertips brushed her belly – 'this will be just for us.'

'And where exactly –'

She tipped her head towards the blackstone altar. 'What do you think that's for?'

Caraway opened his mouth to protest, but something stopped him. There was fear behind her smile. In this place, the weight of her ancestors must press on her as much as it did him – more, in fact. She was trying to conceal it, for his benefit, but she was afraid ... of what? That he would turn and run? That he wouldn't understand the history that was bone-deep in her?

They had broken tradition often enough, the two of them. This time, they'd do things the Nightshade way.

Without another word, he scooped her up in his arms and strode over to the altar. There he proceeded to worship her, with fingers and lips and tongue, until her head tipped back and his name fell from her lips in a breathless cry of delight. Even as her body clenched and shook she pulled him to her, inside her, wrapping her legs around him and urging him deeper, heedless of the bruising stone beneath her. And that was how it went for the rest of the night, until the first grey light of dawn crept through the window of the little blackstone temple, and the candles were all spent.

Now, Caraway smiled in the darkness. They hadn't slept at all, that night. They must have explored each other in every possible way before the daylight came. Yet it shone in his memory not for the act itself, but for the words Ayla had spoken to him. He knew she cared deeply for him. He had long since ceased to doubt that. Yet she had always been reticent with her feelings. Quick to anger, yes, but reluctant to reveal her softer emotions. Another legacy of her father's, no doubt. But on their wedding night, she had let them all show. Words of adoration, of admiration, even of gratitude: they'd come spilling from her lips as if her last shields had finally been cast aside.

It was the first time he could remember her telling him she loved him.

He had responded to her with his own heartfelt words, until it had seemed the two of them were utterly open to each other. It was a strange and wonderful thing, the ability to reveal so much without fear. Most of the time people existed in layers, peeling themselves back gradually, always afraid to show the deep emotional truths at their heart. So to expose that emotion, the love and the need and the willingness to surrender ... that, and not anything their bodies might do, was the greatest kind of intimacy.

Perhaps there was alchemy at work, Caraway had thought later. Some great power in the little blackstone temple, weaving the threads of their two lives into one. Whatever the truth of it, he had known by the time they left that he would never again need to doubt Ayla's feelings. *You are my heart,* she'd told him. And *you unfroze me, Tomas.* And *all of me is yours, forever.* A woman who could say those things – and plenty more besides – was not a woman who loved in half measures.

She loved him. She trusted him. And he would never let her down.

On the way back to Darkhaven, the niggling desire for a cup of ale lay quieted, leaving his mind calm and clear. He needed to bring the war to an end, and he could only do it by uncovering enough evidence to prove to the Kardise that Ayla hadn't killed their ambassador. So even though the investigation had come to a standstill, he had to find a way through it. It was simply a matter of uncovering the loose thread.

Working with Captain Larson of the Watch, he'd arrested the merchants who'd been involved with the shipments of illegal firearms that Sorrow had uncovered. Yet as she'd told him, none of them had been able to put a real name to their investor. And although he'd got a list of their crews and tracked most of them down, Sorrow hadn't been able to identify any of them. So that had ended his hope of uncovering at least one member of the Free Arkannen group that way.

He had also quizzed both Miles and Gil again about the possibility of an antidote to zephyr, yet each man had been adamant that no such antidote existed. The only logical conclusion was that someone in the dissident group had made a discovery about which they were keeping very quiet. He could see no obvious way of pursuing that line of enquiry further.

So where did that leave him? He knew the group had killed the ambassador. He knew they'd used Hana to do their dirty work within Darkhaven, then killed her for it too. He knew most likely they'd done it by poisoning the bottle of taransey and supplying Ayla with an antidote that would protect her. He even knew one of the group was a wealthy investor who used the name Jack Malone to conceal himself. Yet he had no way to prove any of it.

The only plausible course of action he could identify was questioning Mirrorvale's elite in the hope of uncovering the traitor. But he knew, without needing to test it, that they'd close ranks against him. The wealthy investors of the city wielded an awful lot of power. If Ayla had been there, he might have been able to get something out of them. Without her, they would politely point out that he had no jurisdiction beyond Darkhaven, unless he had enough evidence to support arresting them for direct treason against their overlord. And who had the evidence he needed for that? One of them did.

Still, it might be possible. And even if it wasn't, he had to try. It was no more than he owed to the woman he loved.

As the days passed, Ayla's hope of a swift end to the war – her hope that against all the odds, Tomas would find a way to exonerate her and convince the Kardise that Mirrorvale was not to blame for their ambassador's death – began to flicker and fade like a guttering candle. At the same time, the Kardise grew bolder. They began to make raids under cover of darkness, sending small parties to strike at the sentries and deal sudden, bloody death to the nearest handful of warriors before retreating as swiftly as they'd come. Ayla's generals increased the number of people on lookout at any given time, but still the raids continued.

Then, finally, there was a dawn attack. Two cohorts of Kardise riflemen, one on each flank of the army; the first drew Ayla's attention, while the second wrought destruction. The Mirrorvalese managed to drive them off, Ayla-as-Alicorn pursuing them back across the border, but they left scores of men and women wounded or dying in their wake. After that, Ayla walked up and down the front line in her creature form for the rest of the day, all through the night and into the next day, ready to spring into action at even the slightest movement from the Kardise camp – until, unable to resist it any longer, she tripled the sentries, curled up in her bed and fell into an exhausted sleep.

Sometime later, she awoke suddenly without knowing why. She listened, but heard no clash of weapons or voices that would indicate a raid. By the sky outside, it was not yet close to morning. So why –?

Then she smelled it, on the air: the faintest hint of smoke.

She ran to the small, glassless window and peered out, but the Mirrorvalese camp looked as it normally did. Few people were stirring at this time, and the fire-pits had sunk to a glimmer; only the sentries moved through their patrols. She could smell gunpowder and blood and roasted meat and the latrine pits and yes, smoke, but the latter was a different sort of smell from the one that had woken her. Sharp and resinous, not a damp, choking smoke.

When she moved back into her room, she smelled that other smoke again – stronger now. Suddenly afraid, she flung open the door.

'Lady Ayla?' The two Helmsmen on guard outside turned to her in alarm.

'Can you smell that?'

They looked blank; no doubt her senses were more sensitive than theirs. One of them asked cautiously, 'What is it?'

'Smoke …'

Yet even as she said it, a noise exploded below them that was surely loud enough for anyone to hear: the screaming of horses, the stamping of their feet. Ayla turned and ran, her guards hard on her heels.

The fort was a hollow square, with sleeping quarters in the upper storey and rooms used by the border officials below. The upper floor had a covered walkway along all four edges, providing access to the bedrooms, and the only way up to that was a pair of staircases, one to each side. By the time Ayla reached the top of the nearest staircase, she could see the flames licking at the stable door.

'Fire,' she snapped at one of her guards. 'Wake everyone up, get them out –'

But it was too late. In a small explosion of indrawn air, the entire stable went up in flames. First one horse, then another, and then a whole group of them burst out of it, eyes rolling, flanks heaving, forelegs torn and bloody. They were on fire. Their manes and tails streamed with it. They ran, desperate and terrified, seeking only to escape the threat – yet the threat rode them. And there was no way out. The door was bolted and barred. They could only run, round and round the square, while behind them the wooden staircases and the columns that held up the walkway began to burn.

Ayla backed away, the screams of the horses ringing in her ears. *You can't go that way now,* she told herself. *Even if you get down the steps, you won't make it to the door.*

She turned and ran along the walkway, banging on the bedroom doors, trying to wake everyone else whose quarters lay inside the fort – the generals, the quartermaster, the people she relied on to lead her army. Some of them had already come out. Some of them had run back into their rooms, scrabbling desperately at windows that were too small for grown adults to fit through. Yet just like the horses, they had no way out.

'Lady Ayla!' One of her guards caught her arm. 'You have to leave!'

Yes. The fire was spreading along the walkway, eating into the bedrooms beyond. She was the only one who could escape this. Yet, surely, she could do better than that.

Without another word, she leapt off the walkway towards the flames below, summoning the Change as she went. The fire licked at her hooves, but she swept her wings downward and veered away from it, rising back up to the level of the first floor.

Jump, she told the Helmsman. *I will catch you.*

He barely hesitated. It wasn't as if he had much choice. The impact of his landing shook her, but she righted herself. And then two other people flung themselves at her. One caught her around the neck, dragging on her mane and sending her listing sideways; the other glanced off her and fell with a scream, hitting the ground below.

No more, she warned the others. *Find the most stable place you can and wait. I will come back for you.*

She managed four trips before the entire upper floor of the fort was consumed by flames and it was no longer safe to return. She'd carried ten people to safety, some of them suffering from serious injuries. Twice as many again had been trapped in the burning building or fallen to a fiery death. She'd done all she could. It wasn't enough.

By then the army in the camp outside had mobilised themselves, aiding the wounded and fetching water from the canal. Yet they had no way to put out such a massive fire. In the end, once they were sure they could do no more to rescue anyone from within the fort, they had to let it burn itself out.

Back in human form, Ayla stood and stared at it. It wouldn't have been possible to burn down the fort from the outside. The wood soaked up enough moisture from the canal, the air and the springtime rains that it resisted fire, to a certain extent. But inside ... there, everything was dry. The sentries hadn't seen anyone approach the fort, but a small boat had been abandoned on the canal that ran past one side. The Kardise party must have approached in that, creeping through the water undetected. None of the windows on the ground floor of the fort were large enough to admit a person, of course, but they didn't need to be. All they'd required was a gap big enough to fling in their firestarters. Whatever they'd used had been swift-acting and merciless, consuming the inside of the stables and setting the horses alight before anyone on the outside saw a single flame. And then, when the horses had burst through the stable doors ...

Ayla shuddered. In her mind, the trapped animals still circled, desperate and dying, bringing destruction to everything they touched. In her mind, men and horses still screamed.

The fire still raged. She kept staring at it. And a slow, cold anger settled over her like the first frost of winter.

Still in human form, she stepped out onto the battlefield. Two Helmsmen – her two new guards – ran after her, but she ordered them back. She had business with the Kardise.

They had come by canal – so as she walked, she froze it. Tendrils of ice reached deep down and across the surface, swift and relentless, crackling as they went. Let that send a message to them. Let them know she would freeze their fire.

But if I had my father's power – a small thought began. She crushed it mercilessly. She had no room for doubt. She had to be cold.

When she was halfway between the two armies, she stopped. The Kardise had already seen her; she could hear the shouts, the running feet. They knew better than to try and shoot her, by now. Their calls contained as much alarm as they did the possibility of opportunity. They wanted to see what she was going to do before they tried anything.

She sent her senses questing ahead of her, into the wooden fort that housed the Kardise councillors. The fort very much like her own had been, before they burned it. She focused her mind at the base of the walls, and *tore*. Vast cracks opened in the wooden sides. Once more and it shattered, pieces of wood flying everywhere, sending men hurtling through the air. She kept going, ripping and pulling and tearing with her mind, until the enemy's fort was nothing but jagged splinters.

She heard the cries of the wounded men. She heard the cheers of her own army. And yet she felt nothing. Nothing at all.

NINETEEN

Zander had begun to avoid returning to his apartment, spending all his time in the fifth ring. There were a few spare beds in the barracks for weaponmasters and their assistants; someone always worked late enough to want to avoid the walk back to the fourth ring, or needed to make a sufficiently early start to warrant an overnight stay. Some of his students still whispered about him, and some of the other warriors looked at him askance, but enough people knew him in the fifth ring for it to feel like a sanctuary in comparison to the streets of the lower rings.

Then, one morning, as he went through the forms alone on one of the smaller duelling floors, he heard a voice behind him.

'Hey, Kardise boy.'

That wasn't likely to be the opening to anything good. Zander's stomach clenched, but he made himself put down his sword and turn around slowly. A couple of men stood there, shoulder to shoulder, blocking his exit: merchants' guards, by the look of them. One was fair-skinned, almost as fair as a Nightshade, with reddish blond hair and a scowl; the other, cracking his knuckles and grinning, had colouring more like Ree's, amber and brown. In the past, Zander would barely have registered what they looked like in such simple terms, skipping straight to the more important details of build and posture and possible prowess in weaponry. Yet in the strange new world in which he found himself, such things were significant.

'Who, me?' he said, and the brown-haired one's smile widened.

'I don't see any other Kardise boys in here.'

Zander hesitated as the little scene unfolded itself before him in all its tedious inevitability. It wouldn't make any difference what he said or what he did; their intent was clear to read in their aggressive stances, their hard eyes and curling fists. He was a symbol to them, not a person. And as such, all that mattered to them was what he looked like.

'You want to pick a fight,' he said wearily. 'So can we just skip the insults and go straight to the part where you beat me up?'

'Don't be clever, Kardise boy. No-one likes clever.'

'What are you doing here, anyway? Why aren't you back in Sol Kardis with all your traitor kind?'

'I'm a junior assistant weaponmaster.' Though probably not for much longer, after this. He found himself remembering Ree's face when he'd talked to her about leaving, the little frown between her eyebrows as she worried about him. At the time, he'd thought he could weather anything as long as he could stay here in Arkannen. Now, in retrospect, he realised it had been easy to dismiss what he'd never experienced. 'I teach basic swordsmanship and bladework –'

'That can't be right,' the blond one said. 'What're the weaponmasters playing at? We can't have your sort teaching our troops.'

'Yeah. That has to be bad for morale. Serious security risk, too.'

What do you think I do? Zander wanted to ask. *Harangue them about how much better Sol Kardis is than Mirrorvale? Pass on information about how Borro's grip still isn't improving, even after I've shown him fifty times? I'm not teaching troops, I'm teaching rich kids who barely know one end of a sword from the other!* But he held his tongue, because none of it would have helped. Instead, he tried a smile. Surely even these men would respond to a little charm and the application of reason.

'I mainly run errands and fill in paperwork. I'm not privy to any secrets.' He spread his hands. 'Besides, I've been here three years now. Arkannen is my home.'

'So you're sayin' you've turned against your own people? Taken Mirrorvale's side in the war?'

By all the little gods. How was he supposed to reply to that? They'd consider him a traitor either way. But then he saw their faces darkening with a mixture of anger and harsh satisfaction, and realised that was the point.

'Well,' he said hastily, 'I'd really rather it wasn't happening at –'

The punch caught him on the side of the head, sending him stumbling backwards. His ears were ringing. He considered lunging for his discarded sword, but that would lift the fight from a brawl into a duel, and if he killed anyone – even in self-defence – he really wouldn't have a place in the fifth ring any more. All this was against the Code as it was.

Unfortunately, he didn't think he could hold off the two of them in unarmed combat. He had the benefit of Helm training behind him, but that had ended a couple of years ago – and since getting his job, he'd mainly focused on improving his skill with the sword, since that was what he taught. Against two seasoned merchants' guards, he didn't stand much chance.

'Look,' he said. 'Do we have to –'

The blond one threw another punch, which he managed to block before sidestepping so that the other one didn't have a clear line of attack. If he could get them to obstruct each other, he might be all right. He landed a kick squarely on the side of the blond's knee, taking the opportunity afforded by the man's temporary incapacitation to get into a better position. He didn't want to be pinned between them and the wall. Ideally, he'd reach the door and escape. At this stage, he was far less concerned with proving himself than he was with escaping in one piece.

'No you don't, you little shit.' The brown one stepped in to block his path, slamming the heel of one hand towards his nose. Zander barely managed to deflect the blow, and the force of it set him off balance. Before he could right himself, the man brought a knee up into his groin, hard enough to double him over. Gasping, he backed away, knowing it was taking him further from the door but unable to help it –

'That's right,' the blond man's voice murmured in his ear. 'Stay here with your friends.'

Then one of them had his arms pinned behind his back, while the other drove a punch straight into his guts. His body convulsed, trying to fold in on itself a second time, but the tight grip that twisted his wrists up behind his back left him nowhere to go. Gulping desperately for air that didn't seem to be there, he blinked the tears out of his eyes in time to see the man's fist draw back again –

'What the fuck is going on?' The voice was familiar, though

distorted by Zander's own fight for breath. It certainly worked on his assailants; the threatening fist was lowered, and his arms were released. Zander dropped to his knees, unable to keep himself upright, and sucked in a long, blissful draught of air.

'It wasn't our fault,' one of the men said – Zander couldn't tell which. 'He picked a fight with us. We were just defending ourselves.'

'It didn't look that way to me.'

'But, Captain Caraway –'

'Shut up. I know exactly what you were doing. And that kind of shit isn't welcome in the fifth ring, so I suggest you remove yourselves before you get removed.'

'You don't have the authority,' one man muttered. Zander glanced up in time to see Caraway's eyebrows lift.

'I'll force you out of here if I have to,' he said calmly. 'And that's all the authority I need.'

'But you can't –'

'Try me.'

Silence. Then, with a mumbled *yes, sir,* the two merchants' guards retreated. Caraway followed them to the door, and Zander heard a brief exchange of words before the captain re-entered the duelling room and sat down beside him.

'Two of the Helm are escorting them to the Gate of Steel,' he said. 'They won't be back.'

Slowly – because it made his bones ache – Zander turned his head to look at him. 'You know, you're quite scary when you want to be.' *Ugh. What in the name of all the gods did I just say?* 'I mean ... thank you, Captain Caraway. I'm sorry. I'm not thinking straight.'

'How do you feel?'

Zander prodded his cheekbone, then winced. 'Like I just

got beaten up by two men who hate me for where I was born.'

'Do you want me to have them arrested? They broke the Code. I could press for more than a ban from the fifth ring, if you like.'

Zander sighed. 'What would be the point? It wouldn't solve anything. It wouldn't stop people looking at me and seeing the enemy. It wouldn't end this war.'

Clearly the fight had screwed him up worse than he'd realised; he never usually let this much bitterness come out of him. He never usually *felt* this much bitterness. Even when he'd been wrongfully imprisoned for planning Ayla's assassination, he'd never felt so ... helpless. That was the only word for it. As though no matter what he did, no matter who he was, a simple accident of birth meant he would always be wrong in some people's eyes.

Caraway looked at him for a long moment in silence. Then he asked softly, 'Is it very bad, Zander?'

'Nothing I can't handle.' The reply came automatically, even though Zander wasn't sure if it was still the truth or not. He returned Caraway's gaze, seeing brown eyes and brown skin only a shade lighter than his own, and wondered ... 'You don't get it too, Captain?'

Caraway shook his head with a rueful smile. 'Not to my face. Though I did overhear a couple of sellswords discussing the fact that I'm obviously a Kardise agent sent to weaken the Nightshade line with my filthy foreign blood. But there have been people talking that way since I married Ayla, so I'm used to it.'

Zander didn't know what to say to that. He couldn't imagine ever accepting the things some of his students said of him with that kind of easy equanimity.

'I don't know how you bear it,' he muttered, and Caraway shrugged.

'People are far better at noticing how they're different than how they're the same. I see it year after year when I'm training new recruits. And war only brings it out more strongly. It turns everyone into patriots.' One corner of his mouth turned up. 'Not that I object to people being proud of their country, obviously. But there's a difference between that and hating everyone else's.'

Zander nodded. It was all part of what he'd once described to Ree as *believing in things*: start believing in something strongly enough, and you began thinking that anyone who didn't share your opinion wasn't as worthy of respect as everyone else. That kind of thinking was what led to seeing people as labels, instead of individuals: *us* and *them*. And if your belief was strong enough, you'd manage to convince yourself that killing *them* was no worse than killing flies.

He expressed some of that to Caraway, who listened gravely before adding, 'Though of course, it's hard to blame anyone for working themselves into that state. Not when they've just been thrown into a war that's not of their making. What are their alternatives? This war isn't about ideology. It's not about right and wrong. It's a war that neither side wants but neither can avoid. No-one wants to die for that, but they might all the same.' He sighed. 'Thinking of the Kardise people as a homogenous group allows us to hate them. And hating them allows us to kill them when the time comes. If it's that or be killed, what else can we do?'

'We?' Zander echoed.

'I don't hate the Kardise. But given the chance, I will kill anyone who threatens my family. So really, I'm just the same as everyone else: afraid of losing what matters to me.' Briefly he gripped Zander's shoulder. 'Perhaps it would help to remember that, Zander. These people who say cruel things to you, who call you names ... in the end, their words are only fear.'

Easy enough to say, Zander thought. Easy enough to believe, in the abstract. Not so easy to live through. Caraway was a good man, but he was protected by who he was. Even Zander himself had a reasonably secure position, with friends like the Captain of the Helm to look out for him. But other people, like that street vendor, working down in the first ring every day ... what did it matter to them if the cruelty came from hatred or fear? It was hard to feel sympathy for someone while they spat in your face.

'I'm afraid it will go beyond words,' he said. 'You saw what happened just now. And there are plenty of Kardise immigrants in Arkannen. Plenty of people like you, whose families have been in Mirrorvale for generations but who look a bit Kardise. Some of them have already started leaving the city, Captain Caraway. I might be able to understand why people are behaving the way they are, but that doesn't make it right.'

'No.' Caraway gazed out across the deserted duelling floor, lost in thought. He looked tired. With something akin to shock, Zander realised he'd been so caught up in his own problems that he'd forgotten Ayla had gone to the border to fight. In her absence, Caraway was in charge of everything: the Helm, Darkhaven, Arkannen. His and Ayla's three children. He'd sent older, more experienced Helmsmen to the border and kept the younger ones in the city, which Zander had been selfishly glad of on Ree and Penn's behalf, yet he hadn't been able to do the same for Ayla. He must be afraid for her every day. He must be desperate to find the evidence that would prove her innocence and put an end to the fighting. Yet he'd still found the time to rescue Zander from a couple of idiots and tell him *I don't hate the Kardise*, even though he had far more right than most.

That generosity of spirit, as much as anything else, was why Zander was still in Mirrorvale instead of fleeing home with his tail between his legs.

'I'll speak to the Captain of the Watch,' Caraway said, oblivious to Zander's tumbling thoughts. 'See if she can spare more men to patrol the Elbaite Quarter and keep an eye on the Kardise-run businesses in the city. And the Helm can help to keep the peace in an unofficial capacity, though I'm always wary of treading on Larson's toes. As for you – if you have any more trouble, Zander, just let me know. You shouldn't have to put up with this kind of thing.'

'Thank you,' Zander said quietly. But as Caraway made to get up, he stopped him. 'Captain ... is there anything I can do to help?'

'With keeping the peace?'

'With ending the war.'

Caraway hesitated, before settling back down beside him. 'To be honest, Zander, I don't think there is. I'm not sure ...' He closed his eyes for a moment, pinching the bridge of his nose, before finishing, 'I'm not sure there's anything anyone can do.'

'Then there's no hope at all of finding the proof you need?'

'Oh, there's always hope.' Tipping his head back against the wall, he added softly, 'Just not a great deal of it.'

'Why not? If you don't mind me asking.'

'Because although I know there are people in this city who conspired to take Mirrorvale to war with Sol Kardis, I can't find out who they are without the cooperation of a bunch of rich men who make it their business not to cooperate with the Helm. I'm questioning them anyway, but so far it's bloody slow going.' Caraway shot him a sidelong glance. 'It's enough to drive a man to drink.'

Startled, Zander swung round to face him – *but surely it must be all right if he can joke about it.* All the same, just to make sure, he said tentatively, 'Sir, you're not ... I mean, you haven't ...'

'No,' Caraway said. 'Ayla trusts me.'

'It's that simple?'

Caraway's eyebrows lifted. 'Isn't it?'

Unsure whether they were still talking about Caraway himself or something else entirely, Zander said nothing.

'I taught her the sword in here, you know,' Caraway added. 'A couple of years ago. After unarmed combat, it seemed the logical next step. And she'd always wanted to learn, so ...'

'Is she good at it?' Zander asked curiously. In response, the captain's lips curled in a slow smile that was equal parts amusement and pride.

'Damn straight.' After a moment, though, the smile faded. 'But it doesn't matter, does it? I could teach her every combat trick I know, but that wouldn't keep her safe during wartime. Nothing can do that, not for anyone. The only sure way of not dying in battle is not to go into battle in the first place.' He scrubbed his hands through his hair; for a moment, his façade slipped until he was no longer Captain of the Helm, just a frightened young man. 'A few nights ago, there was a raid. The Kardise set a fire. People died, on both sides. I had to send more men to the border, men who hadn't been fully trained. And still, the wealthy investors of Arkannen refuse to help me!'

Zander didn't know what to say. He wanted to know more about the raid – his mind kept jumping from his father to Helmsmen he knew, from the boys he'd grown up with to the boys he was doing his best to train in the city. Yet he didn't think he was even meant to know about it. As far as the citizens of Arkannen were concerned, news from the border was sporadic and largely positive; it was only a moment of stress that had induced Caraway to reveal anything different.

'And you really don't have any other leads?' he asked instead.

'Take a look, if you like.' Caraway fished a small notebook out of his pocket, turning it to a particular page before handing it to Zander. 'See if anything strikes you.'

His tone didn't suggest he believed anything would come of it – more that he was desperate enough to try anything – but Zander took the notebook anyway. The way he felt right now, he was desperate enough to try anything, too.

Caraway had set out all the pertinent points of the investigation across a double-page spread. Zander read through it all, carefully, but the captain was right: there was little enough to go on. Certainly nothing came to his own mind that would be at all helpful.

Absurdly disappointed, he flicked through the rest of the notebook – and then a name caught his eye. *Maurais*. He knew that name, from somewhere in his distant past as the polite and well-behaved son of a councillor. He just couldn't quite remember where.

'Captain?' he asked. 'Who's this?'

Caraway leaned over and frowned at the page. 'Sorry. Terrible handwriting. It was the name of the previous owner of the warehouse where Sorrow overheard a meeting of the

Free Arkannen group. He died years ago, and I couldn't find any connection to the present business. There are certainly no current trade investors of that name.'

'He had a daughter,' Zander said slowly. The story was coming back to him piece by piece, from some long-ago dinner-party conversation that had no doubt seemed interminable at the time. 'It was still being talked about even when I was a child, because it was such a sore point for my father and his friends ... Giovano Maurais's daughter married a factory owner, here in the city. Not just any factory owner: Derrick Tarran, the man who controls the world's supply of taransey. The Kardise were convinced it was their chance to finally learn the secret of how it was made, but Liliane Maurais never told anyone back home. Not even her father, when he was alive.'

'Taransey,' Caraway repeated. He looked dazed, as though Zander's words had hit him like a weapon. 'I'm a fucking idiot. You're sure about this, Zander?'

'I think so ...' Yet even as he said it, Caraway was on his feet.

'I'd better go. I need to follow this up. But, Zander ... thank you. Maybe you've ended the war after all.'

He was out of sight before Zander had the chance to formulate a reply.

TWENTY

A man who was plotting against his overlord, Sorrow thought, really ought to know better than to leave his window open. Particularly when that man was also wealthy enough to be a prime target for every thief this side of the border.

Admittedly, the open window was at the back of the house, top floor, where no-one could reach it in a hurry. And the occupant had gone so far as to station a guard at the back door as well as the front. All the same, she'd known thieves who could have turned over the whole place before either guard or homeowner knew what had hit him.

Of course, *could* have wasn't the same as *would* have. The Charoite Quarter might seem to offer the richest pickings, but in fact it was hardly ever burgled; the best targets were those who were comfortably well off, not extraordinarily so. *Comfortable* wasn't enough to put expensive security measures in place, and *comfortable* couldn't afford to hire some ruthless bastard to find out the name of the thief and make them pay in blood. Sorrow herself had done more than one job like that on behalf of the city's elite, tracking down a petty thief or opportunist who had more intelligence than sense and showing him the error of his ways. The very rich never cared much about getting their money or possessions back; what they cared about was demonstrating their power. Sending a message. In all Sorrow's years as a sellsword, none of them had ever asked her to kill anyone. They preferred to leave their victims alive.

She'd never been bothered by that sort of job. She'd never been bothered by *any* sort of job. But now, she found herself grimly satisfied by the idea of doing to Derrick Tarran what his kind had ordered done to so many others.

We've found out who owns that warehouse, Caraway had said to her, holding out two pieces of paper. *The one where the smuggled firearms were stored and the Free Arkannen group met. I need you to interrogate him.*

Sorrow had taken the papers. One was a will leaving all Giovano Maurais's property and possessions to his daughter and only child, Liliane. The other was a deed recording the marriage of Liliane Maurais to Derrick Tarran.

Tarran, she'd said. *Aren't they the taransey people?*

Yes. Derrick Tarran is the current owner of the taransey distillery. We believe he supplied the poisoned bottle for the group.

Right. She'd shrugged. *Seems like you have enough evidence to make an arrest. So why ask me?*

Because we don't have any time. I need him to talk, and quickly.

Go beat him up yourself. You're perfectly capable of it.

Naeve ... He'd given her a pleading look. *You know I can't. I have to be the law. And the law goes and arrests him, and we have a polite conversation in which he tells me precisely nothing, and I search his house and find no evidence ... and then when I'm forced to release him because I can't make anything stick, he goes home and burns what-*

ever it was he managed to conceal from me in the first place. I can't risk that. This is the only chance we have to end this war.

So – just to be sure – you want me to break into his house and make him talk, by any means necessary?

Caraway had hesitated, then nodded. *Do whatever it takes. But, Naeve, remember ... I trust you.*

She glanced up at the open window one more time. Yes, she had known plenty of thieves who could have made a dramatic entrance through that window. She, on the other hand, was going to take an easier route.

Straightening up from her crouch behind Tarran's outhouse, she hurled a stone at the fence on the opposite side, then emerged from her hiding place. As she'd hoped, the sound of the impact had made the young guard turn his head. She was by his side before the moment's distraction had passed.

'Don't move,' she said softly. 'Unless you want to die horribly.'

He had enough sense to obey, but his eyes cut towards her in a clear demonstration of scepticism. 'I don't think you're tall enough to cut my throat, sweetheart.'

She gave him something akin to a smile. 'It's not your throat that's in danger, *darling*.'

His gaze moved slowly downwards. When he looked back at her, his cheeks were visibly paler.

'I really don't think it's worth losing that on Derrick Tarran's behalf,' Sorrow said. 'Do you?'

'What do you want? Who are you?'

She pressed the pistol into his groin a little harder, and he suppressed a yelp. 'Naeve Sorrow. You may have heard of me. I want Tarran's back door key.'

The guard nodded, sweat on his brow. Ever so slowly, he

slid a hand into his pocket and brought out a set of keys. Sorrow took it.

'Good. Now bugger off and pretend you never had this job, or I'll blow your balls off.'

Once he'd gone – vaulting over the wall as if he feared she was about to use him for target practice – she unlocked the door. Maybe the guard would go for help and come back, but she doubted it. Besides, she'd be gone before then. All the same, just in case, she locked the door behind her before venturing further into the house.

She found Derrick Tarran in a room that looked like an office, sitting at a desk with his back to her. She didn't bother with subtlety. After closing the door silently behind her, she crept up behind him and held her pistol to his head.

'Don't move,' she said, as she had to the guard. 'I'm sure you're filthy rich enough to know what a pistol can do to your skull.'

He had tensed at the first sound of her voice, but now his shoulders relaxed again.

'Quite so,' he said affably. 'But if you want money, you should know I don't have much to hand. We filthy rich don't keep it in the house, you know.'

Sorrow didn't point out that he was certain to have a safe full of valuables somewhere in his office. Instead, she took out the cord she'd brought with her and, as swiftly as possible, began tying him to his chair.

'Is there anyone else in the house?' she asked as she worked.

'My wife is upstairs. My son is out. The servants are doing whatever servants do.'

'All right.' She finished the last knot. 'Then you'd better keep your voice down. Understand? Make a noise that's loud enough to fetch anyone, and I'll kill you.'

Without waiting for a reply, she walked round into his line of sight and sat down on the edge of his desk. His eyes widened, then narrowed.

'Naeve Sorrow. You, of all people, should know what will happen to anyone who steals from me.'

She shook her head. 'I don't want your money. I want information. And *you*, of all people, should know what I'm willing to do to get it.'

'I'm not one of your low-class thugs, Naeve. Touch me, and I'll see you hobbled and blinded. Forced to live out your days without teeth or fingertips. You think you're the only sellsword who can do that kind of work? If I send enough of them after you, even you won't be able to escape.'

Sorrow smiled.

Then, very deliberately, she leaned forward.

'Ah, Derrick. You're a clever man, but you're missing one very important fact.' She put her lips right up to his ear, dropping her voice to a whisper. 'This time, I have the law on my side.'

He scoffed. 'Sunk so low as to accept jobs from the Watch, now, have you? I hate to tell you this, Naeve, but you've been misinformed. The Watch won't touch me.' Abruptly, he turned his head until they were almost nose to nose; his hot breath left flecks of saliva on her skin. 'Money does a remarkable job of proving one's innocence.'

She straightened up, resisting the urge to wipe her face with her sleeve. 'The Watch might be in your pocket, but the Helm aren't.'

'The Helm?' For the first time, she saw unease in his expression. 'What have they got to do with it?'

'I'm here on Darkhaven's behalf,' Sorrow said. 'You've been playing at sedition, haven't you, Derrick?'

'I don't know what you –'

'Free Arkannen.' She rolled her eyes. 'It's not a very original name for a rebel group, is it? Do you actually believe all that shit about reclaiming Mirrorvale for the Mirrorvalese? Or is this war simply a way for you to make money?'

His lips curled contemptuously. 'You're crazy.'

'I was there, Derrick. At the meeting after the ambassador's death. I didn't see your face, but I know it was you. What was it you said?' She pretended to think. 'Oh, yes. *Soon the Kardise scourge will come to an end.* Does your Kardise *wife* know that's your opinion?'

'Prove it.'

She drew Caraway's papers from her inside pocket and held them up. The man's eyes widened a fraction, and she saw the bobbing of his throat as he swallowed.

'Being on the side of the law is a pain in the arse,' Sorrow said. 'You have to have a load of evidence before you can do anything. Look at poor Captain Caraway and his futile attempts to get even the slightest whiff of information from your kind. If it was up to me, I'd have worked my way through every damn investor's house I could find until one of you squealed.' She shrugged. 'But luckily for your colleagues, we discovered this first.'

'I don't see how that proves anything.'

'An investor going by the name of Jack Malone stored illegal firearms in a particular warehouse where the Free Arkannen group met. An investor going by the name of Jack Malone is also listed as purchasing the bottle of taransey they used to kill the ambassador. Since you own both warehouse and distillery, and since you went out of your way to claim the bottle had been resealed despite your own foreman's opinion to the contrary, it's not hard to see the truth. You poisoned it yourself, before you even put the seal on it. Not many people in this city could do that.'

'If you know all this, then why are you here?'

'I need more,' she said. 'That's why. I need evidence that proves Free Arkannen, and not Ayla Nightshade, was behind the Kardise ambassador's death. And you're going to give it to me.'

'Not a chance.'

Sorrow glanced down at her pistol, turning it over in her hands, then placed it carefully beside her on the desk.

'About eight years ago, I was employed by a factory owner like you,' she said. 'One of his supply trains had been robbed, and he wanted revenge. He thought the usual people were behind it – you know, the crime syndicates, the fences and traffickers. The ones who make a profit from other people's loss, just like your kind do, but don't try to set themselves up as respectable citizens in the process. Their existence always seems to piss off your lot. I suppose it's like looking in a more honest mirror.

'Anyway, after a bit of persuasion, I found out it wasn't a syndicate job. The thieves had been employed by another factory owner. Young man, up-and-coming, investing in the same kind of goods. I went after him. But when I caught up with him, he offered me twice as much pay to keep it quiet. So I went back to the thieves.' She shrugged. 'Ever heard a finger break, Derrick? It's quite a distinctive sound. Just like a twig snapping, and as easily done.'

'What's your point?' Tarran demanded. There was an edge of fear underlying his voice, but it hadn't quite broken through yet. He still believed himself untouchable. 'You work for the highest bidder. Is that it? You want paying for your silence? I can offer you two hundred ranols –'

'No.'

'Three hundred –'

'I don't want your money.' Strange, how she could say that with barely a pang of regret. It wasn't as if Caraway was going to pay her anything like three hundred ranols for this job. She would have taken it, once.

But that was before the bastard sitting in front of her had sent her country to war.

'Come on, Naeve,' he said, moistening dry lips. 'Profits are low. I didn't get nearly as much for those firearms as I'd hoped. The most I can offer you is four hundred –'

She snapped the little finger on his left hand.

When he'd finished groaning and cursing, he looked up at her wild-eyed and drenched in sweat. A spreading patch of damp on his trousers told its own story.

'Bitch! Whore! I'll cut out your eyes with a –'

Calmly, she broke a second finger. It really did sound like a dry twig snapping.

'You forget,' she said, over the sound of his pain. 'I work for Darkhaven now. If I so much as graze my knee after I leave this house, you'll find yourself on trial for treason before you can blink. Your only hope of getting away with nothing worse than a few broken bones is to give me what I want.'

'All right! All right. It was as you say. I supplied the poisoned taransey to the group. One of the other men said he could get hold of an antidote to the poison.'

'His name?'

'I don't know. We wore masks, remember? I knew who one or two of them were, but not the whole group. Safer that way.'

'But this man supplied the antidote.'

'Yes. In fact, he was the one to come up with the plan in

the first place. Said he knew someone on the inside. Someone in Darkhaven. Said he could convince her to plant the poisoned bottle, deliver the antidote. I simply supplied him with the taransey to pass on to her.'

'And then you killed her.'

'Not me.'

'But you agreed to it. I heard you.'

'I ... it wasn't like that. The same man came to us after the ambassador was dead. Said we'd have to do something about the girl, stop her talking, or the entire plan would fail. We agreed. And that was when he told us he'd already taken care of it.'

'This mysterious man – do you know anything else about him?'

'Only that he was the one who brought us all together.'

Sorrow thought about that. So the softly spoken man she'd overheard at the warehouse had been the instigator of the group, despite the fact that he'd apparently allowed Tarran to take the leading role. Ideally she'd find him and drag him off to Darkhaven to confess his crimes. But the important thing, here and now, was to get the evidence needed to stop the war.

'This is all very well, Derrick, but I'm going to need proof.' She dug around in his desk until she found a sheet of paper, then scrawled out a summary of what he'd told her.

'Sign this,' she ordered him, sliding it beneath his good right hand and tucking the pen between his fingers. Even with his wrists tied to the arms of the chair, he ought to be able to manage. He looked at her sullenly.

'I'm not signing any –'

'*Sign it.*' She picked up her pistol again. His sullen expression became more pronounced.

'Wrong hand.'

She shrugged. She couldn't have known he'd turn out to be left-handed.

As he wrote his name at the bottom of the page, wincing and cursing at the pain, Sorrow tried to decide if she'd done enough. Ideally she'd hunt down the softly spoken man and, with him, any evidence of this previously unknown antidote to the poison that had killed Tolino. Still, she had a signed confession from one of the perpetrators; surely that would be sufficient to call a halt to the war. She took the confession from Tarran – making sure to remove the pen from him as well – and tucked it into her pocket.

'Anything else?' he growled.

'I suppose,' she said slowly, 'I'd like to know why you did it.'

It was an odd question. Not one she'd intended to ask. She didn't care why people acted in the stupid ways they did; all that mattered was the results.

Yet something was niggling at her. There was something she was missing. And until she'd worked it out, she didn't plan on leaving.

'Why do you think I did it?' Tarran retorted. He'd recovered himself somewhat, now, though his two broken fingers were swelling and darkening. 'To put a stop to Ayla's crazy plans for peace. The city is already overrun with foreigners, and now she wants to usher in more of them? Not that you'd understand –' his gaze swept her contemptuously – 'but some of us don't want to see the Mirrorvalese bloodlines diluted any more than they have been already.'

Since Sorrow had always enjoyed the fact that she had ancestors from every country in the known world, she was able to ignore the insult. Instead, she pointed out, 'You have a Kardise wife. Your son is half Kardise. By your reckoning, you chose to dilute your own bloodline.'

'That was different,' Tarran said dismissively. 'I married for profit, not principle.'

She shook her head, the niggle becoming an itch. While human inconsistency never surprised her any more, the distillery owner's motives were far more inconsistent than most. It wasn't impossible that a man could believe strongly in keeping foreign blood out of Mirrorvale and yet take a Kardise wife – just unlikely. Far more probable that *profit, not principle* was his driving force in everything. She'd said it herself: *is this war simply a way for you to make money?* And the answer was almost certainly yes.

'Profit,' she said. 'That's the truth, isn't it? You're not doing this out of principle, but out of greed ...'

Her voice trailed off. Something was yelling in her subconscious, trying to make itself known. And then, suddenly, she had it.

'But you don't have anything to gain from war,' she said softly.

'What?'

'I can't believe I've only just realised it. You own the taransey distillery. A few other factories around the city, none of them making things that would be relevant to the war effort. You're one of the few investors in Arkannen who stands to earn almost nothing from this conflict! Admittedly there was that shipment of illegal firearms, but that hardly brought in the kind of wealth that people like you are interested in. So ...'

She stared at him, and he stared back. His face was impassive, but small beads of sweat glistened at his hairline.

'So you must be earning money from this another way,' she said. 'Someone's paying you for it.'

'No.'

'They are.' She moved closer. 'Who's behind all this, Derrick? The Kardise Brotherhood? Who is it that's making it worth your while?'

His lunge nearly finished her. She hadn't seen him work his right hand free. She certainly hadn't felt him take a knife from her belt. The only warning was the flash of metal as he drove the blade towards her, aiming beneath her ribcage. She twisted aside, and the knife glanced off her body and cut deep into the flesh of her upper arm. Her pistol was still on the desk; she grabbed it before retreating out of his reach. In the same instant, he cut his left hand free and sprang back, kicking the chair out of the way. They faced each other warily.

'You're not a warrior,' Sorrow said. 'Put that down before you hurt yourself.'

His teeth showed in a snarl. 'Not everyone who lives in Charoite is soft and idle, Naeve Sorrow. I was being trained in the fifth ring when you were still a babe in arms.'

He flicked the knife at her, spraying her own blood into her eyes. She wiped it away with the back of one wrist, stumbling back so he couldn't close the gap between them. Silently, she cursed herself. She'd underestimated him. And, clearly, it was a matter of importance to him not to reveal his paymaster – which meant it was equally important that she get it out of him.

Which, in turn, meant she couldn't shoot him. Not yet.

Perhaps recognising her hesitation, he lunged forward. She knocked his arm out of the way, then transferred the pistol to her left hand and drew another knife with her right. He was fighting with his non-dominant hand. That would give her an advantage, though perhaps a small one. She slashed at his broken fingers, making him cry out.

'Who's paying you?'

'No-one.'

He raised his knife again, but she spun and scored her blade across his inner elbow. Swearing, he dropped the weapon, stumbling backwards away from her. Then she had him pinned against the wall with her pistol against his temple –

I trust you, Caraway's voice said somewhere in her mind.

Her finger tightened on the trigger – and stopped. *Fuck.* If she was going to shoot him, she'd have done it by now. Captain bloody Caraway had done a number on her, and now she was going to drag this bastard up to Darkhaven alive, like a good little girl.

She began to say something, and that was when Tarran's foot hit her in the side of the knee, loosening her hold on him. His good right hand came up over her left, the one holding the pistol. She strove to keep it pointed at his head, but gradually he forced it round towards her. *Shit. He's stronger than me.*

But she had the use of a second hand.

Even as his fingers pressed down hard on hers, she dropped the knife and brought her right hand up to clasp his, wrenching the pistol back round. Heat scorched her cheek. Tarran slammed into the wall and slid down it, leaving a thick smear of blood and brains in his wake.

Dead. Sorrow shook her head in a vain attempt to relieve her ringing ears. *The fucking bastard.* He'd been determined not to reveal who'd paid him to betray his overlord, which meant it was the one thing Caraway probably needed to know. Worse – she'd done her very best not to kill him, and he'd bloody well died anyway. How was she going to explain that one?

Still, for now the important thing was to get out of this house before the servants came to find out if anything was wrong. She holstered her pistol, picked up the pieces of cut cord and her discarded knife, and slipped out of the room.

TWENTY-ONE

Since the attack on the fort and her subsequent retaliation, Ayla had found herself eating more and more quickly, sleeping less and less, and spending as much time in her creature skin as possible. She'd begun to feel the wildness of it even when she was human; her emotions were fading, becoming starker and less complicated. It was easier that way. Easier to become the ice and ebonwood of which her Alicorn-self was made than to stay human and keep *caring*. People were destroyed by war, but Changer creatures throve on it. War was what they had been made for. It would have been foolish not to use that.

Sometimes she wondered if this was how her father had felt, all the time. If that was why he'd been how he was. She'd never thought of it, before. Never realised how the Change could alter her, even when she was human. Maybe she couldn't return to who she'd been before. Maybe she'd discovered her true nature here on the battlefield.

Her children wouldn't know her. But somehow, that didn't matter so much any more.

On the fourth day after the burning of the fort, a cry went up that the beacon fires to the east had been lit. Ayla led a small fleet of airships to investigate, and discovered that a larger fleet of Kardise airships had crossed the border into Mirrorvale. The patrolmen left in the watchtowers had seen them coming and raised the alarm.

Fall back, Ayla told her own pilots. *Await my orders.* And then she went to meet the enemy.

The Kardise ships were armed with guns, but that was of little account to her. If anything, she was amused by the fact that they had thought to outwit her with such fragile toys. Though the envelope of an airship was strong, it tore like paper beneath the diamond hardness of her horn. She ripped three ships from the air, sending them and their crews to crumple and burn on the ground below, before the rest of the fleet fled. Then she led her own ships back to the Whispering Plain, exulting in the fact that not a single one of her men had been lost.

When they got there, they found carnage.

While she was gone, the full Kardise army had attacked. The Mirrorvalese army had stood their ground, but they were outnumbered and outgunned. They were dying. Everywhere Ayla looked, they were dying.

She flew straight over her own people and landed in the middle of the Kardise troops, trampling men beneath her hooves. Her horn pierced flesh and armour alike, catching people before they could charge towards her and throwing them bloody and broken to the ground. A ring of riflemen surrounded her, lifting their weapons to their shoulders as they took aim. She rose up on her hind legs and opened her wings to their fullest extent, presenting herself in defiance. Let them try to shoot her. They would soon discover their mistake.

A hundred miniature explosions. A hundred flashes of light. The air grew thick with the smell of gunpowder. She felt the sting of the bullets as they struck her and bounced off, but they mattered as little to her as the buzz of flies. She flung back her head, letting loose a piercingly sweet cry. And then she ran at them, stabbing and kicking and biting and trampling until they and their weapons were nothing more than twisted flesh and metal beneath her feet. She tore at them and raged at them until, finally, the Kardise army turned and ran.

Victory. She flew back to join her own people on their side of the border. Yet when she landed, she turned and screamed defiance at the Kardise once more. They couldn't defeat her. They would never defeat her. She was invincible.

Later that night, once the bodies had been removed and the wounded taken to the medical tent, Ayla returned to human form for some food. Yet she couldn't stop shivering. People had died. Some she'd killed. Some she'd failed to protect. In a single day, she'd seen more blood spilled than she'd seen in a lifetime. And it could happen again. It *would* happen again. Because she couldn't be everywhere. Because one Changer creature, however powerful, was not enough to defend an entire country.

In the end, she had to retreat to her tent to eat, so that no-one would see her shaking hands. And when she came out, she Changed straight back into her Alicorn form again. It was easier that way.

Accompanied by a handful of his men, Caraway had just carried out his usual checks around the perimeter of Darkhaven, prior to locking it up for the night, when he heard his name being called. He turned to see Naeve Sorrow striding up the hillside towards him, the front and one sleeve of her shirt splashed liberally with scarlet like a warning flag.

'Is that your blood?' he asked her. She gave her left arm a cursory glance.

'Some of it.'

Caraway followed her gaze to the gaping hole in the fabric and the raw, glistening wound that showed through it. 'I'll send for the physician –'

'It won't kill me,' Sorrow said impatiently. 'This is urgent.'

'Understood. And if it's all the same to you, I'd rather you didn't pass out before you've finished telling me.'

He followed her through the postern gate into Darkhaven's central square, ordering one of the Helmsmen with him to run for the physician. Then he turned to her.

'Well? Did you speak to Derrick Tarran?'

'I have evidence for you,' Sorrow said. She handed him a sheet of paper. 'A signed confession from Tarran himself. From what he said, it seems clear enough that your murdered maid was the traitor within Darkhaven. But there's also a man we should try to find, somewhere out there in the city. The one who killed the girl, supplied the antidote and masterminded the entire plan. I think he'd have some interesting things to tell us.'

Caraway noted the *we* and *us*, but made no comment. He was too overwhelmed with relief. Surely this would be enough, if not to make peace, then at least to end the fighting …

Gil arrived at that point, ready to patch Sorrow up, which gave Caraway a chance to fight down the embarrassing lump in his throat. It wasn't long before he was able to ask, quite normally, 'And Tarran?'

'Dead.' She shifted a little under his stare, the closest she ever came to showing discomfort. 'Not my choice, I assure you! I did my best to keep him alive. But the stupid man wouldn't accept defeat. He tried to kill me, and during the struggle ...'

'It was an accident?'

'That's what I said.' Her expression hardening, Sorrow folded her arms, ignoring Gil's faint protest. 'Should I take it, then, that all your bullshit about trusting me was just that?'

Caraway shook his head. 'Of course not. I believe you. But for him to be ready to kill you, even though he knew you were there on Darkhaven's behalf ... he must have been keeping a massive secret. Something that would have ruined him completely, if it had come out.'

The defensive expression faded as she considered that. 'Yes. And my best guess is ...'

'The Kardise Brotherhood?' Caraway said it with her. 'Mine too. If it was ever revealed that Tarran had conspired with the Kardise to bring Mirrorvale to war, the people would be clamouring for his head. Ayla would have to execute him; no way around it, for that sort of treachery. And we would be within our rights to seize every factory he owned – the distillery, too – which would leave his family with nothing.'

'If you find the softly spoken man, you might uncover the truth,' Sorrow said. 'He played a key part in it all, and I got the impression that Derrick knew more about him than he let on. Perhaps he was a representative of whoever was paying Derrick.'

Caraway nodded. 'I'll set some of my men on it. We need to find out as soon as possible. Because if the Kardise Brotherhood were behind the war, I don't know that any amount of evidence will be able to stop it.'

He hesitated, not liking to ask the next question when Sorrow had already been wounded – but it was important.

'Naeve, will you take the evidence to Sol Kardis for me? And tell Ayla everything that happened between you and Tarran. I think she needs to know.'

The physician looked up in alarm. 'Sir, I really don't think she should be going anywhere so soon after –'

'Rubbish,' Sorrow said. She hesitated. 'Is Elisse all right, Caraway? And Corus?'

'Fine. I had another report from their guard today.'

She nodded. 'Then I'll take it. First thing in the morning.'

Miles fidgeted uncomfortably in the shadows of the Sun Lord's temple. It had already been night when he'd received the summons, and he didn't like being in Luka's temple at night. A temple without its god was a strange and lonely place. Not only that, but after greeting him, his contact had fallen into silence. It was only after what felt like an endless wait that the faceless man finally spoke.

'We have a problem. The war may end sooner than we expected.'

Relief washed over Miles like clear spring water on a summer's day. He wanted to leap up and shout his thanks to the absent Sun Lord. The war would come to an end. And since Miles hadn't been the one to reveal the truth, surely the faceless man wouldn't take it out on Art. Unless …

'What happened?' he asked anxiously.

'A man signed a confession. Never fear –' this with an edge to it that suggested the faceless man knew very well what Miles was thinking – 'Parovia was not implicated. But we need to strike now.'

'Strike?'

'This is the only chance we will have to discover the secret of the Change.'

Miles frowned. He knew, of course, that Parovia wanted the secret of the Change. The closer he'd become to Ayla Nightshade, the more pressure he'd been under to supply it. Yet like collars that protected ordinary soldiers from bullets, the secret of the Change was too vast a power to be attained by a large country like Parovia – a country that could use it to conquer the world. And so he had fed back bits and pieces of his research, giving the Parovian alchemists enough to work on without ever revealing some of the most fundamental truths he had uncovered. But if the faceless man thought the secret could be discovered soon ...

'How?' he asked cautiously.

'We need those documents. The ones you identified. We had thought there would be time for you to smuggle them out, piece by piece, but if Ayla returns ... no. We need to act fast. Seize everything in a single raid.'

Miles wasn't sure if the faceless man could see him in the moonlight, but he nodded to hide his relief. The documents he had identified to his contacts in Parovia were valuable and old, kept not in the library but in the treasury, under lock and key. They'd been written in the time of the first Changers and were almost impossible to translate – so much so that he had been able to claim his inability to do so without calling down suspicion. But based on what he *had* managed to decipher of them, they wouldn't reveal the deep secrets that Parovia desired.

All the same, a raid on Darkhaven ...

'You are not going to hurt anyone?' he asked. Then, hastily, because the question revealed too much of his weakness, 'No suspicion will fall on me?'

'Not if you are clever,' the voice said. 'But either way, you could not have hoped to remain detached forever. You have done a good job of supplying us with information, Miles, but this time we need more. This time, you will be required to get your hands dirty.'

'W-what do you want me to do?'

The faceless man told him. Afterwards, he held out two bottles and said, 'If you do this, we will release you from our service.'

'Really?' That sounded too good to be true. 'Why –'

'Because you are no longer of much use,' the faceless man said acidly. 'Just make sure you keep our secrets, Miles, if you want your weaponmaster to live a full and happy life.'

'I will.' Miles took the bottles. He noticed his hands were shaking. Freedom. At last. He could put his guilt behind him and make a real, forever life for himself here in Mirrorvale. In Darkhaven. With Art.

You have this one last job to do first, he reminded himself. *And this is not simply a matter of sitting back and letting a war happen. This is actual treachery ...*

Still, no-one was going to die this time. That was something.

TWENTY-TWO

An airship was approaching from deeper in Mirrorvale. The patterning on the envelope indicated that it was the morning's courier ship arriving as usual from Arkannen, so Ayla didn't rise to meet it. She remained in place, patrolling the front line, while some of the Helm went to investigate.

When they returned, it was in somewhat more disarray than they had left. There was scuffling and jostling, a good bit of swearing, and Ayla heard Naeve Sorrow's voice above the rest.

'Get off me, you blithering idiots! I was sent by your captain and you know it!'

The Helm parted, and Sorrow stumbled out from their midst as though she had been pushed. She shot a narrow-eyed glance back over her shoulder at the offending Helmsman, before turning to find herself face to face with Ayla. It was the first time Ayla had ever seen fear in her eyes.

'I ...' She backed away a step, then caught herself and squared her shoulders. 'Lady Ayla. I bring you news from Darkhaven.'

Go on, Ayla sent into her mind. The woman's eyes widened still further.

'Fuck. I mean – fuck. I didn't know you could –'

How else would we command our troops on the battlefield?

'Right. Of course.' Sorrow visibly took hold of herself. 'Captain Caraway sent me. I have the evidence you need to prove to the Kardise that you didn't kill their ambassador.'

Ayla gazed at her. Even in creature form, even frozen and resolute, she couldn't deny the hot emotion that surged through her. It was relief. Utter, glorious relief.

No more death.

No more *killing.*

She Changed, and as she did so the emotion intensified. By the time she was in human form, with a Helmsman handing her a robe, her eyes were full of tears.

'Thank you,' she managed, blinking them back. She wanted to kiss the woman. But she was still a leader, and still at war; no time for softness. 'Come to my tent, and we'll discuss it.'

Once they were alone, Sorrow handed her the evidence and told her everything that had passed between herself and Derrick Tarran. It was almost overwhelming, but one thing was clear: this was a chance. If the Kardise didn't accept it as enough reason to at least call a temporary truce, there was little chance they'd accept anything.

'I brought you something else, as well.' Sorrow took another package out of her pocket. 'From Captain Caraway.'

Ayla unfolded it. The topmost sheet of paper was grubby and a little crumpled. In Marlon's uneven handwriting, it proclaimed *we love you mama come back soon Marlon.* Underneath that, Katya had printed her name in large wobbly letters, and there was even a faint *W* for Wyrenne.

The second sheet of paper was a letter.

Dearest love.

I have thought it best not to write to you directly before now. War leaves no room for emotion and no time for softness. You are leading an army. I am doing my best to run Arkannen in your absence. We cannot spare any energy for love.

Yet I have every hope that what Naeve has brought you will mean an end to the war. I know it will take time to achieve. I know you will have to start all over again with the treaty. But we have time. As long as the fighting stops, we have time.

Every evening I stand above the main gate and look out across Arkannen to where you are. I try to keep you safe by force of will. Stupid, I know, but it feels wrong that I'm not there to defend you on the battlefield, as is both my duty and my privilege. I would give my life for yours in an instant, Ayla. Never doubt that.

I hold you in my heart, now and always.

Tomas

This time, she couldn't stop the tears falling. She cried for Tomas, and for her children. For all the people who had died and all the people she had killed. Even, a little, for herself. When she finally looked up, Sorrow was gazing at the walls of the tent with a profoundly uncomfortable expression; yet in her outstretched hand was a square piece of cloth. A smudge of something black marked one corner, but Ayla took it anyway and wiped her eyes.

'Thank you,' she said, when she felt sufficiently in control of herself to speak. 'For the messages, and for the handkerchief.'

'It's actually a cleaning cloth for my pistol,' Sorrow answered. 'Lucky for you, I had a newish one on me.'

Ayla surprised herself with a rather watery giggle. In

response, Sorrow's mouth turned up slightly at the corners. Her eyes held more warmth than they ever had before, Ayla thought. Or maybe she was just seeing warmth in everything, now that she herself had unfrozen.

'Well,' the sellsword said. 'I'd better get back to Arkannen.'

She stood up. Battling unexpected disappointment, Ayla stood up too. As Sorrow passed her, she found herself reaching out to touch the woman's arm.

'Naeve!' The sellsword turned to look at her, the usual flat expression back in her hazel eyes, and Ayla bit her lip. 'Sorrow. Will you stay?'

'What for? I wanted to get back and make sure Corus –'

'I know. But Tomas has him well guarded. And I think it would help. I have to take this evidence to the Kardise and convince them to agree a truce. So if you could be there to give your testimony ...'

'They didn't pay much heed to my word before, did they?'

'No,' Ayla admitted. 'But maybe with the evidence *and* you ...'

Sorrow shrugged. 'All right. If that's what you want, I don't have any choice, do I? You're my overlord.'

'I don't recall that ever making a difference before,' Ayla said acerbically, and the sellsword nodded in acknowledgement of a hit.

'Maybe seeing your other form scared the shit out of me. Or maybe ... maybe I finally understand the point of you, Ayla Nightshade.'

'Thank you. I think.'

'Put it this way,' Sorrow said. 'I'm glad you're still not dead.'

Ayla had the fleeting urge to embrace her, but she settled for a smile instead. 'Me too.'

Derrick Tarran's widow, Liliane, projected an air of composure, but her red eyes betrayed her grief. Seeing her for the first time – the brown skin an almost identical shade to Zander's, the dark hair and eyes – Ree understood certain things about Lewis that had puzzled her before. Every feature that he clearly hadn't inherited from his father had just as clearly come from his mother; he was a perfect mixture of the two of them. Half Kardise – because that was where Liliane had come from, according to Captain Caraway. Surely she couldn't have had any idea what her husband was doing, murdering one of her own people and setting her country-by-marriage at war with her country-by-birth.

'We're very sorry to have disturbed you at such a difficult time,' Ree said. She and Penn had been shown into the library of the Tarran residence by the butler, whose chilly politeness had left them in no doubt of his opinion of Helmsmen turning up on his doorstep. Yet once he had consented to deliver their message to the lady of the house, she had arrived promptly and with no outward appearance of similar disdain. Either her servants reflected her husband's opinions more than her own, or she was too well trained to betray any kind of negative emotion.

'I am always happy to help the Helm,' Liliane murmured. 'Particularly with all the current trouble.'

Ree found the euphemism irritating; she didn't stop to analyse how much of that might be because she could imagine her own mother saying something very similar. Deliberately, she chose bluntness.

'The war must be difficult for you.'

Liliane's hands gripped each other in her lap, but her voice remained unchanged. 'I assure you, my loyalties lie squarely with Mirrorvale.'

'I don't doubt it,' Ree said. 'The Tarrans have been loyal subjects of the Nightshade line for centuries.'

She watched the woman's face closely, but saw nothing that might betray her knowledge of Derrick Tarran's activities. Liliane simply nodded, and then – as the pause grew longer – raised her eyebrows in gentle enquiry.

'Forgive me, but you have not yet told me why you are here.'

Ree couldn't decide if Liliane was hiding something or if she herself had been unforgivably rude. She glanced at Penn, who cleared his throat.

'We're trying to find out why your husband died.'

'Is that usual?' Liliane asked. 'For the Helm, and not the Watch, to investigate a death in the fourth ring?'

'No. But as you said, these are troubled times.'

'I see.' The words were spoken with so little emotion that Ree couldn't work out what they meant. Perhaps Liliane had known of her husband's treachery. Perhaps she hadn't known, but now feared what might come to light. Perhaps she was simply a grieving widow whose mind was somewhere else entirely. Whatever the truth, it seemed clear they would gain little information from her.

'We'll need to search your husband's office,' Penn said. Again, Liliane showed no reaction.

'I will ring for someone to show you up.'

Yet when a footman arrived at the main door to the library and gestured them to follow him, Liliane held Ree back.

'You are the girl my son wanted to marry,' she said softly. Startled, Ree only nodded. Liliane touched her arm. 'Thank you.'

'What for?'

'For standing up for him.' She backed away a step, inclining her head in farewell. 'I hope you find what you are looking for.'

Then she was gone, disappearing through the other door, and Ree hurried to catch up with the footman.

In Derrick Tarran's office, she and Penn set to searching. *Anything that might tell us who was paying him,* Captain Caraway had said. *Or anything that might lead us to the other conspirators.* Yet the contents of Tarran's desk were innocuous enough. If there was a clue here, it was too opaque for her to find.

'Ree?' She glanced over her shoulder to find Lewis in the doorway. Immediately she left what she was doing and went to meet him. Purple shadows lurked beneath his eyes, but he managed a smile. 'What are you doing here?'

She hesitated, before giving him the same half-truth that Penn had given Liliane. 'Trying to find out why your father died.'

He said nothing. His fingers crept up to the bridge of his nose and squeezed. Ree put a hand on his arm.

'Are you all right?'

'Not really.' His gaze settled on her hand, then slowly climbed to her face as though he'd momentarily forgotten who she was. 'He didn't understand me, but he was still my father.'

Ree nodded. No doubt she'd feel something similar if her father died.

'It seems quite obvious it was murder,' Lewis said in the same flat voice. 'But from what my mother has said, or what she hasn't said, I think she suspects it was justified.' He grimaced. 'My father was ... not an easy man to live with.'

'And what do you think?'

'I think ...' He looked away from her, shoulders slumping

in a sigh. 'I think the Helm wouldn't investigate a death, however wealthy the dead man, unless he'd been involved in something very serious.'

'We're not suggesting anything at this –' Ree began, but he cut her off.

'I think he got himself into something he couldn't get back out of.'

Her heart rate increased. 'What do you mean?'

'My father was involved in every dodgy enterprise you can think of. Firearms, opiates, human trafficking. He thought nothing of running other investors into the ground – your father, many more. He took the money he inherited from the distillery and multiplied it twenty times over, and he did it by seeking out all the dirtiest deals he could.' Lewis shrugged. 'He always told me, *you have to take the risk to gain the prize.* But it wouldn't surprise me if the risk caught up with him.'

Ree said nothing. Part of her was reeling at the extent of both Derrick Tarran's criminality and his son's knowledge of it. The rest of her was desperately disappointed that Lewis hadn't been able to tell her anything she didn't know already.

'The new man probably had something to do with it,' Lewis added.

'What man?'

'Father was involved in something different, recently. Not with any of his usual people; a man with an accent, wearing a mask. I heard them talking in here, late one night.'

'What accent? What did he say? Did you see his face?'

'No. Only the mask, as he walked down the hall. He greeted my father, and his voice was ... I don't know. Not a city accent. But then they closed the door, and I couldn't hear through it.' He shot her a sidelong glance. 'Though I tried. I've never thought it wise to remain ignorant of my father's dealings.'

'Then can you tell me anything at all?' Ree asked urgently. 'Anything that would help us find him?'

Lewis frowned; then his expression cleared. 'He gave my father a calling-card. Hold on.'

He went to the writing cabinet on top of the desk, pulled out a small drawer that appeared to be full of rectangular cards, and rifled through it with his fingertips. Finally, with a triumphant exclamation, he held one aloft.

'Father left it on the hall table while he was showing the man out. I remembered it because it didn't even have a name. Only an address.'

Ree took the card. It read simply, *12a Crucible La. Obsidian.*

'You do know the Watch will be investigating your father's business affairs?' she said softly. 'Anything that's illegal profit will be seized.'

'I know.' Lewis's smile was more genuine this time. 'And in a way I'm glad. It would have been a heavy weight to carry.'

'You think they'll leave you the distillery?'

'I hope so. That would be an honest legacy. But if not ...' He shrugged. 'Maybe I'm not too old to become a teacher after all.'

Briefly, Ree had a vision of what her life would have been like as Lewis's wife. Derrick Tarran had probably been more pleased than any of them had realised, to be given the chance to have a Helmsman as a daughter-in-law. He'd probably hoped that he could bully or blackmail her into giving him inside information or preferential treatment, using her family as leverage. He'd always been a powerful man, able to buy his way out of trouble and arrange everything in the city to his own advantage, yet he'd never been able to touch Darkhaven. She would have been his way in.

Would she have given in to his threats? Impossible to say. But she shivered, all the same, at how close she'd come to being tested. And as if in echo of her fears, Penn straightened up from the cabinet he'd been searching with a heavy piece of paper in his hand.

'I thought you two weren't getting married after all.'

Ree snatched the paper from him. Sure enough, it was a marriage contract. Not just any marriage contract, but a full, traditional marriage contract in which the fathers of the two parties assumed sole responsibility for making the agreement on their children's behalf. It had been a century since such contracts had been widely used and accepted. The only way you'd use a contract like this was if you belonged to a really rich old family whose children had been brought up expecting to be bartered for profit – or, Ree thought miserably, if you were in a lot of debt and desperate.

Hoping it was just a draft, she examined it carefully, but the document bore all the official seals, as well as the signatures of both Derrick Tarran and her own father. And it was dated the very same day that she and Lewis had met for the first time.

'They must have had it witnessed and sealed even as we were getting to know each other,' she muttered. 'Elements! What do we do now?'

'Can't you just get it cancelled?' Penn asked.

'It's not that easy. Once two merchants have agreed a contract and had it legally signed and sealed, neither can go back on it without being blacklisted by the contract clerks for six months. Which is bad for business.' Ree rolled her eyes at Penn's surprised expression. 'I am my father's daughter, you know. The point is, my father can't break the contract without effectively ruining himself.'

'And I can't either,' Lewis agreed. 'I am my father's heir, so in most cases I'd have the ability to break a contract he signed. But this one names me as a subject.' A wry smile. 'That is, Ree and I are essentially the goods in this contract. And if you're the subject of a contract, you can't act for another party in it.'

'It all sounds very complicated,' Penn said uncertainly. 'So does that mean –'

'It means we'll have to sort it out later.' Ree took the contract and shoved it in her pocket. She couldn't think about all that now. 'Thank you, Lewis. I really appreciate your help.'

Out on the street, Penn frowned at her. 'Ree –'

'I don't want to talk about it, Penn.' She walked off in the direction of the Gate of Steel. 'Let's get this address to Captain Caraway.'

Zander had lost his job, of course – almost directly after his encounter with the two merchants' guards in the duelling room. The weaponmaster in charge of bladework had been very apologetic, to the extent of tripping over his words in his haste to explain the decision. *Nothing to do with your work, Zander, you're very – and we'd certainly have you back in an instant after all this is over, if – I mean, it's really not my choice, but the students are beginning to – and with all the new faces here in the fifth ring for battle training, incidents like the one today are only going to become more ... I'm sure you understand.*

He did understand. But that didn't make it any easier.

All the same, things could have been worse. He wasn't sure if Ree had spoken to Captain Caraway – if she had, she wouldn't admit it – or if it was something the captain had thought up on his own, but either way, his lack of a job hadn't led to him being thrown out of the fourth ring. Instead, he'd been given a place in one of the Helm's safe houses.

You can stay here as long as you like, Caraway had said. *We have other people of Kardise descent in similar situations. And we're working with the Watch to keep an eye out for trouble across the city. I don't know if it will be enough, but we're doing our best.*

Zander was grateful, both on his own behalf and on the others', yet staying in the safe house only hammered home to him how much of a stranger he was in Arkannen these days. And too often he found himself staring at the same four walls, unable to face leaving the house and potentially receiving threats and abuse. His friends visited him, of course, when they had time – but understandably, that wasn't often. So when the knock came at the door, he almost leapt to answer it.

'Hello, Zander.' It was Captain Caraway. 'Can I come in?'

'Of course.' Zander stood back to admit him. 'How is it, down in the city?'

'Like a kettle on the verge of boiling.' Caraway looked even more tired than the last time Zander had seen him. 'Someone set fire to a Kardise-owned shop last night. Nearly sent a whole street up in flames. We had to bring out both water cannons *and* make a bucket chain to the canal.'

'Did you catch whoever did it?'

'No.' Caraway dropped into a nearby chair, rubbing his face with both hands. He blinked wearily at Zander. 'Luckily no-one was hurt. Their neighbours raised the alarm and helped get them out. And people came from all over to help put out the fire. So I haven't completely lost my faith in the citizens of Arkannen.' He shook his head. 'But there were children living above that shop, Zander. And someone was prepared to let them burn.'

'That's more than hatred born of fear,' Zander said. 'That's just simple hatred.'

'I still believe what I said before,' Caraway replied. 'Most Mirrorvalese don't hate the Kardise. But a situation like this ... it brings them all out into the light. The ones who *do* hate anyone different from them, who *do* believe Mirrorvale should have stayed as it was a hundred years ago, before peace fell and the borders opened. War legitimises that. It provides an excuse.' He sighed. 'You warned me this would happen, Zander. And I listened, I really did. But I suppose ... I suppose I didn't want to believe it of my own city. I wanted to believe that after this long, we must have changed for the better.'

'It's not just Arkannen,' Zander said. 'The same thing in reverse will be happening in Kardissak too. And all over both Mirrorvale and Sol Kardis. It's human nature. When we feel threatened, we become more primitive. You taught me that yourself.'

'Yes. But I suppose I thought Arkannen was somehow better than other cities. That we had been open to the world for long enough that we'd left prejudice behind.' His smile was sad. 'Which means I'm just as bad as everyone else, really. Harbouring a secret belief that my own country and people are superior.'

Zander wondered whether to mention the fact that the fourth ring of Arkannen had an Immigrants' Quarter, and that it consisted of small, damp apartments full of Kardise and Parovian workers who spoke their own language and kept to themselves. He wondered whether to mention the fact that even before the war, he'd occasionally been called *mudskin* and *Kardise trash* by belligerent late-night drinkers on the streets of the first ring. He wondered whether to point out that there were many jobs closed to anyone who hadn't been born in Mirrorvale, the Helm being one of them; that it took years longer for foreigners to become accepted as full citizens of Arkannen and given access to the higher rings than it did for immigrant Mirrorvalese; that when the priestesses had proposed adding shrines to the sixth ring for the Kardise, Parovian and Ingalese gods and goddesses, only a handful of decades ago, many of the city's residents had fought a prolonged and furious battle to keep them out. The truth was, mistrust existed on both sides that even centuries of movement across the border couldn't entirely dispel. Yet it seemed unnecessarily cruel to say it. The tolerant, welcoming Arkannen that lived in Caraway's head did exist, after all. It just wasn't the whole picture.

'I was wondering ...' he said instead. 'Did anything come of our conversation the other day? The name in your notebook?'

Caraway's expression cleared. 'It did. In fact, that's what I came to tell you. This morning, at first light, an agent set off for the Kardise border with fresh evidence concerning the ambassador's murder. We hope it will mean an end to the war and a new chance at the treaty.'

'But Captain, that's ... why didn't you tell me sooner? That's wonderful!'

'It's good news,' Caraway agreed. 'But, Zander ... do you remember, back when this first started, I told you about the condition your father had placed on any agreement?'

Dull realisation fell into place. 'That I should return to Sol Kardis.'

'I don't know if it will still hold,' Caraway said. 'But if it does ... Ayla would have spoken to you about it, had the process ever got that far. It was one area where she and Tolino differed. And since she's not here ...'

'I understand.'

'I'm not asking you to leave. It might never come to that anyway. But I thought I should let you know that Sol Kardis might make such a demand.'

'And if they do?' Zander asked quietly. 'Will you have me shipped out on the first skyboat you can find?'

'That's up to you.'

'But –'

'Ayla was adamant we don't treat people that way without cause. If you had committed a crime against Sol Kardis and they wanted you back to mete out their own justice, we would deport you. But we won't allow a single man to hold an entire peace treaty hostage in order to control his grown son.'

Zander was silent, guilt and gratitude tumbling over themselves inside him.

'That's what Lady Ayla thinks,' he said finally. 'But what do you think? What would you do, if you were me?'

Caraway returned his level gaze. 'I don't know, Zander. That's the honest truth. I don't like the idea of your father using the treaty as a weapon against you. I don't know what the other Kardise councillors were thinking, letting him do it. Maybe they'll see sense second time around. But if they don't ...' He lifted a shoulder. 'I'm not sure I'd be able to live with the knowledge that I had the opportunity to secure peace between two countries and didn't take it. No matter the personal cost to me.'

'I understand.'

'Which isn't to say I'd think any worse of you if you

refused,' Caraway added hastily. 'But you did ask for my opinion.'

'Yes.' Zander couldn't bring himself to say any more than that. And clearly the captain realised there was little more to be gained from the conversation; though his expression was regretful, he stood up, gave Zander a nod, and headed for the door. Yet when he reached it, he turned.

'It might not happen,' he said again. 'I'm sure Ayla will do everything she can to avoid it. I just ... I wanted to warn you. Just in case.'

'Thank you.'

'I'm sorry, Zander.'

'I know.'

Then the door closed, and Zander was left alone.

TWENTY-THREE

They met in the middle of the plain: Ayla and her bodyguards, a single Kardise councillor and his. And Naeve Sorrow. Beside them, a pale flag fluttered in the breeze. As long as that flag flew, there would be no more fighting.

Sorrow wasn't really sure why Ayla had asked her to stay. The key evidence would be Tarran's confession, not an awkwardly delivered account from someone the Kardise would almost certainly consider an unreliable witness. Yet there had seemed little point in refusing. In a way, Sorrow thought, she ought to be flattered. It wasn't every sellsword who'd been invited to attend the most important diplomatic event in recent Mirrorvalese history. Shame the event itself would be no more than a load of dull chitchat. Political conversation was all the same: circuitous nonsense that was more about scoring points off a rival than actually getting things done.

'Don Mellor,' Ayla greeted her counterpart when they were still a little distance apart.

'Lady Ayla.'

'We come unarmed,' Ayla said in Kardise. Sorrow could attest to the truth of that; it was only with the greatest of reluctance that she'd agreed to leave all her own weaponry behind. All the same, she'd concealed a knife in her boot. She wasn't willing to go completely unarmed anywhere, even to a peace talk. 'May I approach?'

'We are also unarmed,' Mellor said. 'But before we start, I would ask you please to take off your collar.'

'That isn't a weapon,' Ayla protested.

'It makes you stronger. With it, you could Change and kill us all, and we'd have no way to stop you.'

She raised an eyebrow. 'Unless you've brought a pistol to this supposedly unarmed discussion, I could do that anyway.'

'That is why we would rather you were as close to human as possible, Lady Ayla. You have the power to destroy us all. You cannot leave that behind. But it is only fair that you should be vulnerable like the rest of us.'

Ayla hesitated. Then she took off her collar, dropped it in the grass beside her, and strode forward into the space between the two parties. Mellor left the safety of his own guards and came to meet her. An arm's length apart, they stopped and regarded each other warily.

'You claim to have evidence that proves you didn't kill Don Tolino,' Mellor said. 'You still want peace? Even after we have killed so many of your men?'

His tone suggested weakness on her part. A test, Sorrow thought. But to her credit, Ayla lifted her chin and matched him blow for blow.

'And even after I killed so many of yours. That question cuts both ways, Don Mellor. I hope I have proven to you that I will do whatever it takes to defend my people. But I cannot believe this war is in either of our countries' interests.'

He inclined his head in acknowledgement. 'Let me hear your evidence.'

So Ayla showed him Tarran's confession. She called Sorrow forward to tell her story, which Sorrow managed to do without making too much of a fool of herself. And finally, Mellor nodded.

'All right. It is enough to extend the truce, for now. I will take it back to the other councillors and see what they say. But, Lady Ayla ... you should know that an end to the war will not necessarily mean peace. Even if what you say is true, Tolino was murdered by Mirrorvalese patriots on Mirrorvalese soil. So though you might not have killed him, your country still did.'

'I understand,' Ayla said. 'But I assure you, no-one who kills an innocent man for the sake of manufacturing a war would ever be considered a Mirrorvalese patriot.'

She gave him a Kardise bow. And as she straightened, something caught Sorrow's eye. A movement, up on the distant hillside. A glint of light –

Not even a rifle can fire that far, she thought.

And then, *You don't owe her anything.*

Yet her body was already in motion, hurtling across the gap between herself and Ayla. They collided hard enough to knock both of them to the ground. The crack of the gun echoed in Sorrow's ears. Too late. Was she too late?

But then pain flared up from her guts, white-hot and vicious. It tipped her over onto her side, to curl in on herself like an animal seeking refuge. The earth was red. Her hands were red. Why was everything red?

You've been shot, you stupid woman, she told herself. And before she could think of a suitable retort, she blacked out.

* * *

Ayla sat up, dazed. Beside her, one of her Helmsmen was already tending to Sorrow. The other positioned himself between her and the far-off hillside where the bullet had come from, and said, 'Lady Ayla.'

He was holding out her collar. She took it from him with shaking fingers and fumbled it back into place. He offered her a hand, which she clutched gratefully, using him for support until her legs felt strong enough to hold her. On their side of the plain, Mellor and his guards watched her in silence, their eyes wide and terrified. They expected her to kill them, Ayla realised. And she could do it. A couple of days ago, perhaps she would have. It would be easy enough to Change and run them through –

'I came here in good faith,' she said in her own language, staying calm with an effort, though she couldn't keep the ice from her voice. 'Am I to assume, then, that we are to recommence the war?'

'Lady Ayla …' Mellor looked increasingly frightened as she approached him, and answered in the same tongue. 'I assure you, this wasn't our doing. I will have men sent out to look for –'

'You're saying it was a coincidence?' Ayla snapped. 'That you asked me to remove my collar, and then …'

'Not a coincidence.' Sweat stood out on the man's brow. 'There are some things we do not speak of, but I can only say again that the Kardise government was not behind this.'

'The Brotherhood, then?' Ayla heard the stifled gasps of the councillor's guards, but she waved them aside. The time for tact was long gone. 'Your Brotherhood have tried repeatedly to kill me, Don Mellor. Forgive me if I grow a little tired of preserving their secrets.'

Without waiting for a reply, she turned her back on him

and strode to Sorrow's side. The sellsword remained unconscious, her breath coming in shallow gasps.

'Will she live?' Ayla asked the Helmsman putting pressure on the wound. He glanced up without removing his hands; the tightness around his eyes told her everything she needed to know.

'I hope so.'

'Do everything you can,' Ayla said. 'She took that bullet on my behalf. I won't have her dying for the privilege.'

The Helmsman nodded. Ayla turned back to Mellor.

'We will leave the flag here,' she said. 'You go away and talk to the councillors. But be careful, Don Mellor. If I am to be held responsible for my *patriotic* countrymen, then you must also be held responsible for yours.'

The address on the calling-card that Lewis had given Ree – 12a Crucible Lane, Obsidian Quarter – turned out to be the basement of an ordinary, rather shabby-looking house. Ree and Penn tried knocking on the door, but got no answer, so they stood outside and watched it for a little while. Obsidian was the Alchemists' Quarter, which meant not only alchemists but apothecaries and even physicians lived there. Certainly a good place to find all the ingredients needed to brew up a new antidote to a deadly poison.

'We should go in,' Ree said. 'We haven't seen anyone come or go from the entire house the whole time we've been here.'

'But if there's no-one home –' Even as Penn said it, he realised what Ree was suggesting. 'You mean break in? But the Helm can't just – I mean, we should at least get a warrant from the Watch before –'

'We're at war, Penn. We have to be unscrupulous. I'll just say I found the door open.'

Before he could object further, she'd crossed the street and descended the external steps to the basement apartment. With a strong feeling that he'd live to regret it, Penn followed.

'Zander should never have taught you how to pick locks,' he muttered. 'He's created a monster.'

'Nonsense.' Ree's voice was a little too bright, her actions a little too hasty. She'd been like this ever since he'd found the marriage contract in Derrick Tarran's office: as though she could see her life coming to an end, and it made her reckless. 'Ah! There we go.'

She eased open the door. The basement turned out to be a single room, with a high ceiling and no windows – clearly intended as a storage space, rather than a separate apartment. There was even a hatch in the ceiling, through which the occupants of the house above had once accessed the basement. Penn had expected distillery equipment, yet instead he saw only a bench covered in papers.

'No-one could possibly live here,' he said. 'Or brew an antidote, either. This must just be the address the mysterious man gave Tarran in case Tarran needed to contact him.'

'I suppose so.' Ree looked disappointed. 'Still, now we're here, we might as well take a look around.'

A single oil lamp hung from the ceiling above the bench. Penn lit it; then Ree closed the front door, calling up a curl of cold air from somewhere else entirely. A draught? Penn glanced around the walls and spotted a ventilation block in the corner furthest from the door. That made him breathe a bit easier. He really didn't like the idea of a room with no windows.

Ree joined him at the bench, and together they began to look through the papers. They soon found that most of them were completely incomprehensible, written in a kind of shorthand interspersed with symbols. Alchemists' notation? A secret code? Impossible to tell. Yet at the bottom of the pile lay some large, thin sheets of paper that were rather different. They clearly belonged together, a set of five: each showed a long, pointed oval divided into sections and marked with different words in both a foreign language and Mirrorvalese.

'What is this?' Ree muttered. 'Plans, but of what?'

They frowned down at them together. Then, hit by a sudden bolt of enlightenment, Penn said, 'The *Windsinger*.'

'What?'

'The Parovian airship. You know, the one that's moored over at Redmire. See, it's definitely an airship – here are the engines, the gas chambers, the rudder at the tail. But airships aren't usually built with rooms inside them, so …'

'The *Windsinger*,' Ree said slowly. 'Why would Free Arkannen have the plans for that? It has nothing to do with the war between Mirrorvale and Sol Kardis.'

'No.' Penn kept frowning at the papers. There was a connection there somewhere. Had to be. 'I'm not very good at this kind of thing, but if Free Arkannen have plans of the *Windsinger* … I think we have to assume that there's more to what they're planning than what they've already done.'

Ree nodded. 'D'you think they're going to sabotage the airship? Make it look like an act sanctioned by Darkhaven, and throw us into conflict with Parovia as well as Sol Kardis?'

'Maybe.' It was a clever deduction, and the sort of thing Ree always leaped to far quicker than he did. Her brain made connections at a speed he could only dream about. Yet for all that, something was nagging at him – and after a moment, he realised what. 'Only thing is, these plans … they're top secret. The *Windsinger* is new technology; the Parovians wouldn't share any more information than they had to. So …'

'So for a Mirrorvalese dissident group to have the plans, they must have stolen them.' Ree shrugged. 'Well, couldn't they?'

'It's possible,' Penn said doubtfully. 'But I think there would have been a huge outcry from Parovia. No ... it seems more likely that Parovia *gave* them the plans.'

'In which case, the group is a front for Parovian interference, not Mirrorvalese at all.' Ree looked thoughtful. 'Maybe not sabotage, then. If Parovia wanted outright war with Mirrorvale, there'd be far easier ways to achieve that than building a technologically advanced airship just so it could be destroyed. So if the *Windsinger* isn't a target, maybe it's a weapon ...' She scanned the plans again. Then, in an altered tone of voice, she said, 'You did say it was a passenger ship, didn't you?'

'Yes. Largest in the world.'

'Then it wouldn't carry cargo?'

'I don't know,' Penn said. 'Usually it's one or the other. Cargo ships have a different design from passenger ships. But maybe with a ship this big, they decided it could handle both.'

'Oh. It's just, there's a label here that says *Cargo*. I thought maybe if Parovia did engineer the conflict between us and Sol Kardis, it was so they could smuggle something out of the country while we were otherwise distracted ...'

Penn looked where her finger was tapping one of the plans. Sure enough, a space in the very lowest level of the airship was labelled *Cargo*. Nothing odd about that: if there was going to be such a thing as a combined passenger and cargo ship, that's where he'd expect the goods to be stowed. And yet ...

'It's an odd sort of cargo hold,' he said, pulse quickening.

'There's no loading hatch in the wall. No way in except a single internal door. They can't be intending to carry anything heavy or bulky. Yet there's a window marked on here, look. What kind of cargo needs daylight but no easy way to get it on or off the airship?'

They were silent for a while. Then Ree said, in a voice that shook slightly, 'Maybe a live one.'

'You think –'

'I don't know. But we should take these to Captain Caraway as soon as possible.'

The sudden smashing of glass made them both look up. A broken flask lay on the floor, something faintly green curling out of it like smoke. And at the door –

A man's arm, disappearing from view as the door closed behind him.

'Stop!' Penn ran for the door, dimly aware that Ree had snatched up the plans of the *Windsinger* and stuffed them into her pocket before following. Yet he was too late. He heard the clunk of the key turning, followed by a loud *snap* –

'He's broken it off in the lock,' Ree said, after a short time with her lockpicks. 'I can't get the door open.'

Penn nodded. He felt stupid and light-headed. He watched the last traces of green smoke dissipate into the air from the broken glass, and thought vaguely, *Poison. In a windowless room. We don't stand much chance there.*

'Penn?' Ree said in a small, wavering voice. 'I feel strange.'

'S'because it's windowless.' Penn squinted at her. *Windowless*. It reminded him of something. He took her by the hand, led her over to the far corner of the room, and pushed her down towards the ventilation block. 'Breathe.'

Ree lay down. He could hear her taking great gulps of air. Slowly, he slid down the wall beside her until he found himself sitting on the floor.

'There,' he said. 'You'll be all right.'

And he closed his eyes.

The war had a chance of ending, but he might be the price of peace. Once Zander knew that, he found it even harder to stay in the safe house. He wanted to visit all the places in Arkannen that he'd never quite got round to seeing, before it was too late. He wanted to eat food from a street vendor and practise duelling in the fifth ring. Most of all, he wanted to spend all the time he had left with his friends. But Ree and Penn were busy, and as far as everyone else in the city was concerned he was still the enemy – and so he stayed put, feeling his entire life slipping away from him. As a result, when a message arrived from Art Bryan requesting a moment of his time, he jumped at the chance.

He wasn't technically allowed in the fifth ring any more, now that he'd lost his job. People were admitted through the Gate of Steel for one of three reasons: they worked in the fifth ring, they were training there, or they had legitimate business in one of the higher rings. But maybe the Watch didn't know his status had changed, or maybe Caraway had told them he had special dispensation, because the two guards on duty didn't try to stop him – merely greeted him in the usual way as he passed.

Of course, he could have asked for Weaponmaster Bryan if he'd had any trouble getting in. But it was good to feel, just for a moment, as though he still belonged there.

He found Bryan in his office, and walked in with a kind of bittersweet nostalgia already catching at his throat.

'You wanted to see me, sir?'

'Take a seat, boyo.'

Zander obeyed. Bryan contemplated him in silence for a moment, before saying abruptly, 'Tomas told me what the Kardise are likely to ask for.'

Zander nodded.

'And he told me what he said to you – that if it were him, he'd feel obliged to agree to it for the sake of peace.'

Zander nodded again. Bryan gave a rueful chuckle.

'He's a good lad, Caraway, but he does have a tendency to be noble. There's more than one way to do the right thing.'

'I'm sorry, sir,' Zander said cautiously. 'I'm not sure what you mean.'

'Look,' Bryan said. 'I see a lot of young people in the fifth ring. And more of their lives than you'd think are shaped by what their parents want for them, rather than what they want for themselves.'

Zander didn't argue with that. He had only to think of his two closest friends to realise he was hardly an outlier.

'Most of 'em mean well,' Bryan added. 'The parents, I mean. But there's a damn fine line between guidance and control. Same as in teaching, I s'pose. And more often than not, those who fall the wrong side of it only want the best for their children.'

Zander wasn't at all sure that applied to his own father, who seemed far more interested in maintaining his own reputation than considering his son's needs – but again he held his tongue.

'Want to know what I tell the trainees?' Bryan asked. 'When they come to me for advice? I say, *don't let someone else define your choices*.' He planted a finger on the table for emphasis. 'Ask Ree! She knows that as well as anyone.

You shouldn't have to constrain yourself just to make someone else happy.'

'But it wouldn't be to make him happy,' Zander said. 'It would be to stop the war.'

'Only because your father has pushed that choice onto you. Your life here, or peace. The mistake you and Tomas are making is to believe that's the only choice there is.'

'You're saying I don't have to pick either option?'

'I'm saying you find a way to make your own options.' Bryan raised his eyebrows. 'Have you forgotten everything you learned in training? You used to be a decent strategist, once upon a time.'

'Even if you're right, I'm not sure I'll get the chance,' Zander muttered. 'I'm not likely to be consulted before they ship me off to Sol Kardis.'

'Maybe not. But nothing's ever final until we're dead, Zander. You know that.'

Zander wasn't sure if the abrasive words were meant to comfort him – it wasn't as if Bryan made a habit of being comforting – yet they did, all the same. Because the weaponmaster was right: as long as he was alive, he had options.

'Thank you, sir,' he said. 'Do you mind if I stay for a bit?'

'Be my guest,' Bryan said gruffly. 'Plenty of jobs that need doing.'

Zander smiled. 'There's nothing I'd like more.'

TWENTY-FOUR

Miles stood in the doorway of the mess hall, scanning the room as though looking for someone. The two bottles given to him by the faceless man weighted the pockets of his coat, one each side; his heart struck out a rapid drumbeat of anxiety.

The hall was filling up tonight. Ever since the war started, the Helm had been on double patrol; more than half the sixty-strong force were present in the room, the majority of those who hadn't gone with Ayla to Sol Kardis. The late-evening meal marked the handover between the men who had been on duty during the day and those who were taking the night watch, and Captain Caraway liked them to eat as a group. Men who might soon be fighting alongside each other needed to spend time together, he had told Miles, and this was the one opportunity they had to do it. Breakfast was a different affair, with one group leaving Darkhaven to spend a couple of days training and visiting their families, and another arriving to go on duty. But at sixth bell, when the Helm ate their final meal of the day, the tower was already locked for the night and they were free to gather.

Of course, gathering every Helmsman in Darkhaven into

a single room was madness, from a security point of view ... but only if you expected treachery from within. And as far as Caraway was concerned, the traitor within the tower's walls had already been identified.

One or two of the Helm glanced up at Miles and lifted a hand in greeting before returning to their conversations. They were used to seeing him in the mess hall, though not so often without Art. Yet tonight, Art was down in the fifth ring training the reserves and wouldn't be back until sometime tomorrow – for which Miles was infinitely thankful. He didn't think he would have been able to carry out his task if Art had been there. The physician, Gil, also sat at the end of one of the tables; as Darkhaven's main source of medical knowledge, he knew the Helm quite well and often came down to the mess hall for his meals, just as Art and Miles did. Unfortunate that he'd be caught up in this ... but probably for the best, Miles told himself. The fewer people awake when the raiding party arrived, the less likely that anyone would be killed. What he planned to do to Tomas was bad enough.

We do not want you to hurt him, the faceless man had said. *It must seem as though he has neglected his duty. A sleeping draught should do it. A splash of alcohol on his clothing – he used to drink, yes? And then, you open the gate.*

But –

But what? Your research in our service has already led to a man's death. This is a very minor thing, in comparison.

Miles had wanted to say that it was different. He'd wanted to say that it was worse, because Tomas was his friend, and because Tomas would never forgive himself for what it would appear he'd done. But the man hiding in the shadows of

Luka's temple would have cared nothing for that. It would have been of interest to him only as another weakness to be exploited.

The same sleeping draught supplied to the mess hall will take care of the Helm, the faceless man had added. *And that will make way for a small airship to land in the grounds of the tower without interference. The raiding party will be able to recover what we need from Darkhaven without any bloodshed whatsoever. That ought to please you.*

Please me? Miles had echoed. *No, it does not please me.*

Perhaps he should have tried harder to rein in his sarcasm. The faceless man's voice had dropped to a threatening growl.

Remember your sister, Miles. Remember your lover. The Enforcers require the secret of the Change. And since you have been unable to supply it to us, we have no choice but to come and get it.

And, of course, Miles had capitulated. He'd been able to convince himself that what he was about to do wasn't so very bad. Certainly not on the level of allowing Mirrorvale to go to war with Sol Kardis. At least this time no-one would die – and since he was almost certain that what the raiding party seized would not, in fact, lead to the secret of the Change, it was really nothing to worry about.

But at the very least, Parovia will make a fool of Mirrorvale, stealing into Darkhaven under the noses of the Helm. And Tomas will get the blame for it.

'Sorry, mate!' A passing Helmsman knocked his elbow. Vane, one of the youngest and newest Helmsmen: always ready with a cheerful word. Miles murmured something and shuffled a few paces into the room. His fingers crept up to touch the metal collar concealed beneath his shirt – the latest version of the one he was developing to protect ordinary people, which he wore all the time now because it made him feel safer. Then he looked around again, convinced someone must be watching him with suspicion, but no-one was paying him any attention.

Do it now. For Mara. For Art.

Seizing his courage, Miles crossed to the two massive kegs beside the door that led to the kitchens. Ale for the Helmsmen coming off day shift, water for those going on duty for the night; Captain Caraway was quite strict about that. In a few moments the serving staff would bring out the mugs and start filling them up, and then it would be too late.

With a final glance over his shoulder, he prised the top off the water keg and poured the contents of one of the bottles inside, then did the same with the keg of ale. As always, a thousand doubts filled his mind. Had the faceless man got the dose right? Would it mix properly with both water and ale? Would everyone drink? If some of the Helm didn't receive enough of the draught to fall asleep, what should he do then? Why in Luka's name had he not thought to ask that question sooner?

Stupid with panic, he returned to the tables and sat down next to Vane at the end of a bench. Not long afterwards, several maids emerged from the kitchens, some bearing platters of food for the tables, others with mugs which they proceeded to fill from the kegs. Miles sat in silence as the usual routine of the evening meal swirled around him: Helmsmen helping themselves to meat and bread, sharing banter with the maids, wishing each other good health as they drank. The atmosphere was one of elation. The Helm knew all about the evidence that had been sent with Naeve Sorrow to the border, and they all shared their captain's hope that it would mean an end to the war. As a result, they drank deeply and talked to their fellows with all the carefree abandon of men who believed their lives would soon return to blessed normality.

Miles rejected the offer of a drink, though for an instant he was tempted to take one and avoid the consequences of his actions by falling asleep with the rest of them. Instead, he crumbled bread on his plate and listened to Vane and Tulia talk. The maids left the room, the platters and mugs grew emptier, yet still nothing happened. Had the sleeping draught failed? What in Luka's name was happening?

Then, beside him, Vane began to choke.

Alarmed, Miles slapped him on the back. 'Are you all right?'

The young Helmsman shook his head. His eyes watered. His lips were tinged blue. Miles gave him a harder bang on the back, glancing towards the end of the table where he had last seen Gil, but the physician was no longer in his seat.

Across from Vane, Tulia took a long, wheezing breath and clutched at her throat. And as if in a nightmare, the sound began to spread. Miles looked wildly around him, but saw the same thing everywhere. People turning blue. People fighting to breathe. People dying.

No. No, this is wrong. Horror rushed through him in a hot-and-cold wave, leaving him both sweaty and chilled. *What is happening?*

He pulled himself to his feet, clamber-stumbling over a bench weighted down by gasping, choking Helmsmen. *Help. I need to get help.* Relief hit him as the door from the kitchens swung open and the physician re-entered the room, stopping abruptly beside the kegs as he took in the carnage. Miles tripped over his own feet in his haste to reach the man.

'Gil!' *He will know what to do. He can stop it.* 'Help them. They are dying!'

'Yes, I imagine they are,' the physician said calmly, still surveying the hall. 'Chanteuse tends to have that effect.'

'What?'

Gil turned to look at him.

'I know I promised it would be without any bloodshed.' His voice sounded both stronger and less hesitant than usual; his Mirrorvalese accent had gone, replaced by one more familiar and yet – from his lips – far more alien. 'But I am afraid I forgot the kitchen staff.'

Belatedly, Miles noticed the knife in the physician's hand. The blood soaking the physician's sleeve. Not only that, but he recognised the physician's voice. Sometimes he heard it in his nightmares ... and by now, there was no doubt that this was a nightmare.

'You,' he whispered.

'For an intelligent man, you are really rather stupid,' Gil said.

'*You* are the faceless man?'

'Evidently.'

'And you have just killed ...'

'It was only a couple of maids,' Gil said. 'Waiting to clear the plates at the end of the meal. I could not have them raising the alarm.'

'No.' Miles shook his head, cold unreality creeping further over him with every breath he took. 'This is ... no.'

With a sigh, the physician turned back the lapel of his coat to reveal the Enforcers' token. Miles looked at it blankly, then back at his face.

'But ... the Helm are dying.'

'Yes,' Gil said. 'You did a good job.'

No. No, no, no. 'It was meant to be a sleeping draught.'

'Sleeping draughts are unreliable. You know that. It took

me long enough to get your dosage right. Whereas strong poison …' Gil shrugged. 'That will kill anyone.'

'But chanteuse?' Miles knew all about poisons; his training had seen to that. Chanteuse was one of the many poisons that wouldn't work on a Changer, but for most people it was a reliable path to death. It closed the airways, causing the victim to suffocate. Although there was an antidote, it had to be swallowed immediately to have any effect. 'Did you have to –'

'It had to be something fast-acting if we wanted to be sure of wiping them all out,' the physician said. 'But not so rapid that we ran the risk of it beginning to act before everyone had drunk.' He gave a slight, condescending smile. 'I assure you, Miles, I considered all the options, and this was by far the best of them.'

Best? Best for who? Miles shook his head. 'Why did you make me do this? Why, when you could have done it yourself –'

'I would have thought the answer to that was obvious,' Gil said. 'In case the poison failed to work in all cases. If anyone had survived, I would have told them I saw you putting something in the kegs. You would have had no idea I was anything more than a concerned physician. And I would have been free to finish the job.'

Miles knew he should have more questions. He should have more *objections*. He should be shouting, raging, running for help. But it was too late, wasn't it? They were dead – or if not, they soon would be – and he was the one who had killed them. If he had only checked the contents of those bottles …

The knowledge settled on him like a shroud, leaving him numb – as though he had died alongside the Helmsmen and was just waiting for his body to stop working. *Gods forgive me.*

'Now,' Gil said, picking up a discarded cup and filling it with water from the poisoned keg. 'Anyone who could have interfered is out of action, but we have one more obstacle to deal with.'

Does he mean I have to drink it myself? Miles wondered. The prospect didn't seem so bad. Enforced suicide would at least be an end. But the physician shook his head as if he knew what Miles was thinking.

'Captain Caraway. He is still on lookout.'

'And you want me to frame him ...' Miles began, but even as the words left his lips, he knew they were wrong. If the faceless man had lied about everything else, no doubt he had lied about that too. And sure enough, Gil sighed.

'Of course not. What would be the point?'

'You want me to kill him.' Experimentally, Miles dug the nails of one hand into his palm, but he was still numb. Why was he so numb?

'Technically he will kill himself,' Gil replied. 'Simply carry the drink to him, then take the key to the postern gate from his pocket once he is dead.'

'You could do it yourself,' Miles shot back, but Gil only laughed.

'He trusts you.'

Yes. He does. The thought was enough to lift the numb clouds that had settled on him, a little. *Then ... I will warn him. Tell him what has happened. Tell him not to drink. And the two of us together will overcome Gil ...*

'In case you are getting any bright ideas,' the physician added, 'you should be aware that I have sent an assassin after your weaponmaster. He can be stopped only by a single command, and once Caraway is out of the way I will tell you what it is. Understand?'

You want me to choose between Tomas and Art. Between Darkhaven and Art. Miles nodded. It was no more than the same choice he'd been making since he first found out who was behind the ambassador's death. And once again, he couldn't help but choose love.

'Good,' Gil said. 'I will follow shortly, and I will be listening from the stairs.' He sneered. 'So do try not to say anything indiscreet.'

Miles took the cup without another word, and walked out of the room full of dead men. Yet as he made his way towards the central square, another ray of light broke through the fog, this one dazzling in its hopefulness: this time, he might not have to choose. This time, he might be able to save Caraway's life and Art's. Because his flask full of spiced fruit punch – laced with the sleeping draught he'd been taking every night for weeks – was in his breast pocket.

Once he had that, the rest of it came almost without thought. Glance over his shoulder to make sure Gil wasn't in sight. Tip the poisoned water out of the cup. Refill the cup from the flask. There would still be traces of chanteuse in there, and he wasn't sure exactly what effect they'd have when combined with the sleeping draught, but at least the mixture was no longer lethal.

With the walls of the tower silent around him, he walked steadily across the central square. As expected, Caraway was at the lookout post above the main gate. Miles climbed the outer steps to join him. Caraway glanced back for the briefest of moments, to check he wasn't an intruder, before returning his gaze to the darkening horizon.

'Do you think she's all right, Miles?' he said softly. 'Do

you think Sorrow got there in time? I'm yet to receive any news, so I don't know –'

Miles nodded. 'She has just as good a chance of surviving as we do.' He held out the cup. 'I brought you this. Spiced fruit. No alcohol.'

'Thank you.' Caraway took it, but he didn't immediately drink. Instead, he curled his hands around it and smiled. 'Actually, I wanted to thank you for much more than that. If it weren't for the fact that Ayla has your collar with her, I'd probably be going crazy with fear round about now.'

Choose your words carefully. Remember the unseen listener.

'I assure you, I have been very happy to work with Lady Ayla these past years.' Just for a moment, the knowledge of what Miles had left behind in the mess hall threatened to claw its way out of him. He fought it back and added, rather desperately, 'And of course I am glad to have been of use.'

'You've been a good friend,' Caraway said. He glanced down at the cup in his hands, and Miles thought with relief that he was about to drink, but then he looked up again and asked, 'Did you come from the mess hall? Did you see Vane? I need to speak to him about the night shift.'

Desperate wheezing. Lips turning blue. Fighting for breath –

'Yes, he was there,' Miles said faintly. He could feel a scream building up in his throat; with an effort, he swallowed it and nodded at the cup. 'You should drink that. They sent it over specially from the kitchens.'

Caraway studied him for a moment, a slight frown between his brows. *He knows. He knows something is wrong.* Relief coursing through him that the decision had been taken out of his hands, that Caraway was going to be perceptive enough or paranoid enough to avert the disaster that was about to befall Darkhaven, Miles stood and waited for the blow. But then Caraway shrugged, raised his cup in salute, and drank the contents down.

Sudden, irrational fear gripped Miles that somehow this draught would turn to poison as well. That he would have to watch Caraway die, just as he had most of Caraway's men. But in fact, nothing happened to start with. Caraway placed the cup on the wall in front of him. He returned to his contemplation of the darkening horizon. Miles stood with him in silence, doubt and elation running through him in an endless loop.

The dose was wrong. Too weak for a man who is a warrior rather than a scholar. He will stay awake. But then they will kill him, when they come. No. *He will hold the tower against them. He will stop me.*

I wish he would stop me.

'Miles,' Caraway said faintly. 'I don't feel right.'

Below them, on the hillside outside Darkhaven, Miles saw a torch spark in the night. The small airship had landed safely on the far side of the tower. The raiding party was on its way. In a moment, he would have to descend the steps and hand over the key that would admit them.

Caraway had obviously spotted the light, too; he swayed forward, clutching at the wall in front of him to stop himself falling. 'Do you see that?'

'Yes.' Miles backed away. 'I – I am sorry, Tomas.'

'What?' Caraway turned, clumsily, one elbow sweeping the cup from the wall to shatter at his feet. 'No. Miles. You haven't –' His legs buckled beneath him, sending him lurching forward. Miles caught his forearms, and they stared at each other.

'You bastard,' Caraway whispered. He was clearly having difficulty focusing, but he pushed away from Miles and reached for his sword. He got it half out of the scabbard before it became too much for him; he let it go, falling heavily to his knees. 'You complete bastard.'

'I am sorry,' Miles said again. He slid his hand into the inner pocket of Caraway's coat and fished out the key to the postern gate. Then, letting the captain slump forward on the cold stone, he turned and ran down the steps.

Gil was waiting for him halfway. 'It is done?'

Miles nodded, heart racing. 'Now tell me the command. The one for Art's assassin.'

'All in good time.' The physician took the key, before moving over to the postern. Three men entered, one carrying a burning torch with the gas turned down to a mere flicker. Gil spoke to them softly. Then they headed across the square, and Gil returned to join Miles beside the massive main gates.

Abruptly, Miles found that his numbness had lifted. He was shaking. He wanted to cry, or scream. But instead, he squared his shoulders and faced the physician head-on.

'I do not understand,' he said, in a voice that quavered only slightly. 'Why so many deaths, just for this?'

'So no-one can follow the raiding party, of course.'

'Follow them?' Miles echoed. 'I did not think anyone was even supposed to know they had been here! They were to enter while the Helm slept, break into the treasury –'

'Treasury?' Gil snorted. 'What would they be doing in there?'

'Finding the secret of the Change. Removing the old and valuable documents, the ones I highlighted in my reports. The ones from the time of the first Changers, written in a language I could not translate. That is the point of the whole –'

But Miles stopped, because Gil was laughing.

'The secret of the Change does not lie in *books*,' he said. 'It lies in people.'

'P-people?'

'Oh, come on, Miles. Surely you knew the Enforcers would not go to all this trouble for a few books.'

But he hadn't known that. He valued books so highly, it hadn't even occurred to him that others might not feel the same. And if the raiding party wasn't here for the ancient knowledge contained in Darkhaven's treasury –

'Really, I cannot tell what to make of you,' Gil said. 'Everyone keeps telling me how clever you are – and indeed, you did well enough with the antidote. But the idea that we would send a country to war for the sake of some books ...'

'Then what?' Miles demanded. 'What are those men here for?'

Gil smiled. 'The children, of course.'

For a moment, Miles wasn't sure he'd heard correctly. 'The children?'

'Yes.' The physician sounded impatient now. 'You told us yourself that you can learn no more from Ayla. But with three Changer children as subjects for our testing, we will soon uncover their secret.'

'But –' Every bit of horror and revulsion that Miles had felt at the deaths of the Helm came surging back in full force. It took a considerable effort to hold himself back from attacking the other man, and that only because he knew that if he was to have any chance of stopping this, it would have to be done with reason.

'The children are still young,' he said. 'The youngest is only one. It will be more than eight years until the first of them might possibly Change, and even then it is not guaranteed. I thought the secret was required more urgently than that.'

'Again, your intelligence does not appear to be on display,' Gil replied acidly. 'You have learned all there is to learn from a grown Changer. Short of cutting her apart, there is little more to gain from her. But the young ones ...' He shrugged. 'So many opportunities to learn from what they can do. Their blood alone may give up what we need. If not, Ayla may agree to share the secret as payment for her children's safe return. Either way, we will supply His Majesty with what he has asked for.' A pause, before he added, 'It is a shame, really, that it was necessary to interfere with her reproductive capabilities. Still, too many children would have been difficult to manage, and I had to find a reason for the old physician to retire.'

What? 'But you saved her life.'

'From a crisis of my own making, yes.'

'Then the flaw that runs in the family ...'

'Oh, it is in the blood, sure enough. But Ayla was damnably healthy. I doubt she would have succumbed to it unless I had given her a little nudge.'

He was utterly without mercy. If Miles had only known it this time yesterday, he would never have put anything into the kegs without testing it first. Yet the betrayal he'd thought he was committing had seemed so vast, the idea that it could be masking a vaster one hadn't even crossed his mind. The man in front of him was willing to murder huge numbers of people, send countries to war with each other, put a pregnant woman's life at risk and steal children from their beds – all to obtain the secret of the Change. And Miles had unwittingly helped him with most of it. *What in Luka's name have I done?*

'I know Ayla,' he said. 'And she will not sit still in

Darkhaven while you threaten her and her family. As soon as she finds out what has happened, she will go after them.'

'But she will not find out in time, will she? There is no-one left to tell her. And if she does ...' Gil smiled. 'Maybe we are prepared for that possibility, too.'

There is me. If I can just get a message to Art ... But Miles already knew that wouldn't happen. Gil had told him far too much to allow him to walk free.

'The command,' he said, without much hope. 'For Art's assassin. Please ...'

'Patience, Miles.'

Both of them turned as the three men re-emerged on the far side of the square. Each of them carried a small, wrapped figure over his shoulder. The children were still and quiet, limp dolls with lolling heads. Dead? No, that would make no sense. Drugged.

Miles found himself remembering all the noisy breakfasts he'd shared with the children, over the years. Marlon, gesturing with both hands as he described something. Katya stirring her porridge and humming tunelessly to herself, while tiny Wyrenne shrieked and banged on the table. He had already done far more than he could ever hope to be forgiven for, but this ...

'Stop.' His voice came out inaudible. Cursing himself for a coward, he cleared his throat and tried again. 'Stop! Gil, please ... they are only children.'

'What difference does it make? You are already a murderer.'

'No!' The denial was automatic. He caught himself in time. 'No, that was your doing.'

'Come now, Miles. I may have poisoned the Helm, but your friend Caraway's blood is on your head.'

That is one thing I do not have to bear. Miles shook his

head. 'Caraway is, was, a soldier. He accepted his life was at risk. But the children –'

'Not children. Nightshades.'

'Children,' Miles insisted. 'And they are too young to survive being taken away from their home and family. The littlest one –'

'Is least likely to be of use to us as she grows up. You have already told us of the possible link between the Nightshade phenotype and the Nightshade gift. If the baby is not a Changer, she will yield little in the way of test results, so it does not matter so much if she fails to thrive.'

Nausea clutched at Miles's throat. 'You have lived with these children,' he said hoarsely. 'You have tended to them for more than a year. How can you talk about them as if they are no more than animals?'

'They are constructs of alchemy. You are a man of science; you must have dissected a creature or two in your time. No point getting sentimental about it now.'

'No.' Miles shook his head. 'No, no, no.' As the raiding party and their burdens approached the postern gate, one of the secrets he had been keeping all this time came spilling out of him. 'The Nightshade blood is not enough!'

Gil's eyes narrowed. 'What do you mean?'

Miles hesitated – but better to reveal the truth than to let the children be taken.

'The Changer gift is a result of two things,' he said. 'The alchemy in the Nightshade blood, and the alchemy in Arkannen itself. Without Darkhaven, you can cut those children open as much as you like –' his voice caught in his throat; he forced himself through it – 'but you will never be able to create a Changer. Never.'

'Liar.'

'I swear, it is the truth.'

'You have known this all along? And yet you did not think to tell us?'

Seeing the fury in his face, Miles flinched; yet only for a moment. Then he lifted his chin. 'If I have my way, Parovia will never discover the secret of the Change.'

Gil stabbed him.

Miles tried to evade the blow as it fell, so it caught him in the thigh, yet still the force of the impact drove him to his knees. Pain spread through him in a shocking wave, like an alchemical explosion, turning his blood to fire. He struggled to stand, but his legs were weak and he only scrabbled uselessly at the ground. *I have to get up. I have to –*

'You are the worst kind of traitor,' Gil spat. 'Hoping to play two sides off against each other, and ending up despised by both.'

Gasping, Miles looked up, but the physician's face was hidden by the shadow of his hood; once again he was the nameless messenger in the dark.

'Still,' Gil added, 'you serve your purpose. They will need someone to blame. And better you than me.'

Bending down, he thrust his knife into Miles's stomach and back out again in one quick movement. Miles cried out, clutching at the wound with shaking hands. His own blood was hot and sticky on his fingers, and he could smell it, and the pain was everywhere. Everywhere.

He was going to die.

'Art,' he whispered, and Gil scoffed at him.

'There is no assassin, Miles. I really have no interest in whether the man lives or dies. Though it might have been kinder to kill him, given what he will soon discover about you.'

'And Mara?'

The physician made an impatient noise. 'Your family is already dead. They were killed before you even left Parovia.'

'But the letters –'

'Yes. I daresay writing those gave some junior clerk a moment's relief from the tedium of her usual duties.' He shook his head. 'What purpose would there have been in spending time and resources on giving your family a new life, with all the risk that one day they might slip through our net? Come on, Miles! Do you not think they would have asked questions? Do you not think they would have tried to find you?'

A third burst of pain ripped through Miles as the knife blade cut him open again, but this time he barely felt it. Tears leaked from his eyes. He couldn't see Gil clearly any more; the man was just a shape in a haze of grey.

'No. Everything you have done, every act of betrayal you have committed since you first arrived in Mirrorvale, was for no more than ghosts.' Gil laughed. 'Think on that as you breathe your last.'

Something cold and hard was pressed into Miles's palm, and reflexively he tightened his fingers around it. Then the physician's footsteps moved away. Gritting his teeth against the constant, agonising pain, Miles put all his strength into trying to move. *I have to warn Art. I have to warn Ayla.*

But the world slipped away from him, and everything turned black.

TWENTY-FIVE

Ree had been floating somewhere between waking and dreaming, in a half-hallucinatory state where nothing made a great deal of sense and nothing seemed to matter. Yet gradually, piece by piece, reality was beginning to remake itself.

She was lying facedown on something hard.

Her head ached.

Her lungs ached.

Someone had tried to ... poison her?

The basement. She had been in the basement with Penn. And someone had poisoned them and locked them in and –

Penn had told her to breathe through the ventilation block. She remembered that now, quite vividly: his hand on her back, pushing her down. Without Penn, she might be dead.

But Penn himself hadn't got any fresh air at all ...

'Penn?' she said. It came out as a croak through her parched throat. 'Penn? Are you all right?'

In answer, she heard a groan. It wasn't much, but it was at least enough to know he was alive.

Ree put her mouth against the ventilation block and sucked

in several more deep breaths, enough to make her dizzy. Then, slowly, she risked pushing herself up to a sitting position. The gas lamp still burned, though with a smaller and bluer flame. The air was hazy. Penn lay slumped against the wall nearby.

'Penn!' She shook him. His eyes flickered open.

'I'm tired,' he mumbled, before his eyelids drooped shut again. She tugged on his arm until she'd got him into a lying position, then rolled him over so that his face almost touched the ventilation block. That should help, a little.

She looked around the room. The air seemed to have cleared, a bit. It wasn't as if the basement were completely airtight. But unless she got Penn out, the poison might still finish him off. And if it didn't, they'd both soon die anyway, with no water or food.

She went back to the door, but she already knew it was useless. The poisoner had deliberately broken the key off in the lock. And the door itself was solid wood, with thick metal hinges. No way she could get that thing open.

The other possibility was the hatch in the ceiling. She walked over to stand underneath it, peering upwards. Perhaps the poisoner had forgotten it – the cobwebs suggested it hadn't been used in a long time. But the latch was a simple wooden thing, so if she could only reach it, she might be able to open it.

Of course, she was far too short to do it alone; that went without saying. She didn't think even Penn could have stretched that high. And standing on the bench wouldn't help much either. Standing on Penn's shoulders, on the other hand …

'Penn.' She crouched down beside him and shook him again. 'I need you.'

No answer. She put a hand on his chest to make sure he was still breathing, suppressing a sob of frustration. He needed more air, to clear the poison out of his system. If she could get the hatch open, that might be enough. But she couldn't get it open without him.

Unless ...

She was going to have to shoot it open.

You can't, her inner critic said promptly. *You know how abysmal your aim is.* And it was true, even after years of practice. She carried a pistol, as all the Helmsmen did, but it might as well have been a stick for all the good she could do with it.

Still, it didn't make any difference. She had to get that hatch open. And since Penn couldn't do it, that made her the only chance they had.

No pressure, then.

Ree looked again at the latch, but it seemed impossibly small and far away. Surely she'd never be able to fire a pistol with enough precision to break it and open the hatch. She was more likely to shoot herself – or Penn. And since they wore firearms for defence and deterrence, rather than in order to get involved in a gunfight, they didn't tend to carry the accoutrements around with them. The single bullet in Ree's pistol was the only chance she'd have.

She took a deep breath and let it out slowly. Then, lifting the pistol, she aimed and fired. The bullet punched a neat hole in the centre of the hatch.

'Shit.' Ree stared at the pistol in her shaking hands. *I'm sorry, Penn.*

'Ree.' To her surprise, Penn said her name quite clearly. Perhaps the little bit of air coming through the ventilation block was having an effect. She looked down at him, and saw that he was gesturing at the pistol in his own belt.

As she took it, he mumbled, 'You've got this.'

'But I –'

'Ree.' His hand moved jerkily until it found hers. She felt the tremor in it. There went any lingering hope that he might make a swift and startling recovery in time to take over the job from her. 'Better'n you think you are. Just take your time.'

She straightened. Took aim. Hesitated. *But what if I don't –*

You've got this.

The shot rang out. The hatch fell open, showering dust and cobwebs onto her upturned face. She blinked and spat, but she couldn't help grinning. *I actually bloody did it.*

'Knew you could,' Penn mumbled. She got her shoulder under one of his arms and dragged him upright, using the wall as a support on his other side, until he was standing in the draught of fresh air. As soon as he felt up to it, they'd be able to escape.

In the end, they dragged the bench under the hatch and climbed onto it. Penn boosted Ree up through the gap, before hauling himself out after her. The room they were in now appeared deserted: no furniture, just bare floorboards and more dust. And outside –

'It's dark,' Ree said incredulously.

'Mmm.' Penn still seemed dazed, but he was talking normally again now and breathing easily rather than in gasps, so that was a big improvement. 'Better get up to Darkhaven and tell the captain what happened. You still got the plans?'

'Yep.' She bumped him with her elbow. 'Hey, you know what this means, don't you?'

'What?'

She smirked. 'You can never tease me about my aim again.'

Caraway's head was throbbing, and he was lying on cold stone, and for a moment he couldn't work out where he was. On a street somewhere in the first ring, perhaps. He'd drunk too much and passed out again. That must be it. But then he moved, an involuntary twitch, and though it sent renewed agony sloshing through his skull, it also triggered blooms of memory. Ayla. The children. His captaincy. The entire mundane beauty of his life. He didn't drink. He never drank. This was something else.

He forced his thoughts back through the pain to the last clear moment he could remember, which was the day shift coming off duty. After that it was all fog, but surely ... he would have gone to watch the gate, as he did every evening. Yes. He remembered it now. He'd watched the sun setting over the city. Thought some philosophical nonsense about beauty enduring even in wartime or ... he wasn't sure. It didn't matter. But he'd been alone. No reason there for his pitiable state now.

Alone, until ...

Miles.

Miles had given him something to knock him out.

Miles was a traitor.

And there had been a light, out on the hillside where no lights should be. A light approaching through the darkness, without hesitation, as if its owners knew there would be nothing to stand in their way.

Darkhaven had been compromised.

Which meant the children –

He was on his feet before his body had time to protest, but it made up for that an instant later. He slumped against the wall, breathing hard, as coloured swirls filled his vision and the vice tightened on his brain until he had nothing left but the single basic drive to remain conscious. Yet after an eternity, the pressure eased and he found himself still standing. So that was something.

He kept blinking, and finally the dizzy colours faded to reveal a narrow walkway and a waist-high wall. The lookout post. They hadn't moved him. They'd left him where Miles had let him fall. Maybe that meant they thought he was dead. Or maybe it meant they didn't care, because they'd already achieved their purpose.

Marlon and the girls. Are they captured? Are they hurt? Are they –

With a vast and painful effort of will, he pushed the questions aside. He had to keep going. He had no alternative. If there was any chance ...

Focus. One step at a time. His first task would be to draw his sword. His second task would be to descend the stair into the courtyard. His third task would be not to fall over while carrying out either of the previous two tasks. He'd think beyond that once he got there.

Unfortunately, he soon discovered that task one was going to be impossible. He got the weapon out of its scabbard, but lifting it was another thing entirely. His fingers were numb and weak. His arms shook as soon as he put the muscles under any strain. If he met anyone who showed signs of wanting to dispatch him, the sword would be a liability rather than an asset. He fumbled it back into place, trying not to think about how easy he currently was to kill, and decided to concentrate on task two. *Walking downstairs. Surely I can manage that.*

By the time he'd taken the five or six jarring steps to the top of the stair, he was beginning to think he didn't stand any chance at all. Each step sent renewed waves of agony washing over him. It was worse than the worst hangover he'd ever had – and back then, he'd simply curled up in whatever dilapidated corner he had access to and slept it off. Every single part of his body was begging him now to do the same, telling him he just had to lie down and rest ...

Screw my former self, Caraway thought. *And screw Miles's bloody sleeping potion. We're talking about my* children.

He gritted his teeth and forced himself down the staircase, swearing under his breath at each jolt. By the time he reached the bottom, he'd broken into a cold sweat all over.

This is no good. I'm about as much use as a newborn foal.

He tried to keep moving, but instead he found the ground coming up to meet him. *Fuck.* He caught himself on splayed palms, the impact vibrating up his arms and eliciting another swirl of painful darkness inside his head. His ears rang in the silence.

Silence.

Why was it so quiet? Where were the Helm? Surely if an invading force was trying to take Darkhaven, he should be able to hear resistance. They wouldn't just roll over and let the enemy win! They'd defend the tower to their last breath, as was their duty.

Unless they were incapacitated, just as he was. If an alchemist could brew one sleeping draught, he could brew thirty.

Caraway cursed aloud, long and low and bitter; and in answer, he heard a faint groan coming from the shadows at the foot of the main gate. He didn't think he could stand again, not yet, so he drew a small knife before crawling in the direction of the sound. His hands found the slick of warm blood on stone, then the bulk of a body. Someone was lying there, abandoned in the darkness. Caraway touched the man's chest and felt the rapid rise and fall of his breathing. Wounded, but alive.

'Who are you?' he muttered. Sitting back on his heels, he grabbed the torch from his belt with his free hand and flicked the sparker with his thumb. The wavering flame cast a small light into the night, shaping the wounded man's face in peaks and hollows. Caraway recoiled.

'Miles ...'

'I am ... sorry ... Tomas.' The alchemist's voice was a hoarse whisper. Caraway propped the torch against the wall and grabbed him by the shirt-front, yanking the man up with all the limited strength he possessed to be menaced by the knifepoint in his other hand.

'Fuck your sorry! I don't need sorry! Where are my men?'

'Dead,' Miles gasped. 'Poison, in the mess hall –'

'My children?'

'Taken.'

'Taken where? Damn you, taken where?'

'Parovia.'

Miles sagged, a sigh escaping his lips as he lost consciousness again. Something small and bloody fell from his hand: the key to the postern gate. The one he'd taken from Caraway's pocket.

Down in the sixth ring, the temple bells tolled seven slow, solemn notes. Midnight. Caraway swore under his breath. They were into the seventh bell, now, the double-length period that would take them all the way to morning and the first bell of a new day. He'd lost nearly a whole bell already. And with every chime, his children were being carried further from him ...

Rage and horror rose in him like a dark, destroying flood. His hand tightened on the knife. It would be so easy to drive it home. There could be no doubt that the man in front of him deserved it. So easy ...

Too easy.

'Fuck you, Miles,' he snarled, letting the alchemist's head bang back down onto the stone. 'You don't get to die.'

Of course, he might not have any control over that. The man had lost a lot of blood. But all the same, he took off his own shirt and cut it into strips. A tourniquet for the leg wound. A staunch for the gut wound. When he was satisfied that he'd stopped the flow, he sat back against the wall beside the flickering torch and, finally, let his tears of despair fall.

Dead. All those Helmsmen. He had known every single one of those men as if they were his brothers, and not just because it was his job. Miles had wiped them out, without even allowing them the dignity of fighting back. And the *children* –

Caraway found he had leaned in towards Miles, knuckles white on the hilt of his knife. Although everything in him screamed for revenge, he forced himself to sheathe the weapon and sit back against the wall. As soon as he had enough energy, as soon as his head cleared and his limbs worked properly, he'd be going after his children. And he intended to use Miles to do it.

Marlon. Katya. Wyrenne. He tried not to think about their fear, because that would only destroy him. Instead, he repeated their names over and over, silently, as if somehow they might know he was thinking of them and be comforted by it. *Marlon. Katya. Wyrenne.* They were alive, at least. If Parovia wanted them dead, they'd already be dead. And that meant he still had a chance.

TWENTY-SIX

Penn kept pace with Art Bryan as they walked through the Gate of Death and began to climb the hill towards Darkhaven. He and Ree had intended to bring along any Helmsmen they came across on their way through the fifth ring, in case what they'd uncovered proved to be serious enough to require the presence of the entire Helm, but instead they'd found Bryan and Zander. Penn wasn't sure whether either of them would be much help, but he had to admit it was reassuring to have them along. His lungs still didn't feel quite right, and Ree sounded hoarse too, so it was good to have people with them who were at full fighting strength.

'You definitely agree this can't wait till morning?' he muttered to Bryan.

'I don't know,' Bryan replied. 'But there's no harm in taking it now. Your captain'll be awake anyway, no doubt. He doesn't sleep much at the moment.'

Penn nodded. To be honest, he always found it odd when people could sleep a whole night through. It was as though they didn't have anything to worry about.

He glanced up at Darkhaven. Though the seventh bell had rung, light still blazed from the mess hall windows. That was odd. And he couldn't make out any guards at the various lookout points around the outside of the tower. Still, the main gates were closed, just as they should be, and all seemed quiet and still. Perhaps the Helmsmen on night duty had been called away for some reason. No cause for alarm, necessarily – but his spine prickled, all the same.

The postern gate was locked, as he would have expected at this time of night, but there should have been a guard in place above it. Still, Bryan was one of the few people entrusted with a key. He pulled it out of his pocket, muttering something under his breath at the awkwardness of it in the dark, and fumbled it into the lock.

As soon as the gate swung open, they saw the flickering light of the torch across the central square. And the body it illuminated. And the man slumped against the wall beside it as if his bones had lost all rigidity. He lifted his head at their approach, revealing a face streaked with dirt and blood and ... tears?

'Ree ... Penn ... you're alive. Thank all the elements for that.'

'Captain Caraway?' Penn dropped to a crouch beside him. 'What happened?'

'He told me the Helm were dead. But I forgot that some of you, at least, were outside the tower.' Caraway grabbed Penn's shoulders, searching his face. 'Did you see any more –'

His gaze slid past Penn to Bryan, and sudden horror widened his eyes. 'Art. Don't – Miles –'

Penn glanced back over his shoulder, and for the first time recognised the body on the ground. Bryan saw him at the same moment. He pushed past Ree and dropped to his knees beside Miles, cradling the alchemist's head on his lap, heedless of the blood.

'He's alive,' Caraway said. 'I did the best I could. But –'

Bryan looked up, murder in his eyes. 'Who did this, Tomas?'

'One of his fellow Parovians, I suppose,' Caraway said wearily. 'He's a traitor, Art. He poisoned me. He poisoned the Helm –'

'No.' Bryan's denial was instant. He stood, taking a step towards Caraway, hands balling into fists. 'You've got it wrong. You're lying –'

'Art, please.' The captain struggled to his feet in turn, using Penn's proffered arm as a crutch. His voice started soft, but as he spoke it rose in volume and intensity until he was almost shouting. 'My men are dead. My children are gone. I can't walk ten paces without falling down. I know it hurts, and I'm sorry, but you have to believe me when I say I'm pretty fucking sure about this!'

They stared at each other. Penn could feel how heavily Caraway was leaning on him; if the captain and the weaponmaster came to blows right now, Bryan would surely come out on top. Desperately, he fought to understand what had happened.

The Helm are dead.

The children are gone.

How –

The *Windsinger*. It hit him with full force. This was what he and Ree had feared when they saw the plans, though at the time they hadn't known exactly what or who to be afraid for. But if the Nightshade children had been taken, that must be how.

Penn gazed at Bryan, willing him to understand. They'd told him what they'd found. He must understand its significance. Yet the weaponmaster looked close to breaking, and if he did ... Penn exchanged a silent glance with Ree. The two of them would stand with their captain, if necessary. But then Bryan's fists unclenched, and deep devastation touched a face that looked suddenly old.

'What are you going to do?'

'I'm going to get my children back,' Caraway said. 'Art, listen. I know this is a shock. I know you're grieving. But I don't have time for any of that. I need information from him, and you're the best person to get it.'

Bryan closed his eyes. His voice was a hoarse whisper. 'All right.'

'What do you want us to do, Captain?' Ree asked quietly. Caraway looked up and gave her a grateful nod.

'Ree. I need you to go back down to the fifth ring and find any more of the Helm who weren't in the tower when – when it happened. This is going to be a stealth mission, I think, but a few more men would be welcome. And I'd like to know ...' He glanced down at his shaking hands for a moment, before curling them into fists. 'I'd like to know that some of them survived.'

Ree nodded. Tears shone in her eyes. Penn knew how she felt. After two years in the Helm, he and Ree had become close to the rest of the men. The idea that most of them were now dead was too large and too terrible to comprehend.

'Penn,' the captain continued. 'I'm sorry, but I need you to check over the tower. Confirm that the nursery is empty. Make sure the Parovians are really gone, that I won't be leaving Darkhaven in enemy hands. Go to the mess hall and see – see if anyone is still alive in there ...' He shook his head, swearing under his breath. 'I'd do it all myself, if I had the strength. But I haven't. I just haven't.'

'It's all right, Captain Caraway,' Penn said. His palms were already sweating at the prospect of having to walk into the mess hall and *look* – but Caraway was right. It had to be done. 'You can count on me.'

'First, though,' Ree added, 'I think we'd better give you this.' She reached into her pocket and pulled out the messily folded plans she'd snatched from the basement. 'Long story, but if the children are gone ... well, Penn and I have reason to believe this is where they're being taken. The *Windsinger*.'

'The airship?' Caraway took it. 'You're sure?'

Raw hope cracked his voice. Penn exchanged another glance with Ree. If they were wrong – but they couldn't be wrong. The mysterious man who owned the basement had done his best to prevent them escaping with this particular secret.

'Sure as we can be, sir.'

'Right, then.' The information seemed to give Caraway new energy; he stopped leaning on Penn, standing with only the merest hint of a sway on his own two feet. 'If that's where they've gone, we have until dawn. Monster like that can't fly at night. We'll sneak on board, get the children back, and escape before the Parovians even notice we're there.'

'They will notice,' Bryan said heavily. Meeting Caraway's glare, he shook his head. 'I'm not trying to throw obstacles in your path, lad. You know I'm on your side. But they will notice, and they will come after you, and you'll be back to the reason you wanted it to be stealth in the first place: too few of you, and too many of them. That airship's crawling with Parovians, and you can bet more of them are soldiers than we realised. You need –'

He stopped abruptly, but Caraway finished the sentence for him. 'Ayla.'

They looked at each other; then the captain slammed his fist into his palm.

'Damn it. You're right. I don't think we can do this without her. But if she leaves the Kardise border now ...'

Bryan frowned. 'The evidence you sent with Sorrow –'

'Is enough to show that a Mirrorvalese dissident group, and not Ayla herself, killed the ambassador,' Caraway said. 'It should have been enough to halt the war. But with Mirrorvale still apparently to blame, I don't know that Ayla will have been able to swing Kardise opinion all the way back round to the possibility of peace.'

'But now we know the mastermind behind the plot was Parovian, not Mirrorvalese,' Ree said. 'Surely that will make a difference.'

'Yes,' Caraway agreed. 'If I had a way to prove it. But the connection between Parovia's actions tonight and the activities of Free Arkannen is based purely on hearsay. Given that I'll be sending a Helmsman to the border to call Ayla away in haste, any attempt to claim Parovian involvement in the ambassador's murder will be viewed as desperation. The Kardise will have no reason to believe it, or to rush through the signing of a treaty. And without that, if Ayla leaves the battlefield ...'

'Does it have to be a Helmsman?' Zander asked. He'd been standing in the shadows, silent – keeping out of Helm business – but now he stepped forward. 'Or could I go?'

'You?'

'Yes. I thought ... you are right that it will be hard to convince the councillors. They will suspect a Mirrorvalese trick. But since I am my father's son ...' His smile was a ghost of itself. 'Besides, as you know, my father wants me back. So sending me would be a token of good faith on your part.'

'Zander?' Ree said in a small voice. 'You are coming back, aren't you?'

'I don't know.'

'But –'

'If me staying in Sol Kardis is what it will take to convince the councillors to sign the treaty and release Lady Ayla to go after her children, I have to do it.' Zander turned pleading eyes on her. 'Don't I?'

She hesitated only a moment, before nodding. 'Yes. You do.'

'Thank you, Zander,' Caraway said softly. 'We'll need to find an airship and a pilot, assuming there's anyone willing to fly in the middle of the night –'

'Actually, an airship alone would be enough.' Zander smiled rather sheepishly. 'A councillor's son doesn't get to my age without knowing his way around the controls of a skyboat.'

'All right. Use the courier ship. The one that would have set off at first light. Ree, go with him. Take horses if it'll get you to the third ring faster. Soren is on guard down there tonight; tell him he's released from that duty. Instead, he's to take the duty roster and the address ledger and call up the off-duty Helmsmen from their homes.' He paused for a moment's thought. 'One of them had better go straight to the Mallory farm and make sure Corus is safe – alert his guard. The rest'll defend Darkhaven while we're gone. In the meantime, you grab anyone you can from the fifth ring and get back here by the third chime. We need to reach the *Windsinger* before dawn.'

'I could ring the warning bell,' Ree said. 'That would bring them up here –' But Caraway was shaking his head.

'No. The Parovian force believe they've put Darkhaven out of action. I want them to keep thinking that.'

Ree nodded. She looked at Zander. 'You ready, Zander?'

'Yes.' He touched his fingertips to Caraway's in farewell. Then he walked over to Penn and gave him a hug. 'You and Ree take care of each other.'

Not trusting himself to speak, Penn hugged him back. Without another word, Zander and Ree jogged off in the direction of the postern gate. Swallowing a lump in his throat that felt very much like tears, Penn turned his back on them and went to see if anyone in the mess hall was still alive.

Miles was alive. That was the first thing. It hurt more than anything he'd felt before, but he was alive.

He tried to open his eyes, but his body wouldn't cooperate. It was too busy screaming, all over, silently. Fractured signals reached him in between the waves of pain: cooling stickiness beneath his hands – his own blood? Hard stone beneath him. The unintelligible murmur of voices –

That was the second thing. He wasn't alone.

He concentrated on breathing, though his lungs protested with every rise and fall. Gradually the voices became clearer. Mirrorvalese accents, not Parovian – so he was probably still in Darkhaven. Which meant someone must have found him. But did they know – had they realised – the children –

Once again, he tried to open his eyes, but he was a prisoner in his own body. *Take it slowly, Miles. Just listen ...*

'... all I could find in the fifth ring.' He recognised that voice. Ree, one of the younger Helmsmen. The one who couldn't shoot straight. 'There must be more of us who were neither at the border with Lady Ayla nor here in Darkhaven when – when it happened, but I expect they're either at home or elsewhere in the city. Soren has gone looking for them, like you said, and he'll bring them up as soon as he can.'

'Thank you, Ree,' a man's voice replied. This one was

even more familiar. Captain Caraway. *So I did keep him alive, at least.*

In the warm aftermath of relief, Miles managed to lift his eyelids a fraction, but light pierced his skull like a dagger and he squeezed them shut again. Orange light, it had been. A lamp. Still night-time, then. Even though Darkhaven had been locked up for the night, and Gil had thought himself safe until morning, Ree must have come up to the tower unexpectedly, discovered the situation and raised the alarm.

'It will be enough,' Caraway said. 'It will have to be enough. A handful to go after the children, a handful more to stay here ...' Then, abruptly, his voice changed to something sharp and anxious. 'Penn? Did you –'

'I'm sorry, sir.' New footsteps sounded, approaching from further away. 'They're all dead.'

Miles could hear how much it cost Penn to say those words with even a semblance of composure. Guilt poured through him, awakening another silent scream from his battered body. Then Penn added, 'I did wake the physician before I went to the mess hall, just in case there was anything –'

His voice cracked, and Gil spoke into the pause with the soft Mirrorvalese tones he usually affected. 'We thought perhaps the effects of the poison might have varied. Perhaps some of the men might have survived. But sadly, it wasn't so.'

Now Miles lay still by choice rather than necessity, trying not to let his breathing show. Gil couldn't have expected Caraway to be alive; he must be thinking on his feet, working out how this affected the overall plan. But it wasn't an insuperable problem for him. Whereas the continued existence of Miles himself ... as soon as Gil discovered that, he would have a single goal in mind: to put an end to it before Miles could reveal the truth. The only advantage Miles had was that Gil certainly wouldn't expect *him* to have survived. The man was a physician, for the Sun Lord's sake! He knew how to stab someone effectively. If Miles hadn't been wearing the latest prototype of the collar he was developing for the Helm, he would have bled out a long time ago. Even with it, he'd be dead before morning unless he received medical attention.

Just stay quiet, Miles. He thinks you are already dead. The others believe you unconscious. With any luck, you will gain enough time to –

'I understand you have been poisoned too, Captain,' Gil said. 'Let me give you an antidote.'

Flaming Luka. Without another thought, Miles lurched into a sitting position. 'No, Tomas! You cannot trust him!'

The movement forced a fresh gush of hot blood from his wounds, and the pain that belatedly gripped him was fierce enough to bring tears to his eyes. He wrapped his arms around himself and ducked his head, gritting his teeth to keep his moan unvoiced.

'Deal with him, first,' he heard Caraway tell Gil. 'I need you to keep him alive.'

'I'll do my best.'

He is going to kill me. Miles jerked his head up again to find Gil almost within arm's reach. The man was dressed in bedclothes, for all the world as if he'd been sleeping, but he'd flung his coat on over the top. Miles wondered how he'd explained away the bloodstain on the sleeve. He must have expected to have the whole night to clean up, not – judging by the position of the moon in the sky – a mere handful of chimes.

Their eyes met, and Miles began to babble.

'He is one of them. One of us! He wants to keep me quiet. He tried to kill me.' Then, as the physician knelt down beside him with a small bottle, 'Tomas! Please! Your children. He is the only one who knows where they are. I swear –'

'He is feverish,' Gil spoke over him calmly. 'You won't get much sense out of him until I give him this dose. If you wish, Captain, I can take half of it myself.' He laughed. 'Prove it isn't poison.'

Miles understood. The draught wouldn't kill him after all; that would raise too many questions. It would merely knock him out for a bell or two, long enough for morning to come and the children to be well on their way to Parovia. That was all that mattered to Gil. Suspicion would fall on the physician after the event, of course, but by then it would be too late.

For the first time, Miles risked taking his eyes off Gil. If he could just find someone to listen to him, someone who might be willing to take his side – but of course there was no-one. The circle of light shed by the lamp revealed only a few faces: Gil to the right, with Penn standing at his shoulder, and Caraway to the left. Behind the captain were Ree and the men she'd presumably brought up from the fifth ring, perhaps three or four of them; hard to make out in the shadows. Darkhaven's main gates loomed above them. They were still in the central square where Gil had stabbed him, and there was no-one else around.

Which meant his only hope was the man he'd poisoned less than a bell ago.

'Please.' Miles fixed his gaze on Caraway's face, willing him to accept it, but the captain wasn't even looking at him. 'If you want to find them –'

'Can you hold him down for me, Penn?' Gil spoke over

him again, unstoppering the bottle. Penn moved into position behind Miles, his hands on Miles's shoulders.

'You are running out of time –'

'When I give you the signal, tip his head back and hold his mouth open.'

'Please, just trust me –'

'Enough.' Caraway said only that one word, but everyone else fell silent. Miles studied his face, barely daring to hope, but he was looking at Penn. And Penn ...

Penn's hands were fast around Gil's wrists, keeping him from moving.

When Miles turned his head back in Caraway's direction, finally the captain met his gaze.

'Give me one good reason, Miles. One good reason why I should trust you.'

Miles didn't blink. 'Because I have nothing left to lose.'

Caraway laughed, but it was a harsh sound like metal grating against bone. 'You think that makes you trustworthy? A man'll say and do anything when his life is on the line.'

'Just turn back his lapel.' Was the physician arrogant enough to be wearing it still? Miles rather thought he was. 'You will see the Enforcers' token he carries. That will prove I am telling the truth.'

At a nod from his captain, Penn let go of one of Gil's wrists and lifted the lapel of his coat. Silver glinted in the lamplight, and Miles released a long-held breath. It was there. The Parovian crown. Surely Caraway would believe him now.

Yet Gil's free hand was already moving, snatching the bottle out of his other hand and lifting it to his lips. Penn caught his wrist again, wrenching it back down, but too late. The little bottle fell to the ground, spilling a final few drops of liquid across the stone; a dazed, stupid grin spread across the physician's face.

'Damn you, Gil.' Caraway stumbled forward a couple of steps, but he was still unsteady on his feet. 'Tell me what you've done with my children. Tell me!'

Yet it was no use. Even as Caraway took another step towards him, Gil's eyes rolled back in his head and he slumped against Penn. The bottle had contained something to knock him out, just as Miles had guessed. Not an ordinary sleeping draught; something far stronger. There'd be no waking him for some time ... which meant no way he could give up his secrets.

Caraway swore. Leaning on Ree's shoulder, he stared wild-eyed around the circle as though at a loss for what to do next. But then his gaze settled on Miles, and decision returned to his face.

'Is there anything you can do to bring him out of it?'

'No.' Miles really wished there had been. At least that way he would have been able to prove his good faith. 'Or rather ... I could perhaps analyse the drops left in that bottle and come up with an antidote, but it would take more time than you have. I am sorry, Tomas.'

Caraway looked at him in silence for a moment longer. Then, turning his head, he said, 'Art?'

Relief and fear hit Miles in quick succession, leaving him breathless.

Art is here.

He knows what I am.

He didn't want to watch as Art left his place in the shadows by the gate, behind the Helmsmen, and came forward into the light. He didn't want to see the expression on Art's face. Yet he couldn't help himself. He huddled on the ground and waited, motionless except for his trembling hands, until Art stood directly in front of him – and all the while, he couldn't look away. He saw the new lines in Art's face. He saw the hurt and the bitter disappointment. And his heart seemed to slow to nothing in his chest.

'Are you sure you're happy to do this?' Caraway asked.

'Yes.' Art's gaze never left Miles's face.

'All right. Then we'll go and prepare ourselves.' Caraway touched Art's shoulder, briefly, before moving away in the direction of one of the doors that connected the tower to the central square. His steps were slow and uneven, and Ree remained at his side to support him; yet even so, a single sharp whistle sent the rest of the Helmsmen scurrying in his wake, two of them carrying the physician's recumbent body between them.

'Tomas!' Miles called after him, turning away from Art with considerable effort. The captain stopped walking and glanced back over his shoulder.

'Yes?' His tone was not encouraging.

'T-try eating something. It will help with the after-effects.'

Caraway hesitated, frowning, as though he were trying to decide which of several stinging retorts to give. But in the end he simply nodded, before he and the Helmsmen disappeared through the door.

Miles was left alone with Art.

Tentatively, he looked up once more. He didn't even know what Art had been asked to do, he realised. Interrogate him? Torture him? Kill him? The people you loved made the best weapons against you – he'd learned that already. But had Caraway?

Either way, the important thing was to offer Art some kind of apology, however inadequate, before it was all over.

'Art?' he whispered hoarsely.

'Shut up, Miles.'

'But I –'

'I said shut up. I'll ask the questions when I'm ready. In the meantime, there's not one damn thing you can say to me that I wanna hear.'

He wasn't looking at Miles any more – he was staring into the middle distance as though preparing himself for an unpleasant task – and somehow, that was worse even than the intensity of his previous stare.

At least it is not torture. Or death. Yet that provided Miles with no consolation at all. He was going to have to tell Art everything he had done; faced with that prospect, he thought death would almost certainly have been the better option.

He gritted his teeth and waited in silence. Finally, Art cleared his throat, folded his arms and met Miles's gaze once more, his face wiped clean of all expression.

'How did they get in here?'

'Airship.' It hurt to talk, but Miles pushed himself through it. 'A small one can land on the hill outside the tower. The Enforcers have known that since the mercenary, Sorrow, crashed here three years ago.'

'Because you told them.' Art's voice was flat, but Miles flinched all the same.

'I th-thought the information would be of no use,' he said, stumbling over his words, 'because surely Captain Caraway would do something to prevent it happening again. But he never did. There is only space for a two-seater, after all. Hardly an invasion. And the Helm would see it coming long before it was a threat. But the Parovian pilot was trained in night-flying and precision landing ...'

He was talking too much. He dug his nails into his palms, forcing the flow of information to slow.

'Three men came in through the postern gate and took the children out the same way. It would have been terribly dangerous, flying a two-seater airship with six passengers at night. They must have landed as soon as they were beyond the walls of the city, transferred the children into some other conveyance ... they will be heading for the border. But how they plan to cross, I do not know. I promise.'

Art just looked at him.

'I promise!' Miles repeated. 'If I knew, I would say so. Gil did not tell me any of the details. You have to believe me.'

'I don't have to believe anything. But lucky for you, we think we know how they plan to get the children out of the country. They're using the *Windsinger*.'

Of course. It made sense. A large airship visiting Mirrorvale for fully legitimate reasons, one that had enough space for three illicit passengers ...

'What we need to know,' Art added, 'is what they're going to do with them. Demand ransom? Use them as surety against invasion? What?'

'They want the secret of the Change.' Gripped by renewed shame, Miles mumbled the words in the direction of his own lap. 'That is what I was sent here to find. But I failed to deliver it, and so ...' He winced, pre-emptively. 'They believe they can discover it by ... experimenting.'

'Experimenting.' It was an emotionless echo.

'They do not see the children as people,' Miles whispered. 'They see them as subjects for testing.'

He looked at Art, waiting for the next question; yet when Art said nothing, just returned the gaze with a grim frown that was worse than anger, more words came tumbling out.

'Art, I need you to know – I tried to stop them taking the children. If I had known that was what they intended, I never would have consented to it. And the Helm ... that was not my choice, either. I never thought the potion would ...' He faltered to a halt beneath the contempt in Art's eyes. 'I saved Tomas's life, at least!' he said desperately. 'I gave him something different, something I knew was safe –'

'So you draw the line at murdering your friends,' Art said. 'Good to know.'

'That is not –'

'I'm sure Tomas is very grateful you spared his life. Gives him the chance to bury his men.'

'I did my best –'

'Of course, he'll probably get himself killed going after his stolen children, but that's not your fault, right? Your hands are clean.'

'No, I –'

'And Mirrorvale, well, Mirrorvale will be fine! Sure, we'll be a vassal state of Parovia now, and Ayla will live in lonely misery for years while your masters experiment on her family to discover the secrets of their blood, and once they have those secrets they'll kill all remaining Nightshades and put their own overlord in place – but none of that matters, right? Because you didn't mean to murder anyone!'

Miles buried his face in his hands. '*They threatened your life, Art!* What was I supposed to do?'

Silence. After a time, Miles risked a glance upward, but the raw shock – and, worse, fury – in Art's face made him look away again quickly.

'Are you trying to say,' Art said in a low, fierce voice, 'that you did all this for me?'

Unable to find appropriate words, Miles nodded.

'For fuck's sake, Miles! Didn't you stop to think how I would feel about it?'

'What?'

'You let war and murder and invasion happen for my sake. You put me before hundreds of other people. Didn't it occur to you that I would never, ever want my own life to be preserved at that cost?'

'And if it had been my life?' Miles whispered. 'What would you have done?'

Art was silent for a time. Then he said heavily, 'Here's a novel thought: I would have talked to you. Told you what was happening. Between us, we'd have decided the war had to be stopped, whatever it cost. And then maybe, just maybe, the two of us would have found a way to protect you from the threat of assassination, like you did for Ayla.' He sighed. 'We'd have made our own options. And we'd have done it together.'

'But if I had told you that,' Miles said, in an agony of regret and self-recrimination, 'I would also have had to tell you the rest of it. Confessing to my situation would also have meant telling you I was working for Parovia, and ...' He bowed his head. 'I did not want to lose you.'

Art snorted. 'Then perhaps you should have been honest in the first place.'

'No. No, it is not that simple.' Miles wasn't sure why he was bothering to defend himself, except that this was *Art*. And though he knew what lay between them was dead, now – perhaps worse than dead, a twisted and bitter mockery of itself – he desperately wanted Art to understand. Not absolve him. He wasn't that naïve. But at least be able to see why he had done what he'd done. 'By the time we fell in love, it was already too late to tell you –'

'Love?' Art echoed. 'Without honesty, love means nothing.' He ran a hand over his head. 'Not that it matters much, now, but why *have* you been betraying us to Parovia all these years?'

'They had my sister. My brother by marriage. A nephew and another on the way.' Miles looked pleadingly at him. 'I did fall in love with you. All of you. But how could I let my family die?'

Art returned the gaze, and Miles saw the mirror of his own anguish in his eyes. 'You didn't have to. You just had to trust us.'

'But –'

'As soon as you knew us well enough, you should have talked to me. To Tomas and Ayla. Told us what was happening, in secret, so that we could look into bringing your family here. We would have done everything in our power to help you. Because we loved you too, you stupid bastard. We loved you too.'

Miles couldn't find an answer. Tears soaked his face; he wiped them off with the back of his hand, but they kept falling. Art watched him cry.

'Was it worth it?' he asked finally. 'The family you destroyed our whole world for – are they safe?'

Miles shook his head. 'They were killed before I even reached Mirrorvale.'

'I'm sorry,' Art said. He sounded as if he meant it. And then he stood up and walked away.

Miles sat and stared at nothing. After an indeterminate length of time, he heard footsteps and lifted his head – heart beating with a hope he knew full well was ridiculous – but it was only Caraway. He was moving with greater ease than he had before, and some of the colour had returned to his face. A couple more lamps hung from his hands, and in the crook of his arm was one of the Helm's medical kits.

'The food helped?' Miles said humbly. Caraway crouched beside him and began to tend to his wounds.

'Yes. Thank you.'

'Is Art –'

'He told me everything you told him. I'm leaving him in charge of Darkhaven while we're gone.' Caraway glanced up. 'He's never going to forgive you, Miles.'

'No.'

'Nor will Ayla.'

'No.'

'And if any of my children are harmed,' Caraway said, busily winding a bandage around Miles's torso, 'you'll wish you'd died tonight.'

Miles nodded. None of that was any more than he deserved. He was surprised Caraway hadn't beaten him bloody – though he supposed he shouldn't be. He'd known Caraway for years. Long enough to know that although he was a fine swordsman and a formidable warrior, he didn't actually enjoy violence. Not like some of them did.

Long enough, also, to see the captain's tight-pressed lips, his clenched jaw, and recognise that he was equal parts furious and terrified. *He'll probably get himself killed going after his stolen children,* Art had said, and Miles couldn't deny it. Whatever happened, he'd ripped a family apart. The knowledge made him heavy all over, as though guilt had transformed his bones to lead.

'I really am sorry –' he began, but Caraway glanced up again. Only for a moment, but the expression on his face was enough to stop the words unspoken in Miles's throat.

'Save it for your gods, Miles.'

'Can I ask what you are going to do?'

'*We* are going to get my children back.'

'We?'

'I need someone to get me on board the *Windsinger*,' Caraway said. 'The damn physician would have been better, because at least three men there know him, but since he's knocked himself out beyond hope of revival, you'll have to do.' Sitting back on his heels, he pinned Miles with a stare. 'So if you mean even the smallest bit of that *sorry* you're so ready to give me, this is your chance to do something about it.'

'Yes. Of course. How –'

Caraway reached into his pocket. Something flashed in his fingers, gleaming in the lamplight. The Enforcers' token.

'Tonight may have got away from you,' he said, 'but you knew full well what you were doing when you let Ayla go to war. So I might as well tell you, Miles: I won't forgive you either. But you spared my life, and my children are moving further from me with every passing heartbeat, and those are reasons enough to take a gamble on trusting you now. Will you help me?'

Miles nodded. He considered making a sacred oath, to prove he was telling the truth, but in the end he said simply, 'I promise.'

'Good,' Caraway said. 'Then let's go.'

TWENTY-SEVEN

As Zander piloted the skyboat in the direction of the Kardise border, a single thought played on his mind: *This is it. The best chance I'll ever have to win back my father's approval.*

Of course, it was a chance that depended on betraying the people who were relying on him. Darkhaven already teetered on the edge between disaster and catastrophe; failure to deliver Caraway's message to Ayla would push it over completely. Because without Ayla's help, Caraway and Ree and the few Helmsmen remaining in Arkannen were unlikely to retrieve the Nightshade children – or if they did, there would be nothing to stop the Parovians coming after them. Zander was well aware of the importance of his errand.

On the other hand, he was unlikely to get another chance to impress his father so thoroughly. Let this one slip by, and he'd almost certainly be disowned. In his father's eyes, just carrying this message to Ayla was enough to mark him a traitor to his name and to his blood. And for what? A country that viewed him with permanent suspicion. A country whose citizens spat on him in the street.

But most people aren't like that, he told himself. *There's*

Ree, and Penn and the others. They accept me without any doubt. And Captain Caraway has been good to me.

Though, admittedly, not so good as to trust him with a role in the Helm.

He's trusting me now.

But was that merely out of necessity? If the ambassador hadn't been killed, most likely Zander would have been sent back to Sol Kardis in acquiescence with his father's demands. Reluctantly, perhaps, on Ayla's part – but when it came down to it, her first loyalty was to her own country and its people. Surely Zander's must be too.

And there was no denying, it would be very easy. All he had to do was land on the far side of the border and deliver Caraway's message to his own father rather than Ayla.

I couldn't do that to Ree. They'd been given no time for long farewells, but she had embraced him, briefly and fiercely, before he climbed into the gondola of the skyboat. She hadn't said anything, but he'd understood it all anyway. Ree and Penn were the best friends he'd ever had. How could he betray them?

Yet it wasn't as if he'd ever see them again. Whether he delivered the message to Ayla or to his father, the result would be the same: he'd have to stay in Sol Kardis. Either because he'd sold Mirrorvale to the Kardise, or because his father would demand him back as proof of Ayla's good faith. He knew that. He'd accepted it as a price worth paying. But if he was never to leave Sol Kardis again, perhaps he owed it to himself to return as a hero, and not as a reluctant sacrifice.

Not much of a choice, he thought wryly. And as if in answer, he recalled Bryan's words to him earlier that evening. *Find a way to make your own options ...*

By the time he spotted the glow of the Mirrorvalese campfires up ahead, his mind was made up. He held his ship at a steady speed, passing right over the camp and across the border to Sol Kardis.

Some airships were tethered on the far side of the Kardise camp; his lamps picked out their curves. He gave them a wide berth, not trusting himself to avoid them in the darkness – no point meeting his end in a fiery snarl of wood and canvas. Beyond them, the grassy plain continued flat and featureless. Plenty of space for a night landing.

He brought the skyboat down safely, albeit with a bit of a bump – he might have grown up flying, but during his time in Arkannen he'd rarely had occasion to go anywhere – and vaulted out of the gondola. As soon as his feet touched the ground, a pistol was shoved in his face. Well, he had come from the Mirrorvalese side of the border.

'Put that away,' he said irritably in his native tongue, extending a hand to display the signet ring on his finger. 'And take me to my father.'

The man behind the pistol frowned at the ring, but as soon as he recognised it, his expression became one of deference. 'Your father is sleeping, Don Alezzandro. He is to begin negotiations with Mirrorvale in the morning.'

'Wake him up,' Zander said. 'This is important.'

The man hesitated, then nodded. He led Zander through the camp to one of the larger tents in the centre, where he indicated that Zander should wait outside, before entering himself. There was a muttered conversation. Then the same man emerged again, bowed to Zander and gestured him inside.

'Alezzandro.' It had been years since Zander last saw his father, but the man hadn't changed one bit. His expression remained entirely neutral, even a little bored. 'I trust you have a reason for this sudden reappearance.'

'Good to see you too, Father.'

Marco Lepont's eyebrows lifted a fraction, but he made no reply.

'Yes, it was a difficult flight in the middle of the night,' Zander said. 'No, I won't have a drink, thanks for offering.'

'Why are you here, Alezzandro?'

Catching the underlying hint of impatience, Zander reined himself in. He wanted his father on his side, after all. Best not to needle him, however hard a habit it was to break.

'I flew here at Captain Caraway's behest,' he said carefully. 'I have urgent news to deliver to Lady Ayla.'

'And yet you came to me.' Marco Lepont's eyes narrowed, studying Zander's face. Then, for what was possibly the first time in a decade, he smiled at his son. 'Then I have misjudged you, my boy. You are cleverer than I realised. All this time I thought you disobedient, and yet ... This is information we can use against them, yes?'

Yes. The word hovered on Zander's lips. It would be so easy to say it. Say yes, give his father what he hoped for, and bask in that smile a while longer. Yet he had chosen to follow a particular path, and he had to see it through.

'Father, you have to listen to me.' He gripped Marco's forearms and looked him straight in the eyes. 'As soon as I give Ayla this news, she will leave. Now. Tonight.'

'And leave her men undefended? Before the ceasefire is even made permanent? She wouldn't do it. Not when she has fought so hard to end this war.'

'She will do it,' Zander insisted. 'Her children have been taken. She will go after them.'

'Taken? By who?'

'Parovia. They are seeking to acquire the secret of the Change.'

Marco's eyes narrowed once more. 'Then we must strike as soon as she leaves. Wipe out the Mirrorvalese force and take over the capital before Parovia can –'

'No,' Zander said quickly. 'That's not why I came to you. I want you to help her.'

'Help her?' Marco took a step back, his expression closing. 'Have you really lost so much loyalty to your own people that you would –'

'Father, please listen.' Zander took a deep breath, compressing every bit of emotion he felt into a tiny, hidden ball at the heart of him. He couldn't afford to make this personal. His father would be swayed by logic, and logic alone. 'Sol Kardis can't afford to let Parovia take the Nightshade children. Even if we gain Mirrorvale, we will have lost its greatest secret to the enemy. We might increase our territory, but Parovia will have something much more valuable: three potential Changer creatures, growing up under their command! Mirrorvale may be small, but it provides a buffer between us and Parovia. You know that. If Mirrorvale falls, Sol Kardis and Parovia will tear each other apart.'

His father shrugged. 'Let Ayla regain her children from the Parovian force. When she returns to Darkhaven, we will be waiting for her.'

'You can't take Darkhaven,' Zander said. 'Not in a night. Not with the Helm defending it.' It wasn't a lie, not exactly – but if Marco found out that the majority of the Helm had been eliminated, there'd be no holding him back. 'If Ayla succeeds, you will end up embroiled in the same war again, except on Mirrorvalese soil, with no hope of treaty the second time round. If Ayla fails, Parovia becomes far more powerful. Neither outcome is good for Sol Kardis.'

'Then what, Zander? What do you propose?'

'Sign the treaty,' Zander said. 'Do it tonight. Lend Ayla whatever aid she requires. And once she has her children back, Sol Kardis and Mirrorvale work together to prevent the Parovians from discovering the secret of the Change. Because the Parovian agent was the royal alchemist, Father! He has been passing them information about the Nightshade line for years. And if there is one thing none of us can afford, it is for Parovia to create their own Changers. Because the Changer power in a small country like Mirrorvale is an effective deterrent, but in a large country like Parovia it could be the weapon to subdue the world.'

'We cannot let Parovia gain the secret of the Change,' Marco agreed. 'But I doubt the other councillors will agree to a full treaty with Mirrorvale. We have been shown some evidence, now, that Don Tolino's murder was not Ayla's doing. Yet if Mirrorvale is so unable to control the rogue elements within its borders –'

'That's the other thing,' Zander said. 'The dissident group, the one behind the murder, was set up by Parovia.' That was how Ree had explained it to him, anyway. She and Penn had found the plans of the *Windsinger* in a basement owned by the man who had masterminded the entire plot. 'They engineered this war for their own ends. They have been manipulating us all along. They are the enemy, Father. Not Mirrorvale.'

Marco studied his son, impassively and in silence. Zander couldn't tell what he was thinking. In the past, such an expression had been far more likely to herald a rebuke than a modicum of praise, but there had always been a chance that Zander had got it right for once. That was what made it so unbearable.

'All right,' his father said finally. 'Take the truce flag and cross the border. I will gather the councillors. But, Alezzandro –'

'Yes?'

'You will stay in Sol Kardis after this.'

It was not a question. Zander nodded, feeling the weight of inevitability settle on him like fallen snow. He had no place in Mirrorvale. He would return to Sol Kardis, put his own desires aside, and try to be the dutiful son his father wanted.

'Yes, Father,' he said. 'Whatever the treaty requires.'

Shouts awoke Ayla. She was up and out of her bedroll in an instant, running for the front line, cold air slapping her in the face. Several of her men had gathered beside the scorched hulk of the ruined fort, peering through the night in the direction of the Kardise camp.

Surely not an attack. Not now. We're due to begin again with the treaty in the morning –

But then the group of soldiers opened up, letting her through, and she saw the blur of a pale flag in the darkness. That was why no shots had been fired, though several of the patrolmen had guns in their hands. Not only that, but her sharp eyes made out what theirs could not: the face of the person carrying the flag.

'Stand down,' she said sharply, gesturing at the patrolmen. 'Let him cross.'

'Lady Ayla?' The flag-bearer stepped into the light shed by the Mirrorvalese fires. She nodded a greeting.

'Zander. What –?'

'Captain Caraway sent me.' He glanced uneasily around

at the gathered soldiers, then lifted his chin and spoke directly to her. 'Urgent news from Darkhaven.'

'Go on.'

'You should know, I've spoken to my father and the councillors are willing to sign your treaty. Now. Tonight –'

'*What's happened?*'

'It's your children,' Zander said. 'They've been kidnapped by a Parovian force. It was Parovia that arranged Don Tolino's death. They murdered all the Helmsmen in the tower tonight and took the children to the big airship. The *Windsinger*. The captain believes it will take off at first light.'

Several of the men swore; ice ran through Ayla's veins, leaving her paralysed. Through numb lips, she managed, 'I don't understand. How can the entire Helm have been overcome?'

'Poison.'

'But who –'

'Miles. I'm sorry.'

This time, she couldn't speak. Miles was a traitor. He must have been working for Parovia all along. Sharing her secrets and plotting her downfall, when she'd welcomed him into her heart and home ...

And her children were on the way to Parovia.

She turned and ran, summoning the Change the instant that she was far enough away from everyone else to do no damage. Her legs tangled beneath her in her hurry, wings half unfurling for balance, but she was already preparing to launch herself into the air –

'Lady Ayla!' The boy hurried after her. The fear in his voice held her back, despite her own urgency. She turned.

'Please. You can't leave yet. Not before the treaty is signed.'

I will not put duty above my children. Not this time.

'I'm sorry,' he said. 'But you have to. I've convinced my father that helping you is best for Sol Kardis. That the treaty should be signed now, tonight, before you leave. If you go …' He shrugged. 'There will be nothing to stop the Kardise army overcoming your men and marching straight for the heart of Mirrorvale.'

I could kill them all, she sent at him savagely. *Your father. The other councillors. Anyone who dares to oppose me. What then?*

'Then you will find yourself fighting a war on two fronts. And you will be destroyed or you will become a tyrant, but either way you will lose.'

He wasn't talking about losing the war, the human heart of her realised. He was talking about losing herself.

She wavered. Every muscle in her body strained towards flight; towards racing to her children as fast as her wings would carry her, and tearing down anything that stood in her way. That was both her instinct and her desire.

Yet, perhaps, her will was stronger.

She Changed back into human form, though she had to fight herself every step of the way to do it. Her legs buckled beneath her, sending her into a crumpled heap on the earth. Zander approached cautiously, holding out her robe. Behind him, the gathered warriors looked on.

'The airships are waiting for your men,' he said. 'The councillors have gathered. You will be able to leave as soon as the treaty is signed. I swear, Lady Ayla, you will still reach them in time.'

She didn't reply. Her children's faces swam before her, and still she fought herself: her fear, her instinct, her blind, driving love. Only once she had compressed them into a small, burning coal lodged under her ribcage – only once she had forced the tears back from her eyes and stopped her hands shaking – did she stand up and take the robe.

'Half of you will make ready to leave,' she ordered the warriors. 'The rest must stay. Whatever the outcome of my discussion with the councillors, I fly to Parovia tonight.' Then, as they sprang to obey her orders, she belted her robe tighter around herself and took a deep breath. 'Thank you, Zander. Please take me to your father.'

Sitting across from Don Mellor in the Kardise campaign tent, with the surviving councillors ranged behind him and several Helmsmen at her back, Ayla had to dig her nails into her palms to keep herself in the here and now. Words. Words. So many words. All she wanted to do was fly away. Yet the Kardise had agreed to peace. They'd drawn up a treaty and they were willing to sign. She couldn't ignore that opportunity, no matter how much it hurt.

'Are you satisfied, Lady Ayla?' Mellor asked in careful Mirrorvalese. 'Shall we sign?'

She looked at the treaty once more. It was almost exactly what she'd discussed with Don Tolino, six weeks or a hundred years ago. Even down to –

No, she told herself. *Don't question it. Just let them have what they want. The children –*

But she couldn't let it go. Even now, when every single muscle in her body was screaming at her to Change, to fly as fast as she could to the rescue of her loved ones. Because it was Zander, and it wasn't fair.

'This last clause ...' She tapped the paragraph that demanded the return of Alezzandro Lepont. 'I can't agree to this.'

Mellor threw a glance at Zander's father, whose face was

already sharpening into a frown. 'But Lady Ayla, it is one of the conditions –'

'Mirrorvale does not treat people like criminals unless they *are* criminals. The young man in question has committed no crime.'

'Surely, for the sake of the treaty …' Mellor spread his hands and tried an ingratiating smile. 'He is not, after all, one of your citizens.'

'I don't care where the people in my country come from,' Ayla said. 'Only what they do when they get there. You should try it sometime.'

At the back of her mind, she was aware that what she'd just said wasn't strictly true – that Zander had wanted to join the Helm, but had been unable to do so precisely because of where he came from – and that she would have to remedy that particular point. But she didn't let the knowledge show on her face, just kept looking at Mellor until he lowered his gaze.

'He's my son!' Perhaps sensing Mellor's weakening, Marco Lepont stepped forward. 'I agreed to help you in the belief that the treaty would be signed as written. If that isn't the case, then –'

Ayla barely looked at him. 'It is my understanding that *your son* is an adult. As such, I don't see that you have any say at all in what he does.'

'Certainly more than you,' Lepont retorted. 'Are you really going to risk your own children's lives on this point?'

She entertained a brief fantasy of taking her other form and stabbing him through the heart. Instead, she pinned him with a glare and spoke every word with ice-cold clarity.

'I don't like blackmail, Councillor Lepont. I will go through fire and death to get my children back. But if I let my care for them override my care for my people, I do not deserve to remain overlord. Your son reminded me of that, this evening. It's why I'm here with you now. And it's why I will not sign this treaty until it offers what is best for everyone. Including Zander.'

'Alezzandro is not one of your people.'

'He has lived in Arkannen for three years. Through choice, rather than birth. That makes him as much one of my people as anyone else in Mirrorvale.'

He was silent. Seizing the opportunity, Ayla softened her tone. 'Your son wants to be a Helmsman. He'd make a damn good one. And if our countries are allies, I will gladly welcome him into Darkhaven.'

'My son is not an employee,' Marco Lepont snapped. Ayla arched an eyebrow at him.

'Most of us are someone's employee, Don Lepont. Who pays your wages?'

She didn't need to mention the Brotherhood. The knowledge was there in his carefully restrained anger, in Mellor's sideways glance. Placing both hands on the table, Ayla leaned forward.

'Do I have to remind you,' she added softly, 'that your people tried to kill me under a banner of truce?'

Neither man replied, but she saw the sweat on the elder Lepont's brow. He was scared of her, she realised. They all were. It was a highly satisfying thought. She straightened up and, in one swift slashing motion, crossed through the paragraph of the treaty that mentioned Zander.

'I could ask for far greater reparation,' she said, 'but I will accept this. Now, are we going to sign?'

Once it was done, the Kardise seemed determined to make the best of it. They offered her airships. They offered her men. They even offered her a physician. Ayla declined both airships and men, preferring to take her own, but she accepted the physician. Her own battlefield physicians were still busy tending to the Mirrorvalese wounded, and she'd need someone knowledgeable with her in case – in case –

But she didn't let herself think it. Her children would be unharmed. She had to believe that, because what else could she do?

The night sky was blushing into pinks and greys as she left the campaign tent and strode out across the plain towards her own camp. Dawn. She would have to be quick.

Zander ran after her. 'Lady Ayla!'

She slowed enough for him to catch up. 'Yes?'

'Thank you. I didn't expect –'

'I know.'

'It's about time someone flung the Brotherhood in my father's face.'

'I'm glad you approve,' Ayla said. 'Now, get some sleep. And in the morning, you can fly Sorrow back home to Mirrorvale. She's been grumbling about wanting to get back to the Mallory farm ever since she was shot. You can check on Corus at the same time and bring a report to me tomorrow. All right?'

'Yes, Lady Ayla.' Zander saluted. His smile told her that he knew quite well what she was doing, and he was grateful for it. Yet as she turned to go, he added quietly, 'Good luck.'

'Thank you,' she said. Then she was off, running across the plain, summoning the Change as she went.

TWENTY-EIGHT

The airship landed in a field just outside Redmire as the first glimmers of dawn began to streak the horizon. It carried six occupants in total, as many as it could hold: Penn, Miles, Ree, two of the three Helmsmen she'd fetched from the fifth ring, and Caraway himself at the controls. A few other members of the Helm had begun to arrive at Darkhaven even before their little party left, so Ree had no doubt it would be well defended if anyone tried to take advantage of its current weakness. Whether she and her five companions would be enough to retrieve the Nightshade children safely was another matter. Still, there had been no time to gather a larger force – and little point, either. A direct confrontation would have far too much potential for ending badly.

The six of them approached the small town's airfield through the trees that bordered it on one side, but the caution turned out to be unnecessary. Even after all the days the *Windsinger* had already spent moored in Mirrorvale, and despite the fact that the sky was only just beginning to lighten, a crowd had gathered beside the ship. With their striped coats discarded in Darkhaven and their weapons kept to a minimum, Ree and the others would blend in with ease.

As they got closer, the reason for the early attendance became clear. A large board stood outside the airship; a poster reading *Airship Tours: Last Day Today!* was plastered across it, one raggedy corner curling and uncurling in the breeze. Even as Ree watched, a man descended the gangplank and tore the paper away, wadding it into a ball, before folding the board and carrying it back onto the ship under his arm. The crew were packing up to leave. The crowd were here to watch the take-off.

Although she'd expected it, Ree's stomach dipped in a mixture of relief and anxiety: relief, because she and Penn had brought back accurate information; and anxiety, because that meant they were up against the entire crew of a very large airship. She scanned the field, searching for threats, and spotted a much smaller balloon tethered in the shadow of the *Windsinger*. Another confirmation. That must be the ship that had landed in Darkhaven's grounds, the one that had carried the children away.

Beside her, Caraway swore under his breath. Ree glanced at him, but he was staring at the name painted on the side of the airship.

'Captain?'

'The *Windsinger*.' Slowly, he turned his head to look at her. 'What killed the Kardise ambassador, Ree?'

'Zephyr.'

'And all those Helmsmen?'

'Chanteuse ...' It hit her, then, just as it must have hit him. 'You mean they named their ship after the tools they planned to use to destroy us?'

A muscle twitched in his jaw. 'And no doubt someone somewhere thought that was *really fucking hilarious*.'

Ree shivered. It showed a frightening arrogance, for the

Parovians to paint their intentions in such plain sight. It suggested they thought they couldn't possibly fail. And maybe that meant they were right.

No, they're not, she told herself fiercely. *They have no idea what they're dealing with.*

'All right,' Caraway said. 'Miles, you're with me. Ree and Penn round the back. Lonnie and Riba ready with a diversion. You all know what to do.'

It wasn't a question. They'd been through the plan on their way over. But everyone nodded anyway.

'Good,' Caraway said. He looked at each of them in turn. 'I know I don't have to tell you this, but the children are all that matters. We keep them safe, whatever happens. Not because they're my children, but because they're the future of our country. Understood?'

'Yes, sir.'

'If any of us are caught, the rest of you keep going. Take the children back to Darkhaven. Nothing else is important. All right?'

'Yes, sir.'

'Then let's go,' Caraway said. 'I have every faith in you.'

He gestured Miles to follow him, before striding off in the direction of the gangplank that led onto the *Windsinger*.

As Caraway neared the gangplank, he slowed to allow Miles to catch up with him. The plan was to pretend that Miles had been retired home to Parovia with honourable injuries after losing his cover in Darkhaven, and that Caraway himself was Miles's assistant. Which meant –

'You need to go first,' he muttered. Miles threw him a frightened glance, but stepped up readily enough to take the lead. Caraway gritted his teeth and hoped, desperately, that

Miles wouldn't lose his nerve. That he really did regret what had happened the previous night, and would do whatever it took to make it right.

As soon as Miles set foot on the gangplank, the airship captain appeared at the top of it. Perhaps he was coming to greet them – but as he got closer, Caraway saw his face was contorted into a scowl.

'Traitor!' he snapped at Miles in Parovian. Caraway glanced at Miles, searching for the telltale signs that he'd known this would happen all along, but Miles looked more bewildered than anything. Clearly the original plan wasn't going to work. He needed to improvise.

'What's going on?' he asked in the same language, stepping between Miles and the angry airship captain, knowing a moment of gratitude that his position as Ayla's husband had required him to brush up on the languages he'd learned as a boy. The man turned a glare on him, which faded when he saw the token in Caraway's hand. Caraway hadn't been willing to hand it over to Miles, however penitent the man was; he'd argued that it would be natural for an aide to take care of his employer's most important possessions. Lucky, given the turn that the conversation had just taken.

'This man is a traitor,' the airship captain said. 'The retrieval team saw him stabbed in Darkhaven for refusing to carry out his orders.'

'I'm well aware of that,' Caraway replied brusquely. 'But he still holds information that's of interest to the Enforcers. *My* orders are to escort him back to Parovia for interrogation.'

Where are the children? he wanted to demand. *What have you done with my children?* It was excruciating, playing some damn fool part when all he wanted was to run on board the ship and force the bastards to give his family back.

Only the knowledge that stealth would succeed where action wouldn't kept him focused on the conversation – and every muscle quivered with the willpower it took to hold himself in check.

'Yes, sir,' the airship captain said.

'Show us to a berth, please.'

'Yes, sir.'

'Go on, then,' Caraway said roughly to Miles, playing the part, and shoved him forward up the gangplank.

As the captain led them through the airship, Caraway concentrated on matching his surroundings to the plan he had memorised. Once he and Miles had been shown to one of the best rooms the *Windsinger* had to offer, a spacious two-bunker complete with armoire, washstand and even writing desk, he thanked the airship captain and listened as his footsteps receded. The ladder that led down to the lowest deck wasn't far from here. All the same, he didn't have much time.

'Stay put,' he told Miles. 'Lock the door if you want to.'

Without another word, he left the room. Miles would have to take his chances when the airship reached Parovia. No doubt he'd end up being executed, but Caraway could find little sympathy to spare for that. It was likely, after all, that he himself would share a similar fate. When he'd come up with this plan, he'd focused on getting the children to safety, no matter what the cost.

He stole along the narrow passageway, descended the ladder, followed another passageway where it branched to the left – and finally there he was, at the room deep in the bowels of the airship that on the plans had been marked *Cargo*. Without hesitation, he knocked on the door.

'Who is it?' came a muffled voice from within.

'Message from the captain,' Caraway replied.

A moment's pause, before the door swung open. It wasn't as if the man on guard could be expecting any trouble. Presumably he was there to keep an eye on the children, not fight off angry Mirrorvalese. As far as the crew of the *Windsinger* were aware, anyone in Darkhaven who might have opposed them was dead.

Making full use of that element of surprise, Caraway pushed forward as soon as the door began to move. In his original guise as Miles's aide, he hadn't been able to wear his sword, but there had been space for a knife in his pocket. He had it pressed against the guard's belly before the other man even thought to draw his own weapon.

'Step back slowly,' he murmured, and the guard obeyed, backing away with hands raised. Caraway followed, never letting the gap between them widen. As soon as he was through the door, he kicked it shut behind him and threw a quick glance around the room.

And saw the cages.

There were three of them, simple barred cubes, and each contained one of his children. Wyrenne, the baby, lay on her front with eyes glazed, whimpering and hiccupping with the aftermath of tears. Katya was curled in a tiny ball in the corner of her cage, face tucked against her knees as though she sought to block out the world. And Marlon stood upright, holding onto the bars, his face pale and tear-stained, his eyes blazing defiance. Yet as soon as Caraway's horrified gaze caught his, that defiant look crumpled; one hand came up to scrub at his nose, and his voice cracked as he said, 'Papa?'

Caraway stabbed the guard. Not once but three times, methodically, gripping the man's shoulder to keep him upright as the blade drove into his guts, making sure he was totally incapacitated. *They were crying for me. All night they were crying for me, and I wasn't there.* He let the guard's body fall with the knife still in it, and ran to the cages.

'Papa,' Marlon said again, stronger than before. 'Papa.' And Katya was uncurling and turning to face him, trying to smile though her eyes were big and haunted; and Wyrenne blinked, her glazed expression vanishing as the tears welled up once more. They were all crying, now, all saying *Papa*, their pleading fingers reaching through the bars to him. Caraway touched their hands and hushed them, blinking away his own tears, comforting them as best he could – and all the while, a frantic corner of his mind kept telling him that if anyone heard the noise and came to investigate, their escape would be over before it began.

'The key,' he said, as soon as he thought at least Marlon and Katya were calm enough to pay attention. 'My loves, I have to find the key –'

'There's a bolt at the top,' Marlon said, sniffing. 'I watched 'em close it up.'

Caraway scrambled to his feet and discovered the truth of that disclosure: there was no lock on each cage, just a bolt beyond the reach of little fingers. He opened Wyrenne's cage first, because she was still distraught, and scooped her up. She clung to him like a small, frightened animal.

'I tried, but I couldn't reach,' Marlon added with a scowl that didn't quite hide his residual fear. 'They wouldn't even let me look after my sisters, Papa.'

'I know.' Caraway released Katya and Marlon in swift succession, before sinking down onto the floor and gathering them into his arms. 'I'm sorry I wasn't there for you,' he told them, kissing them fiercely. 'I came as soon as I could.'

'I knew you'd come,' Marlon said stoutly, though with a quaver in it. And Katya added in a tiny voice, 'I waited and waited, Papa.'

Caraway couldn't help crying a little, then – both for what had been, and for what he knew would have to come. But though his throat ached with it, he didn't let himself indulge in emotion for very long. They weren't safe yet. Which was why now, almost as soon as they'd got him back, he was going to have to ask them to leave him again.

'Listen, my loves,' he said. 'I need to get you out of here. And the door isn't safe, so I need you to climb through the window. All right?'

Three pairs of eyes looked doubtfully at him. But the window was plenty big enough even for Marlon, though not for Caraway himself. And if he lifted them high enough, they'd be able to pull themselves through it.

'Ree and Penn are waiting on the other side to catch you,' he added. 'You like Ree and Penn, don't you?'

Marlon nodded. Katya sniffed. Wyrenne buried her face in his shoulder. Caraway hardened his heart against their distress. He had to get them out. That was all that mattered.

Beneath the window, he sent up a soft whistle and heard Penn whistle in response. Good. They were in position. He tried lifting Wyrenne first, but she screamed and clung to him with all her strength.

'Wren, please –'

'I'll go first, Papa,' Marlon said stoutly. Caraway deposited Wyrenne on the floor, where she howled even louder and clung to his legs, then hoisted Marlon up to the window. The little boy wriggled through without a moment's hesitation, his legs vanishing suddenly as – presumably – Penn caught him under the arms and pulled him down on the other side of the wall. Seeing that, Katya followed without a whimper. But Wyrenne ...

Caraway picked her up again, humming a soothing tune under his breath, but it was no use. Hard enough at the best of times to settle her once she was overtired, let alone in a situation like this. And no matter how he coaxed and soothed her, still she clung to him.

'Penn!' he called up softly. 'If Ree stands on your shoulders –' But already he could see it was impossible. Even if he lifted the sobbing baby as high as he could, and Ree could reach through the window towards her, there was a good gap in between. Wyrenne could have climbed through by herself – fire and blood! He'd seen her clamber up the vast stone staircases of Darkhaven without any fear or sense of self-preservation whatsoever – but she wouldn't leave the safety of his arms.

Should have sent Penn in here, and waited on the other side myself. But Caraway knew he couldn't have done it. As usual, he had suffered from an overabundance of believing that he was the only man for the job. *You're a damn fool, Tomas Caraway. And if Wyrenne has to pay for it –*

'Hush, Wren,' he murmured, cradling the little girl's head against his shoulder. 'We'll find a way out. Don't you worry.'

As if to prove him wrong, the ship lurched around them, and Penn hissed, 'Captain! They're preparing for takeoff!'

Fuck. Caraway thought about it very briefly, but there was only one course of action that he could see.

'Fall back,' he ordered Penn. 'Stay out of sight. Keep Marlon and Katya safe.'

'I swear it,' Penn said. 'Sir ... what are you going to do?'

Caraway sighed. 'If I try and break out with Wyrenne now, they'll realise the other two are missing and come after you on the ground. I can't take that risk. So she and I are going to take a little trip to Parovia.'

'But, Captain –'

The ship lurched again, and Caraway gritted his teeth. 'Just go, Penn.'

'Yes, sir.'

He sat down on the floor, rocking the baby in his arms, and waited for the ship to take off.

Wyrenne was asleep by the time someone came to relieve the guard. Caraway had been expecting the change – even watching *three children in cages* wasn't a task a man could perform indefinitely – so he was already waiting behind the door when it opened, the sword he'd taken from the dead man in his free hand. He ran the new guard through with it before the man even had the chance to turn around. It didn't sit well with him, but the cages made it easier. The cages, and the murdered men back in Darkhaven. Even if he were to stand here killing people all day, it would pay only a fraction of what he owed Parovia in vengeance.

Once he'd closed the door behind the second dead man, he stooped to search his pockets and was relieved to find a key – something the first man had been unable to supply. Wyrenne stirred at the movement, but he murmured her back to sleep before easing the key into the lock. The two of them might still be trapped in a room with a pair of corpses, but at least Caraway now controlled the entrance. They'd be able to overcome him by weight of numbers, of course, but it was a marginally better position than the one he'd held before.

'Stay asleep, Wren,' he whispered. When she woke up, she'd be hungry. Thirsty. She'd need clean cloths and a change of clothing. And when he couldn't provide what she wanted, her crying would summon the crew of the airship as surely as an alarm bell.

At that stage, if Ayla hadn't arrived yet, Caraway would have to decide what to do next.

Ayla was his only hope of escape: he knew that all too well. Assuming that Zander had made it to the border, and assuming that Ayla had been able to leave a delicate and potentially lethal situation unfinished, she would come after the *Windsinger*. Caraway's job was simply to keep Wyrenne safe until that happened. Yet he had nothing to bargain with; the Parovians would know that as well as he did. And once they discovered that Wyrenne was the only Nightshade child remaining to them, they would be anxious to get her back under their control. Alive, of course, which was one good thing – they had no desire to kill her – but given that Caraway had the self-same lack of desire, he couldn't use that against them. Most likely, they would find a way to take the baby from him and bring him down. He didn't see how he could hold them off, not if they threw enough men at him. Not if he wanted to keep his daughter from getting hurt.

Of course, if they succeeded in getting her back to Parovia – if he himself was killed, if Ayla didn't arrive in time – she'd be hurt anyway. Miles had told him a little of what they intended. Experiments. Blood. Pain. Wyrenne would grow up in a cage just like the one he'd found her in, treated as no more than an animal. A rare and valuable animal, but an animal all the same. She'd cry herself to sleep every night, until one day she'd forget what she was crying for. And then finally, once she'd given the Parovian alchemists what they wanted, they'd dispose of her.

Either that, or they'd bring her up as one of them, then

set her against her family as soon as she was old enough to Change ...

Wyrenne whimpered in her sleep, and Caraway realised his arms had tightened around her. He'd have to choose. If it came to it, he'd have to decide whether it would be better for her to die than to live the life they'd give her.

I could never kill my own daughter, his heart said. *Never.*

But if the choice is between a clean death and a long, degrading, painful one? his head replied. *What then?*

I don't think I have the courage.

Of course you do. You're Tomas Caraway. You're a hero, remember?

Shut up.

You're going to die anyway. The only question is whether you'll take Wren with you or abandon her here on her own.

I said shut up.

For a wonder, his turbulent thoughts obeyed. He rested his cheek on Wyrenne's hair, hummed a lullaby, and prayed for Ayla to arrive.

TWENTY-NINE

A fight had broken out in the crowd on the opposite side of the *Windsinger* from the window that led to the cargo hold. One man had stepped on another man's toes, or perhaps the second man had elbowed the first in the ribs; now they were hurling insults and trying to get each other in a headlock, drawing all eyes as they did so.

That much was according to plan. When they'd discussed it in the airship coming over, Caraway had given Lonnie and Riba the task of causing a distraction while he, Penn and Ree took the children to safety. Yet that part of it had always been impossible, Penn realised now – and Caraway must have known it. Even if all three children had been retrieved in secret, as soon as Caraway tried to escape the *Windsinger* he would have raised the alarm and the Parovians would have come after them. So right from the start, Caraway must have intended to stay on board, relying on his team to take his children home safely while he ... what? Went to his death, most likely. Discovering the failure of their entire mission was unlikely to leave the Parovians feeling benevolent.

Penn wasn't sure how Wyrenne's presence would complicate that situation, but he thought he probably shouldn't mention it to Ree. She might well argue that they couldn't leave their captain behind – but Caraway himself had always told them that their loyalty was to Ayla and her children, not to him, and Penn intended to follow that directive.

'You're arguing with me in your head,' Ree panted. 'I can tell.'

'How?'

'You get this particular look on your face.'

She was carrying Marlon on her back, while Katya was nestled in Penn's arms. He'd soon discovered that there was no good way to carry a small child. Her arms and legs were too short for her to cling on like Marlon was, and she had objected strongly to being put over Penn's shoulder, so in the end he'd settled on an inefficient one-armed hold that made his muscles ache – and he wasn't exactly unfit.

'Parents must be made of steel,' he muttered, and Ree grimaced at him.

'Don't change the subject. Tell me what you were thinking before.'

So he did. To his surprise, Ree only looked sad.

'I'd figured that out for myself, you know,' she said. 'And I wouldn't have argued. I mean, even if I was more loyal to Captain Caraway than to the Nightshade line – which I'm not – it comes out the same. Loyalty to the captain *means* putting Ayla and the children first. That's the way he's set it up. Isn't that the point?'

Penn nodded.

'Anyway, I wouldn't bet against the captain, even hopelessly outnumbered,' Ree said. 'Really, it's worse that we've left Wyrenne. Remember that training exercise we did, all the way back when they were first assessing us? We had to get a Nightshade baby to safety.'

'And you said it didn't matter how many of us were left behind, as long as the baby was safe,' Penn agreed. It was the first time he could remember liking her.

'Right. Yet here we are, running back to Darkhaven and leaving Wyrenne in danger.'

'Only because we have Marlon and Katya to protect,' Penn objected.

'I know. But even so.' Almost to herself, she added, 'I can't see how he'll get her out. Not once they've taken off.'

'He doesn't have to,' Penn said firmly. 'He just has to keep her alive until Ayla gets there.'

Doubts chased each other across Ree's face, but she only nodded. Over her shoulder, Marlon looked up at Penn with big, shadowed eyes and said in a small voice, 'Is Mama coming?'

'She has to fetch your sister first.'

'And Papa?'

'Yes. Of course.' Briefly Penn met Ree's gaze. 'Don't worry, Marlon. Everything will be all right.'

It was a useless platitude, but apparently it was enough for the little boy; he rested his head back down on Ree's shoulder, though his watchful eyes still scanned their surroundings. In Penn's arms, a residual sob shook Katya's slight frame, making her whimper even through her exhausted half-sleep.

'Nearly there,' he whispered to her. 'The airship's just up ahead.'

They would lie low in their own little airship until the *Windsinger* was out of sight, then take off themselves and set a course for Darkhaven. Lonnie and Riba would remain behind to make sure no-one had followed. Best not to think about Caraway or Wyrenne. Best not to think about anything other than getting Marlon and Katya to safety.

Everything will be all right, Penn repeated to himself, yet not even he believed it.

Ayla had never flown this fast before.

There had been times when she was anxious to get somewhere. Times when she'd been in a hurry and taken advantage of the speed her wings had to offer. But she'd never pushed herself. Fear and urgency had never driven her to find out exactly what her limits were.

As it turned out, her limits were *high*.

She outstripped the airships before they were even out of sight of the Kardise border. That was no surprise; even a leisurely Changer creature was faster than an airship. But then she continued to accelerate. Her lungs expanded. Her wings beat the air. The ground below became a blur. And still she felt no strain or tiredness, only a fierce and exhilarating joy. She was made for this. She would find the people who had dared to take her children, and she would kill them. The desire for retribution burned through her veins, driving her onward. She saw the traitors dying. She imagined the blood and heard the screams. And in response her senses expanded further, until she could hear every tiny animal movement on the surface of the earth beneath her, see every wisp of cloud in the sky. A corner of her brain caught and discarded each one of those myriad distractions, searching for anything that might be relevant to her goal – and all the while she kept pushing forward, faster and faster, steam rising from her body and rolling off her wings until she felt herself made of fire, not ice.

Then she heard Marlon's voice.

A small airship lay ahead of her, a dot on the horizon but growing fast. It wasn't anything like large enough to be the

Windsinger, and it was travelling deeper into Mirrorvale rather than heading away, and so Ayla didn't attack it. It wasn't as if Marlon had sounded frightened or hurt, only sleepy. All the same, she kept moving forward at a fair speed, anxious to find out whether all three of her children were safe.

As the gap closed between her and the airship, she made out Penn at the controls, and heard Ree murmuring a story to Marlon. There was just one other person in the ship – Ayla could hear them breathing. Not Tomas. A child. *Katya or Wyrenne?* A fretful whimper gave her the answer: her elder daughter was curled up against Ree, dozing fitfully. Tomas and his little Wren were missing.

She didn't slow as she neared the airship, but Changed in midair, pouring herself over the side of the gondola to land in human form within.

'Where is Wyrenne?' Her voice sounded harsh and strange in her own ears. During her journey, she had inhabited her other form so intensely that some of that fierce wildness still lingered – and she couldn't afford to let it go, not yet. Not while her baby was missing.

'S-still on board the *Windsinger*,' Ree stammered. 'Captain Caraway couldn't get her out like the other two.'

One arm held Katya on her lap, while the other was around Marlon beside her. Both children were asleep now. Ayla kept her gaze firmly fixed on Ree's; looking at her children's faces would only melt her fully back to human. Of course, that meant she was intimidating Ree, but she couldn't help it.

'Tomas is with her?'

Ree nodded, biting her lip as though she feared Ayla would destroy her.

'He told us to go,' Penn added, without looking away from the controls. 'We thought it best to get the children to safety.'

His expression was resolute. He would do anything for her family, Ayla realised. Even if it meant abandoning his captain. And just like that, she finally made complete peace with the fact that one of her protectors had once kidnapped her son. He was making up for it now.

'The *Windsinger* took off?' she asked.

'It'll have crossed the border by now,' Ree said. 'Lady Ayla ... what do you want us to do?'

As if in answer, Katya stirred; a small, sleepy voice said, 'Mama?' But Ayla hardened her heart against it. She couldn't stay. Marlon and Katya were safe, so that only left Wyrenne. And Wyrenne was in Parovia.

'Keep going,' she said. 'Back to Darkhaven.' Then, fixing each of them with a fierce stare, 'Their lives are in your hands.'

She was already summoning the Change again as she vaulted back over the side of the airship.

Her wings unfurled. The air rushed. The ground rolled away beneath her. She reached Mirrorvale's eastern border and crossed it without a thought. And then the *Windsinger* was ahead of her, visible even through the rain that had started to fall. She didn't need to read the name painted on the side, or identify it by size. She could have found it with her eyes closed. Because deep in the heart of the ship, surrounded but not concealed by the babble of voices and the creak of the gondola and the roar of the engines, Wyrenne was crying.

An instant later, a note of alarm entered the voices on board the ship: they had seen her coming. Ayla heard their running footsteps, smelled gunpowder as they readied their firearms. But she didn't hesitate. She barely slowed beneath the onslaught of bullets – bullets which, thanks to the Parovian alchemy that had created her collar, bounced off her like hailstones on a window. She felt their sting, but it didn't turn her from her course. Instead, she plunged her horn straight into the upper edge of the airship and ripped it open, just as she once had with smaller Kardise craft.

The *Windsinger* wasn't small enough to be torn straight out of the sky, but the rupturing of several of its gas chambers caused it to list alarmingly. The hail of bullets ceased as the Parovian crewmen realised they were in very real danger of setting their own ship on fire. Ayla circled and stabbed, releasing ever more of the buoyant gas from within the airship, and it began to sink.

Bring her in to land! she heard the cry go up. *Before we lose her!*

Lurching drunkenly through the sky, the vast airship descended into a flower-dotted meadow beside a river. Ayla followed, Changing even as her feet touched the ground, snatching up the simple garment she'd carried with her and thrusting her arms inside. The rain was falling harder now. Good. Water meant ice, and ice was a weapon.

Even in human form, she knew exactly where Wyrenne was. She could still hear her crying, deep in the heart of the ship. And so she extended her senses into the wooden frame and ordered it to crack. Fissures ran up the sides, the entire structure listing and groaning. Raising her arms in the air, she gestured wide, and pieces of wood flew up and out at her command. The entire airship shattered like a dropped bowl, raining splinters down on the ground around it. Men shouted and screamed as they dived free of the collapsing ship or struggled to free themselves from beneath the fallen wreckage. Yet right in the middle of the carnage ...

Right in the middle, a single room remained intact. And within it, Tomas Caraway was singing his daughter a lullaby.

Ayla started forward. A man lurched through a gap in the broken wall to her right, but she used her power again without a second thought, cracking one end of a loose beam and bringing it down on his head. Around her, she sensed a few people moving in the wreckage, rearming themselves with pistols and moving towards her; that was more difficult, but she followed the scent of gunpowder back to its multiple sources and *froze* the falling raindrops around what she found there. A pistol couldn't be fired if its flintlock mechanism was encased in ice. The men cried out as the intense cold crackled across their pistols and into their hands. Ayla smiled and kept moving.

She heard Tomas stop singing. She heard the key turn in the lock of the incongruously intact door. And then he walked out, Wyrenne in his arms, and Ayla forgot everything except the need to reach her child as soon as possible –

Chill metal touched her wrist, and her senses deadened. Instinctively she wrenched her arm away, turning ready to defend herself, but it was too late. The man who'd crept up behind her had put a manacle on her wrist made of ... what? She wasn't sure, but there was steel in it. Glass and amber, too. A manacle created by alchemy, made with the same knowledge that had created her collar but for a very different purpose. And until she could get it off, all her Changer powers were lost to her.

She spun on the ball of one foot and kicked him as hard as she could, then turned and ran for Tomas and Wyrenne. But now other men were emerging from the wreckage of the

Windsinger: their clothing tattered, their expressions grim, some of them streaked with blood. They were moving to intercept her. And there, nearby, where it had fallen from the broken deck –

A cage.

THIRTY

Miles lay motionless under the shattered pieces of Parovia's greatest engineering triumph. One of his legs had been trapped by falling timber, but he didn't have any inclination to move anyway. He simply lay there, and wondered why he was still alive.

He had watched the short air battle from within his cabin: the golden alicorn, untouched by bullets, using her strength to tear the *Windsinger* from the sky. He had given her that protection. He ought to feel something about that.

Later he had seen Ayla, back in human form, standing on the ground with arms spread wide as pieces of wood rained down around her. He had helped her to discover that power. He ought to feel something about that, too.

And now his countrymen had trapped her with an alchemical combination derived from his own research, pinning her in human form while they dragged her back towards the cage that had also been created using his research, and he ought to feel something about that – but he didn't. All he knew was that people were dead because of him. Lots of people, starting with Mara and her family and leading all the way up to the crewmen lost in the rubble of the

Windsinger. He had left destruction wherever he went. And Art ...

Art. Forgive me.

If the Sun Lord had any purpose for Miles at all, he was having a hard job understanding what it was. As far as he could see, the world would have been better off without him.

He closed his eyes, but something made him reopen them. Half the crewmen still standing were advancing on Tomas and Wyrenne. The other half were hustling Ayla towards the large cage – bent and twisted out of shape, but still functional – that had been built at the heart of the ship. As Gil had said, the Parovian crew had prepared for every eventuality. Their primary goal had been the children, but they'd take the mother if they could.

Short of cutting her apart, there is little more to gain from her, Gil had said. Was that what they intended? To experiment on her, slicing her open in an attempt to understand the alchemy in her blood? Miles shuddered. *We treat people like animals and call it science. This is what I have been working for, all these years.*

His hand moved slowly across the ground, passing over crushed grass and a broken flower until it found what it was looking for. A long, jagged piece of wood. A piece of the broken *Windsinger*. A stake.

They would pass right by him, on the way to the cage.

Ayla's death would destroy Mirrorvale. More to the point, Ayla was his friend. Did that mean anything, after all he'd done? Perhaps not to her. But to him ... yes. Though Art had mocked him for the lines he refused to cross, they were still part of him. He wouldn't let Ayla or any of her family die, whether quickly now or slowly in a laboratory. He'd allowed a war to unfold, and caused untold harm to

Mirrorvale, for the sake of a lie; now he knew the truth, he owed Parovia nothing.

As the two crewmen with Ayla between them drew level with him, he rose up and drove his makeshift weapon hard into the nearest of them. The man yelled, his grip on Ayla loosening as his hands went to his bloody thigh. Ayla twisted free. Miles had a moment to see that, to see her twisting free.

Then another crewman kicked him backwards, planting a boot on his chest, and stabbed him, reopening the bandaged wound that had already come close to taking his life. Miles saw the man's face above him, drawn into a snarl. He felt the hot splash of saliva hit his cheek. And then the man was gone.

The colour had begun to bleach out of the sky, now. The sounds of angry men faded to a wash and hiss, like the random ebb and flow of the wind. Miles had little sensation left in his hands, or anywhere for that matter, but he reached into the inside pocket of his coat for the letter he had written to Art while he was on board the ship: the one that told Art how much he loved him, truly, and how much he regretted everything he had done. He hoped Ayla or Tomas would find it. He hoped they would take it back to Art. Maybe Art would never read it, but if he did, perhaps he would find a measure of comfort in the knowledge that whatever else Miles had lied about, he had never lied about what lay between them.

The numb feeling had spread throughout his body, now, and he was thankful for it. He fumbled the letter to his chest and closed his eyes. The end was coming, and his overwhelming emotion was one of relief.

He would die on Parovian soil. Somehow, despite everything, there was peace in that.

* * *

As Miles fell, and Ayla broke free of her distracted captors, Caraway was already running. Two of the Parovians tried to block his path, but he punched one of them and, as the man staggered back, plucked the short Parovian sword from his belt and used it to stab the other one. Then he wrenched it back out without any finesse whatsoever and ran on, flicking the blood from the blade. Still clutched in his left arm, Wyrenne screamed relentlessly.

Good testing exercise for future Helmsmen, some small, sarcastic part of his brain observed. *If they can fight holding a distraught one-year-old, they're in.*

Ayla met him halfway, taking the Parovian sword from him without a word and spinning to face her pursuers. Caraway drew the sword he'd taken from one of the guards, earlier, and turned as well. Back to back, they gripped their weapons as the remaining crewmen encircled them. Spotting her mother over Caraway's shoulder, Wyrenne stretched out her arms and screamed louder than ever.

'Stay still, Wren,' Caraway bit out. *Make that a distraught, wriggling one-year-old.* If she wasn't careful, he was going to drop her. He hitched her further up his shoulder and – as the Parovians advanced – began yet again to sing her favourite lullaby.

'The moon is up ...' *Two of us and four of them – no, five if you count the one with the broken nose.* 'The stars are bright ...' *It's not impossible.* 'The owl has come to say goodnight ...'

He spun to block one attack, converted it into a lunge that sent his opponent reeling backwards, then turned in time to meet the next man's blow. Wyrenne still cried, but it was a grumbly sort of cry rather than the utter outrage of before. The song was working – either that or the constant movement.

But what came after the damn owl? He must have sung it a thousand times, today alone, and yet he couldn't remember. He started from the beginning. 'The moon is up ...'

Every so often, out of the corner of his eye, he caught sight of Ayla. She wasn't used to the short swords of Parovia; he'd only ever trained her with the Mirrorvalese Helmsman's standard issue. An omission, perhaps, though he could never have imagined these circumstances. Still, she was holding her own. What she lacked in technique, she made up for in feeling. He recognised the feeling, because it was one he shared: *I'll be damned if I let you have my daughter.*

'Will you stop – bloody – singing that?' one of the Parovians panted. Caraway smiled and ran him through. *One down.*

He did have to stop singing, though, shortly after that. It was that or drop Wyrenne, or drop his sword, neither of which were acceptable outcomes. But as soon as he faltered, Ayla picked up the lullaby. She kept singing while she hacked a man's hand off at the wrist. She kept singing while Caraway blocked a thrust and, through more luck than skill, deflected it to injure his second opponent. She sang until, finally, the last man fell and they were able to turn to face each other.

Ayla's thin tunic was torn and bloodstained in several places; she had a gash on one cheek and a deeper cut down one arm, but Caraway couldn't see any damage more significant than flesh wounds. He knew he'd been cut in multiple places himself, and the knee he'd injured racing after Ayla six years ago – which had never been quite at full strength since – throbbed in a way that told him he'd suffer for it in the days ahead. But they'd survived it. Against all odds, they'd survived.

'Is Wyrenne all right?' Ayla asked.

'Yes. She's angry, but she isn't hurt.'

'Can you get this off?' Ayla held out the wrist that bore the manacle. He handed her Wyrenne, before wrenching the strange metal apart with his bare hands. Something in her expression eased, a hint of tension dissipating as her full abilities returned to her.

'Thank you,' Caraway said. 'You got here just in time.'

She managed a smile. 'I thought it was probably my turn to rescue you.'

'Oh, Ayla.' He rested his forehead against hers, careful not to crush the baby between them. 'You did that a long time ago.'

For a moment they stood in silence, just breathing each other in. But only for a moment, because Wyrenne's cries – which had died down to exhausted, hiccupping sobs – were beginning to ramp back up again.

'She's tired,' Caraway said. 'And hungry, and wet. I wish I could have done more –'

Ayla shook her head. 'She's alive.'

Sinking to her knees, heedless of the carnage around her, she put the baby to her breast. Caraway took off his coat and draped it over her shoulders. Then he stood on guard beside them, but there was no sound or movement from the wreckage. The three of them were alone with the dead.

He had seen far too much death since this time yesterday morning.

He walked in a slow circle, fighting the heaviness of his limbs, scanning the battlefield for hidden threats, and that was how he stumbled across Miles. The alchemist lay on his back, eyes closed. His hands clutched a folded paper to his chest – and scrawled across the outside, clear to read despite the bloodstains, was the name *Art Bryan*.

Caraway stood and looked at that piece of paper for some time. Perhaps he should leave it behind, or destroy it ... but it wasn't his decision to make. When it came down to it, all he could do – all he had the right to do – was deliver the message to Bryan and deal with the consequences.

He leaned down to pick up the letter, and caught the shallow rise and fall of Miles's chest. *Alive.*

Again, Caraway ran through his options and just as quickly discarded them. Leave the man behind ... but that would run the risk of him surviving to fall into Parovian hands, and no doubt there were still Nightshade secrets that could be extracted from him. Kill him ... but without Miles, they'd all be in captivity right now. He was the one who had kept Ayla from being locked in a cage; Caraway couldn't repay that with murder. Which meant the only choice they had was to take the man with them back to Darkhaven. But how?

By the time he returned to Ayla and Wyrenne, the baby had finished feeding and had drifted off to sleep. Ayla looked up at him with a question in her eyes.

'We need to get back across the border,' he answered it softly. 'We're vulnerable here. It shouldn't take long to walk –'

She shook her head. 'There's a Mirrorvalese force coming by air, somewhere behind me. I can carry us to meet them.'

'It's not just us,' Caraway said. 'Miles is alive.'

'Miles is the reason we're in this situation in the first place.'

'I know. But ...'

'We can't just leave him to die,' Ayla finished for him. 'All right. I'll carry all three of you.'

'Are you sure? You must be tired after –'

'I can rest when we're safe.' She stood up, a practised fluid motion that barely jolted the baby at all. 'Here, take Wyrenne.'

Caraway accepted his coat and his daughter, then stood in silence as Ayla Changed. He thought he probably should be protesting more. She'd come all the way from Sol Kardis, destroyed an airship, fought by his side, and now she was proposing to carry them all to safety? Surely she didn't have the energy for it. Yet there was no denying he longed for home – and since he had no transport to offer, Ayla's solution was by far the best one.

The last swirls of black smoke condensed into gold, and the alicorn gazed at him steadily. Even after six years at Ayla's side, Caraway hadn't lost his awe of her other form.

'How should I –'

In response, she dipped her knee. *Put Wyrenne between my wings while you fetch Miles. I'll keep her safe.*

He did so. The baby was so exhausted that she barely stirred when he placed her on the alicorn's broad back; the great golden wings folded over and round, covering Wyrenne in a blanket of soft feathers.

Caraway bound up Miles's wounds as best he could, then hoisted the man over his shoulder. There was room to lie him across the alicorn's neck, with head and arms hanging down one side and legs the other. Caraway vaulted into place behind him, then turned round to scoop up Wyrenne and settle her against him. Tentatively he reached out to grasp a handful of the alicorn's flowing mane, but dropped it again when she snorted and tossed her head.

'I'm sorry.'

I won't let you fall. Any of you.

'I know.'

And then they were in the air.

She had never carried him this way before. She'd never offered, and he'd certainly never asked. A Changer creature wasn't a common beast of burden. But after a while, with Wyrenne sleeping peacefully in his arms and the landscape unfolding below, he forgot to be awkward about it. He felt the cold wind in his face, listened to the silence of the air, and let himself enjoy the fact that this was as close as he'd ever get to knowing what it was like to have wings.

He wasn't sure exactly when they crossed the border. But the grassy meadows became orchards and fields, the red soil of Parovia became the more familiar dark earth of Mirrorvale, and shortly after that he spotted the approaching airships. Ayla snorted when he pointed them out, in a way that suggested she had noticed them long before he had, but she flew swift and straight to meet them. And then –

Then, he wasn't sure. By the time they climbed aboard an airship, he'd been smothered by a thick, heavy blanket of exhaustion. He was vaguely aware that Resca was there, tending to Miles. That one or two of the Helmsmen he'd sent to war were with him. But all that really mattered was that he had Ayla beside him, sitting with her head on his shoulder and Wyrenne on her lap. They drifted in and out of sleep, broken by the random snatches of conversation that were the result of two people drained beyond their natural capacity.

'Half the Helm are dead,' he said at one stage, and Ayla squeezed his hand.

'I know. I'm sorry. I –' Her breath hitched in a little sob. 'I'm really sorry.'

Then, later:

'I met Ree and Penn on the way,' Ayla said. 'They were taking Marlon and Katya back to Darkhaven by airship.'

Caraway nodded. 'I knew they could do it.'

And later still:

'Do you think it must be war?' he asked softly. 'Mirrorvale and Parovia?'

'Not if I can help it.'

'They'll be expecting a declaration. They've given us enough cause.'

'Yes. But with Darkhaven so weakened ...'

'That's why we have to appear strong.'

'I know,' Ayla said. 'But I did destroy the *Windsinger*. And we have Sol Kardis on our side, now. Perhaps that will be enough.'

After that they must have fallen asleep completely, because Caraway wasn't aware of anything else until the airship landed outside the tower. Straight down onto the hillside outside Darkhaven. He made a vague note, somewhere at the back of his mind, that he'd have to do something about that. As the Parovians had proven, a skilled pilot could do it at night. What use the rings of Arkannen, if an airship could land directly in the seventh?

Bryan awaited them, along with several Helmsmen. His relief and happiness went a long way towards showing – if Caraway had still possessed any doubts on the matter – that the weaponmaster was his friend, and not simply his old mentor. Yet when Miles was unloaded from the airship, Bryan's face went completely blank.

'Is he –?'

'He's alive,' Caraway said. 'Just.'

Bryan nodded silently. But as Caraway turned away, the weaponmaster muttered, 'Don't let him die.'

'I don't think he will,' Resca said, unaware of the deep emotional currents running around him. 'His blood is far less swift to drain from his body than anyone else I've seen. I gather this remarkable collar has something to do with it.'

His swift, keen glance left Caraway wondering whether the Kardise physician's presence was going to cause more trouble than it was worth. Secrets were spilling out all over the place at the moment. But Miles needed medical attention, and he was really too tired to think much beyond that.

As alchemist and physician retreated in the direction of the infirmary, he remembered the folded paper that Miles had been holding in the wreck of the *Windsinger*. He fished it out of his pocket.

'Art!' he said, turning back on his heel. He wasn't sure this was the right time to mention the letter. He wasn't sure he should mention it at all. But if he didn't deliver it to its intended recipient now, he probably never would. 'He was holding this. When I found him.'

Bryan took it in silence. Then Ayla was there with Wyrenne in her arms, and the Helmsmen who had returned from the border were awaiting orders, and Caraway forgot all about Miles and his letter.

As soon as they could manage it, he and Ayla went in search of their other two children. They found Ree and Penn standing guard in the nursery, one at each bedside, and sent them off to one of the empty bedrooms to get some rest. Then Caraway and Ayla carried all three of their slumbering children into their own big four-poster bed, and curled up around them. After a while, Ayla reached across the three small bodies for Caraway's hand, and that was how they fell asleep.

THIRTY-ONE

Sorrow settled herself more comfortably against the banked-up pillows in Elisse's double bed, and sighed in satisfaction. At times like this, when she was still recovering from a kiss with death, she could really appreciate the simple comforts of the Mallory family farm.

'Behold Mirrorvale's new hero,' she drawled, and Elisse rolled her eyes.

'So are ya finally going ta tell me what happened?'

'I took a bullet for Ayla Nightshade.'

Elisse looked at her with an expression that said *Pull the other one*, which altered slowly into *You must be out of your mind*. 'Why?'

'Because ...' Once again, Sorrow tried to pin down the reason for her unexpected slide into patriotism. *Because she's my overlord* was the official reason, but official reasons seldom had much to do with the truth.

'Because she's family,' she said finally.

'I never knew ya had royal connections, Naeve.'

Sorrow ignored the sarcasm. She was feeling unusually earnest, and she planned to make the most of it while she could. She'd probably never feel like having this conversation again in her life, but that was what nearly dying did to a person.

'Family isn't what makes us,' she said. 'It's what we make for ourselves. Corus is my son – close as I'm ever going to get, anyway. And Ayla is his sister, by blood and by choice. If I'd let her die, I'd have let him down.'

It wasn't the whole of it, of course. Thinking about it rationally, there were a hundred reasons why she'd been right to act as she did – not least among them, the need to prevent a war and keep Mirrorvale under Changer protection. But when it came down to it, in the brevity of the moment between seeing someone under threat and responding to it, there was only ever room for a single instinctive decision: *do I value their life at least as much as my own?* Reason came later.

'Anyway,' she said hastily. 'I took a bullet for Ayla, and then while I was busy having it dug out of me, she signed a peace treaty with the Kardise and flew off to rescue her stolen children from Parovia. So really, I missed all the good bits. Instead, I got to lie around in a crappy infirmary tent and then get flown back to Mirrorvale by Ayla's newest Helmsman.'

The truth was, she'd liked Zander, as much as she ever liked anyone – *ah, who are you kidding?* some mocking part of her interrupted. *You like all kinds of people these days. You're almost making a habit of it.*

Anyway, she'd liked Zander, mainly because when she'd smirked at him and said, *Oh, you're Ree's boy,* he'd thought about it for a moment and then said, with a little smile, *Yes, I suppose I am.* After that she'd felt quite comfortable talking to him about weapons and more weapons and his strange, inexplicable happiness at being made a Helmsman. Bit of a waste, really. That one had a streak of mischief that could be put to good use.

He'd also made her feel old. As far as she'd been able to estimate, from what he'd said, she was fourteen years older than he was. *Fourteen years.* Aside from certain obvious logistical difficulties, she could have been his mother.

'You know what?' she said glumly. 'I'm about ready to retire. Give up the business and settle down in the country.'

She meant it. She thought she meant it. And she thought Elisse would be pleased. But the other woman only grinned and shook her head.

'Sod that, Naeve. Soon as Corus is old enough ta be left with his gran for a week or two, I'll be coming with ya.'

'You what?'

'Give it another year, and I reckon we'll be there. He'll be nearly eight by then. They're sending that tutor from the city, so I won' need ta teach him any more …' Elisse's fingers moved to brush Sorrow's. 'I wan' ta be your partner, Naeve, if you'll let me.'

Sorrow gazed at her hand. Then, after a while, she lifted her head to gaze at Elisse's face.

'You want to be my partner,' she said flatly.

'Yeah.' A hint of uncertainty crept into Elisse's eyes. 'Is that all right?'

'I'm quite respectable these days, you know,' Sorrow said. 'It won't be as much fun as it used to be.'

'I dunno. Working for Darkhaven didn' stop ya nearly getting killed.'

Sorrow snorted. 'You think nearly getting killed is fun?'

'Don't bullshit me, Naeve Sorrow. The danger of it is the whole point. Being shot is no fun, I'll give ya that. But *nearly* being shot …'

Sorrow considered that a moment. Then, slowly, her fingers curled around Elisse's. *A partner*. Someone who'd be there alongside her when she got herself into another situation she couldn't quite handle. The more she thought about it, the less her wounds seemed to throb. So she raised her eyebrows at Elisse.

'Want to come and nearly get shot with me?'

Elisse smiled. 'I thought you'd never ask.'

Before Ree and Penn left Darkhaven, the morning after they returned from the *Windsinger*, Caraway summoned them to the small receiving room where he'd once given them secret instructions about the murder investigation. As before, Ayla was there with him; she greeted them warmly and asked them to sit down.

'I wanted to thank you both,' she said. 'For the part you played in rescuing my children, and before that as well. Tomas tells me that without you, we wouldn't have known where they were being held.'

'Are they all right?' Ree asked.

'Yes. Thank you. All three of them are fine.'

'And you?' Ree wasn't even sure if she should venture that question, but a shadow lingered in Ayla's eyes, and she couldn't help but ask ... yet Ayla only nodded gravely.

'Well enough. Thank you.'

She wasn't really, Ree thought. She'd aged since she went to war – not outwardly, so much, but it bled through from somewhere inside her. Still, it was clear she didn't want to talk about it, and so Ree asked her other burning question.

'Please ... what happened to Zander? Did his father make him stay in Sol Kardis?'

Ayla and Caraway exchanged a smile.

'He tried,' Ayla said. 'But in the end he saw reason.'

'Then Zander came back with you?'

Ayla shook her head. 'As the newest member of my personal guard, I sent him on an errand. He should be back in the city by now, though.'

It took a moment for Ree to understand what she meant. 'You made Zander a Helmsman?'

'He's good enough,' Caraway said. 'He's certainly proven his loyalty. If it hadn't been for the Kardise situation, he'd have been in already. So now that we have peace ...'

'They didn't try to make him a condition of the treaty, then?' Penn asked. That was what both of them had believed Zander was flying back to.

'Actually, they did,' Ayla said. 'But I argued them down.'

Ree didn't know what to say. That argument must have taken place when Ayla already knew her children had been taken. When she had every reason to agree to Kardise demands for the sake of reaching her loved ones sooner. And yet she had fought for Zander, who wasn't even part of Darkhaven ...

'Ree?' Caraway cut in while she was still trying to formulate a response. 'Can we speak to you alone for a moment?'

'Yes, sir ...' That was odd. She shot a sideways glance at Penn, but he only gave her an ambiguous little smile before leaving the room. Frowning, Ree turned back to her captain.

'I found this,' Caraway said. 'You handed it to me with the plans of the *Windsinger*, though I didn't notice at the time.'

He was holding her marriage contract. Ree found herself suddenly hot all over, as though she'd been dipped in boiling water.

'Is there something you want to tell us?' Ayla added gently.

Ree opened her mouth. She hadn't planned to tell her captain about this, let alone Ayla. It had been an awkward, embarrassing problem she'd been determined to deal with alone. Yet now, unexpectedly, the entire story tumbled out of her. The bargain her father had made with Derrick Tarran. Her own encounter with the man. Penn's discovery of the contract in Tarran's office.

'But I don't want to leave the Helm,' she finished. 'I don't want to be married. And nor does Lewis! But my father can't afford to pull out of the contract and get blacklisted for six months, even if he wanted to, and Lewis can't do it because he's one of the subjects of the contract. And I don't –'

Ayla held up a hand. 'Ree. I've already terminated the contract. And,' she added reflectively, 'I really need to see about making this kind of thing illegal. No-one should be signing unbreakable marriage contracts on their children's behalf, however traditional the practice may be.'

'But –'

'I spoke to Lewis earlier this morning,' Caraway said. 'I would have spoken to you, too, only I didn't want to wake you.' His smile was warm. 'And Lewis was adamant enough for both of you that the marriage wasn't your choice.'

Ree opened her mouth. Closed it. Opened it again to say faintly, 'What about my father's debt?'

'I paid it off,' Ayla said.

'But – but –' Ree couldn't find the words. She was close to tears. Finally she managed, 'I would never have asked you to do that, Lady Ayla.'

'I know you wouldn't. But Lewis Tarran is about to lose a great deal of his father's wealth, and I can't have the taransey business failing now; it would be bad for the city. Besides ...' For the first time Ree could remember, Ayla looked unsure of herself. 'I didn't want to lose you. Is that all right?'

'We wouldn't have done it if we hadn't been certain the marriage was against your wishes,' Caraway added. 'I asked Penn about it, too, and he said the same.'

So that explained the little smile Penn had given her as he left. Ree shook her head, feeling stupid with confusion. She thought maybe she ought to be angry. Caraway and Ayla might be her employers, but they had no more right to interfere in her life than her parents did. Yet she couldn't deny that they'd done it for the very best of reasons.

'Is that all right?' Ayla asked again. Impulsively, Ree stepped forward and hugged her. It was probably inappropriate, but she didn't care. And Ayla hugged her back, so it wasn't as if she could have minded all that much. Ree hoped not, anyway.

'Thank you,' she mumbled. Backing away again, she looked down at her feet, suddenly aware of her hot cheeks. 'Both of you.'

Caraway touched her arm. 'Ree.'

She raised her head.

'Next time you have a problem like this, please tell me about it before you get to the point of being forced into marriage.'

'It didn't seem that important,' she said. 'Not with war coming.'

'That's exactly why it was important. Anything that could distract you from doing your job, I need to know about. A distracted Helmsman is a defeated one. You know that.'

Ree nodded. 'I'm sorry, sir. I just ... I was ashamed.'

'Of what?'

Good question. She struggled to articulate it. 'Not being able to handle it myself. Having some stupid problem that none of the others would ever have. I know you want to keep me safe, Captain, but –'

She stopped, because he was shaking his head.

'Of course I want to keep you safe,' he said. 'But it's not because you're a girl, if that's what you're implying. It's because you're one of my men. I want to know if someone's trying to force you into marriage in the exact same way I want to know if Lonnie's brother has died of fever or Riba's baby was born two months early or Soren has lost his home after a dispute with his landlord. I care about your lives, Ree. All of you. We're a family.' He hesitated, then added sadly, 'We *were* a family.'

Ayla rested her cheek against his shoulder, briefly, in recognition of the amendment. Ree nodded. She managed a salute, before turning and leaving the room.

Outside, Penn was waiting for her. She walked right up to him and punched his arm. 'Why didn't you tell me?'

'It wasn't my place.' He shrugged. 'But you're happy, though, aren't you?'

'Yes. It's brilliant. I just – I wish I could thank them properly. Not just for that, but for –' she struggled to find the words – 'being who they are. You know.'

'I know,' Penn said. 'And we thank them by being good at our job.' He gave her one of his rare smiles. 'Come on. Let's go and see if we can find Zander.'

They were nearly at the Gate of Steel when – just as she had all those weeks ago – Ree spotted her parents waiting for her. Penn must have worked out who they were, too; a shade of alarm entered his eyes.

'I'll just wait for you over –'

'Oh no you don't,' she said firmly, linking her elbow with his. 'I need backup for this one.'

Her parents stepped forward as she approached, both of them shooting speculative glances at Penn. He was a good-looking boy, Ree thought with detached amusement. And very … Mirrorvalese. No wonder her mother was looking at her as though she'd finally solved an age-old secret.

'Good morning,' she said breezily. 'Did you hear the news about the treaty with Sol Kardis? This is my friend, Penn Avens.'

Penn managed to mumble something vaguely suitable. Ree's mother fixed her gaze on him as if she were about to subject him to interrogation, but Ree's father got in first.

'We received this,' he said, holding out a thick piece of paper covered in elaborate black ink. Ree recognised the Darkhaven seal at the bottom. 'A termination of your marriage contract. By order of Ayla Nightshade.'

Here we go. Ree sighed. 'Can we talk about this another time? Only I really don't have the energy to –'

'A letter came with it,' her father went on as if she hadn't spoken. 'Informing me that my debt to the Tarran family has been paid in full and thanking me for the excellent service of my youngest daughter, who has … where did I put it?' He fished a second piece of paper out of his pocket, this one in Ayla's energetic scrawl rather than the beautifully inscribed lettering of a legal clerk. '*Rendered herself indispensable to the Nightshade line.*'

He looked up; to Ree's surprise, tears gleamed in his eyes.

'She says you helped stop the war,' he said softly. 'That you rescued her children. Is that true?'

Ree was about to be self-deprecating when she realised there was really no reason why she should be. Her parents had taught her that a well-brought-up young lady never boasted about her accomplishments, yet her parents had also never seemed to understand that she'd actually accomplished anything. So she lifted her chin and looked her father in the eyes.

'Yes. That's my job.'

He regarded her in silence for a moment, a smile tugging at the corners of his mouth. Then he said, 'I'm proud of you, Ree.'

'Both of us are,' her mother added.

'And we wanted to apologise. For what we've said and done these past few weeks. We hope ...' He hesitated, then said it in a rush. 'We hope you can forgive us.'

Ree didn't even have to think about it. She opened her arms wide. Then all three of them were hugging, and her mother was crying, and Ree found that she was crying too. It had been a long few days. A long few weeks. And people were dead, and she'd very nearly died herself a couple of times, and Zander had come back to Mirrorvale, and she didn't have to get married ... and she wasn't sure if she was happy or sad, but sometimes it was good to cry with your parents. Even if you were a nineteen-year-old woman in charge of your own life.

'You're sure this is what you want, chicken?' her mother asked finally, wiping her eyes. It was the easiest question in the world to answer.

'Yes. I am. I really am.'

'Then I'm happy for you.' She darted another glance at Penn, who had retreated a little way when the hugging started, and a hopeful smile curled her lips. 'Now, tell me all about that young man over there.'

'Penn and I are just friends, Mother.' Ree considered her words, decided *just* was a stupid word to use for a friendship that was as important to her as any romantic relationship could be, and amended, 'Close friends. The best of friends. He's a wonderful person. But as for what you're thinking ... no, I have absolutely no desire to sleep with him.'

'Ree!' That single, scandalised word sent her into a fit of laughter. And perhaps her mother realised her own reaction had been one of habit, rather than genuine feeling, because after a moment she shook her head and said with the hint of a smile, 'Well. It's good to know you have friends in the city.'

After they'd gone, with many promises to visit again soon and have her to stay at home – *you can wear whatever you like, Cheri, but do bring that nice boy if you want to* – Ree turned to Penn with eyebrows raised.

'They'll never change. My mother has already married us off in her mind. But at least they're trying.'

'Did you mean it?' Penn asked gravely. 'When you said we're the best of friends?'

She looked at him in surprise. 'Of course. You and Zander ... you're like my swords. It's not that I *need* either of you, exactly. It's just that the two of you make my life better when you're in it.'

Penn considered that, and a slow smile spread across his face.

'Ree Quinn, I think that might be the nicest thing you've ever said to me.' Linking their arms together once more, he looked down at her with affection. 'Come on. Let's go find Zander.'

THIRTY-TWO

Caraway spent the best part of a day on the hardest task of his life: accompanying each of his dead men on their final journey to be returned to their families. Some of them would end up in the Temple of Death, the only place in Arkannen where it was possible to return someone to the earth with all the appropriate dignities; others would be taken to the pyres outside the city, or carried home to a family estate or village burial grove. But in each case, Caraway had to speak to a parent or a child, a lover or a sibling, and explain why their son or father or husband or brother wouldn't be coming home.

To start with, he encountered a lot of denial. Everyone knew there had been a war, of course, but the Helmsmen who had stayed in Darkhaven should have been the ones to survive, not the ones to die. Over and over again, Caraway had to explain how it could be that an entire cohort of warriors in the heart of their own domain had been so comprehensively destroyed. And over and over again, he was forced to confront his own failure. He had retrieved his children unharmed, and he was thankful for it. Yet for thirty-three men and one woman, he had failed to be the captain they deserved. He had failed to protect them. And they had died.

As dusk fell, he dismissed the surviving Helmsmen who had helped him to deliver the bodies and the news, and trudged back up to the fifth ring alone. A long list of urgent tasks spooled through his mind, starting with the need to recruit more men to replace those who had fallen, but he couldn't bear to face them now. Instead, he went in search of the one person he thought would truly understand his guilt.

He found Bryan keeping busy: too busy. Caraway recognised the signs. He bore the weaponmaster off with him to the sixth ring, where they sat outside the Shrine of the Moon and listened to the priestesses singing.

'You all right?' Caraway asked finally. Bryan shrugged.

'I'm not gonna fall apart, if that's what you mean. I'm a soldier. I know how the world works. People die. People betray you. Shit happens.'

'Fall apart as much as you like,' Caraway said. 'You can't do it worse than I did.'

He sensed, rather than saw, Bryan look at him from beneath heavy brows. 'Want to bet, boyo?' A rusty chuckle, which turned into a sigh. 'Nah ... the truth is, I'm not all right. I keep thinking, how could I not have known? And also –'

Caraway waited, but there was no more.

'Also?' he prompted.

'I can't stop loving the bastard.' It was a barely audible mutter, with a defensive edge that suggested Bryan half expected Caraway to mock him for even mentioning the word *love*. But really, Caraway thought, his friend should know him better than that. Fifth-ring banter was one thing, but Caraway made no secret of the fact that much of the time, love was the only force holding him together.

'Of course not,' he said. 'That isn't how it works, is it? You don't stop fighting just because someone stabs you in the heart.'

'Then what? Stab him back?' It was said flippantly, but Caraway heard the deep underlying sorrow in it.

'No,' he said softly. 'Because love means throwing away all your weapons. All your armour. Love has no room for defences. That's why it hurts so much when you realise the other person had a knife after all.'

Silence. Bryan sat with his forearms propped on his knees, hands fisted, head bowed. His shoulders shook. Caraway put a hand on his back and said nothing. Sometimes it wasn't possible to do anything more than be there.

'And you, lad?' Bryan asked, once he'd got himself under control. 'Are you all right?'

'No, not really.' It was easier to say it in the darkness, with the stars above him and music in the air that made the conversation seem almost like a dream. 'More than half the Helm died under my watch. Most of those I sent to the border with Ayla returned unharmed. They were safer in a war zone than with me in Darkhaven. I'm not sure I can live with that, Art.'

'You have to,' Bryan said gruffly. 'What else can you do?'

'I don't know. But ale is looking pretty damn good right now.'

'It won't help. Look, I know how you feel. If not for me, Miles would never have come to Darkhaven in the first place. No war, no massacre, no stolen kiddies. Don't you think I've been aware of that ever since I found out he was a traitor? Don't you think it's been playing on my mind, the what-ifs?

Your murdered Helmsmen are just as much on my conscience as they are on yours.'

Caraway shook his head. 'If Miles hadn't been there, Gil would have done it himself – in which case, I'd be dead too. So if you're going to take any responsibility, you can take it for my continued existence.'

'You're quick enough to absolve me,' Bryan said. 'Try applying a little of that forgiveness to yourself. *You couldn't have known, Tomas*. This wasn't your fault. You fought the war as best you could. It just turned out to be a different war than you were expecting.'

Again they were quiet. Then Caraway said, 'I hope you'll come back to Darkhaven. If not now, then ... sometime.'

'You still want me living there? Without ...'

'Of course. If you want to come.'

'Thank you,' Bryan said. 'I'd like that.'

When he got back to the tower, Caraway ignored the comforting call of family and bed, instead taking the quickest route to the cells where Gil was being held. Ayla didn't know he was doing this. He wasn't even sure why he wanted to. It wasn't as though it would change anything. But the man had killed half the Helm, and Caraway couldn't leave that alone. It scratched at him like a ragged nail. He knew Gil was the kind of man who would never feel any remorse. He knew a confrontation would achieve nothing but tear the fragile scab from a barely healing wound. And yet he couldn't help it.

He dismissed the Helmsman on duty, then carried a chair down to the furthermost cell. Gil was shackled at wrists and ankles; no-one had wanted to take even the slightest chance that he might escape before his execution. He looked tired and uncomfortable, but not in pain. Ayla had insisted on that.

'Good evening, Captain.' The greeting was polite, a little

sombre. No hint of fear. The Parovian accent was clear, now; he no longer had any reason to conceal it. Caraway dropped the chair just beyond the doorway, sat down, and met Gil's steady gaze.

'I have to know,' he said. 'I have to know why you did it.'

'I love my country, Captain, just as much as you love yours.'

'My love for my country doesn't extend as far as entering someone else's country and committing mass murder.'

'I had to keep the Helm from interfering. It was the logical thing to do.'

'Logical?' Caraway was on his feet before he could hold himself back, hands curling into fists. The physician was cuffed and chained; it would be easy to make him pay, a little, before his death, and certainly none left in the Helm would fault their captain for it ...

But Ayla would.

He turned away, walking to the door and back again to give himself enough time to regain control. Once back at the chair, he gripped its back and stared at Gil.

'You killed thirty-six people.' Most of them Helmsmen, but there were the two murdered kitchen maids as well: their throats slit, their bodies left to lie where they fell. 'Not in wartime, not in retribution, not in self-defence. Men and women with lovers, children, friends. And you don't see anything wrong with that?'

'It was my job, Captain Caraway. I saw no other way.'

'A sleeping draught –'

'Would not have prevented the Helm from going after the children once they awoke.' Gil shrugged, and repeated, 'It was the logical thing to do.'

'Logic didn't get you as far as it should have, though, did it? The children are safe. Ayla is safe. Darkhaven didn't fall.'

Incongruously, a small smile crossed the physician's face. 'Unfortunately, people and logic rarely go hand in hand. All the same, Captain, if it had not been for the damned alchemist and his unwillingness to let you die …'

Caraway didn't want to discuss Miles. He brushed that aside. 'And Hana?'

Gil looked at him blankly. 'Who is Hana?'

It was as close as Caraway had yet come to punching the man. It took him every last drop of self-control to hold himself in one place, though his heart pounded hard enough that he could feel the blood rushing past his ears.

'The first girl you murdered,' he said with taut calm. 'She gave Ayla your antidote. She made sure your taransey reached its destination.'

'Miles's antidote,' Gil replied. 'And Tarran's poisoned taransey. All I had to do was persuade the girl to deliver them.'

'How? And don't try to tell me she was a traitor too, because I won't believe it.'

Gil shrugged. 'You really ought to be stricter with your maids, Captain Caraway. I only had to drop a friendly word in her direction and she was blurting out her whole life story.' He affected a squeaky voice. '*Me and Sia are best friends. We always go down to the cellar together because we hate the rats. I like my job, but I'd rather work in the nursery. I love the children. It's so sad Lady Ayla can't have any more. Yes, I have the fifth day of each week off, did you want to meet for a drink sometime?* Blah, blah, blah.'

Caraway gritted his teeth. 'So …'

'So I told her I thought I had discovered a cure for Ayla's

weakness in childbirth, one that required her to drink taransey of the newest possible vintage to work most effectively. And that she wanted to keep it a secret from you to avoid raising your hopes. After that, the girl fell over herself to carry out my instructions. Deliver the antidote in Ayla's morning tea. Take the right bottle of taransey from the cellar. Easy as that.'

'And then you killed her.'

'I had to. She was very much the weak link in the chain. Really, Captain, I do not know what you expect from me.'

'She thought she was doing something good for her country,' Caraway said. 'For Ayla. And you murdered her without a second thought.'

Gil snorted. 'Hypocrite.'

'What?'

'You cannot tell me you would not kill one, ten, fifty girls to save Ayla's life. And what about the crew of the *Windsinger*, Captain? Correct me if I am wrong, but I rather think they are dead.'

'They had my children –'

'That makes it better, does it? No. We are both willing to shed as much blood as it takes to protect what we believe in. That is what war is, what it means. So what gives you the right to say your kills are virtuous, and mine are not?'

'We're not at war.'

'Oh, we are. We have been at war since you planted your baby in Ayla Nightshade's belly and continued a line of tyranny that should have died with her. Your refusal to recognise it does not make it any less true. And in war, Captain Caraway, people die.'

'Tyranny?' Caraway echoed. 'It's all Mirrorvale can do to stand against Parovia. Against Sol Kardis. Against every larger power that threatens our borders. We do what we can to survive, and no more. What part of that is tyranny?'

'But you are no longer standing against Sol Kardis,' Gil said. 'You have allied yourselves with them. You have changed the balance of power. Perhaps you thought you were seeking peace, but what you have made is war.' He shook his head. 'We would have been content to let Mirrorvale remain small. The pivotal point, the unchanging centre holding the rest of us in tension. Do you think I have not heard Miles spout his alchemical theories? But now ...'

'Now what? We stop losing men to an endless war of attrition along our southern border. We agree new trade deals. What difference does that make to Parovia?'

The physician sighed. 'This is what happens when a mere soldier becomes the second most powerful person in an entire country. Anyone who had been through even a fraction of a political education would have advised Ayla against making peace with Sol Kardis. Because like it or not, she is a weapon. She is the one thing neither we nor Sol Kardis possess. And the only way you could have kept us both reasonably happy with that situation was to remain neutral. Whereas now you have opened your borders to Kardise trade and Kardise influence ...' He shrugged. 'If the enemy of your enemy is your friend, Captain Caraway, what does that say about the enemy of your friend?'

'But our borders are already open to Parovia,' Caraway said. 'We've been trading with you for decades. We let you bring the *Windsinger* to Mirrorvale! If anything, the Kardise treaty only puts us on the same footing with Sol Kardis that we're already on with Parovia. That's fair enough, isn't it?'

'You keep bringing up fairness,' Gil said. 'As if fairness has anything to do with politics. We were happy when you and Sol Kardis were keeping each other occupied. It left us free to focus on our own plans. We protected Ayla from assassination, three years ago, because we did not want Sol Kardis getting stronger. We tried to prevent you making an alliance with them because we did not want you to be too strong either. But we failed.' He smiled. 'As I said, you have changed the balance. You have chosen strength. And the thing about strength is, you have to be prepared to prove it over and over.'

Caraway looked at him in silence.

'Tomorrow, I will be dead,' Gil said. 'But Parovia will not be. His Majesty wants the secret of the Change, and his agents will not rest until they have procured it for him. You might believe you have won, but you came within a hair's breadth of disaster on our very first attempt, and we will only become cleverer. Take that as a warning, if you will.'

'Why?' Caraway snapped. 'So I never trust anyone again?'

'You are in charge of Darkhaven's defences. Ayla Nightshade's protector. Father of Mirrorvale's future. Given who you are, it would be foolish to trust.'

Caraway shook his head. 'Given who I am, it would be foolish not to.'

'A trite reply, Captain,' Gil said. 'Do you have an argument to back it up, or are you just throwing empty words at me?'

If I don't trust my people, they won't trust me. If I don't trust Ayla, I might as well abandon her now for all the good I can do her. If one man in a hundred is a traitor, and I allow that knowledge to close my heart to the other ninety-nine, who is the winner then?

Suddenly, Caraway found that his need to hold this conversation was over. Straightening up, he smiled: a sad smile, but a smile nonetheless. 'I don't have to explain myself to you.'

'You mean you cannot.'

'I mean I see no point in trying. Ayla and I, our children, the Helm – all of Mirrorvale – we're as far beyond your understanding as you are beyond mine. You sought to take something from us because you were envious and afraid, and now that you've failed, you want us to be afraid too. But in the end, love will always be stronger than fear.'

The physician scoffed. 'Love? You are a fighting man, Tomas. Surely you know love is just another form of weakness.'

'Anyone can hate,' Caraway said. 'It's love that requires courage.'

Zander lowered the most recent letter from his father to stare blankly at the opposite wall.

'Well?' Ree asked. 'Has he disowned you?'

The words might be flippant, but her voice was anxious. She genuinely cared about the answer. Beside her, Penn wore a small frown. A smile fought for control of the corners of Zander's mouth, but he managed to keep his expression blank.

'I'll read it to you.' Raising the piece of paper in front of his face once more, to hide his irrepressible amusement, he began the letter in solemn mockery of Marco Lepont's rather pompous tones.

Alezzandro –

I am not sure what you expect from me. You left home against my express wishes. You stayed away for three years, despite my repeated requests to return. And when you finally did come back to the country that made you, it was out of concern for Mirrorvale, not Sol Kardis. Clearly your godless new friends mean far more to you than your own blood, so much so that you are willing to take a job the sole purpose of which is to protect the unnatural magics we Kardise have long abhorred. What else can I do but disown you?

I have considered this question long and hard, and come to the conclusion that I might have been too hasty. You are a wilful, disobedient boy, but you have far more intelligence than your tutors led me to believe. I realise, now, that perhaps you have not been completely wasting your time these past three years. After all, the support and respect of the most powerful woman in Mirrorvale has to count for something, unnatural magics or not.

Thus you have my permission to stay in Arkannen and be a Helmsman, for now. By the time you are of an age to leave soldiering, you will just about be of an age to start learning the business of running my estate. But if Sol Kardis and Mirrorvale should come to war again in the meantime, Zander, I expect you to stay out of it. That is an order.

Marco Lepont

Zander put the letter on the table in front of him and raised his eyebrows at his friends.

'You have his permission?' Ree said, but she was smiling. He grinned back at her.

'Let him give me his permission if it makes him feel better, the old windbag. He's accepted my life and he hasn't cut me off. That's a huge concession as far as he's concerned.'

'Guess you'll be around a while longer, then.'

'Guess so.' Zander glanced at Penn. 'Think you can cope with that, Avens?'

'I suppose I'll have to,' Penn said. 'Reluctantly.'

And he too smiled.

The day of the execution dawned bright and clear. Ayla saw it happen; she'd been awake since well before first bell, pacing between her bedroom and her children's until, finally, she'd made herself stop. Made herself settle in the deep window seat and watch the sky change from ink-dark to grey to blushing blue, and not think about what lay ahead of her.

It could have been two executions. Some of the Helm had called for Miles's head, as well as Gil's. He'd been passing on Darkhaven's secrets for years, they'd pointed out. He could have stopped the war, but he hadn't. And he'd been the one to kill their colleagues and friends, however unwittingly. Gil might have given the orders, but Miles was the one who had carried them out.

Ayla could see their point. Part of her agreed with it. Yet she thought it was probably more complicated than that. He had saved Tomas's life and helped him to rescue the children. He had helped her break free in the wreckage of the *Windsinger*. He was a traitor, yes, but at least he hadn't been a willing one. She herself had felt the impulse to protect her children at all costs, even if it meant abandoning her people to war. She knew what it was like to be caught between different kinds of love.

Sitting on the window seat, watching the sun rise, she found herself remembering a conversation she'd held with Miles, once, while they were doing research together. While he was researching her.

Love is like alchemy, he'd said.

What do you mean?

The combination of two distinct elements to make something completely new. Something stronger than either of them alone. And more than that ... the same two elements can react in different ways, depending on the environment. Love is not a single predictable reaction. Even between the same two people, it changes and mutates over time. New love is not the same as long-standing love. But if the elements are compatible enough, they will never repel each other, no matter what the circumstances. He'd frowned. *Really, love is such a vague word as to be almost meaningless. It is a whole collection of different emotions and experiences, tied together with a messy bow.*

She'd thought about that. Certainly her love for Tomas, which was passionate and complicated and fluid, was quite different from the love she felt for their children: something fierce and fundamental that lived deep down at the heart of her. Her love for Myrren had been another kind of animal again, a love born of history and shared experience, a love patterned in her bones. And yes, Miles was right: each of those emotions had evolved over time to become something richer and more complex than it had been before. But there was more to it even than that. She could see, in that complexity, how easy it would be for darkness to creep in and turn love to hatred. Because it was the people you loved who had the greatest capacity to destroy you.

She'd expressed that thought to Miles, who had nodded. *That is like alchemy, too. Often the elements that are strongest in one configuration are also the most explosive in another. The potential for the greatest acts of creation comes hand in hand with that for the most terrible destruction.*

Do you have a family back in Parovia? she'd asked, suddenly curious. Suddenly wondering why she'd never asked before. His mouth had turned down at the corners.

Not any more, Lady Ayla.

She wanted to hate him, but she couldn't. He had done terrible things – she would never trust him again, let alone forgive him – but he had done them to protect the people he loved, and that was something she understood far too well. Besides, he still lay in the infirmary, treading the knife-edge between life and death, and no-one could yet say with any certainty whether he would recover. If he did, all she could say with certainty was that she hadn't signed a warrant for his execution. Whatever else his future held would have to wait.

Gil, on the other hand, was a very different case.

There has been a lot of death already, she'd said to Tomas, trying to make sure she was being as fair to Gil as she had been to Miles. Trying to compensate for her own hot desire to exact a drawn-out and bloody vengeance by setting herself on the side of mercy.

Most of it his doing, Tomas had replied.

And that was all. That was as far as the conversation had gone. Both of them knew there was only one appropriate punishment for a man who had used his position as a trusted physician to commit mass murder and betray the children under his care to a foreign power. And both of them also knew it must be for that reason alone, and not as a result of their own desperate, seething emotion, that the sentence was carried out.

Perhaps that had been a benefit of her father's approach to such things, Ayla thought. His judgements had been bloody, but at least they had been quick. Acting with decision, rather than impulse, had also given her time to become inventive. Some of the execution methods she'd found herself contemplating had shocked her with their cruelty.

That couldn't be right. She didn't think so, anyway. If she wanted it to be justice, and not murder, she had to make it clean.

She couldn't eat. She wasn't hungry. She stayed at the window, looking out at the sky, until the second bell rang. And then Tomas came to fetch her, and it was time.

Side by side, they walked down to the cells. There was no Helmsman on duty; no doubt the man who would have had that task today was dead. Shuddering, Ayla stopped with her hand on the cell door and looked at Tomas.

'You know I've never done this before. At war, yes, and in self-defence, but not an execution in cold blood ...'

'No,' he said simply. 'But I'm with you.'

Their former physician was sitting on the narrow bed in a corner of the cell, elbows on his knees, manacled hands dangling between them. He looked up as they entered, his expression composed and a little grave. As if he had just lost a game of skill. He didn't say a word as they escorted him out of the cell and up the steps into the daylight.

The surviving members of the Helm waited to one side of the central square. They didn't rush the traitor physician and beat him to death, as Ayla had almost expected they would. Not so much as a hiss disturbed the silence. Only their grim, set expressions revealed the extent of their feelings. On the other side, the housekeeper and the servants had gathered – all except Cathrin, up in the nursery with the children. They too had lost friends. They too were here for justice.

Tomas touched Ayla's hand. Neither of them needed to speak. He led Gil away from her, into the middle of the open space. Then he retreated to join his men.

'Well?' Gil straightened his shoulders, but the hint of a quaver touched his voice. 'Get on with it, damn you!'

Ayla looked at the man in front of her for what felt like an eternity. He had been her physician. He had tended to her and her children. Because of him, good people were dead.

Because of him, countless more lives had been destroyed. Because of him, she felt nothing even close to whole.

And yet, she found that most of her anger had drained away. She was just very, very tired.

She summoned the Change, letting all her muddy human thoughts fall away. For the first time she saw alarm in the man's eyes, but it gave her little satisfaction. It was simply a relief to feel clean emotions again; to know what was right.

She lowered her head, and pierced him straight through the heart.

Acknowledgements

This one is for everyone who knows how much harder it is to achieve *anything* with a one-year-old in tow.

You go through an entire day doing everything one-handed because she refuses to be put down. You spend nights on end snatching half an hour of sleep at a time because he's sick and needs constant comfort. You sing the same lullaby until you're hoarse, read the same book until you can recite it from memory, and watch the same show until you've forgotten the world is populated by anything other than multicoloured animals with strangely enormous eyes. Occasionally, you catch a glimpse of yourself in the mirror and are surprised at the sight of an actual adult human, albeit one with dishevelled hair and an unidentified crusty substance smeared across its shoulder. Sometimes you wish for a little light swordfighting and a life-or-death situation or two ... you know, just so you can have a bit of a break. And yet you'll get up and do it all again tomorrow.

My heartfelt gratitude goes to Marc, Nikki and all the team at my local Waterstones, for being unfailingly supportive and making me feel like a real writer.

Also to Harriet: for the generous gift of her time and

intelligence, for performing an impressive act of last-minute alchemy, and (which is very important) for telling me not to panic.

And finally, I suppose, to the original 'Gil'. What doesn't kill us, etcetera.

Printed by RR Donnelley at Glasgow, UK